The Spearfisherman

Ric Szabo

Pytheus Press

ebook edition © 2022 ISBN 978-0-6454119-0-4
paperback edition © 2022 ISBN 978-0-6454119-1-1

A catalogue record for this book is available from the National Library of Australia

www.ricszabo.com

. . . and halfway across the river the scorpion stung the frog, dooming them both.

'But why?' implored the frog.

'I can't help it,' replied the scorpion. 'It's just my nature.'

– The Scorpion and the Frog –

Prologue

I stare into the mirror a bit longer tonight.

I wear my navy wool tuxedo. The last time I wore it was about five years ago. Before that, the same. It's a tighter fit now, and well past its day, but I cling to it like the memories it inspires. We go back a long way.

I recall a deeper shade of hazel in my eyes. The corners of my lips point a little more down and I think my cheeks are starting to sag. The grey in my hair is no longer the odd streak in an otherwise healthy sprawl of brown. Tonight, I will trade the same scrutiny with faces I haven't seen in almost three decades. Perhaps I will wonder if what I see bears testimony to wiser choices, happier lives.

It is a night to ponder what might have been. If things would have been better any other way. If those deceptively significant decisions hindsight tells me were critical turning points in my life were the right ones. In my formative years I embraced the notion of destiny with religious zeal. We all meant something back then, we were all going places. Tonight is one more reminder that humbles that line of thought.

We are not rich. There are scratches on my car I have learnt to ignore. My mortgage balance looms heavily in my mind whenever I try to gloat over my two-story, brick veneer house. My wife collects shopping dockets and scans junk mail for specials. I stress over the wastage that inflates our bills. I like my job only as much as it takes to appreciate all the more the life I have outside of it. As I look deeper into my face I search for signs that I am not happy, that I am the type of man who must convince himself by telling himself so. That this is the only way to make it real, when in fact it ended long ago, without me realising, and I progress under the momentum of some former glory.

I am thrilled about tonight. I will laugh and rehash old stories and shake lots of hands and get melancholically drunk and tell my friends I love them for about the hundredth time. But tonight is a portal into a part of my life best left alone. The past shapes what we are, like soil to our roots. I look into the mirror and wonder how many wrinkles, how many grey hairs are owed to what happened back then. The things I can't bury deep enough.

For a long time now, I've been trying to shake myself of a dream. I am back in college standing around with my friends, and *he* is there. But there's something odd about him; he is not as we knew him. And he's acting strange, saying weird things. He has this child-like innocence about him and doesn't pick up what we are thinking: *you shouldn't be here*. We start to look around nervously, scared perhaps, because we know something's wrong; there's been a mistake. It all feels so real that I start to think it's the other way around; that I'm not dreaming at all, that everything else is the dream. I feel good then, all is well. Until I wake.

I wonder how different my life might have been if I'd never met him. If Manners had never lost his necklace at the party, if we'd never gone to the Grange that night. That and a thousand other things.

I wonder.

One

Before

nvitation was word-of-mouth. School holidays were almost over and I thought this would be a great appetiser for Uni O-week just around the corner.

Six of us packed into Peter Grigg's Holden Monaro, three in the front and three in the back. I rode front and middle on one of those long vinyl seats three people can slide onto. The seatbelt in the middle goes around your waist. With guys like Grigg driving, I'd always wonder if the dash would be the last thing I'd see. Gaunt-faced and heavy-lidded, he looked forever sick or forever stoned. I'd never seen him with a lot of friends until he got a car.

On my left sat Saunders, a tight-muscled goon with restless energy and an erratic, darting gaze that was the mark of his attention span. Throughout primary school athletics had been his thing, track mainly. I used to be in awe of the guy. Sportsman of the year twice, made it to state championships in year six. High school got in the way of a promising career, so he claimed. Truth being that by age fifteen he'd taken up binge drinking and smoking anything that caught a flame. To look at him you'd never pick it. He was one of those freaks that didn't lift a finger in exercise, ate every piece of junk food imaginable, and didn't have an ounce of fat on him.

Behind Saunders on the passenger side was Kep. The smallest and quietest amongst us, he was loyal as a puppy dog and my best friend at the time. At peace he looked like a nerd, fired up he was all bullterrier. Directly behind me, flicking my ear now and then just to annoy me, was Manners. The biggest of our group, he'd grown a barrel of a chest and had arms like fire-hoses. The eyes that plugged his puffy

3

face were dark and always glistening. Unlike Saunders he was built for strength, not speed. Or much else, I often thought. He played rugby league for a local club; no skill, all brawn. We joked that he spent more time on the bench than on the field, either injured or serving a stretch for some cheap shot. His name was Barry Mannering and we called him Manners for the irony. He was anything but.

Then there was Jarrod Finlay. Like Manners he was an apprentice mechanic, which is how they met and how I got to know him. He had a lazy, mirthless manner, and unless you talked cars his brain rarely engaged. If not for Manners' sake, he wouldn't be there.

Apart from him, the rest of us had been friends since primary school. Good fortune had seen us live a short bike ride from each other and we'd kept in touch these past years, even though we went to different high schools. Part of the reason I wanted them along on this night was because I felt we were drifting apart. Every one of them had opted for apprenticeships after year ten and since then some emergent differences were wedging their way into what was once an inseparable friendship. The last couple of years at high school I'd made a lot of new friends and these guys were becoming an afterthought. The loyalty was still there, however. It's hard to forget something you earned from some pretty tough knocks and a greater share of mischief than most.

AC/DC's *Hells Bells* bellowing out an open door, party heads out front, and blazing porch lights spared us the need to count house numbers looking for the place. Cars with P-Plates lined both sides of the narrow road, forcing us to park a street away.

The house was an old fibro, no garage, and a pathetic front yard with plants that looked like they'd taken root by accident. The air was vibrating *What Do You Do For Money Honey* when we entered through the front door all harmless and smiling. We negotiated our way past pimply-faced kids sipping beer and West Coast Coolers, and I politely acknowledged one or two guys I wouldn't go as far to call friends but were useful now if our presence was questioned. We reached the dining room where there was a table spread with the usual stuff; neat little triangle sandwiches, bowls of biscuits and chips, a dip or two. We settled into some chairs in a corner and Saunders handed each of us a VB. One by one we popped them open. 'Cheers,' we chorused.

That was our place for the next couple of hours. A few boys we knew came over every so often. They were careful with their words, all polite and respectful; my company had a reputation.

The first warning came just before 11pm. Manners had just gone to the bathroom when a skinny guy with long fringe came over and nabbed the chair he'd vacated. I watched him take it over to his friends near the food table but was too caught up in an argument with Saunders about Alan Border's batting form to care.

Manners came back and asked where his chair was. I showed him. Beer in hand he walked over to the group, biceps knotted beneath his T-shirt.

'Hey,' he said matter-of-factly. 'I was sitting on that.'

The guy flicked the fringe out of his eyes and looked up. His shoulders weren't much wider than his head. His two buddies weren't any bigger. Two girls were sitting among them, puffing on cigarettes.

'Sorry,' he replied, all polite and trouble-free. He stood obediently.

Manners came forward to take the chair. 'Ask next time, prick.'

That's all it usually took. The funny thing was that in all my early years growing up with him I'd never see this side to the guy. I'd seen plenty of it since his testosterone kicked in.

Wisely the kid didn't rattle, just shot him a look of disappointment mild enough to keep it below a provocation. Manners slid the chair back to our corner but as if to make a point, didn't sit in it. He lifted his can to his lips and drained it, then threw it clunking into a corner.

'Anyway,' he said, resuming his former discussion with Finlay and reaching down to pull another can from the case, 'you soften those dodgy springs of yours you'll bottom out over every hump. You may as well replace the lot.' He popped the tinnie and took a swig. I saw the fringed guy drag another chair in from nearby.

All was quiet for a while.

Manners said he was hungry. He went over to the table and Saunders followed. For a moment he eyed the offering greedily before reaching for a sandwich. By then they looked pretty soggy, having sat in whatever had spilled onto the tray.

'Just like you to pick the one soaked in piss,' Saunders commented.

Manners' sandwich landed on Saunders' chest with a splat. Saunders immediately armed himself with his own and took aim. Manners, howling with laughter, tried to skirt around the table. Saunders threw and the sandwich skimmed over Manners' head as he ducked.

'Slut!' Manners threw another sandwich that missed and slapped against a wall.

Pieces of bread flew back and forth in rapid succession. One of the guys in the corner straightened in his chair. 'Hey guys,' he said, a soft note of appeal in his voice. Manners and Saunders faced off, threatening each other with sloppy sandwiches.

'Drop it!' Manners warned, beaming.

'You drop it,' Saunders replied.

Manners held up his hands, like it was a pistol he was surrendering. 'Truce?'

Saunders smiled wickedly and did the same. 'Truce.'

Manners put the sandwich down. 'Okay then.'

Saunders' hand was a blur; full of beer he could be just as quick as when he was sober. Manners tried to duck but a slice of bread glanced off his scalp and left white crumbs in his hair. Laughing hysterically, he sprayed beer from his can at Saunders, sending it frothing all over the place, some of it over the group near the table.

'Hey!' one of the girls complained loudly, and stood up. She was a solid girl with makeup on thicker than clay. 'Do you mind? Some of us went to a lot of trouble here. If you're going to behave like animals then go!'

'Oh shut up woman,' Manners said. 'Go and lose some weight.'

Saunders used the distraction to score a direct hit and Manners returned fire. Slices of bread bounced off the wall, others skidded and broke apart on the floor, leaving trails of cheese and ham and lettuce and other healthy goodness.

I stayed on the girl as my two friends resorted to chips here, crackers there. The flare left her face and I could see the shiny moistening of her eyes.

'Hey Manners.' Tempting as it was to tell him to check his own scales, I said instead: 'Give it a rest. I was going to eat some of that.'

Still grinning, my two friends gave up and returned to our corner, not so much at my request but because there was nothing left to throw.

Behind them, the group sat huddled like a litter of stunned kittens. Tears were rolling down the girl's cheeks and she was wiping them away in a distressed, awkward motion. Her friend hit us with the death stare, then slid her chair forward and put a hand on the girl's shoulder and whispered into her ear. The fringed guy regarded us with a brave frown; his two buddies tried not to make eye contact.

A little later I noticed Fringe stand from his chair and help the girl up. They walked away without looking back.

We were sitting in our corner discussing the whereabouts of old friends when they returned with two others. The lead guy was oldish, I'd say mid-twenties. I'd seen him pulling things out of the fridge and cupboards with the liberty you'd expect from someone with a stake in the place, so I tagged him as one of our party hosts. A red T-shirt with 'Porn Star' printed on the left breast was tucked tightly into his jeans, giving his gut a pregnant look. His mate had a face as harmless as a teddy bear and legs that flapped inside his jeans.

The girl lifted a finger at Manners. Makeup smeared her face and her eyes were dry and angry now. 'That's him.'

'Hey buddy, why'd you go saying something like that to the lady?' our party host asked, using a tone clearly intended not to inflame the situation.

'Just mucking around,' Manners said.

'That's not mucking around, mate.'

Manners frowned up at the girl. 'What's your problem, woman?'

'Oh, piss off,' she retorted.

'Mate, you'd better leave,' Party Host said.

'No thanks,' Manners answered coolly. 'We're just warming up.'

'We'd like you to go. This is our house. You weren't even invited.'

'Hey buddy,' I decided to step in. 'I'll keep an eye on him.'

The bloke ignored me, kept his eyes on Manners and his voice calm. 'Whoever told you to come got it wrong. You need to go.'

'Me friends ain't finished their beers,' Manners said.

'Then finish them outside.'

'Okay. Show me the way.'

'Fine.'

The guy didn't get it. A blind man could find the front door.

Manners stood up. 'Grab the case boys,' he said cheerfully. Kep was the closest and he leaned down to pick it up, by then a light load cradled under his armpit. The others stood from their chairs obediently, all show.

Party Host led the way through the house, and Manners followed directly behind. I tailed the last of our merry bunch, with Fringe and his friend and the girl dripping makeup behind me to boost the procession with a show of authority.

We marched out onto the front veranda. A girl stood between the legs of a guy seated on a low wall, resting her bangled hands on his thighs. Two other chaps were standing around, both of whom I recognised as local boys I was on good terms with. By the kerb two sizeable guys were leaning against a sedan. Two girls stood in front of them, giggling and playing up.

We stepped off the veranda and Manners stopped abruptly. 'Changed me mind,' he announced.

Party Host looked us over. 'Ok, but stay out here and don't come back inside.' He gave Manners a parting glare and turned to leave.

Saunders said, 'Send out some sandwiches,' and Manners hooted with laughter.

'You with these guys?' Fringe asked me, having caught on I was the least trouble. Party Host turned around in support.

'Guess so,' I answered.

'Then watch your mate, will you?' Party Host said, flicking a finger at Manners. 'There's plenty of people here want to enjoy themselves. Any trouble and we call the cops.'

It wasn't a smart thing to say. It told us loud and clear what he thought of any troops he had.

'We'll just stand here,' I promised, 'drink our beer.'

'What about your mate?' he replied. 'Is that going to keep him happy?'

Manners turned on him sharply. 'I'm getting pretty fucking tired of being happy,' he snarled. It was a familiar turning point; face glowing red, chin thrust forward, hands balling into fists. He was looking straight into the guy's eyes, spitting sparks out of his own.

'Woah Manners,' I said. 'Too early.'

'I don't give a shit,' Manners growled. 'This prick here's going to be real sorry anytime now.'

There followed a lot of swearing and posturing from Manners, and some fairly impressive diplomacy from our party host and his two buddies. Though these friends of mine weren't the sharpest tools in the shed, what they were good at they did very well. They were sharks. They could sniff out fear and weakness as good as anything that lived by the tooth; a skill they'd acquired through a lot of trial and error. It was part body language, part common sense. They knew a threat, and there simply wasn't anything of that design out here. Enough guys stood around to match us in numbers, but those on the veranda were fringe acquaintances of ours and weren't going to step in, swinging at least, so you could rule them out. The only ones worth serious consideration stood at the kerb, and the girls they were working on looked too classy to risk having their night spoiled by sticking up for a couple of nobodies. You couldn't always put your finger on it, you just knew.

Saunders, Grigg, and Finlay moved to the flank, glancing around to keep Manners covered. I stood back a bit with Kep, close enough to show where our allegiance lay, far away enough to let the opposition know we were neutral. I could see Manners fast losing patience, could see that the party boys had picked up on it too.

Fringe nudged Party Host. 'Come on, just leave him.'

For a moment, the man seemed to oblige. 'Take a chill pill,' he said, and let his scowl linger on Manners a bit longer. He shook his head contemptuously and made to turn. I felt sorry enough for the poor sod to almost say out loud: *Mate, do not turn your back*—

Manners moved before I finished the thought. His torso twisted and there was the blur of his arm I could never follow. All I caught was the flash of white knuckles the moment they smacked into the side of the guy's face so hard it made me wonder how the human skull could take such punishment without caving in. He went over like a tree, so quick his legs hardly bent, and no arm came up to break his fall. There was a mild thump as his head hit the turf and bounced once or twice. He'd fallen facing my way and I saw that his eyes were half-open. The emptiness behind them told me they saw nothing.

The girl shrieked. Not a true, deep-lung scream, more a high-pitched groan of utter disbelief. She was over him in a second, her shrieking giving way to loud sobs. Manners stood over his victim, snarling down with his fists cocked.

'Take a close look, boys,' he hissed at the other kids. 'Anyone else want to bite the dust?'

'Jesus . . .' Fringe moved forward in slow steps. He crouched down and put a hand on the guy's forehead; I could see his fingers trembling. 'Amie, can you go and get some ice?' he said to the girl in a soft, shaky voice. I put it down to shock. Ice. A fat lot of good that'd do.

He looked up at Manners. 'What'd you go doing that for?' he asked in a subdued voice.

'Watch your mouth mate, or you'll get the same,' Manners warned.

'Just fucking leave, will you?' Amie yelled, her eyes a flood of tears. 'Go! Get away from us!'

Right then I noticed two guys hurrying toward us. They must have just come out of the house. Both had the bulk to fill their clothes but they had a sozzled look and their steps weren't as sharp and straight as they should have been. Fringe stood up, buoyed by the arrival of numbers.

'Go on! Get out of here!' he said loudly, a sight braver than he was before.

'What do you reckon boys?' Manners said to us. 'We ready to go?'

'He didn't ask us very nicely,' Saunders said, like he meant it.

The new guys came up to us and stopped. One of them knelt by

Party Host and checked him over. 'What happened?'

'This one hit him,' Amie blubbered, pointing.

The guy stood up and faced Manners off. It was a bold gesture but his eyes lacked courage and he kept his body well out of arm's length. Manners gave him ample time to have a shot, but the guy just stood there.

Manners turned to go. We all turned to go. It was all over, we were leaving. So why did this guy just have to say, 'Mate, I know you. You're Barry Mannering. We got plenty of friends, dickhead. Better not show your face local.'

Manners and Saunders turned on him with relish. The bravado on the guy's face flashed with annoyance, that *what the hell do you want now* look. Like this had nothing to do with him.

My two friends put an end to his confusion with a flurry of punches before he could raise his hands. They were more vicious with him because he tried to stay standing. Didn't put up a fight though, just tried to grapple with the two of them. His buddy came to his aid with a clumsy swing of his arm that brushed Saunders' head, and Finlay reached him in two steps. A few smacks in the head later the guy was scurrying away on his knees and Finlay and Grigg kicked him into some bushes where he curled up tight as a fist and wisely stayed that way.

As usual, the few party-goers on the front lawn and veranda just stood there watching. With a coordinated effort they could have assembled some troops and beat the stuffing out of us, or at least stopped it, but as usual they did nothing. Like watching prisoners of war, thousands of them sometimes, march past a handful of guards. United you stand, divided you fall. We lived by it.

The guy Manners and Saunders was beating into finally dropped and curled into a ball with his arms and hands protecting his face from the boots that started in. There was a lot of loud thumping and there'd be a few nasty bruises, but like his mate in the bushes he'd be walking out of there as long as he stayed curled and brassed it out. Might need a stitch here or there, and a check over Party Host from a doctor wouldn't be a bad idea, but all three would be hobbling out of here . . . eventually.

The kicks got softer and Manners stepped back panting. 'Hey,' he said, looking down at his feet. The guy peeked up at him from between his arms. His face was bloodied and he had an eyebrow as mangled as squashed grapes.

'Yeah, I think I know you too,' Manners went on. 'What's your name?'

The kid stared back and didn't answer. Manners leaned down, grabbed his jacket and lifted him to his feet. 'I'm talking to you!'

'That there's Jacob,' Saunders said. 'Hangs around Dinos and his losers.'

'Jacob!' Manners cried, lining him up with his fist. 'How you going mate!'

Jacob tried to turn his face away as Manners' fist lunged forward. It cracked loudly on the back of his head and he dropped but didn't lie flat. He gathered himself up on all fours, dazed but still with it. One hand came up and felt the side of his head while the other stayed on the ground keeping him steady.

The back of the head is where the skull is thickest, apparently. Never one to give up easily, Manners stooped down and hauled him to his feet again. 'You listening?' he said, the smile on his face stretched ear-to-ear. 'Hey!' he shook him roughly, 'You listening?'

'Yeah,' Jacob said feebly.

'Watch your mouth.' This time Manners aimed for the cheek and got him better. Jacob dropped again and lay face down. I couldn't tell if he was out or not, but this time he stayed there.

'Righto!' Manners said. 'Let's go boys.'

We headed off to the car. A few beers never stopped Grigg driving; he actually claimed they made him drive better. I slid into the back and Manners got in beside me and closed the door. As we pulled away from the kerb he felt around his neck. 'Aw shit, me chain come off.'

We pulled up at the front of the house. The same crowd was there, along with several girls sniffling and weeping. The guy from the bushes was up and about, Jacob was sitting on the grass nursing his head with a wet towel, and Party Host was on his back now with his arm over his face like he was blocking out a bright light. It appeared he was coming to. Fringe and a new guy were kneeling beside him. Manners stepped out of the car and I saw the new guy unfurl. He was impressively built, about an even six feet with lumps and bulges beneath his shirt in all the right places.

Head down, Manners began looking for his necklace. The new guy calmly came forward. Manners would have had him at the corner of his eye, but he pretended not to see him.

The new guy said, 'This the guy, Rob?'

'Yeah,' said Fringe.

If fear and timidity are easily sussed, likewise is balls. It took all of about a nanosecond for Manners to see the game wasn't over. He straightened out of his slouch and looked straight at him.

'You're all man, arsehole,' the new guy said. 'King-hitting blokes when they're not looking. Going to go brag about it later, you gutless piece of shit?'

The sloppiness left Manners' posture. You could see he wasn't intimidated – it took a hell of a lot more than that – but I saw that flash of surprise on his face that came with knowing the fun had come cheap up till then.

Saunders, Grigg, and Finlay were out of the car in an instant. My following them was part reflex, part habit. Kep followed behind me. That was the thing about Kep; he did whatever I did.

'What a surprise!' the new guy said. 'Three . . . four . . . five more dickheads! Because where there's one, there's always more.'

I quickly stepped ahead and stood alongside Manners. The new guy glared at us with eyes to make a demon pause. I put a hand on Manners' shoulder to usher him away but I doubt he even felt it.

'Mate,' I appealed to the new guy, 'you'd best back off. You'll regret it.'

'No, my regret is that I wasn't here about five minutes ago.'

I tightened my grip on Manners' shoulder but he brushed me off and stepped forward with a snarl on his face like a tabby cat. The new guy's hands shot up and balled into fists, his shoulders hunched and his head sunk a fraction. A foot came forward, leg slightly bent, and his expression turned into something that sobered you quicker than a dunking of ice. This guy meant business.

'Just me and you?' he growled. 'Or are you too piss-weak to fight one-on-one?'

In the short lag that followed, I wondered what he was thinking. Surely he knew that someone who king-hit a bloke from behind wasn't going to do him the honour of fighting one-on-one. Surely he knew that guys who didn't think twice about busting someone's nose or knocking someone's teeth out or giving someone brain damage had it in them to fight by some sort of code. Maybe he thought he was Bruce Lee or something.

I knew Manners well. If he'd been sober, he would have backed off a step, taken off his shirt perhaps. He'd do a dance with the guy, use the precious seconds to size him up, wait for an opening. Manners was no athlete but he knew how to use his size and weight to advantage.

If he'd been sober. With five mates behind him and about ten beers under his belt he did away with the formality and went at him like a bull. A step or two away from him he twisted slightly, cocked his thick arm and lunged at him in a wild overarm swing, fist heading for the guy's face like a cricket ball on middle stump.

I didn't see the new guy move. His fist shot out like a muzzle flash and there was a sharp crack as Manners' head jerked backwards. He staggered a bit before regathering his feet. The big guy stepped lightly to the side, arms up like a praying mantis.

Saunders sprang at him. He came in low for the tackle, head down to protect his face. Just as he made contact the big guy hopped a little to the side, put a hand on the back of Saunders' head to stabilise it and lifted his knee with precision timing.

Ever the athlete, Saunders managed to twist his head at the last instant. The guy's knee brushed the side of his face enough to take a bit of skin with it, but it lacked the weight behind it to send him into dreamtime.

Saunders caught the leg and held on. There was an insane dance between the two, then Finlay and Grigg barrelled into the guy from behind and all four of them were on the ground. Manners came up and waited his moment. At the first gap in the writhing mess, he drew his leg back and sent a heavy boot into the guy's ribs as he got to his knees. There was a deep thump and I saw his face contort with pain, but not a tweak left his lips. Manners kicked again but this time the guy caught it, got to his feet and drove his shoulder into Manners' waist, lifting him clear off the ground. Manners hung on tightly, curling his body to break his fall as the ground came up to meet him. They hit the ground with a loud thump and there was an audible whoosh of air from Manners' lungs.

Then the boots came in. One after the other, thick, meaty sounds that reminded me of hitting the tackle bags at rugby training. Around this time my mind usually flashed with an image of some macho-hero belting the bejesus out of the bad guys like some action-movie cliché. A part of me always hoped to see it, but it never happened. Not to this team.

The guy rolled off Manners and somehow got to his feet again. Hopelessly outnumbered he still managed to get the odd punch in, but his gallantry only raised the anger of my friends laying into him. No matter how hard he tried he couldn't deliver that knockout punch, couldn't land a good kick between the leg-arch. He fought off my friends better than anyone I'd ever seen getting a thrashing but in the end reality prevailed. It was an ugly, unbalanced affair and he'd feel the cost of his bravery for a few days yet. But I'd never seen anyone last as long on his feet, I gave him that. One-on-one he'd have been more than a match for any of us.

This probably only went on for a minute or so, it always felt longer. As usual, I stood back with Kep in neutral territory.

There was a break in the melee when the guy managed to throw Saunders off balance and step out of reach of Grigg and Finlay. Manners was having a breather, standing back and wiping blood from a split lip. There was a growing lump under his eye too. All four friends of mine had caught a fist or elbow by the look of it, but nothing worse than a tough day on a rugby paddock.

Manners stepped forward with his arms cocked in boxing mode, the side of his mouth flecked with blood and spittle. 'Keep it coming,' he invited.

There was a voice behind us. 'Hey, don't you reckon he's had enough.'

It sounded like an instruction, not a question. We all turned. The two guys that were over at the kerb were approaching calmly.

There was a brief stand-off as my friends did the arithmetic, simple even for them. Three or four now to our six . . . the numbers were getting uncomfortable. Without making a show of it, my four brave buddies turned and headed for the car.

I kept my eyes on the new guy. His brow was split and dripping a fair bit of blood down his face, and panting deeply he wiped some of it away with a couple of fingers and flicked it dry. His shirt was flapping open and missing most of its buttons. Personally, I was happy for him that we were leaving. The guy deserved a break.

Not far away, Amie was watching us. There was a triumphant glint in her eye that irked me. I walked on over and stopped a couple of metres away. She didn't flinch; she knew she was safe.

I made a broad gesture at the carnage lying around us – the concussed, the bleeding, the weeping. 'You just couldn't let it go, could you?' I said.

I glared at her long enough to drive the point home, saw pure hatred shine in her eyes. I turned on my heel and followed my friends to the car.

Two

The old man drove me in that first Monday morning. We pulled into the college carpark and soon as he yanked the hand-brake I was out the door, a second later and I'd scooted round to the back. The boot popped open and I reached inside to grab a bag. Dad came up from behind.

'Just let me know if you've forgotten anything,' he repeated for about the fifth time. 'I can drop by anytime.' He pulled out a suitcase.

'Ok, thanks.' I grabbed a small carry-bag and slung the strap over my shoulder.

'Ring us tonight, okay? Tell us how you're settling in.'

'Sure.' I took out the last suitcase.

'Here, let me help.'

'It's okay Dad,' I groaned. 'It's not my first day of school.'

'Right.' Dad grinned and held out his hand. I dropped a bag and shook it. 'Starts here though,' he said, 'all over again.'

With a heavy suitcase in each hand my trapeziuses were aching when I reached the main entrance of college. There I paused, took in the Gothic-style architecture. For the early founders of the country's first university, reviving the medieval fad might have been as much a statement as a student residence; for one of its boys a century and a half later it conjured troubling images of the traditions he was in for, passed down from the dark ages as well no doubt.

The admin officer was all cosmetics and smiles as she took my details, ticked me off on some list and handed me a plastic bag. I reached inside and flicked through some maps, a booklet of Sydney University I had already, membership forms for the student representative council, and student union stuff. After signing a form and handing over Dad's cheque for a full term I was told to head for the dining hall. She started to give me directions and I told her I'd been shown the place on Open Day the year before.

Fresh-faced students nodded my way, an older boy or two smiled conspiratorially, and year photos lining each side of the corridor went from black and white to colour as I walked through. I entered the Junior Common Room and saw a TV in a wall unit at the front playing to empty chairs. Dominating the walls were sporting team photos. A white noticeboard hung prominently by a dozen or more steps that led up to another level.

A tall guy with neatly combed hair came over to me wearing a T-shirt that read 'St Phillips O-Week Committee.' Beneath the scrawl was a cartoon of a guy doubled over and retching.

'G'day,' he greeted me pleasantly. 'Signing in?'

'Guess so.'

'Up the stairs. You can leave your stuff here.'

I dumped my suitcases and carry-bag by a wall and climbed the steps into the massive dining hall, lined by a series of long mahogany-coloured tables with cushioned benches. The place had the feel of a cathedral. The walls were decorated with framed portraits of past college elders and polished wooden boards with the glittering names of former presidents, university medallists, sportsmen, politicians and such; an impressive amount of whom would be familiar to the most ignorant Antipodean.

There was a table manned by two older boys, one of whom was writing stuff down with a fresher sitting opposite. My runners squeaked over the polished floor and voices seemed to echo as I headed for the guy with the free spot in front of him. I stopped there and two squinty eyes peered up at me from behind thick glasses. He had greasy blonde hair, a boxer-flat nose, and wore a blue-striped rugby jersey. A card in front of him read: 'Senior Fellow Roland Hardy.'

'How's it doin?' he asked.

'Good.'

'Sit,' he invited, and I slid onto the bench opposite. He flipped open a manila folder and took out a form. 'Name?'

'Steve Chambers'

'Steve . . . Stephen?'

'Just Steve.'

He filled in my name at the top. 'Do any rugby?'

'Not for a couple of years.'

He lifted his pen and cocked an eyebrow. 'Anything else?'

'Cricket.'

'Batter or bowler?'

'Batter.'

'How long you played?'

'Most of high school.'

'Grade?'

'Firsts.'

He twiddled with his pen. 'Any rep stuff?'

'CHS.'

'Yeah?' His eyes twinkled with sudden interest. 'What grade?'

'Firsts.'

'But not rugby.'

'No.'

His nod of approval faded. 'What else?'

I shrugged. 'Bit of this, bit of that.'

He studied me a moment, then slid over a piece of paper. 'Fill this out and bring it back here.'

'Can't I do it in my room?'

'Nuh. Do it over there,' and he pointed to a table where another boy was scribbling away.

I went on over and sat down opposite him. We exchanged short greetings and I started on the paper. I filled in date of birth, high school, undergraduate degree. There were a series of questions beneath. The first asked if I played certain sports: rugby, cricket, soccer, tennis, basketball, rowing, athletics, swimming. Beside each was a yes/no box with an asterisk beside the 'yes' that invited you to elaborate with information about how long, who for, and level attained. I circled 'yes' to rugby and gave myself a slightly embellished version of what I'd given Hardy. For cricket I didn't think I needed to. Beneath this was an alphabetical list of other sports to tick, everything from archery to yoga. I smiled at things like blind skeet-shooting and nude limbo-dancing.

The next question asked me to list any other extracurricular pursuits, and I wrote: 'chess.' The one after that asked if I owned a car: 'no.' After that the standard deteriorated: how many drinks per week, if I owned things like Y-fronts, books by Germaine Greer, music by George Michael, a cat, a signed Australian Rules football or jersey . . . One question read: If you could spend one hour with anyone of your choosing, alive or dead, who would it be and why?

My pen hung above the sheet at this one. I'd heard it before and I don't think my answer ever changes. What I would give to pick the brain of Pytheas . . . Da Vinci. What I would give to stare upon the face of Jesus, kick the living shit out of Stalin. I twiddled with my pen, looked at the other guy. He frowned down on his sheet as if it was an exam paper. In the end I just wrote: Linda Lovelace. Why do you reckon?

As soon as I wrote it down, I regretted it. It was lame and embarrassingly unoriginal. Just like the rest of this imbecilic questionnaire. I felt like I'd fallen into some kind of trap. I went to cross it out, but then it occurred to me that'd just make it look worse.

I lost my enthusiasm for the thing after that. More questions followed – music tastes, what my goals in life were. It all seemed free of conspiracy so I filled it out quickly and truthfully without giving it much thought. The bottom of the sheet read:

Thank you for filling in this form. Rest assured your answers will be held in the strictest of confidence. Welcome to the Phil. Now go get your keys.

I handed my form back to Hardy, who read it over without expression. 'Okay, let's go,' he said after a bit.

I picked up my bags and followed him out to a cropped rectangular courtyard enclosed by the four wings of college. A game of cricket was in full swing. A guy threw a wobbly spinner and the batsman whacked the tennis ball into a multi-layered flower garden. Petals leapt into the air as someone stampeded in after it. We entered B-Wing staircase and climbed a flight of stairs and I followed Hardy down the corridor until he stopped at a door. He inserted a key and pushed it open.

'Not a bad floor here,' he said. 'Your Resident Fellow is Wes Metcalf. He'll catch up with you shortly.' Then he gave me a key.

I walked into the room and was hit by a musty aroma as unique as a person's own. The smell was unlike anything that had found my nose before, a curious blend of matter that disguised any trace of its individual constituents. I threw my bags onto the bed and Hardy started off.

'Dinner is from five-thirty,' he said over his shoulder.

'Hey . . .'

He stopped and turned around. 'Yeah?'

'These room allocations – anything to do with the answers to that questionnaire?'

He grinned and walked away.

I waited until about quarter to six before going down for dinner. I wasn't keen on sitting at a table on my lonesome, dork written all over my face. I needn't have feared. When I got there a long line had already formed. No one was moving.

'What's the wait?' I asked the last guy in the line.

'No older boys here.'

'What?'

'Freshers can't get served until a second year or above gets here.'

'Is this a joke?'

'Nope.'

Such was my introduction to what I would come to know as St Phillips's unique version of contemporary bastardry. Not that I was ignorant; I shouldn't have acted so surprised. One doesn't sign up for a college without doing the homework. Mild and harmless as the stories sounded, they didn't disclose the nitty-gritty of how ruthlessly rules were enforced. Some of it sounded like a hoot, some of it sounded out of order, the rest sounded harmless. Mind you I hadn't heard the one about having to wait in line for dinner until some demigod graced us with his presence.

Bugger it. I walked down the line to the kitchen entrance where stacks of plates and wooden trays were neatly piled on a table, along with utensils upended in little mesh cups. On the wall at eye-level was a display board with the night's menu: chicken or veal. A large notice stuck prominently below this warned:

Freshers not be served until venerable second year or above has taken seat. And no trespassing. You are being watched.

After piling utensils and plates onto the tray, I made my way past frowning faces to the front of the queue into the kitchen serving area where steaming chicken and veal and mash and pumpkin and peas and carrots and other mother's-choice delicacies fogged up the glass panels. I placed my tray onto the shiny aluminium counter and images of M.A.S.H. came to mind. A plump young ponytailed girl wearing a white frock and apron was fussing about on the other side with her back to me.

'Hi there,' I said with a boyish smile.

She turned around with a pot in her hand and smiled back. 'Hello.'

I held out my plate. 'Are we early?'

'Are you a first-year?'

'That's right.'

'You should wait.'

'For what?'

She grinned. 'You *are* a first-year.'

'Aw, come on.'

'We've been given instructions.'

A line of freshers watched me with faces like cows. For a moment I felt like one too. 'Shit.' Prudence demanded I not be the one to put this rule to the test. I took a step back.

'Hey,' some big bloke quipped, 'back in line.'

'Yeah M A O.'

I returned to my place. We stood around fidgeting, not saying much to one another. A few minutes later, right out of the blue, my eardrums nearly burst at the shock of three notes that turned soundwaves physical. We all jumped as if a bomb had gone off.

DA . . . DA . . . DA!

The booming intro to *Jesus Christ Superstar* had no equivalent.

DA . . . DA . . . DA! Second bar, a pitch higher.

All heads turned toward the steps of the JCR where a bunch of boys appeared, led by a guy wearing junk necklaces, a gold-painted paper crown, and a white robe that looked made from bedsheets. The din thumping out of the loudspeakers strung up on the walls was so loud the floor vibrated. One or two boys covered their ears with their hands.

I could only assume it was our college president, Trent Finch, known to me thus far by name only. He walked slow and ceremonious, like a bride approaching the Alter. On passing by he looked us over with an expression of supreme arrogance, like Herod would have himself, screwing his nose and grimacing like we were the scum of the Earth. A couple of kids clapped as they moved past. Anyone that didn't give him enough space received an enthusiastic nudge from one of his entourage.

The all-important point made, someone mercifully turned the volume down. The group reached the table with its trays and cutlery, took what they needed and walked past everyone to the front of the line. The Pres slid his tray onto the counter and spoke in a voice loud enough for all to hear.

'Chicken, mash, carrots, no peas . . .'

And on it went until all his cronies had been served. They moved away and we lesser mortals were served. I had my dinner slopped onto the plate and stopped at the kitchen exit wondering where to park. By sitting where they did, our advance party showed us which side of the room was out of bounds. I elected to sit amongst the group making the most noise but once we'd swapped names it didn't take long for me to realise I was in a different gene pool. I kept my questions brief and left as soon as I'd chewed my last mouthful.

That evening I sat up with about fifty others watching *Trading Places* and *Aliens* in the JCR. Seniors clustered at the front on seats with the backrest marked 'Reserved,' joking about and drinking beer like lords of creation. An O-week schedule of activities posted on the noticeboard drew a lot of attention. I waited until the credits to *Trading Places* started to roll before stretching my legs and checking it out. I ruled out things like tours of the university, sports club meetings, and offers to join obscure groups, and made a mental note of others. A bow and arrow competition on our college oval next morning sounded interesting, and prizes in the form of drink vouchers for our Saturday Night Welcome Cabaret settled it. Too late I learnt that a couple of minutes at the noticeboard were enough to forfeit my chair. I squeezed in amongst some freshers on a stained lounge at the back.

When Ripply tucked Newt in, I took her lead. At the foot of my staircase the door to my Resident Fellow's room was open and a few guys were hanging about out front and inside. A stocky guy stuck out a hand as I walked past. 'Wes Metcalf,' he said with an iron-grip handshake, and his sharp eyes never strayed from me in the conversation that followed. He offered me a glass of what he called rocket fuel and answered my look of enquiry by pointing to a plastic garbage bin. A glimpse at the concoction inside made me wonder if they'd emptied it first. I passed on the offer and he regarded me like I was some kind of weirdo.

My first night in college was spent listening to the muffled thump of Cold Chisel, the slap of feet on courtyard tiles, the banging of doors and lunatic laughter that jarred me awake every time I managed to slip under.

About fifty guys and a good smattering of women had already assembled on the oval when I turned up for this bow and arrow event. Leading the show was an RF with a merry face and Friar-tuck belly who introduced himself as Jeremy Franks.

It was a glorious summer's day. A fluffy breeze played against our skins and the occasional cloud put us in the shade. My interest in bows and arrows paled at the sight of a good many girls dressed in tight-fitting shorts, t-shirts and singlets – pink everywhere. What was it about pink?

About a dozen bows and a large pile of target arrows were piled on the grass beside a Holden Ute for people to help themselves. About thirty metres away a series of targets had been set up on some stands. They'd picked the place on the merits of a safe backstop; empty oval marked by a boundary of witch's hats you'd have to be blind to walk into. For added safety beside the targets were bales of hay. It impressed me that our college might own such stuff until I learnt it was all on loan from the archery club.

From the start I could see I wasn't the only one who'd never fired a bow. We stood around testing our muscles, pulling on the string and letting it snap back.

'Hey,' Franks said when he saw what we were doing. 'Don't dry-fire the bows.'

'What?'

'Don't shoot them empty. Buggers the stock.'

It was way too early in the morning for some of us. We put ourselves in a good cheer with a fair amount of jibing. My RF, reeking liquor from every pore, was a walking zombie. He fumbled with a bow like it weighed a bit, prompting someone to joke, 'There a PCA level for shooting these things?'

'I'll give him a point for standing straight,' Franks answered. He had a clipboard tucked under his armpit, assumedly for scoring.

I was waiting for the fun to begin when I noticed three guys coming over. Two were freshers I'd already met, frail and short and nothing to draw attention. The guy in the middle was the type that did. He walked with the effortless gait of a professional athlete, and a halo of calmness floated about him. *Jesus H Christ.* It was the big guy at the party my friends had beaten into.

All things considered, he had to a part of our happy frat. I wouldn't have missed him at dinner or during the movies, so I figured he got in late last night or early this morning.

Shit.

I went through the motions of pretending I hadn't seen him. The three of them joined the group of another RF.

'Right, let's get started,' Franks declared, picking up a bow. 'Listen carefully. These aren't toys. At full draw they might be twenty pounds max but they'll put a target arrow through you from a mile away. So no stuffing around.'

There were another two or three minutes of prep talk before he demonstrated. It surprised me that fitting an arrow onto a bowstring wasn't as easy as Franks made it look. Incompetence made us equals; no one seemed to be able to find the right grip or pull the arrow back without it slipping from the nock or dropping it.

'We'll keep this simple,' Franks went on. 'Depending on how quick we get through, we'll do two or three rounds. You get three shots each and score points depending on where you hit the target, just like a dartboard. Yellow bullseye is fifty, red circle is twenty-five, blue is fifteen, and black is ten. Hit on the board gets you five points, miss it completely you get ten deducted. Team with the most points at the end gets drinks vouchers for our Saturday night cabaret. We've thrown in a couple of jackpots, those two balloons you can see. The yellow one up close gets you a drink voucher, the orange one behind gets your team an entire case. You pick what you shoot at.' Then he did a quick count. 'Divide yourself into teams of five.'

'What if someone hits a jackpot early?' a goofy-looking guy named Spike asked.

'Then I'll blow up another balloon . . . *imbecile*.'

Metcalf pointed a finger my way and motioned me to join his group. There he introduced me to several bods, one of whom was a lean, bleach-haired dude named Joey Prentiss. There was a bit of discussion between the team leaders as to which team would go first, amicably settled by the flip of a coin.

After watching the first team, I knew I wouldn't be embarrassed. The standard seemed to drop every other shot. Any arrow that thumped into the target was followed by a solid round of claps. The scores would have been mighty impressive if there'd been points for hitting the bales.

Three teams took their turn before mine. Metcalf swayed as he tried to keep balance. 'Be easier to hit the target if I could see the bloody thing.'

Every so often I glanced sideways at the guy we'd beaten into. He seemed the quiet type. Didn't offer anything in the way of hooting and hollering that followed whenever an arrow flew wide. There was something about him at odds with his team, and everyone else for that matter.

My turn came. I aimed my face away from the big dude as I took position at the mark. I picked up the bow and saw he'd taken up chatting to a girl. He still hadn't seen me.

I focussed on the task ahead. Unlike a lot of the other guys, I didn't act like I knew what I was doing. My first arrow flew wide of the board, but by then everyone had exhausted their one-liners and it barely drew a chuckle. My two next shots made up for it, thumping into the board to take my total to a whopping ten points. This enviable score attainted, I heard someone say we were coming second last.

Franks' team went next. With a show of nonchalance that fell well short of genuine, he elevated his team into first place with two shots and wasn't shy about declaring a total score of eighty-five points. Once the congratulations died down – most of it from himself and his team – he lined himself up for the furthest balloon, the closest evidently not worthy of his skills. We did hush though as he lifted the bow and pulled back the arrow, but even to my inexperienced eye it didn't look right. Perhaps it was his stance – the angle of his arms, the height of his elbow – but that faraway balloon looked too ambitious a distance for the image he presented us with. He let loose and sure enough, the arrow flew wide. It was a good shot, but a miss is a miss and his team deflated with an exclamation of despair immediately drowned by a cheer from the crowd that was only fitting for the arrogant bastard.

Then the big dude's team took their turn. Three of his teammates went first and distributed their arrows more or less evenly between target and bales, and then he walked forward to take the bow.

Something about the way he moved hushed everyone up. His movements were precise and tight, and an air of lazy confidence floated about him. Maybe it was because we'd had enough of skylarking, but voices dried up as he took his place. I looked closely for any war wounds he carried from the other night and saw not a single blemish on his square-jawed, chiselled face.

Pointing the bow down, he nocked the arrow onto the bowstring and guided the shaft onto its rest without the slightest fumble. 'Case of beer, huh?' was all he said, and no one answered. His keen eyes made a random sweep, and he saw me.

At once his entire body stiffened; that unconscious tensing of muscles that came with someone seriously sizing you up. A sober look appeared on his face and I knew he'd made the connection. The sinews of his forearm holding the bow tightened and for a moment I thought he was going to bring it up and take aim at my face.

A fly buzzed around his face, his hand left the string and he casually swatted it away. Then, as if I was of equal consequence, his gaze left me and he turned his attention onto the target.

I knew it was all over when I saw what happened next. In one snappy movement, he drew back the arrow and raised the bow. His hand stopped alongside his cheek and didn't budge the instant the bow was levelled. There was absolutely no difference between him and what you saw in an Olympic archer.

That one, precise movement had us all piqued. Everyone stood as statue-still as him. His eyes were narrow and intense, as if nothing existed but what he was aiming at. The arrow might have been glued in place.

It shot out and stuck into the bullseye. Immediately his team exploded with a cheer, followed by a cacophony of laughing and clapping and swearing and crying foul. I did a quick calculation. With one shot his team was leading. He might have got himself a shag too, the way the girls in his team hopped up and down like teenagers at a pop concert.

'Get the—' Franks lamented, cutting himself short '—out of here.'

The big dude picked up his second arrow and again the noise died. As effortlessly as his first aim, he pulled back and took aim.

Before I could turn my head to follow I heard a snap and instantaneous pop. It had been done too quickly for anything more than a half-hearted aim, and again the crowd burst into a cheer.

'Aw, piss off already!' Franks cried.

I glanced at the closest target, now only a tiny piece of yellow rubber flapping in the breeze. I turned back to him and saw that he'd already fitted his third arrow into place. He lined it up for the furthest balloon and again the crowd hushed.

He took a bit longer with his third shot. Even my RF lifted with a whiff of energy. While most people were watching the target, I was watching him. His forehead was slightly contracted, and there was a shine in his eye that wasn't from the early morning sun. I saw the corner of a lip lift slightly, a twitter of amusement you'd only notice if you were watching carefully.

Fifty people stood around in complete silence, and I wondered how many were actually thinking he was going to miss.

The bow sprung back with a snicker and I stayed on him. I didn't need to see where the arrow went, didn't need to hear the far-sounding pop of balloon followed by another eruption of hooting and clapping and laughing. The guy's poise never faltered. He followed through straight as a tree, then his arm slackened and the bow came down. The girl he'd been talking to threw her arms around him, knocking him off his rock-solid balance.

The only team left now was Spike's, and given the standard up till then it didn't matter how many rounds would follow. The show was as good as won.

'Hey Franks,' Spike said. 'You gonna blow up another balloon now?'

'Nuh.'

'Hey! You said—'

'I make the rules here Spike, I can change them. One case of beer's enough. You're the one complaining our JCR subs are too high, tight arse. Get your freebies Saturday night from William Tell here.'

Three

That evening I was waiting in a line for dinner with other docile freshers when this guy walked by, bound for the front with a look on his face that said no one was going to get in his way. I'd seen this kid already – a runt like the rest of us. His face was roundish and puffy, like baby fat, his body the same. All that was missing was the dummy. He stopped at the front of the queue and held up his plate.

The grey-haired matron of our kitchen staff slopped some curried sausages onto his plate. 'Vegetables or fries?'

'Fries.'

A guy behind me said, 'S'posed to wait, Schiffers.'

Schiffers took his plate and headed out.

'Way to go, bro,' someone commended with a clap. It sounded more like a gesture of condolence than support.

Schiffers sat down at a table on his lonesome. A minute or two later two boys strode into the dining room. One was a senior with a bloated gut and beaked nose called Alex Pronk who I'd already met. His mate was new to me; well-rounded, broad-shouldered and cauliflower-eared. Classic front-rower type. Their gaze fell on this brazen new kid and stayed there. Surprise lit up their faces momentarily, followed by wicked grins. They went on over.

The dining hall fell quiet. Schiffers was the only one not watching them.

Pronk sat down with his mate opposite. He clasped his hands together and leaned forward with his elbows on the table. Schiffers cut off some sausage and steered it into his mouth without looking up.

'Hey there,' Pronk said. 'Meal to your satisfaction?'

'Yes, thanks,' Schiffers mumbled through a full mouth.

'Not too hot, not too cold? We can take it back for you, if you like.'

'It's fine.'

'Hmm . . . Schiffers, right?'

'Schiffer, actually.'

'Settling in okay?'

'I guess.'

'Anything we can get for you, anything we can do to make your stay here more comfortable?'

'I'm good.'

'Hey Jeffro,' Pronk said to his companion. 'Don't we have a rule here?'

'Which one?' asked Jeffro.

'Something about freshers not getting served until one of the esteemed has taken seat.'

'I do believe we do.'

Pronk looked confused. 'But this guy's a fresher.'

'I do believe he is.'

'Hmm.' Pronk raised his eyebrows, pretending surprise. Without a word, he slid from the bench and stood. 'Hmm,' he repeated, then walked away with Jeffro to the front of the queue. They got served and sat down on their side of the hall.

Schiffer ate away quietly. I thought it worth an enquiry and so after getting served I walked over, followed by a chap who'd been waiting behind me.

'You're in the shit now, Dave,' the guy following me said. We sat down.

'What are they gonna do?' Schiffer answered in a bored voice. 'Beat my head in?'

The new guy held his hand out to me and I shook it. 'Mick Reiner.' He was a well-groomed boy with cheery lines on his face, and when he smiled you knew it was for real. I connected with him from the start.

'Steve Chambers.'

Schiffer put his fork down and offered me his hand. 'David Schiffer,' he said as I shook it. He scooped up his fork and another piece of sausage disappeared into his maw.

Prentiss and some guys I'd seen at the bow and arrow competition joined us and there were handshakes amongst those who hadn't met. Hardy dropped by to let us know he was one of a bunch of returning students tasked by the Student Club Committee with helping freshers find their feet. He asked us if we had any particular questions.

'Yeah,' I said. 'What other rules they got around here?'

'You'll find out.'

Schiffer said, 'I thought we did away with this Dickensian, boarding-school bastardry about a century ago.'

'That's because you went to a government school, Schiffers,' Reiner said. 'Most boys here come from private ones.'

'Yeah well, what if I just told them to stick it up their ring? What are they going to do?'

'Try it and you'll see,' Hardy suggested.

'We'll be told when we can go piss next.'

'Ease up,' Hardy said. 'It's not that bad.'

'What happens if things turn nasty?' I asked. 'Isn't there some kind of . . . I don't know . . . regulating body or whatnot?'

'Uni's governing body has nothing to do with the colleges,' Hardy explained. 'They're all independently owned and run. Someone'd have to be murdered before any of them showed up here, and even then it'd be just to make sure the mess was cleaned up.'

'What about this rector I keep hearing about?' Reiner asked.

'What's a rector?' I asked.

'Someone who's supposed to look into these sorts of things,' Schiffer answered.

'We got rectors, principals, senior tutors, chaplains even,' Hardy explained. 'Whatever. They move in different circles. You'll see them walking around, and even then you'll wonder if they see you.'

'So how bad does it get?' I asked.

'Depends what you call bad,' Hardy resumed. 'Not bad enough to stop people coming here, or staying here. If you don't like it, find somewhere that gives a toss.' He shook his head at some private thought. 'It happens now and then, not that that stops anyone. We got a shortlist of bods ready to fill an empty room.'

The dining hall filled. It always intrigued me how some dumb fish, or bird, or bug, without the slightest notion of what it was or how it looked, knew exactly what it wanted when it grouped with its own kind. Here we were, a few meals in, and the same principle was on display. Of the dozen or so guys seated around me I sensed a like-minded way of thinking and a smattering of common interests, and I was grateful the next time I collected dinner I wouldn't have to deliberate over where to sit.

Seniors came in and took their tables, not a head turned our way. I sat through dinner primed like a warthog at a waterhole, half-expecting a glob of mashed potato to come flying toward our brave Schiffer – and anyone dumb enough to make his acquaintance – any second.

By dinner's end Hardy had talked us into going to The Grange, our primary college sponsor. A tall, spindly fresher nicknamed Rajah, one of the few students with a car, offered to save me and a couple of boys the walk in. His real name was too difficult for we of the Anglo-Saxon. He was Indian and his name included an 'R' and at least one 'A.' That was close enough.

At the end of an uneventful evening I staggered into the courtyard with Rajah, Schiffer, and a couple of wobbly lads to find a perfectly made bed on the nice green lawn. A set of drawers sat next to it with books stacked neatly on top. Trousers and shirts hung from a make-shift frame and shoes were neatly laid out on the grass at the foot of the bed. We got closer and Schiffer stopped.

'Oh great,' he lamented. 'These are mine.'

We broke out laughing. Poor Schiffer, he was the only one who didn't see the humour. After a moment or two to gloat over his misfortune we left him to his own devices and scooted off probably thinking the same thing: tired and half-drunk was no condition to help drag a bed and gear up who know how many flights of stairs back to his room.

Back in my room I struggled into my pyjamas and stumbled to the bathroom to brush my teeth. Upon returning to my room I heard laughter through my window, muffled words were exchanged and I took a peek outside. Down in the courtyard an older boy was walking off, laughing all the way. Behind him Schiffer crawled into bed and wrapped himself up tight as a baby, cementing the nickname I had in mind for him forever.

One has to muse at a descriptor like *orientation* for a week that passes in a blur. My chief order of business passed unceremoniously early in the week when I joined a long stream of students in the McLaughlin Hall to finalise my enrolment. I proudly handed my forms to a bored-looking woman at a desk who shoved them in a tray and mumbled something about how I could get my timetable for the semester. With that ado I was now, officially, an undergraduate of the Faculty of Science.

Good intentions to attend faculty and school welcomes, information session tours, student transition workshops, inductions and the like were soon abandoned in favour of higher callings, most of which took the form of some alcohol-fuelled romp. A little posturing and chest-beating introduced me to the friendly rivalry between the all-male colleges whenever we passed them on our rounds, while a game of nude touch footy here, a kangaroo court there, and a string of humiliating underground rituals set the tone for what we could expect as the year progressed.

A scavenger hunt showed me into places I'd never see, the rest I explored at leisure. I'd wander lawns festooned with flags and banners, drifting from marquee to marquee, gathering to gathering, losing track of whose society or association or club was beckoning. Poster after poster showcased something to enrol in, somewhere to go. Smells and fragrances new to my nose danced in the air, and now and then a turn of breeze carried the beat of music and voices over loudspeakers, and I'd home in on some college lawn or courtyard to stare at scantily-dressed girls with painted hair, puppy-fat bellies and outrageous body-piercing, swaying about with plastic cups in their hands; girls dressed as nurses, schoolgirls, French maids. Back in my all-boys college bedroom each night I'd lose sleep over how many I'd met who didn't turn their back on me within the minute I started talking to them.

I followed slow-footed tourists through stylish cloisters,

quadrangles and courtyards; through vaulted halls portraited by erstwhile greats and into an unlikely museum to ponder the craftwork of ancient empires, bandaged body parts, and what role chance must have played to land Sir Nick's priceless relics into as improbable and far-flung a resting place as what was, back then, a slight advance on a dumping ground for convicts. I familiarised myself with lecture theatres and prac rooms and noticeboards where students flogged second-hand books; I learnt what discounts my student card entitled me to and which cafeterias made the price of a toasted cheese sandwich or meat pie respectable. I toured the gymnasium seeking inspiration and left it with the matter unresolved. I stopped in front of the Fischer Library and smiled at it without going in. More on that later.

It was a refreshing exercise. There was a carnival atmosphere to it all, an energy in the air akin to the onset of spring, unique in its burst of youth and health and colour of which I contributed. It felt good to know I was part of the place, as opposed to just looking in or passing through. I gave the place its purpose, it gave me mine. One likes to think that centuries, or even millennia from now – assuming we make it that far – if technology wins over lecture theatres and exam halls, some part of places like this would be spared the demolition of progress for our future bioforms to shuffle within and wonder, as we do when camera-clicking our way through some medieval castle, what it was like to actually people its walls.

Perhaps, if they listen closely, they'll hear our ghosts.

We were here.

We cleared the dining hall of its tables and benches on Saturday afternoon and converted it into a dance hall for the Welcome Cab. The first soundwaves thumped across the courtyard just after 7pm. I headed down, handed a twenty-dollar note to someone at the JCR doorway and went straight for a set of tables that served as our makeshift bar. I handed a dollar coin to one of the boys serving and he pulled a can of Tooheys from an esky.

The DJ was parked at one end of the dining room behind a table with a stack of equipment and a revolving ball that sent multicoloured light bubbles swirling across the ceiling and walls and portraits of our austere-faced gentry. I took my beer over to some boys near the doorway shamelessly checking out the talent as soon as it walked through. Our O-week committee had been mighty diligent in handing out invitations and drink vouchers to the girls' colleges indiscriminately.

It wasn't long before the talk turned to rugby. It sent out a blip and within minutes Hardy and a troop of seniors joined us, keen to see how many recruits they'd scored. We talked about the First Division comp of which Sydney University fielded five grades (6 in some years), the intercollege cup, end-of-year tours and bouts of debauchery. Talk turned to positions and predictably there was a glut of flankers.

'Played any other position?' Hardy asked when I nominated this as my preferred spot.

'Not really,' I lied. I just wasn't interested in playing any other position.

'If you play for the Phil, they'll be a few of you competing for the one spot. This chap here's got the other one, that's a given,' he said, gesturing at the guy who was becoming an issue for me. He stood amongst a small group of freshers.

'Who *is* that?'

'Jason Keogh,' and Hardy gave a summary of his football credentials to match his archery skills and make me crook. As we watched a guy headed over to a case of beer and helped himself.

'How did they get their own stash of beers?' someone asked, and Franks updated him on the outcome of the bow and arrow event. 'Anyone wants a freebie, better move fast,' he advised, and Joey and a couple of others went over. I saw Keogh shake hands with all three before bowing down and collecting a can for each.

'Say, Reiner,' Franks asked. 'What noise does a pig make?'

Mick stared back long enough to pass for ignorance, prompting Franks to belch loudly into his face. Mick staggered back a step.

'Thanks,' he groaned.

Franks turned to Schiffer. 'Speaking of which . . . Babs! What noise does a cat make?'

If a couple of days were all it took for seniors to start calling him Babs, I knew the nickname had stuck. I was proud of myself. Schiffer shook his head and answered laconically, 'Nuh.' After that he retreated to a safer part of the room.

Franks glanced around for his next mark, reading faces. When he stopped at mine I shook my head and told him I was initiated to that one at an age when it was soft drinks.

Franks nodded thoughtfully. 'I'll get back to you, then.'

I grinned back at him. 'Good luck.'

He filed it away with a meaningful look. Then a nuggety fresher with a joker's grin carved into his face joined us. He was a likeable fellow for someone who could talk your ears off.

'Flip!' Franks took him up. 'What noise does a cat make?'

Flip's face went blank. Frank's lips lifted triumphantly; there's always one in the crowd.

And so poor Flip mumbled *mee-ow* and *woof* and *neigh* and *baaa* down the list of familiars until Franks got to a whale. Flip paused uncertainly and Franks repeated the question, 'What noise does a whale make?' and Flip shrugged his shoulders naively, the signal for five seniors that had filled their cheeks with beer to spray him like a carwash. We laughed because we've had it done to us before. Flip shook his hair like a dog on leaving the water and headed for the toilets to rinse himself over and reflect on life.

'Does this go on all night?' I asked Hardy.

'Just at the start,' he said. 'They'll tire of it and move onto chasing women.' We settled back into discussion but I took what I'd witnessed as fair warning to stay vigilant for some time yet.

The others dispersed and I found myself alone with Hardy. There was a group of tight-jeaned girls over at a corner with things on their clothes that glittered in the dark. One in particular had the sort of face that didn't need a Uni degree to get her places in life. She kept glancing my way, dainty fingers curled around her plastic cup. At one point I gave her a smile and a nod, and to my astonishment she nudged one of her friends and they wandered over.

'Hi,' she greeted me sweetly. Her eyes flashed like diamonds.

I almost gagged on my beer. In my short career of clubbing around the North Shore no girl had ever come up to me out of the blue and said hello. If this was college, I'd lap it up.

'Yeah, hi. Pleased to meet you.'

She offered an elegant hand. 'What's your name?'

'Steve,' I said, taking her hand and giving it a light shake. 'Yours?'

'Jade,' she said kindly. 'Do you live here?'

'If that's what you call it.'

'What are you doing?'

'Science.'

She took a sip of her drink. 'Why don't you ask me to dance?'

'Okay,' I said with a shrug. 'Would you like to dance?'

'No thanks,' she answered smugly, and her friend giggled. They kept their eyes on me long enough to savour the moment, then walked away swinging their arses.

It had to be a setup. I glanced around but no one was watching. Only Hardy seemed privy to the exchange. 'You got to be kidding,' I groaned.

'Man,' he chuckled lightly, 'that's cruel.'

'Did you put her up to this?'

'No mate, I swear,' he said, holding a hand up reassuringly, and I believed him. He couldn't stop chuckling, but I believed him. There were no gloating faces, not a head turned my way. No, I thought, this bitch was for real.

'It's just payback,' Hardy explained. 'Don't get in a twist.'

Too late for that. *You stupid tart*. I almost screamed it out. *You conceited, full-of-yourself, spoiled brat.* If she'd tried that stunt with Manners, or Saunders, or pretty much any of my home crew, right about now she'd be getting a beer can emptied over her face. And woe-betide any guy who tried to defend her honour. A good night would be ruined for a lot of people.

I checked my anger and took a swig, fighting the urge to go over and give her a piece of friendly advice. Hardy finished his can of beer and lobbed it basket-ball style into a nearby bin.

'Time for a freebie,' he said, and walked off to the gathering around

Keogh. That left me by myself, watching them and mustering the courage. Time to get it over with. I braced myself and went over.

Keogh saw me coming. The talk stopped and a space opened up, mouths shut politely and a silence that was probably only peculiar to me followed. Something stopped me holding out my hand – pride or shame or both. It was an uncomfortable moment, made more so that he studied me intently.

I settled for, 'Hey, how you doing?'

Keogh gave me a barely perceptible nod. We were on the same page. Not a few seconds had passed, it felt a lot longer.

'Am I right for a beer?' I asked politely, gesturing down to the case.

'What, just like that?' he answered flatly. He didn't move, just stared at me with the same gleam in his eye I'd seen at the archery contest. It was the look of someone in total control.

I knew what he was waiting for. I guess I could have said something like *Hey buddy, sorry about the other night at the party. It was stupid, really. You were right and my friends were dicks.* I could have kissed his butt right then and offered to buy *him* beers all night. In front of everyone too, for added humility. Yeah right.

'Is that a problem?'

'You tell me,' he said. 'Think you can handle it?' The silence deepened around me as the boys watched attentively. They'd picked up on something.

'Up yours too then,' I said, and walked off. I had no idea where I was headed. A decent chap I'd met earlier came into view and I made a beeline for him and said the first thing that popped up in my head. 'Hey Jack, see anything you like?' I lifted my empty beer can to my lips and pretended to take a swig, turning my head sideways as part of the same motion to check Keogh's group. No one was watching.

I spent the rest of the night wandering from here to there, watching with amusement as the boys tried their luck. At some point in the evening I either forgot about the talent or gave up on it, preferring instead to join some older boys rumbling on the floor and throwing drinks over each other. I'd see Keogh standing by himself watching us, the beer in his hand seeming to take all night to drink.

Normally I wouldn't have an eye for this type of thing but I stayed on him more than anyone else in the place. He had me curious.

By midnight I was wasted. Reaction time was down and the boys had me on the floor easily. My shirt was soaked and I stunk of beer. I was at the stage when every joke sounds funny, every guy I met was the best bloke on earth, and I felt way ahead of myself. We were catching our breath after a bout of rumbling when God knows how but the talk turned to chess. I took it up keenly; I'd been part of the school chess team and was rather vain with my skills. Sounded like I'd be hard-pressed finding competition inside Phillips but there'd be plenty around campus. Up there with the best was a woman. Franks filled me in. For someone who took little interest in chess I thought it odd that he knew these finer details.

'How do you know so much about this woman?' I slurred suspiciously.

'That's her brother,' he said, pointing to the meaty chap who had accompanied Pronk to Babs' table earlier in the week. Keeping him company were Metcalf and some others. 'Jeff Fuller. You wouldn't think the two were related.'

'What do you mean?'

'She's got everything he don't. Looks and brains. Do your homework because if you ever meet her, you'll fall over yourself.'

I didn't really care, but responded dutifully. 'She a good sort?'

'Mate, she makes Miss Universe look like the Medusa. Go ask Jeff about her. Just be discreet. Don't make it sound like you want to shag her, because he's sick of that. Ask him how she went in her Mensa tests, that's harmless enough. She did them last year and I think she got accepted by the Society. She got an IQ of about a hundred and fifty, so I'm told.'

I still wasn't interested, but Franks urged me. 'Go on, introduce yourself. You'll be playing alongside him, sooner or later.'

I staggered over to him. 'G'day buddy.' I held out my hand. 'Jeff, is it?'

'Howdy,' he said. Wide at the shoulders and wider at the waist, he had a beefy pink face and brown buttons for eyes. He held out his hand

and I shook it. 'Settling in okay?'

'Yeah, good. Say – how'd your sister go in with the Mensa tests? She get in?'

He gave me a puzzled look. Beside him, Metcalf screwed his face as if he'd heard something completely unexpected. The music was loud and I figured neither heard me. I leaned closer and Fuller dipped his head more my way. 'I said – how'd your sister go with those Mensa tests? I hear she's pretty brainy.'

His expression took a turn for the worse and a frown gathered. 'I suppose you're going to tell me she's good-looking, too?'

'Well, yeah . . . but that's not the reason I—'

'This some kind of joke?'

'Oh shit,' Metcalf groaned. The seniors around him looked just as appalled. 'Forget it Jeffro,' he followed quickly. 'He must have got it wrong.'

Fuller ignored him; his frown grew heavier. 'You trying to be funny?'

I was as confused as he seemed to be. 'What do you mean?'

'What sort of dickhead says something like—'

'Mate, leave it,' Metcalf waved a hand dismissively. 'He's just a fresher.'

'I don't give a shit who he is,' Fuller said, raising his voice. 'What is this?'

'What is what?' I asked, feeling a mounting horror.

'You know what, dickhead.'

'No . . . I . . .'

Metcalf put a hand on his shoulder. 'Mate, I said I'd deal with it.'

'What in God's name is going on?' I asked.

'His sister has cerebral palsy,' Metcalf said gravely.

I felt the cold hand of shock slide up my spine.

'That's right,' Fuller fumed. 'She sits in a wheelchair getting spoon-fed every day. I'll put you in a wheelchair, you fucking smartarse.'

For a second or so I had time to feel angry. I looked over at Franks, standing there with a filthy grin on his face. It was a wicked grin, a sadistic grin. The grin a sadist gave when pulling the wings off a fly.

'Hey, don't blame me!' I pleaded, and pointed to Franks, who turned his head and pretended to ignore me. 'Franks put me up to this, just go ask—'

'Oh, what a load of horseshit!' Fuller retorted, poking my chest with a forefinger so hard I staggered back a step. My bowels went loose and my limbs started shaking.

Metcalf tried to step between us. 'Mate, let him go,' he said. 'I'll vouch for him. It must have been a mistake.' He put a hand on his shoulder and had it flicked away.

'Like hell. Everyone knows about my sister.'

Other seniors tried to step in; he shoved them aside roughly and walked around them to get at me, red-faced as the devil. 'Still think it's funny, *dickwash?*' he spat as I backed away out of reach. I was still holding my beer, in my panic ridiculously trying to find somewhere to put it. Everyone I could see was watching us. Of course none of my fresher friends took a step forward, but I did take heart that several older boys came to my aid.

I held up a hand, trying to show him I meant nothing by it. My voice had the pitch of a pleading kid. 'Look . . . I'm sorry man . . . I didn't know . . . I just got told.'

Fuller took hold of himself. 'What was that?' he growled.

'I said sorry, Jesus, I didn't know your sister—'

'Hey Chambers,' someone said behind me.

Tickling with adrenalin, I swung around and saw Franks standing there with a beer in his hand.

'What noise does a whale make?'

I stared at him stupidly, shaking all over. A weird quietness descended that allowed my attention to divert around me. Half a dozen seniors stared back at me, eyes twinkling. Then I noticed their bulging cheeks.

'Oh *shi*—'

Spray blasted my face from every direction. I shut my eyes in reflex and tried to duck but it was too late. I was drenched. The stink of it made my stomach churn.

A roar went up. I opened my eyes, beer trickled down and made them sting. As I wiped them clean Fuller cackled like a hyena and slapped a hand on my shoulder.

'Mate,' he said with glee, 'I don't even have a sister.'

The whole room was filled with the sound of clapping and high-fiving and merciless hoots of laughter. Franks had a grin on him wider than a happy clown.

'Gotcha.'

Other than the ritualistic fresher crap, it had been a good week. The next morning my stomach felt like an acid-bath and my head a woozy water balloon, and I still had to sign up for the pub crawl. They had a score sheet and various tests to do at each pub, and compared with the iron-guts soldiering on I felt like a pansy. My batteries were flat. It had been a creative week, but I was glad it was over.

We had a whole three days break until our first formal dinner on Wednesday night, followed immediately by our inaugural JCR meeting. The last of our impressively garlanded officials graciously departed after dinner and we rounded up all leftover carafes and jugs and took them down into the JCR. President Finch took centre table with his team on both sides and gave a moving speech that differed little in substance from what we'd heard from the Principal et al during dinner. Our duly-elected student leaders were then introduced and clapped, blurbs from each followed and I was tuning out by the time Treasurer Franks explained in a tone of voice that put the blame on everyone that we'd overspent the previous year and we'd be tightening our belts this one.

The last chap to be introduced was the Secretary; a squat fellow with a round, pudgy face. Evidently his speech required him to step away from the tables and take centre stage.

'Good evening gentlemen and freshers,' he said, puffing himself up with self-importance and pacing back and forth like a drill sergeant. 'To those of you who don't know me, my name is Carl Sproule. On the books I am secretary and first-year student coordinator, off the books please think of me as XO, master-at-arms, and badass of this wonderful college. Now that you have all taken residence, it is time to enlighten you on a number of rules. No questions, no whining. You are here because you asked to be, not the other way around. You applied and you were accepted. Your continued stay in this unique abode is conditional. A few home truths – there were far more applications for residency here than our two hundred and seventy-two rooms allow. Our halls are full. There are boys banging at our doors. You will have to earn your right to walk these hallowed walls. We have rules. If you don't like these rules, tough shit!

'You will be watched. You will be assessed. We are not looking for high distinctions, university medals, or notches on beds for how many women you shag. Your previous achievements mean nothing now'— and at this he turned his head conspicuously toward Babs standing by a wall— 'so forget your former life. What we are looking for is the four R's. Respect for the college. Respect for those above you. Respect for our traditions. Respect for our rules.

'These are our rules, our ten commandments you might say. You are expected to memorise them. If you do not comply, you will be punished accordingly.'

He flicked a piece of paper open and began to read.

'Rule number one,' his voice boomed. 'The Senior Common Room is strictly out of bounds. Entry is only by permission of a Senior Committee member.

'Rule number two. You do not get served, eat, or sit down at a dining room table until a second year or above has taken seat. Any of these boys arriving late for breakfast, lunch, or dinner, has priority over any fresher in the queue. He may at any time go in front of any fresher. You shall also when seated stay on your side of the room throughout the meal.

'Rule number three. No drugs. No exceptions, no excuses. You get caught with bongs, green sprinkles on your bed, powder that doesn't smell like Talcolm, or tablets with those little dolphin or bullshit yuppie imprints, and you will be flogged severely.

'Rule number four. Alcohol is mandatory. You shall acquire your preferred nectar and always have it on your shelf. Should any Resident Fellow wish to sample your nectar, you shall without haste acquire a drinking receptacle and pour him a drink. You shall then thank him for having chosen you to oblige.'

Someone raised a hand. 'Can I ask a question?'

'No you may not,' Sproule answered without breaking rhythm. 'Rule number five. No commies, lefties, cross-dressers or crack-waxers. You subscribe to that sort of shit, go someplace else.'

Beside me a guy mumbled, 'This guy's a goose,' and I disguised a snicker.

'Rule number six,' Sproule went on, 'see rule number five. Rule number seven. No women on the premises after ten pm. Those who wish to exempt themselves from this rule may do so only under the following conditions. First, after signing in lady of choice you must present her to RF for approval. Fresher will then wait outside RF's room until further notice. If woman does not come out within thirty minutes, the fresher may leave. If the woman does come out before then, she will have instructions. These may include consent to enter college after hours, subject to conditions, or a nominal gratuity, or both.'

He looked us over with a sly grin. 'Good luck to you all. Please note that we do encourage this close and most meaningful association with our fresher members.

'Rule number eight. In the next day or so, every fresher will be given a personal pet. Like all pets it will need love and care. You will need to carry it with you at all times. You will take it to lectures, you will take it to bed. You will produce it when asked by any senior. This rule has a subset of more rules. You will hear more of this in due course.

'Rule number nine. You will regularly check the notice board in the JCR where you will read your mandatory obligations. Starting with tomorrow. There are a number of formalities each and every fresher is expected to comply with over the coming weeks. Ignorance is no excuse.

'Rule number ten, last and most important. You will attend all JCR meetings, briefings, sessions, gatherings or hearings as directed by myself or the Senior Committee. Excuses for absences must be lodged in writing and approved by myself or a Senior Committee member prior to the event.'

He put his paper into his pocket. 'Thank you, that is all. I shall look forward to meeting every one of you personally. Until then, stay safe compadres.'

We all stayed hushed as he returned to his seat. His was the only briefing that no one clapped.

Four

Our pets turned out to be bricks we had to carry around for two weeks. To lectures, to the dining hall, to bed. I put mine in my backpack and it stayed there. I took it to the bathroom, slept with it at the foot of my bed. There were regular inspections, like walking out of the dining room, minding one's business in the courtyard, coming out of the toilet. Get caught out, have another brick. Within a week, guys like Babs were walking around with sacks like Santa Claus.

I got used to the dining room routine. Freshers learnt to go down to the dining room fifteen minutes after it opened. Rarely did we beat a second year or above to breakfast, lunch or dinner. Not a biggie. Be it saluting the RFs whenever you passed them, walking backwards across the college lawn, or wearing your academic gown around college for those first couple of weeks – if it meant your room wasn't turfed, your eyebrow wasn't shaved, or a raw egg didn't explode on the back of your head, I for one played ball. I wasn't going to dodge them, run from them, or hide from them.

Only *he* could make me do that.

If Keogh was at the dining table, I'd sit at the far end. If I saw him walking in the same direction, I'd change tack. If his head ever swung my way, I'd turn mine the other. On one occasion I walked into the JCR with wonderful timing to see him coming straight at me. For a heartbeat or two my stride faltered and I subconsciously squared my shoulders, lifted my chin and looked him square in the eye. I felt silly sizing him up like some bull to butt heads with, so I tried to blur it all with a half-smile and a nod as we passed each other. Keogh didn't bat an eyelid. I thought he might have dipped his head in a manner resembling a nod, but I was probably wrong.

It was infantile, I knew. More than that, futile. We were dovetailing toward some form of interaction through having the same friends, living in the same college, and of course rugby.

I'd decided to make a comeback. Though my immediate goal was grade with Uni, the big deal on campus seemed to be the intercollegiate games. On account of my presumed batting ability I'd qualified for our college cricket team and padded up in that department already, scoring well enough to earn my share of praise for the wins that followed. Buoyed with confidence, I committed myself to trying out for the game they allegedly played in heaven.

By a rough count there were over seventy players at training that first Tuesday night. We started with a couple of warm-up laps, tossing the ball around and skylarking, stopping here and there to plant our butts on the grass for a rest under the guise of stretching. The standard speech about pride and commitment from our club captain followed but I was too preoccupied with wondering how to avoid Keogh to pay much attention. Being new to the team I figured we were destined to be grouped accordingly, which meant some form of contact with the guy during the session was a given. That both of us wanted to play in the forwards reduced the odds even further.

Basic drills followed no tougher than running back and forth in lines of five or six passing the ball from one end to the other, and from there we moved onto fitness work. Thirty minutes was enough to give our chin-rubbing coaches a fair idea of the newbies who'd be struggling to make fifths. I was encouraged to see plenty of guys blowing long before I did.

I wondered what our elite players thought of it, putting us to shame with their precision passing, hands of glue, and uncanny coordination, with nary a drop of raised sweat between them. Now and then they'd stand aside with the coaches and mumble in low voices, presumably lending their thoughts to the talent. They even called Keogh over once or twice, which helped my agenda. Apart from tossing the ball to him a few times I'd done a good job of avoiding him.

By the time they called it quits I had a feel for the lower grade standard at least, and was confident I'd be competitive. As we did our warm-down stretches I watched Keogh from the corner of my eye, keeping to himself over on the fringe. It seemed to go with a lot of what he did. The guy was a bit of a loner. It occurred to me then that he was the only college boy present that I hadn't shaken hands with, introduced myself to, or shared passing comment, and part of me regretted not making an effort.

It went the same at Thursday night's training. I might have imagined it but people were starting to notice. Word had gotten around about some altercation between the two of us at a party before O-week, and by continually avoiding him I was feeding an image of embarrassment and shame.

The thought consumed me as I headed back to college that night. I barely took part in, let alone heard, the conversation going on around me. I for one wanted to put that unfortunate night behind us and training was a great opportunity to break the ice. I just didn't know how to do it.

I needn't have worried. The seniors sped that up for both of us.

A large contingent of freshers had mustered in the JCR long before the scheduled time of 8.30am. With breakfast possibly our last meal for a while we'd stuffed our stomachs to capacity well before then. Right on time, Sproule walked in with his bodgies and switched off the morning program. A few older boys looked over their shoulders and arched their brows irritably.

'Okay, listen up,' he barked, holding up a piece of paper. 'It's all been sorted. When your name gets called, go to your driver and do what he says. Any bitchin and you'll be treated like one.'

He looked down at his list. 'First cab off the rank – Broker and Camilleri, you're with Hardy. Arses away.' They stood and headed out. 'Garibaldi, Duggan – go with Grimshaw.'

As names were called, I wondered if there was any rationale for the pairings. When my own name was read out, I figured there was.

'Chambers,' he chuckled, 'you're with Keogh.'

A rush of blood warmed my face as we swapped sideward glances. He looked as keen as I did.

'Off you go with Lanky Shanks,' Sproule instructed, and I stood.

'Schiffers!' Sproule continued as I marched out. 'You go with

49

Meadows. You're on your own. You get special treatment.'

We followed Shanks out to the main carpark where his beat-up Ford Fairlane sat in a car spot for the privileged. He pointed to Keogh's wrist. 'Watch off. I'll give it back later.'

Keogh took it off and held it out for him. I wasn't wearing one.

'Got any money?' Shanks asked.

'No,' I replied. Keogh also gave him the negative.

'Turn your pockets inside out,' Shanks said anyway.

We proved it. Satisfied, he opened the boot of his car and pulled out two dresses. One was a bright red, buttoned down the front and frilly around the neck. The other was white and more modest, shorter too, great for nice legs.

'Don't fight over them,' he advised.

'No way,' I said.

'Go get changed.'

'Are you kidding?'

'Rules of the game, buddy.'

'Christ.' Full of horror I scrutinised both dresses, trying to determine the lesser of the two evils. I picked up the white one.

'That'll be yours then,' Shanks said to Keogh, pointing to the red dress.

Keogh shook his head. 'I don't think so.'

'Put it on.'

'It's not going to happen.' Keogh put his hands in his pockets and leaned on the car with an expression that said that was the end of it.

Shanks just stood there, staring at him with a hard face. 'Mate, it's the way it is. Don't whine to me, whine to the committee.'

'Go get em, then.'

'Just put the bloody thing on. Everyone has to wear what they're given. We ain't leaving till you do.'

'Guess we ain't leaving then.'

'Just put it on,' I chimed in. 'If I got to, so do you.'

Keogh glared at me like he was going to take my head off. 'Do I owe you something?'

I shut up then.

'I suggest you listen to your mate,' Shanks said.

Keogh put tone into his voice. 'He's not my mate and you don't get it. Do what you want – turf my room, send me to Perth, pull my fingernails out. I don't care. I ain't wearing no girl's dress.'

There was a quiet, unevenly balanced standoff. I figured Keogh had more going for him than most of us fresher scum, what with his rugby credentials. I'd already overheard talk of him earmarked for the higher grades of Sydney Uni. As he stood there unflinching it was easy to see what Manners and Saunders and the rest of us boys had already seen. He was a tough nut.

Shanks sighed. 'All right, you asked for it.'

He walked away. I sat down on a small retaining wall and contemplated the pretty yellow flowers in the garden bed behind it. I thought they looked just swell.

Joey and Mick came into the carpark dressed as clowns. In spite of myself I had to laugh. Joey wore a billowing suit gathered at the ankles, a blinding yellow wig, jolly red nose, ruffle at the neck and oversized shoes, while Mick's outfit consisted of oversized pants held up by brightly coloured shoulder suspenders, a neck-tie, dashing white gloves and a massive derby hat.

'You clowns,' I said drolly.

More guys came out. They'd certainly been creative, our seniors. It was the height of summer and poor Rajah had been made to wear a fake fur coat and hat that would have been the envy of the elite at a Melbourne Cup festival. Flip was dressed in a black dinner suit and whoever accompanied him was bandaged head to foot like a mummy. Others were fitted out just as mercilessly. There was a lot of jibing in the spirit of the occasion.

Boys got into cars pale-faced, as if bound for slaughter. I thought *Christ,* if this is what they got for doing what they were told, what were we dissidents in for?

'What are you guys waiting for?' Joey asked as he opened the door to a vehicle.

'Not sure,' I replied. 'But it was nice knowing you.'

Engines were coming to life around us when Shanks returned with

Sproule. 'We got a couple of rebels,' our secretary said unhappily. 'We went to a lot of trouble to find you those dresses. Look at those frills! Those hems! You gonna put 'em on or what?'

'Nope,' Keogh said casually.

'Are you special or something?'

'It's against my religion.'

'I see.' Sproule nodded regretfully. 'And we were going to make it easy for you.' He turned to me. 'What about you? You gonna put a dress on?'

'I ain't his bitch.'

'Suit yourself. You're going to the same place anyway. Cappo!' he called to a guy opening the door to a shiny blue Renault. 'Swap your two for these guys.'

Cappo came over and had a private conference with Sproule. When I saw the two blokes Cappo had been assigned, I despaired. They'd already been labelled as trouble, probably earmarked for the toughest of locations. And now it was ours.

'All right, over you go,' Sproule told us merrily.

'Don't lose my watch,' Keogh reminded Shanks.

We followed Cappo to his car and he reached into his pockets. 'Blindfolds,' he said, and handed each of us one of those elasticised eyepieces you get on airplanes.

Keogh took it and muttered, 'I hope you're not wearing one.' He got into the backseat, fastened his seatbelt and slipped the eyepiece on. Then he folded his arms and settled back.

I got into the front passenger seat and wound the window down before putting mine on. It was bloody hot already. The engine kicked over and we were moving. Sproule's voice followed us as we pulled away.

'Don't forget to add a couple of hundred K's to their drop-off point.'

A few turns later we were into the stop and start crawl of Parramatta Road, I figured.

'Where we headed?' I asked.

'You're no better off even if I did tell you,' Cappo answered.

No one spoke after that. I settled back into my seat and dreamily tuned in and out to the stops and starts. Gradually they became less, traffic toned down and the sound of the engine steadied into a low hum. Wind blasted into my face as we rode smoothly on what I assumed was the start of the freeway. I felt for the window handle and wound the window up a bit. The heat of the morning sun bit into the back of my neck, supporting my guess we were heading west. After a while the radio started to fade in and out, eventually it clicked off altogether.

By then I was getting fidgety, not being able to see a thing. Pretending to scratch my nose, I slipped my index finger beneath the blindfold and lifted it a bit.

'Hey, no peeking,' Cappo warned.

I dropped my hand. 'How far do you usually send people?'

'Depends. A couple of years ago they put someone on a plane to Melbourne. Mostly though it's just local.'

'You go out of your way a lot to make it difficult for us.'

'No skin off my nose. I was going home this weekend anyway – mate's wedding. I'll be dropping you boys off before I get there though.'

'And where's that?'

No answer. I let him be for another five minutes or so, and then, more from boredom than interest, I got him talking on the safer subject of himself. This was his third year, doing mechanical engineering, been going with a girl named . . . who cares. I thought Keogh was asleep until Cappo raised his voice.

'How you doin Keogh, you awake back there?'

'I'm awake.'

'What's your story mate, from Newcastle I hear?'

'That's right.'

'Vet science, yeah?'

'Yeah'

'Don't do it up Newy way?' he asked, referring to Newcastle Uni.

'Sydney's better.'

'Had enough of Newcastle?'

'That too.'

A few questions later, Cappo must have realised all he was going to get were one or two-word answers. He changed the subject to rugby.

'Play a bit of rep up there, did you?'

'Yep.'

'Who for?'

'Newcastle City . . . Hunter Region Schoolboys.'

'What position?'

'Open flanker,' he said. I thought it curious he included the word 'open.'

'You know we have a combined college side that plays Newcastle Uni every year?'

'I know.'

'Guess you'd know some lads that play for them, yeah?'

'Yeah.'

'You gonna play for the Phil?'

'Sure.'

'Good man.'

What felt like an hour or more later I heard the gear crunch down into fourth, the car hiccupped and the engine bawled as we tilted up what had to be the Great Divide. I popped my ears and reclined the seat further back in anticipation of a snooze. Stops and starts for another hour or more and then we were brake-squealing down the long slide and sharp turns of the descent. Soon as we flattened out and rode smoothly the drone of the motor played like a lullaby on my ears. I'd almost fallen asleep when the car slowed to a crawl.

I roused myself in the hope this might be our drop-off point. Cappo spoke for the first time in ages. 'You boys stay put while I fill the car. And no peeking.'

I stretched an ache out of my spine. 'I need to take a leak.'

'Not here. I'll pull over soon as we're out of town.'

I heard the door open and the motions of fuelling. I suppose I could have snuck a peek when he went to pay, but I played ball. A peculiar sensation, blind obedience. A hundred clicks or more from college and still its mighty hand doth reach.

True to his word our driver pulled into a lay-by once we rolled out of town. Temporarily freed of my eyepiece I squinted in towering eucalypts and got a glimpse of the road as it arced through the scraggly forest and gave out to straw-coloured fields far ahead. Though I couldn't see the mountains for the trees I could feel their looming influence in the moisture and coolness of the surrounding forest. The faint roar of distant vehicles sounded like background surf. A bellbird gave us a nice ping.

'Don't mean to pop your balloon,' I said as I lined myself up in front of a tree, 'but we could have started this blindfold business here. It's not like we don't know we've just come down the mountains.'

Cappo looked at me like I had two horns.

Soon after taking off again, I fell asleep. A half-full bladder and a cramp in my neck when I woke suggested I'd napped for over an hour.

'What time is it?'

'Another hour or so.'

It felt like a lot longer than that when the car slowed and gravel crunched beneath the tyres. 'Okay, you boys can see where y'are now,' Cappo said.

I slipped the blindfold off and saw the thirsty-looking hills of our eternally drought-ridden state. The sky above was a blue contradiction. The land was gently undulating, freckled with solitary eucalypts and motionless cattle and sheep. I put us a couple of hundred kilometres west of the ranges and a stretch short of the flat western plains. Narrow winding road with a single broken white line, stunted trees crawling up the hills, and not a house or a sign in sight. A few sucks of the air and my throat was dry as dust.

'Where are we?' I asked.

'Don't forget your survival kit,' Cappo said cheerfully, holding out a box of matches and a cheap compass. I don't know why I took them. 'See you back at college.'

We got out of the car and he drove off. The road went empty and quiet.

I turned around. Keogh stood there watching me with his piercing gaze, letting the moment sink in. The guy we'd tried to beat into pulp about a month earlier. And here we were stuck in the middle of nowhere with nobody but each other for company. Satisfied with some point made, he turned around and started walking.

A swarm of bush flies appeared out of thin air. I swatted them from my face as I went over to a tree to relieve myself. Keogh didn't wait for me, just walked off.

'Where you going?' I asked over my shoulder.

No answer. It was a steady, sure-of-oneself pace for someone headed nowhere.

'Don't want to hitch?' I suggested. Still no answer. Okay then. I finished my business and walked briskly to catch up.

It sure was quiet. Our footsteps scraped loudly over the gravel and a cloud of pink galahs screeched high overhead.

'You don't even know how far it is to the next town, or which way you're going,' I said.

'Neither do you.'

I slowed to check the compass. 'You're heading west. It might be better the other way.'

'See yuh.'

I stuffed the compass into my pocket and followed him about five paces behind. A soft breeze rustled the saplings by the side of the road and the air cooled a little. The stench of a bloated roo followed in my wake long after I'd passed it.

'Come on,' I tried. 'Let's give hitching a go. No point walking ten kilometres and getting picked up down the road anyway.'

'You know what a pair of weirdos look like?' Keogh asked, glancing behind briefly. 'Two guys without a bag between them, hitching out middle of nowhere.'

'You reckon we look less weird if we don't?' I mused back, and got no answer.

We kept walking, swatting at flies and saying nothing. A car or three sped by and I saw the drivers turn their heads and watch us as long as they could without running off the side of the road. After half an hour or so we rounded a corner and I saw a house on top of a hill.

Down the bottom, a dirt track joined onto the main road.

'We ought to try that house up there, at least find out where we are,' I suggested.

'That's what I'm doing,' Keogh replied, congenially enough.

We got to the bottom of the hill and turned into a long, rubble-coated track that led to the house. The walk was steep and I was panting as we reached the top. Strewn each side of the track were the sad relics of trucks and cars that must have rolled off the floors mid-century, and further away, the gleaming shell of a large bus beside a shed that leaned at a precarious angle. Twisted metal, tyres, and rusted machine parts littered the ground like plane crash wreckage. Everywhere empty white containers poked from the overgrown grass. I passed one close enough to catch the word 'Fertiliser.'

We approached a flaking weatherboard house and a crumpled dog took to its feet slowly and gave a sick bark. A guy came at us from the corner of a shed. Keogh held up his hand in a friendly greeting.

'G'day buddy,' he said with a smile. 'This is going to sound a bit weird, but we don't know where we are and we need to get to the closest town. We were dropped off down the road. Part of a Uni prank.'

To look at the guy was enough to remind a city boy like me what a life out here can do to a man. His eyes were bottomless holes in a face ruined as much by the elements as the secret bottle, I suspected, pockmarked by sun-lesions and folded with sags where dirt and grime had collected to form dark lines. Age seemed irrelevant; he was part of the landscape. He dragged one leg a little slower than the other, though he tried not to show it, and when he stopped a few metres away he stood with a slight lean to one side. He wore crumpled baggy pants and a dusty polo shirt peppered with holes and soaked with sweat at the armpits. Thongs as thin as pancakes were moulded to the soles of his feet. Flies crawled around the sides of his mouth and eyes with impunity.

'You dunno where yuh are?'

Keogh stopped. 'Nope, we were blindfolded.'

'Blindfolded?' His lips were too tight to stretch beyond a weak smile.

'Like I said – Uni prank. We have to find our way back to Sydney.'

'Sydney?'

'Yep,' Keogh replied patiently. 'Listen, we didn't see any signs. Where's the closest town?'

The man gaped at us, the question apparently a bit hard. 'What, Forbes?'

'Forbes!' Keogh and I traded glances. 'Okay, guess that's where we're going,' he said enthusiastically. 'Any suggestions on how we might get there?'

'There's no buses. Buses don't come by here, 'cept the school'ns, and you don't look like school kids.' He grinned then, exposing teeth that resembled black-and-white boiled lollies. 'They don't pick up just anyone. Anyway, it's Sat'dee.'

'That doesn't matter. We got no money anyway.'

'You got no fuckin money neither?'

The cheer slipped from Keogh's face and his gaze hardened. He had eyes that shone too brightly for a dark set; a wild shine that evoked an image of rage. 'How's the neighbours?' he asked flatly.

'Neighbours?'

'Yeah, you know. People that live nearby.'

The change in Keogh's demeanour surprised me. The man tilted his head at an uncertain angle, as if trying to work out if he'd been patronised, or insulted, and not knowing what he should do in either case. 'Got plentya neighbours.' As he spoke his lips puffed away a fly.

'Who lives closest?'

'There's Steppy, down the road.'

'Steppy? That short for . . ?'

'Steptoe.'

'Which way?'

The man pointed up the road, the way we'd been heading. 'Bout four or five K thataway.'

'Is that the way to Forbes?'

'Yeah.'

'Okay, thanks.'

Keogh walked away. I stayed put, half-inclined to make a better attempt, but when I turned around and saw the guy standing there with that deadbeat look on his face, I decided against it. I flipped my hand goodbye and caught up to Keogh.

'Why didn't you ask him for a lift?' I asked.

'The guy was a dense prick. We can do better than that. We'll try down the road.'

I stopped. 'What, five kilometres away?'

'You in a hurry?'

I looked behind and saw the guy standing there with his hands on his hips, watching me. I kept walking.

About an hour later the road turned into a gully and we saw a house about a kilometre away at the end of a long track. We got to the turnoff and headed up the track, watched by cows with a look slightly more intelligent than the guy we'd left.

Whoever lived here held living standards in higher esteem. The road was smoother and there wasn't a sign of junk. Even the air smelled fresher. The dogs went schizo from way off and when we reached the house the hackles were stiff as a wire brush. While I waited for permission to proceed Keogh walked through without breaking step, the dogs growling bared-teeth at his heels. As he stepped onto the veranda the door opened and an older woman wearing gumboots and overalls came out. The colour of her face was the brown of the outback and her skin was clean and shiny with perspiration. She shut the hounds up with a gruff command and Keogh approached her with his hand extended.

'Mrs Steptoe?' he asked in a polite manner.

She shook his hand and the smile on her face shone as brightly as the sun. He went through a similar dialogue as before, but her response was far less vapid. She asked a lot of questions, more out of curiosity than suspicion I figured, and once she got all she needed she chuckled heartily.

'Well, aren't you in a pickle? How you gonna get to Forbes?'

Keogh shrugged. 'Guess we can hitch. But we were hoping for something a little more reliable, now it's getting late.'

'Geez, you don't ask much. A lift to town is about an hour each way.'

Keogh watched her with that same gentlemanly face. I wanted to laugh.

'You might get lucky though,' she went on. 'A lot of boys around here go into town Saturday nights, and this here's on their way. I know Dozer's boy does. I can give him a ring if you want.'

'That'd be great, I'd really appreciate it,' Keogh responded with charm.

'I'll bet you do,' she said happily, and went inside.

Standing there alone with Keogh left me twitchy. I moved away and feigned an interest in the flowers in the hedgerow, the only thing I could see with any real colour. Keogh leaned against the veranda rail and for about five minutes we managed to avoid conversation.

When she came out she was grinning. 'I guess you got good luck and bad. Dozer's boy Brian can swing by on his way in but he won't be here till around seven-thirty or so, he thinks. That's almost three hours away. You guys wanna wait, or do you want to take to the road?'

'Got any work we can do?' Keogh offered.

'Work?'

'Sure. You've been a big help and we got a bit of time to kill. Seriously, if you need a bit of muscle for something, we can give it.'

I didn't know whether to protest or puke. For a long moment she stood watching us. To look at the two of us you wouldn't have heard the word *psychopaths* ring in your mind. Can't speak for myself, but Keogh looked like a poster boy for some sports product or other. He made as convincing an axe-wielding psycho as Jamie Lee Curtis did as a prostitute.

I saw the look in her eyes go from mild astonishment to genuine admiration. If she'd been any younger I reckon his reward might have been more than a lift to Forbes.

She laughed. 'Son, you do have manners. You want to help me with some fencing?'

About ten minutes later I found myself inside a large shed loading up the back of a ute with bolt cutters, thick gloves, pliers, star pickets, a heavy coil of galvanised wire, a twin-handled tube I learnt was a picket hammer, and a heavy, cumbersome-looking thing I learnt was a wire-strainer. I was still in a state of delusion when we pulled into a paddock a hundred meters or so from the house. Dry grass crackled under our feet as we followed a series of stumps until they stopped in the middle of nowhere. By the eagerness she put into the briefing it must have been one of those jobs she'd been putting off for ages. Keogh of course took to the task in earnest.

'This what you had in mind?' I asked him after we'd rolled the stack of wire out of her earshot. Keogh gave me his first grin and said nothing.

We didn't speak much after that. Keogh and I took turns hammering pickets in until there was a line of five or so, then Mrs Steptoe showed us how to fasten the wire and tighten the slack with the wire-strainer. Simple stuff for city boys and after we'd hammered in another set of pickets she gave us a final instruction or two and left us alone. I kept glancing at the sun, willing its descent toward yonder hills. Sweat streaked into my face and stung my eyes. The insufferable bush fly lapped it up.

I was feeling my hand for blisters when I heard a car crunching over gravel. A white tabletop stopped at the house and disappeared behind the dust overtaking. A guy got out of the car and looked our way. Mrs Steptoe met him at the front door and they talked briefly before going inside.

Keeping one eye on the house, I gave fencing another ten minutes until at last I saw the guy step out of a side door. He gave us a whistle and a wave and I dropped the picket hammer and took a well-earned stretch.

We left everything where it was and walked over. 'You boys from Sydney?' he asked as we came up.

'That's right,' Keogh said, holding out a hand. 'Jason Keogh.'

'Tony,' he said as he shook it, then swapped to mine and I gave him my name.

'Brian coming to pick you up around seven-thirty, is he?' he asked.

'Yeah,' Keogh said. 'Your missus was nice enough to call around.'

61

Tony looked over our shoulders at the hundred metres plus of fencing we'd put in. 'You boys wanna feed before you go?'

Tony kindly let me use the phone to ring the old man. I gave him the story and within the half-hour he'd rung back to tell us he'd organised two tickets to Sydney on the 6.40 morning train, paid for by credit card. We could collect the tickets at the station. That left the overnight stay issue. I'd give him a ring reverse-charge once we'd checked into a room somewhere and he'd sort.

Mrs Steptoe cooked up a cracker of a meal; steak and potatoes and a salad pulled straight from the garden. Tony poured us each a beer to help get it down and told his story. Fourth generation local farmer, mainly cattle and sheep, fields of sorghum and the odd crop of maize when conditions were right. Three kids, who like so many baby-boomers of the bush had opted for lives off the property at the first opportunity and seemed happier for doing so. The guy picking us up was Brian Dorman, he'd gone to school with their kids and worked his old man's excavator business for a living.

We were into our third beer when I saw through the sliding-glass doors dust kick up down the track. The car pulled up out front and we stood when we heard a knock. Tony opened the door and was met by a square-shouldered, flat-stomached boy with eyes that crinkled at the sides when he smiled. His skin was stained reddish-brown from the sun with a sharp 'V' on his neck that showed the extent he buttoned his shirts.

'G'day Tony,' he said. 'These the boys?'

Keogh and I shook his hand, and there was a bit of a delay as Tony talked to him about a hydraulics problem with his harvester. They finished up and I thanked our hosts.

'No problem,' the old man said as I shook his hand. 'And if you wanna come back sometime and finish that fencing, I won't argue with you.'

I almost shoved Keogh in the direction of the car; he looked ready to take up the offer. Thankfully he said nothing but I only relaxed when we pulled out of the driveway for good.

As we turned onto the main road Brian asked, 'Where you boys staying?'

'Don't know,' Keogh answered, and briefed him on our situation.

Brian took it in with a wry smile and rattled off some possibilities. I asked which places might take us in on credit and he told us to have a few drinks with him at the Royal first and worry about that later.

We talked about local footy clubs, what they got up to. He spoke in the slow drawl of the bush and kept his language clean. He was an agreeable country boy in his denim jeans, half placket shirt, and polished leather boots. It was about seventy kilometres to town and I reckon he did about five of them under the speed limit.

We got to the Royal just before nine and Brian led us to a table of his buddies and introduced us. I asked what the chances were of the publican running up a bar tab I could fix up later somehow, and Brian waved the offer away.

'What do you want?' he asked.

'Mate, we can't go in a shout.'

'Shutup. What do you want?'

By the third round he'd stopped asking altogether. As soon as my glass went empty a beer appeared from nowhere. I don't know what Keogh said that I didn't, but after a couple of beers he had a schooner of water in front of him and not a taunt was uttered.

We played pool in doubles, City vs Country. Took me a couple of games to find my aim, then Keogh and I had the table and it didn't take long before I'd lost count of games and beers. To my surprise, Keogh was no better at pool sober than I was half-tanked.

It was a pleasant, easy-going night.

A girl paired up with some guy and took a turn against us. Nothing about her drew my attention earlier, only now did I take interest in the way her jeans tightened and her cleavage sprang to life whenever she leaned over the table to take a shot. She had a flashy smile that made dialogue between us inevitable. She introduced herself as Felicity and said she worked in town as a hairdresser. The way her eyes went mushy every time she looked at Keogh convinced me she was interested in him, but thankfully he didn't respond with the signs she was after. I took up the slack and thought I was doing okay when Keogh sank the black. We shook hands with the opposition and I held onto hers a little longer than normal, and I do believe I caught an invitational sparkle in her eyes before she walked away. My eyes stayed on her nicely rounded bum and when I lifted my hand to scratch my nose a wonderful perfume-mixed-with-her smell followed. I felt a tweak of regret at not having drawn the game out longer.

She sat down at a table with a couple of other girls. I watched her from the corner of my eye as I played the next two games all over the place, picking shots at random and bashing at balls I should have nudged. Keogh made the comment, 'You had enough or something?'

At last, we lost to the competition. I shook the guys' hands and went straight for Felicity's table. At that stage it wasn't just my head giving me warning signs. When you have to consciously aim yourself in a straight line, you should know you've had enough.

For the next hour it was great. We joked, we laughed, and I never noticed the beers had stopped coming until she asked if I wanted a drink. She knew Keogh and I didn't have a cent between us, and I wasn't so far gone to expect a lady to buy me drinks I couldn't repay, and this I told her. She stood up and winked at me over her shoulder on her way to the bar.

The next thing I knew Keogh was tapping me on the back. 'Best leave it,' he warned.

'Leave what?' I slurred.

'The whole pub knows what you're up to,' he said, and motioned with his hand. 'Come on. We're a long way from home and her ex is on your case.'

'Who?'

'Doesn't matter. Leave her alone.'

I looked around the pub, searching faces and swaying on my seat slightly. 'So what? He ain't with her now.'

'He thinks he is.'

'And what, I need his fricking permission?' I pointed to the bar. 'Look! She's buying me a beer.'

'Then bring it over there, with us.' Keogh eyed me long enough to show he meant it before he left.

I belched and muttered under my breath, 'Not going to happen.'

Felicity sat down with our drinks and we continued where we left off. Two or three sips into my beer and I knew I'd hit the wall. The glass took too long to drain, the slurring of my speech was getting worse, and my head felt too heavy for my shoulders. Wherever I turned it my body leaned the same way.

Her friends sat down and I learnt it was nearly midnight. Talk turned to what they were doing next and I caught the gist of the virtues of a nightclub called *The Mint*. Then, right out of nowhere, a guy pulled up a chair next to me and dropped into it heavily. I scrunched my eye in a wink.

'G'day,' I said.

His face was set hard and his eyes were vigilant. I waited for a response but he just sat there motionless, staring at me. I diverted to Felicity and she turned her head away in what I thought was a poor attempt at ignorance.

'How do you like your teeth?' the guy said.

I turned my head back his way. He didn't blink. 'What'd you say?' I asked dumbly. The ears had worked fine, the brain had failed to compute.

'I said,' his voice dropped a notch, 'how do you like your fucking teeth?' His lips curled as spoke. I couldn't tell if that curl was a smile or a snarl.

That part of me alert to this sort of thing sobered instantly, but I wasn't fazed. He was no bigger or uglier than me, no blemish or scar marked his cleanshaven face, and it looked like his nose hadn't caught anything over the years worse than the wipe of a handkerchief. Sitting himself down at a table of girls and puffing himself up like that . . . I was disappointed he didn't top it off with a bit of chest-beating.

'Same as you like yours, I'd reckon,' I said conversationally.

Last drinks were hollered. His wicked grin flattened out and he stiffened in his seat, eyes smouldering. I glanced at Felicity who was still pretending not to notice. 'Say Felicity, what's the name of that nightclub we're going to?' I only said it to goad him.

She said nothing. The girls at the table said nothing. The guy said nothing.

I caught movement at my side and looked up to find Keogh towering over me. His gaze went over me, and when I swivelled my head to follow I saw a look on the face of my new friend sitting next to me like a schoolboy sprung by the teacher. There was a moment of hush as everyone waited for Keogh to speak, but he stayed quiet.

'Hey Jase,' I broke the spell, 'take a seat.'

For a few seconds more Keogh made his presence felt, then he gave the girls a friendly look-over. I thought he might be about to try his own luck, a thought quickly quashed when he said, 'Nice meeting you all. My friend and I have to go. We got an early train tomorrow.'

'Everyone's going to the'—I swung my head toward Felicity—'where we going?'

'The Mint.'

'That's right. The Mint!'

Keogh put a hand on my shoulder to urge me up, but I stayed put. The next thing I knew his hand was under my armpit and I was lifted to my feet and swaying like a tree in the wind.

'Aren't you coming to The Mint?' Felicity asked, more to Keogh than me.

'Yeah baby!' I cried. 'Point the way!' and I saw the guy's scowl turn meaner than before.

'No,' Keogh assured us both, using a little more muscle on me now. He pulled me away from the table and spoke in a low voice. 'Listen – when blokes buy you beers all night you don't repay them by cutting in on one of their women. Especially when it's late and they're full of piss.'

I put a hand on his shoulder for balance. 'I reckon . . . I can talk this girl into letting us stay at her place.'

'I got us a room.'

'What?'

'Here in this pub, while you were sleazing.'

Keogh kept my feet moving to the doors at the rear of the pub. He pushed them open and we were into the empty courtyard with a star-flecked sky overhead.

'Just let me . . . go back for a sec.'

More doors opened and banged closed, and I found myself being led up some stairs. 'Piss off, I can walk,' I said, shaking myself free. Keogh let go and marched up the stairs. I put both hands on the rails and hauled myself up, one step up . . . use hand to pull . . . other foot up . . . reposition foot . . . next step . . .

'You mongrel!' I drawled. Keogh disappeared at the top of the stairs. I lifted my foot another step and it slipped on the lip and I fell forward, swinging into the wall with my hand clutching the rail. With some difficulty I staggered back into position.

'I was in! Like Flynn! I'd hit a homer! Shut the gate! The fat lady was taking a bow—'

'Keep your voice down,' Keogh called from somewhere.

I reached the top of the stairs and fended myself along the wall of the dimly lit corridor to where Keogh stood frowning at me in front of a door. He pushed a key into it and disappeared. A second later a light came on, which I thought handy.

I got to the room and noticed it was higher than long. There were two single beds opposite each other and a basin at the far end. I bellyflopped onto the closest bed and bounced up and down on squeaky springs.

'You mongrel!' I repeated. The bed spun wildly beneath me.

'You're not going to throw up, are you?'

'Urrrrrrrr,' I groaned, eyes half-closed. 'Hope not.'

'Bathroom's down the hall. Please don't use the basin.'

Vaguely I heard him fuss about. There was a soft thump like a shoe hitting the floor.

'I bet you snore, too,' he said.

'Serves you right, you bastard.' That was the last thing I remembered.

It was a painful march to the station the next morning, made worse on an empty stomach. A couple of clicks felt like a marathon. We collected our prepaid tickets and I lay claim to a bench on the platform. I stretched out and told Keogh to wake me when the train came. About three-quarters of an hour later it squealed to a halt and I followed him zombie-like into an empty carriage. He chose a free seat and I flipped the one opposite so that it faced his, then I stretched out on my back and told him to wake me when we reached Sydney.

The best I could manage was to drift in and out between stops. There were too many of them and I found it hard to sleep knowing Keogh would give me a kick as soon as the carriage started to fill. Eventually he did.

'Ticket-man.'

I sat up, winced. The carriage was fuller now and our two seats were the only ones left with one bum on each. The ticket man punched our tickets and handed them back. I waited until he'd left before stretching my legs out and settling my feet on Keogh's seat.

I yawned painfully, rubbed my screaming head. It didn't work, never did. I don't know why people did that. 'Was that girl's ex really there?'

'Ready to rip your head off.'

'Why didn't he, then?'

'Yeah, good question,' he said. 'We talked him out of it.'

'Was he big?'

'You should know, you met him.'

'When?' I asked dumbly, and then it came to me. 'That guy at the end?'

'Yep.'

I scoffed. I didn't know whether to be sceptical or thankful. 'Was she any good? I can't remember.'

'Not worth busting a chin over,' he assured me. Then he settled back and closed his eyes.

'Who paid for the room?'

'Told them I'd send a cheque,' he said, eyes shut. They'd have taken his word for it too. The guy had talked his way into everything else that weekend, getting a room on credit would have been as easy as a handshake. Honesty dripped from the guy's jowls smooth as honey from the comb.

'How much do I owe you?' I asked.

'You pay for the train tickets and we'll call it even.'

We talked between dozes, like regular folks. I watched the Blue Mountains grow taller, trees turn greener, and cows turn fatter. Towns turned less scanty and station names became familiar until I recognised them all. Keogh was a hard nut to crack, with his monosyllabic short answers. He was the type of guy most people would think arrogant by his sheer evasiveness. But I suspected more to it than that. He just didn't like talking about himself, which was a pity, because now that it was just the two of us I was seeing a side to him I hadn't expected.

I was beginning to like the guy.

It's a twenty-minute walk from Redfern to college and the timing couldn't have been better. We made it to dinner with time to spare.

We walked into the dining room and were greeted with big smiles and a stab or two about how miserable we looked. There was a happy hum in the air, like at the end of a wonderful day's outing. We took our meals to the boys' table and got straight into our stories, laughing and joking as we heard about other experiences. Pick of the trophies was Babs. They'd put him on a plane to *Brisbane*, hadn't heard from him since. I listened in awe, not just because they'd sent him that far but that some rich kid or kids had the gumption to fork out the dollars to send him there.

When the guys asked about our experience, I did most of the talking. Every now and then I glanced over at Keogh, but he just sat there biting heads of his chicken drumsticks and grinning in his own, quiet manner.

We sat there having a good laugh long after the dining hall emptied. Any lull in the laughter was followed by a well-timed crack at someone's expense and we'd break into fits again. The first face I'd turn to each time was Keogh, and he'd grin back at me in a way that made me think I'd gotten more out of this *Walkabout* than just a good weekend.

The ice was busted. I'd made a good friend.

Five

The next Friday night a popular Aussie band was set to play in the Manning Bar. I'd passed on seeing the gig, preferring instead to save some bucks and head on up once they were done.

I put in a few hours on a chemistry assignment, got myself cleaned up was heading across the courtyard when I glanced up at C-wing. Keogh's window was second from the end of the first floor, one of only three or four with the light on. I stopped to think about it.

In a few short weeks he'd acquired a fairly solid reputation for keeping to himself, a vibe that seemed to stop a lot of guys from making more than a token effort with him. In my opinion he was just more serious about studies than he needed to be, if not more serious about everything than he needed to be. I wondered if any of the boys had spoken to him about our plans tonight.

A minute or so later I was banging on his door. On hearing a 'Yeah' from inside, I opened it and leaned in. Keogh was sitting at his desk, papers all over the place and radio going softly. He gave me his attention and nodded. 'Howdy.'

'The boys went to see the band,' I said. 'Should be finishing up shortly. I'm going to meet up with them when it's over. Wanna come? Should be a good night.'

He turned his head away and I thought he was going to decline the offer. But then he flicked his pen across the table, stood up and had a stretch.

'Sure,' he said. 'I'll put some shoes on.'

The band had finished when we arrived. We pushed our way through the crowd until we found the lads settled comfortably on the top-floor balcony. The night was warm and the doors were kept open. The place filled quickly and clouds of cigarette smoke billowed into the clean air I was enjoying.

We noticed a swelling of girls in one corner of the bar, pressed up against each other tighter than those queuing for drinks. I checked to see what the attraction was and saw that the band had joined our merry student establishment. A bunch of other guys – roadies by appearances – were also lapping up the attention.

'Guess we'll have to wait,' I commented. Keogh stared at the grouping and grunted.

About twenty minutes later, three girls surrendered their places and went to sit at a table of two others. You knew they were students; they just had that look. And it wasn't a bad one either. We passed compliments that would have made their heads swoon and Keogh went quiet. He kept his eyes on them but I didn't know he was that interested until I saw his gaze follow a blonde to the bar.

'Yeah, not bad,' I agreed. In one movement he tilted his half-empty glass up and drained it. He put it down on a table and went for the bar.

I had to see how he did it, the smooth peacock. He took his place behind the blonde and nudged up alongside when she got served. Within the minute she turned her head his way and they were talking. The barman came back with her drinks and I saw Keogh's lips moving and the barman poured a beer and added it to the round. Keogh handed a note to the barman while the blonde fumbled inside her wallet, as if going through the motions. Keogh pocketed his change when he got it and made a triangle out of three glasses. The girl took the remaining two and they headed over to the table. Her friends saw them coming and smiled approvingly. Keogh put the drinks down, slid out an empty chair and greeted them with a circular hand wave. The girls shifted their chairs to make space and I found it curious that the blonde chose to sit two seats away from Keogh.

We lesser boys kept chatting away, content with our own company. A couple of beers later, inspired by my friend's example, I wandered over.

My bold advance was met with barely a sideward glance. I stopped at the table and no one was talking. Keogh and the blonde were glaring at each other like two boxers in a pre-fight press meet.

'Hey,' I said to no one in particular, 'how you all doing?'

There was frosty silence, then the blonde said to Keogh, 'What you're saying then is we poor dumb girls can't think for ourselves.'

'Case in point.' Keogh gestured toward me. 'My friend here introduces himself and you ignore him. If he was our lead singer, you'd fall off your seat.'

The expression on her face went from anger to murder. I tried to fan the tension away like a true gentleman.

'Steve Chambers, pleased to meet you.' I held my hand out for her to shake but she snubbed me. I dropped it quickly, pulled out a chair and squeezed into a space.

An overweight girl with dyed red hair, pierced nose and a ring of studs in each ear said to Keogh, 'And you don't fall off your chair when some big-titty thing comes along.'

I used the pause that followed to say jokingly, 'I'm an arse man, myself. What about you Jase?' Still everyone ignored me. 'Did I walk into something?'

'Just trying to figure what it is that makes guys like us leftovers,' Keogh replied.

'That's not what I said,' the blonde responded.

'Didn't have to.'

'What makes you—'

'There's any number of guys in here,' Keogh cut in, 'decent guys, who would actually give you the time of day, while you prefer to waste your time on them.' He flipped his wrist at the celebrities in the corner. 'And for what? I'm confused.'

'What you're saying is we shouldn't even talk to them.'

'There's a difference between talking and queuing up like groupies.'

'We're not groupies.'

'Yeah, I'm sure they don't think they are either.'

'Define *groupie*?'

'Women who hang around a band after a concert, pushing other girls out of the way so they can make eyes and giggle at everything they say.'

'That's insulting.'

'Hang on,' I interjected. 'He said *like* groupies. Not that you *are* groupies.'

'Excuse me,' the blonde said crossly. 'Who are you?'

'Sorry, I mustn't have said it loud enough the first time.' I held out my hand, again. 'Steve Chambers. Another leftover.'

Again she didn't take it. 'That's not funny.'

'No, I'm not laughing either.'

She gave me a glare to damn me to hell and turned back to Keogh. 'So if I find someone interesting, their life interesting. If I like what they do, that makes me – what?'

In the short spell that followed, I thought she had him. 'Yeah,' I said. 'I always wonder what those girls have in mind when they go into hysterics at rock concerts. Boy, that Mick Jagger is so interesting if we can't talk metaphysics, I'll settle for tossing my undies and ripping my hair out.'

'Shutup,' she hissed, and turned back to Keogh. 'Well?'

'Depends,' he said.

'On what?'

'What your intention is, obviously.'

'And what do you think my intention is?'

'You tell me.'

'What if it's completely harmless?'

'So you're going to tell me that if the lead singer invited you back to his pad, you'd say no.'

'Why would I?'

'What about a date?'

'Same.'

'Is that a yes?'

The pierced-ear girl said, 'You think we're all that easy, don't you?'

'Some, yeah,' Keogh answered with a snort. 'Definitely.'

'Then why aren't we still over there?' the blonde persisted.

'Maybe you got brushed off.'

'God, you're so—'

'You're just cut up because you think you wouldn't.'

'Hey listen,' I butt in. 'How are we for drinks here? I can—'

'What do you have against them?' a brunette sitting beside Pierced-nose chimed in.

'Nothing,' Keogh said.

'Yeah you do. What is it? Lost a girlfriend to some singer?'

'No.'

'Jealous then, is it?'

'Not as much as you'd like me to be.'

They had a breather, which Pierced-nose took advantage of. 'We're the slutty ones, right?' she said bitterly. 'Like it's never the other way around. How typical.'

She gave Keogh a stare someone like me would have bit into. At the same time, making it look casual, she put a hand on the knee of the brunette in a manner I thought highly irregular. The brunette didn't seem to mind, or notice.

'Hey look,' Keogh put his beer on the table and spoke diplomatically, 'I'm not having a go at you.'

'So why,' the blonde asked, in an almost bored voice, 'the third degree?'

'Just want to hear you admit it.'

'You're an arrogant bastard, aren't you?'

'Well, since we're all getting to know each other,' Keogh said with a grin, 'I don't want to leave anything out.'

A smile gathered on her face, but she quickly brushed it aside. 'In that case I'll follow suit,' she said snidely, and leaned forward. 'I *have* a boyfriend.'

The brunette gave a laugh and a clap that sounded a little forced. At the same time, very discreetly, she brushed Pierced Nose's hand away. It was well-timed; I suspected most people at the table weren't in a position to notice. Pierced-nose picked up her drink and fidgeted with the straw, unable to look at anyone.

'Yeah?' I turned my attention back to the blonde and answered for Keogh. 'Where is he?'

'Back home,' she answered.

'And where's that?'

'Orange.'

'That where you come from?'

'Obviously.'

'What are you doing here? At Uni, I mean.'

'Law.'

'That figures,' I said with a nod. 'First-year, right?'

'Yeah, so?'

If I hadn't had a few belts, I wouldn't have said what came out next. 'Just a wild guess, but I'd say you've had it pretty good most of your life. Good enough for mum and dad to pay most of your way through here, correct?'

She gave me a hostile look. 'So?'

'Where are you living?

'University terraces.'

'Which ones?'

'Why would I tell you?'

'What does your boyfriend do?'

'He's a printer.'

'A printer! Wow!'

The intensity of her frown thickened. 'What's that supposed to mean?' There was an edge to her tone, the sort that dared a person to say what they were thinking.

'How long have you been with him?' I asked.

'Over a year.'

'One year! How cute. So, you're here doing law while your boyfriend's back in Shitsville drinking at the local pub, working weekends and dreaming of owning a printing shop one day. You're living in student housing alongside . . . you tell me . . . how many other students? Plenty of fellas . . . partying . . . going out . . . letting guys buy you drinks after what – a month? And you got four years of Uni in front of you. Wake up and smell the roses.'

That stung her. The spark died in her eyes and she sank back into her chair. Pierced-nose spoke up for her. 'You really are a heartless prick.'

It didn't matter how many beers I'd had; I couldn't let it go now. 'I gotta ask – you got a problem with men, don't you?'

'Ones like you, definitely.'

'No. You don't have a problem with me, I think you got a problem with men. Which means you got a problem with nature. It's all been a big mistake. Of all the species on earth, ours has this genetic imperative for males to be bastards and for females to be the victims of some unjust, evolutionary conspiracy. Right?'

'Gee,' she said, a deep note of sarcasm in her voice, 'aren't you the prime example of what you're talking about.'

Another girl at the table said, 'Memorise that, did you?'

I met her eyes. Until then I hadn't really noticed her. Unlike the girls around her she wore little if any makeup, and her frizzy, auburn-coloured hair was tied in a neat ponytail. She wore a plain shirt, unbuttoned at the top and stretched to near-bursting beneath. She might have come straight from lectures.

'Look,' I said, a little harsher than intended, 'all I'm saying – perhaps badly – is that our gripe is just as valid as yours. You obey your instructions, we obey ours. If you wanted us any different, you'd have bred it out of us long ago.'

'And visa-versa, right?' the frizzy-haired girl said.

I raised my glass to her. 'Damn right.'

She leaned forward and I caught a peek of her assets squashed together like marsh-mellows. 'But there's always room for improvement, isn't there?' she said coyly.

'No, you're perfect just the way you are.' It was my peace offering.

'And I bet you take credit for that too, don't you?'

'Hell yeah!'

'Then you're just as arrogant as your friend.' She'd used a humorous tone though, and the flash of a smile backed it up.

'Like I said, you can thank yourself for that,' I said. 'You wouldn't want it any other way.' I noticed the frown on Pierced-nose go deeper. 'Sorry, you might,' I said to her with a chuckle, making her stiffen even more. If she'd been a guy, I wouldn't have lifted the beer to my lips. I'd have kept my hands free, my focus sharp and my reflexes primed. She wanted to take my head off.

'What the fuck is that supposed to mean?' she snarled.

'I'll let you figure that out.'

'Steve,' Keogh said, 'go get another beer.'

'Sure,' I said, inspecting my glass. It was a quarter full but I'd finish it on the way to the bar. 'Any of you ladies like one?' They looked at me like rattlesnakes. All but the frizzy-haired girl, who watched me with a smile on her face I thought curious.

Pierced-nose said, 'If you're going to the bar, just stay there.' The aggressiveness in her tone sounded very un-lady like.

Keogh chuckled. 'Peace, sister.'

'Fuck off, we're not your sisters.'

He sharpened then, stared her down in the same manner he did with the deadbeat farmer of Forbes. 'I said already I'm not having a go at you,' he said. 'But you don't get it, do you?'

Now she looked like she wanted to take his head off as well.

'Not from blokes, anyway,' I said.

There was the flash of a bangle and I caught a silver arc of liquid headed my way. With my reflexes shot I barely managed to shut my eyes in time. It hit my face with an icy cold splash and I felt ice cubes bounce off my cheeks and nose. My shirt soaked up the rest. Sound around me seemed to turn down.

My eyes stung when I opened them. 'Thanks,' I said, pinching them shut and giving them a wipe. They teared over from the sting and I had to keep rubbing, licking my lips and tasting vodka. I was more surprised than angry. It wasn't the first time I'd been baptised – gee whiz – just a couple of weeks ago a bunch of seniors had emptied their cheeks over me, but this was the first time someone had fired at me in anger.

I stood from the table and gave the girl a glare to match what she gave me. Her friends reminded me of a bunch of mothers having witnessed an unruly kid smacked. They didn't even offer me the sensitivity of a show of embarrassment.

I went to the bathroom and did my best to wash the stink out of my hair and shirt. I ripped off some paper towel and gave my hair a ruffle with it. No amount of washing could take the stickiness out of my neck, and my hair was left frazzled. I left it that way; it passed as being gelled.

When I got back to my friends, Keogh was there. The grins the boys greeted me with told me they'd either seen or been briefed on what happened. Joey held out a beer and I took it. 'Cheers,' he chuckled, clinking my glass. The women over at the table were carrying on as normal. Not a head was turned our way.

'Sorry about that,' I said to Keogh.

'Yeah, thanks mate,' he said, but he was smiling forgivingly. 'That how you help me pick up women?'

'You were struggling.'

'At least I don't turn it into a train wreck.'

'Just backing you up. Hell, I didn't even mean what I said.'

'Couldn't you have told them that?'

'I especially didn't want to tell them that.'

Keogh turned his head back toward their table. 'Something about that woman.'

The night wore on and he couldn't keep his eyes off her. At one point I saw her notice and they locked eyes, faces still as ponds. A devilish smile fluttered on Keogh's lips, and then her gaze fell away.

Shortly after that she stood with the frizzy-haired girl and made for the door. Keogh near bolted after them, bailing them up at the doorway. The frizzy-haired girl dutifully walked out of earshot, and we both watched them for about three or four minutes. Keogh did most of the talking. At last he held out his hand. His love-interest cast her head down, shouldered her handbag and offered up her hand slowly. Keogh took it and gave it a shake.

He came back and I asked what all that was about. 'Making peace,' he said.

A few days later he told me he paid her a visit. Sounded like it had gone a lot better than their introduction. I learnt her name was Lisa, and they'd be catching up again on the weekend.

Six

On any blue-skied day the cropped lawns dividing the rise of sandstone walls were sprinkled with students taking a break; reading books, going over notes, chatting gayly. As my routine settled I'd keep an eye out for individuals as habitual as me: on this particular day the cute little red-haired girl sat cross-legged at the same spot out front of the Faculty of Law, Styrofoam coffee-cup in one hand, paperback in the other. The fastidiousness about her was at odds with the mature-aged, hippy-type throwback sprawled on his back reading a newspaper nearby, the bench where he usually sat occupied by two lovebirds letting the world know they were in the early days of romance.

I pushed through the turn-styles of the Fisher Library; a nine-story modern wonder compared with the local libraries I was accustomed to. Deep inside you don't have to be blind to wander around in circles looking for an exit, let alone find what you're after.

The elevator took me to the eighth floor, not where I'd find my course material. The doors opened to instant silence and a turn or two later I was deep inside a labyrinth of steel shelves stacked floor to near-ceiling with faded books. As usual, no one was about. A student or two at most strayed by. The university took around fifty thousand students a year, and whenever I pondered how many were bumping past each other on the grounds below, I'd think of shoppers in Westfield Mall on Christmas Eve. I found the location I'd tagged for further perusal and filled my arms with a stack of books. I only had two hours.

I loved the place. I craved my peaceful hours here as much for its therapeutic effect as for the joy of reading. No better haven opened its doors freely for people seeking solitude. In my younger days I made a habit of skipping games of touch or cricket with my friends to lose myself in the local library, fibbing about it later when asked where I'd been. Add to this my geekish love of history and I'd be drawn like a papyrologist to the Letters of Paul. Here I could devour the lifeworks of people whose efforts are never fully rewarded. But I heard them. Sometimes I'd take a deep breath and draw their spirit in – this peaceful wisdom with shelf-lives as deservingly endless as the aisles they fill.

My favourite desk sat along the eastern wall. Before sitting down I checked my surrounds, made sure my anonymity was complete.

I perused the books laid out in front of me like a jeweller might his rare gems. I picked one at random and started reading. If it didn't grab me, I'd try another. I'd been doing this for weeks now and found I rarely had to. I set the timer on my watch. If it wasn't for an alarm, I'd be there all day.

The Fatal Impact – the Invasion of the South Pacific, by Alan Moorehead.

I didn't see pages of ink. I saw an ocean as brilliant in its shade of blue as the sky above it. Time had no feel, just the roll of ship, the sting of salty spray, and the push of breeze. I'd be eating weevil biscuits, swaying with each step. Below deck the air tasted musty; I'd hear the kiss of water beneath the keel and the creaks and groans of a leaking hull. In the crow's nest the tropical sun felt closer, the wind cleaner. A bump showed on the horizon and I felt the excitement of the lookout – a slum-kid perhaps – on sighting a fabled paradise not even the eyes of kings are privy to. And then I felt its pull, like the moon's on the tide, strong enough to draw men from the far side of the globe. It steered the albatross wheeling silently overhead, the fluke of the whale, the—

'Hello,' a girl's voice dragged me back.

I looked up and saw the frizzy-haired girl from our night at the Manning Bar. 'Hey . . . hi.'

'You can run, but you can't hide, huh?' I cringed at her wit and it must have shown; her smile flattened out and she dropped her gaze sheepishly.

I hadn't taken much notice of her the other night; she wasn't the type to bowl a guy over with beauty. Her face was roundish and her cheeks a bit puffy, but it was a warm face with a natural look, and her chocolate-coloured eyes were sharp and friendly. Her hair was tied into the same ponytail as before and a couple of wispy strands bobbed in front of her eyes. She wore faded jeans, a white t-shirt and a light brown cotton jacket.

'I'm Natalie, I met you the other night.'

'Yeah, I remember. How are you?' I asked out of politeness.

'Okay,' she said, grinning. 'How's the shirt?'

'In the wash.'

'What about you?'

'Fab.'

'That was . . . an unusual night.'

'Not for me,' I said with a shrug. 'Get drinks splashed over me all the time. A few weeks ago was beer, chased it up the other night with vodka. I'm working my way through the shelves.'

She giggled a bit. 'What do you do?'

We swapped specifics and I learnt she was doing visual arts and living in the same Uni-run terraces as Lisa, a bit further down the road. They'd both signed up for Uni hockey which is how they'd met. I wondered what she was doing here on the eighth floor but didn't care enough to ask. I kept my answers short and my questions at a minimum. At one stage I saw her eyeing the books on my desk. Her forehead crinkled and a bemused, if not surprised look showed on her face. Her mouth opened briefly, shut again, opened again.

'You said science, didn't you?'

It impressed me, I had to admit. In less than five minutes she'd discovered an interest of mine akin to a fetish not even my best friends knew about. 'Yep.'

She opened her mouth to speak, but any words seemed stuck inside. I dipped my head and flicked a page or two, hoping her astuteness extended to taking a hint.

I was grateful it did. 'Okay, catch you around,' she said, staying put and shuffling her feet. She dropped her head down and hugged her books to her chest. I knew she had something on her mind, but I kept reading.

'Your friend Jason . . .' she faltered '. . . seems like a nice guy.'

'That he is,' I agreed. So that was it. She and her friend were bitch-fighting over him already.

She cleared her throat. 'That bit you said about Lisa's boyfriend, that they wouldn't last. Why did you say that?'

'I don't remember saying it in those words, but I guess I implied it.'

'She cried later on, you know.'

I sniggered. 'Was that before or after she agreed to see Jason during the week?'

She tensed a bit, watched me closely. 'Don't you think two people can continue a long-distance relationship if they love each other enough?' The note of derision in her voice raised a hackle in me.

'If you don't mind,' I said with a grimace, 'I got a good serving the other night, thanks.'

'I'm sorry,' she said, and her gaze dropped to her feet. Her face took on a fragile appearance, which I thought humbling. A strand of hair danced back and forth in front of her nose that she seemed not to notice.

'Look . . . from what I can tell,' I explained, 'the odds of sticking it out with the same person here for more than a year are tough enough, let alone someone geographically impossible.' She kept her head down, and then it struck me. 'What is it, you got a boyfriend tucked away somewhere too, have you?'

Her head came up quickly. 'No,' she answered, looking away at the same time. To me that was a giveaway. I looked down and flicked another page.

'Do you have a girlfriend?' she asked.

Now *that* caught me off guard. I didn't know whether to feel embarrassed or flattered. 'No.'

She regarded me in a way that suggested she'd have used it against me if I had. In the silence that followed I thought that was the end of it.

'Okay,' she said. 'Nice talking to you. I suppose I'll see you around.' She'd said it a little too composed, with tight lips.

'If Lisa's your friend, and Jason's mine, I'd say that's inevitable.'

She smiled then, a sad sort of smile with a story behind it, and walked off. By habit my gaze went to her butt. There was a tad too much girth about it for my liking, and I figured it wouldn't take more than a donut or two to send it south.

No, I concluded. Not my type.

I'd always taken the view – perhaps a lazy one – that the best relationships require the least effort. Let them happen, like friends. If it's meant to be, there's nothing you can do to stop it. If it's not meant to be, there's nothing you can do to make it last.

That Saturday night Keogh led us through a tight crowd in the Grange to the back of the room where Lisa stood amongst a group of girls, two of whom I recognised from our night at the Manning. One was Natalie. I closed the distance with a sure step and eyes aimed straight at them, no more embarrassed about my behaviour that night than they would have been about theirs.

Keogh and Lisa pecked lips, then he introduced Joey, Mick, Flip and Rajah. There were handshakes all around and I saw a light go on in the boys' eyes; the girls had dolled themselves up nicely. When my turn came Keogh gave me a superficial flick with his hand.

'You've met Steve already,' he said. Lisa regarded me with those tiger eyes of hers, and despite everything I still envied him. She had the looks to make me drool.

I shook hands with the balance and heard names that went in one ear and out the other until Natalie stuck her hand out. 'Hello Natalie,' I said, taking her hand.

'Hello Steve,' she said, giving me another one of her sweet smiles. With a touch of makeup and that curly hair floating about her shoulders, she held my attention a little longer than last time. There was a bubbliness about her that set her apart from the others. Everyone stands back on first introductions, measuring each other and guarded with their words, but Natalie's mind didn't seem to be working that way. The shine in her eyes was as bright as a playful puppy.

'You two know each other?' Keogh asked.

'We talked the other day, in the library,' I said.

'Right.' He regarded me curiously. 'Okay, who's for drinks?'

When Keogh came back from the bar with a tray of beers, I took mine and left my friends to their own devices, catching up with some students from the faculty while keeping an eye on my group when it was time for another round. I'd wander back over, grab my drink and take off again. By the third round I realised Natalie had me under surveillance.

At first, I wasn't sure how to feel about it. I'd never considered myself movie-star material and my scorecard with women suggested they didn't either. For the most I kept side on to her, glancing every so often in her direction to catch an eye aimed my way. The first few times she looked away, after that she held my eyes and it was my turn to look away. It was a weird experience, left me rather self-conscious. The way she locked onto me made me think she was in total control.

Two or three beers later, I wandered back for my round. 'You all in?' I offered, waving an empty glass. I received an affirmation from everyone except Keogh and as I made for the bar a sudden volition stopped me. I turned around and saw Natalie watching me, no one else was.

The noise was loud but I took it for granted she'd lipread the obvious. 'You right for a drink, Natalie?' I said, miming the offer with my hand.

'I'm okay, thanks,' she called back, raising her glass to show it was half full. 'Maybe later.'

When I returned from the bar she wasn't there. The boys took their drinks and I sparked up a conversation with Mick and the girl he'd been hitting onto, all three of us leaning close to hear better. I took an instant liking to the girl's fizzy candour and by the signals the two were sending each other, I knew I'd be seeing more of her. At the first passer-by she got talking to, I gave Mick a discreet nudge with my elbow and bent my head confidingly.

'What's her name again?' I asked from the side of my mouth.

'Gabriel,' he replied, not so loud that she'd hear.

A couple of minutes later it was back to just the three of us. 'So, Gabriel,' I started up again, 'how do you fit into all this?'

'I went to high school with Natalie.'

'Oh, okay,' I said, nodding. I glanced around, making sure it looked casual. 'She still here?'

'She went to the bathroom. The line's about a mile long,' she replied, and smiled at me knowingly.

All part of the game, I conceded, and I was tipsy enough to play along with it. 'She partnered up?'

'Give her a break. She's still getting over her last boyfriend.'

'Oh?' I asked, mildly interested. 'How long ago was that?'

'About a month ago, right when Uni started.'

'What happened?'

'He went to Bathurst to do Communications,' she explained. 'Dumped her at the train station the day he left, right when she went to see him off.' I took it in silently. 'Yeah,' she agreed, in a tone that sounded abrasive, 'they'd been going out with each other for three years.'

I took a moment to mull it over. I knew the proper sentiment was sympathy, and perhaps I nodded with that in mind. But the honest side to me would have stopped it from looking genuine. *Wake up and smell the roses*, I'd said. I meant it then, I thought it now. Part of me welcomed she'd been dumped, if not for her own sake, then for mine, if indeed I intended going down that path. Was I going down that path?

Just then Natalie stepped into view over Gabriel's shoulder. Knowing that the words I'd used on Lisa at the Manning probably stung her equally, I did feel a tweak of regret for having used them. But more than that, I felt an admiration for the girl. I had a healthy respect for anyone that could keep a relationship going, puppy love or no, for three years at an age when you were still learning what your parts were for.

Natalie picked up her glass from a nearby table and joined Lisa and Keogh. I kept my eyes on her, not caring if she noticed. In fact I wanted her to notice, and I suspect she did, although she pretended not to. I knew I should have gone over. But I also knew I had to be cautious. The girl hadn't exactly lit me up when I was clean, and I was seeing her now in that hazy sort of glow that grew more radiant with each chugalug of beer. I wasn't that far gone not to heed this troublesome phenomenon, but this time I felt differently. Half drunk or no, I found myself genuinely intrigued. Three years? They must have started at what – fourteen? Fifteen?

I finished my beer and put the glass down. I walked to the door and the barman pulled it open for me. 'Thanks buddy,' I said, and glanced behind on my way out. Natalie was in the same spot with Lisa and Keogh and I don't think she saw me. One of her friends did though, which was all that mattered.

I stepped into the night and the door closed. About twenty metres away was a bus-stop and bench. Perfect. I walked over and sat down facing the door, arms folded over my chest for warmth.

Within the minute the door opened and Natalie strode out. She stopped and swept her head in a direction opposite to where I sat. Slowly it began turning the other way and I watched with amusement as it crept closer.

At last it completed its arc. Our eyes met and I saw her face flash with embarrassment. I stood and walked over.

'Sprung,' I said, and she tucked her chin onto her chest. The lighting outside the pub wasn't dim enough to hide the pink filling her cheeks.

'Wanna go somewhere we can hear ourselves talk?' I asked, using my most boyish, charming grin.

She looked down, and I do believe she was nervous. 'Okay.'

We went to the Manning Bar. The place was full but much quieter; there were people we both knew, but not as many. I bought her a tequila and lemonade, myself a beer, and we chose a table in a corner. One of my first questions was if she had been seeing a guy for three years, and she nodded in a dismissive manner. I asked her how it was possible and she said it could happen to anyone. Could we change the subject, please?

I crossed my arms, looked her over. 'You don't think it was more than that?' I persisted. She didn't answer and I leaned forward, unable to resist giving her my theory. 'I think it was more than that. How many of us get together and nut it out for that long, at so early an age? It demonstrates a tolerance, an easygoingness most people don't have, to stick it out for as many years as you guys did. I raise my glass to both of you.' I picked it up and did just that. 'You especially, since you wanted to keep it going.'

'You're overanalysing. We were lucky. It worked, we got on. He was right for me.'

'Bollocks. He dumped you, didn't he?'

Her face drooped and a film of water coated her eyes. 'Why are we talking about this?'

'Trying to give you a compliment, I guess,' I replied in a placating tone, worried she was going to burst out crying. 'I mean – what, three years? I couldn't do it.'

I picked up my glass and took a swig. Her gaze dropped then, and she stayed quiet long enough to make me uncomfortable. 'Hey . . . sorry . . . but would you be offended if I said it was the best thing for you?'

'Oh,' she hardened a bit, 'how's that?'

'Well for one,' I gave her a wink, 'it opens the door to other opportunities.'

'Can we stop talking about it then, please?'

'Deal.'

Once we started talking properly, I saw the side in her I'd hoped to see. She laughed at jokes I didn't think I had in me, put a smile on my face easier than anyone yet, and drew words out of me that made me feel clever and good about myself. She probed me with questions I was busting to answer, her compliments sounded genuine and the talk flowed as smooth as the waters of a deep river. We were on the same page about everything. There was no time lag in her catching onto some vague comment I made, and if we veered off at tangents we'd hit upon another common interest and an entirely new discussion opened up. She had me talking so much I couldn't shut up, while she just sat there listening with her perfect white teeth flashing in the dim light, a twinkle in her eye and those cute little curly wisps dangling in her face. The only interest we didn't share was cricket, which I made a show of reluctantly forgiving. She even shared my love of history, albeit modern rather than ancient, and then, for no real reason and not expecting anything but a no, I asked if she knew who Pytheas was.

'Wasn't he that ancient Greek mariner . . . whose scrolls were thought to be lost when the library of Alexandria burned down?'

I nearly fell off my chair. It was too good to be true. Something wasn't right here and I regarded her suspiciously now. Ignoring that Pytheas bit, I began to wonder if everything else she'd said was a pretentious ruse to try and impress me. Sure it was uncanny how we shared so many views and interests, but in that hazy glow of attraction these are the things you make yourself believe. I feared then that she was one of those insecure, needy girls that couldn't stand being single. Maybe her esteem was so low she thought she couldn't afford to be fussy about anyone. Maybe she just felt like a bit of sympathy sex. Maybe all of the above.

I looked around and was surprised to see how much the place had emptied. There were only about half a dozen patrons left. It was time to leave.

'Okay,' I said, turning serious and rubbing my chin thoughtfully. 'Okay then.' I looked her shrewdly in the eye. 'If you could spend an hour with anyone, alive or dead, who would it be and why?'

I settled back, proud of myself. This was the clincher. I picked up my glass and waited for her to answer. She studied me for so long I thought I had her, that she was sorting names through her head and wondering which I'd approve of most. One word from her mouth and I'd see through her, know it all had been a farce.

I felt a soft graze on my shin and jerked in my seat; I thought a mouse might be crawling up my leg. I bent down just in time to see her big toe retreating.

I straightened up, feeling like a dunce. She half-closed her eyes, leaned forward and put a gentle hand at the back of my head to draw my face closer. Her lips grazed my ear and I almost fell off the chair a second time.

'You,' she whispered.

She never said why. In that dark corner of the bar, we had our first kiss.

It was bliss. I learnt more in the leadup to Easter than I did in two years of backseat fumbling. I hadn't come to university completely green but my limited experience with girls always led me to believe they were doing *me* the favour. Nat didn't make it feel that way. She wanted it as much as me, which I didn't think possible in females. She never said no, offered the things a fertile mind like mine lost sleep over until she came along.

The terraces she lived in were run by the university, which bound its tenants to a residential agreement far more relaxed in its policy toward overnight visitors, amongst other things. Those last couple of hours before our tryst I'd sit at my desk and give it everything, like busting myself in that final lap with the finish line in front of me. The walk to her place was ten minutes but the spring in my step clipped it by two at least. Not long after I'd walked through her door we'd be done with the pleasantries and be at it like rabbits. I was all of eighteen and felt like I was making up for lost time.

If you want to graduate with that hot little holy grail clenched in your fist though, you got to discipline yourself. Central to that discipline is sticking to a routine. Lectures. Study. Dining. Training. R & R. Noise within these walls changes throttle but in between you hear the silence it was made for. Open most doors in this place and you'll see someone beating their brains out in a fashion that stood them out during the HSC. Distraction was the ever-present menace. That a fair proportion of us made it to this venerated place at all spoke some merit for the single-sex institutions that launched us, and I was wary of the female factor. The beauty of the deal with Nat was that there was no pressure, no demands. I'd gone in with a casual attitude, taking each day as it came. We found time for each other when it was convenient.

Didn't take long for that convenience to find a regular spot or two in my weekly schedule. The drift towards routine was so natural and quick I didn't realise I'd slipped into it until she handed me a small paper bag as I headed for her bathroom one night.

'Present,' she said. I reached inside and pulled out a toothbrush, still in its packaging. I'd been using hers up till then.

Just before Easter a flyer advised us to assemble in the JCR pre-dinner midweek to listen to a special presentation. Once Sproule passed the word, it became compulsory. They told us the speaker was on a rigorous schedule with the colleges and he'd only take up about ten minutes of our time.

A man in his mid-forties with thinning hair and a face that scowled easily introduced himself with a fancy title I interpreted as some type of shrink that did work for the police. He got straight into it.

'Guys, thanks for coming. I'm going around other colleges with the same speech, so please don't think we've singled out yours. Before I start, be advised that we view this seriously. You might think this is funny, and you'll probably make jokes, but the fact is the women affected don't think it's funny at all, nor do the police. When I heard about it, I didn't think it was funny either. Apparently it's been going on since last year. Underwear has been stolen from some girls in Women's College. These girls have been getting it posted back to them in the internal mail with the crutch cut out of them. Now you might think this is just a joke, and hopefully whoever is responsible is doing it as a joke, but in my experience this can also be the work of a psychopath. So it's not a bloody joke. If it's anyone here,' and with this he waved a finger like a school teacher, 'I suggest you bloody well stop it. Because if you get caught, you'll be treated as a sex offender. You'll be charged and there'll be nothing funny about it then. Hopefully it is just a prank. Regardless, I'm warning you now to give it up.'

As he reiterated the seriousness of it all and told us to watch out for anything 'unusual' I wondered if everyone was thinking the same as me. Of course it was a bloody prank. And if it weren't for this type of tongue-lashing, sooner or later someone would have 'fessed up and boasted about it. We discussed it over dinner that night.

'I don't get it,' Flip commented. 'Watch out for what?'

'Blokes with scissors and a stash of girl's undies,' Mick replied.

'Gosh,' Joey said, 'that narrows it down.'

'You gotta wonder,' Flip resumed. 'It's not like a fella can stroll unnoticed into the laundry of an all-girls college.'

'Must have a girlfriend in there,' Mick speculated. 'Wouldn't be too hard for him to sneak into one then.'

'Speaking from experience, mate?' Joey asked.

'You got me. But I prefer to keep the undies I steal.'

'I thought you wore them.'

'That too.'

It drew a chuckle from everyone at the table, except me. I found it irritating that I was the only one taking it seriously. 'That guy got it right,' I said. 'Who does something like this? How do we know we don't have some sick psycho here?'

'You won't find him in this college,' Keogh joined in.

'What makes you so sure?' I invited.

'This is the Phil. Honour . . . integrity . . . dignity . . . all that garble. They'd have weeded him out by now.'

The next issue of our college magazine *The Drawl* would include a poorly drawn cartoon of a leering face and forked tongue darting out toward a string of knickers on a clothesline. The caption underneath read: Wanted: Stylist for team jockstraps. Enquiries Chris Lane, President Sydney Uni AFL Club.

A few jokes would circulate for a while, then it would be forgotten. For a while.

Seven

Rajah's parents owned a house at Collaroy. Sounded like his dad had made it big in real estate and this was one of many investment properties. They'd kept it vacant over Easter and my cricketing buddy invited a few of us to stay. Joey jumped at the opportunity for a surf, Mick jumped at the opportunity for anything, and Keogh was into spearfishing and said Long Reef did it for him. Not that interested in either, I was undecided until he talked to me into it.

'Do any spearing?' he asked one lunch while I was mulling it over.

'A little bit, as a kid.' I then briefed him on my vast experience chasing undersized bream and whiting with a handspear in the shallows of Balmoral Beach.

To my surprise he didn't make fun of it, just said in a sincere voice, 'Well, come for a splash over Easter and see if you can do better.' I told him I needed a gun and he said he had a spare. He'd brought all his gear to college on account of someone telling him Uni had a spearfishing club, and he wasn't impressed on learning that they didn't.

To make sure I wasn't missing out on anything with the homeboys I rang Kep and had my expectations confirmed. It was all go for Rajah's. Mick, Keogh and I had rugby Easter Saturday and Gabe would drive us in from there via my place after that to pick up my dive gear. She'd made Mick work a lot harder than I had to with Nat but he'd gotten there eventually, and she had the invite too. A high-school flame of Joey's he denied he was serious about was also coming. Nat had an aunt flying in from Perth, which suited me fine. I needed the break. Though we got on great, I suspected I'd fallen into the trap a lot of us do, that being to bide my time until someone better came along. I justified myself on the grounds that she was probably thinking the same. Keogh though seemed happy enough. The guy had a shell of stone but I could tell this girl of his made him soft as putty inside.

To my genuine regret, Lisa and I just didn't get on. The only chemistry between us was the sort that led to flying sparks and a rather loud bang. For the sake of harmony we did our best, and she was pretentious enough to put on a better show than me, but then one of us would make a remark that had the other steaming at the ears, and if it weren't for the sake of our plus-ones we'd unload at each other every other day. Put us both in an awkward position; her as best friend to my better half, and visa-versa.

I reckon he could have done better for himself. The way she had it over him made me think she was his first proper girlfriend. Or that he'd come to college a virgin; he was certainly moralistic enough to fit the profile. On appearances both were prize catches, worthy of anyone's best effort. Lisa seemed to think she was worthy enough without it. Those little spur-of-the-moment affections that might have suggested otherwise were lost on her. She never took his hand, sat on his lap, hugged him for the sake of it. I'd even seen her stiffen up and shake him off when he tried to, like it was an embarrassment. By his efforts alone might one assume they were a couple. Though it was only early days, and I knew I was comparing her with more passionate girls blossoming campus – mine included – I suspected her motive for being with him was fashion. Barbie needs her Ken – or G.I. Joe in this case – and it must have done her ego wonders to see the rest of us fall into their wake.

I was actually looking forward to hanging out with the guy. Almost two months at Uni now and he didn't have a lot of close friends. People liked him plenty, but the distinction that advanced a friendship beyond mutual convenience seemed to be the exclusive privilege of people like me. The guy was hard work. I'd heard more than one person, including so-called friends of his, say he was full of himself.

Our Saturday rumble passed injury-free and we arrived in good spirits at Collaroy just after 6pm. 'Took your time getting here, boys,' Rajah said when he greeted us at the door. 'Gabe and Mick, you get the room next to Joey and Sal.' He introduced Joey's girl and I shook her hand. With her lithe figure, tanned skin, proverbial belly-button stud and tattooed dolphin nosing it like a playball, she was the picture of the beach.

'You two boys,' he said to Keogh and me, 'get the dungeon out back.'

We walked through the neatly furnished house until we came to a set of sliding doors. Rajah opened it up and I saw a sunroom with two single beds.

'Snore like you did in Forbes, mate,' my bunkie warned as he tossed his bag onto the closest bed, 'I'll stuff a pillow down your throat.'

Rajah cooked up a fantastic tandoori chicken and everyone pitched in cleaning up. Afterwards we collapsed onto an assortment of sofas, chairs, and stained beanbags pulled out of the garage. Rajah flicked through the TV channels with the remote until he landed on a rerun of *Ben Hur*. Over on the lounge Joey pulled a coffee table closer and rolled two joints. One he passed to Sal, the other he lit and promptly sucked down to half its length. Having filled his lungs to capacity, he leaned forward and held it out for me. I took a few long drags and offered it to Keogh, who shook his head.

'Not my thing,' he said.

'Your loss,' I croaked, lungs tight as a balloon.

Rajah asked Keogh, 'Would you like a beer?'

'No thanks.'

'Scotch?'

Keogh shook his head.

'Don't drink, don't smoke . . .' Mick commented.

I watched Keogh to see how he'd react. He just sat there in his watchful stillness, like it all meant nothing. I let my breath out in a long plume of smoke. 'Don't talk much, neither,' I added, and saw his cheek twitch in a show of indifference.

There was a relaxed atmosphere in the room. It felt good. Here I was with friends, it was Saturday night, the horror of my assignments was behind me and Uni commitments were the furthest thing on my mind. Two days of simply hanging out here were in front of me, then a lazy week doing what I pleased. When Rajah made noises about the stink we opened all the windows but the smoke in the lounge stayed thick as fog.

We smoked the reefers down to their butts and sat sprawled where we were, too lazy to move. Joey stroked his guitar as Macedonian and Roman galleys rammed each other on TV. Keogh was filing the tip of his speargun shaft.

'Going out tomorrow, Jase?' Mick asked.

'Ooh yeah.'

'I wouldn't mind giving it a go.'

'Leave it to the experts, mate,' I said.

'Got another gun?' Mick asked. Keogh thankfully shook his head no.

Joey stopped strumming. 'What it is with you and those bloody fish?'

'Same as you and those bloody waves,' Keogh answered.

'Seriously,' Joey added, and you could see he was interested.

Keogh replied without looking up. 'In that darkness camaraderie does not hold: Nothing touches, but clutching, devours . . .'

'What?' Mick asked.

'He's quoting Hughes,' I said, and Keogh gave me a lopsided grin.

'Who is Hughes?'

Keogh stopped fiddling with his gun and stared into space. 'Look around you,' he said dreamily. 'Everything bent to our will. All bitumen and bricks and things made up or torn down. We live in a city of over three million people, and we can step into the ocean beside and be on the edge of a frontier. Stick your face into it and you're eye-to-eye with creatures as wild as anything in the jungle, staring back at you like they know how many millions of years they got on us. Never a world more savage, more tameless. Life hangs on the flick of a tail . . .' his voice faded to a murmur '. . . and yet it's so peaceful down there.'

We sat there in a dopey silence. I don't think any of us had heard him string together so many words in one breath. Joey gave his soliloquy a couple of quick riffs from his guitar and we all broke out laughing; the timing was perfect. I tried to hold it in and it burst out like a pressure cooker, making it all the louder. It wasn't that funny. Stoned laughs never are.

'Shit,' laughed Joey, 'and I thought I was high as a bird. You sound better sitting there with your mouth shut.'

Keogh smiled sheepishly and sought diversion with his speargun.

'Guess that's why you don't talk so much,' I said.

It was that time of morning when you could look at the sun without going blind. It hung a hand-span above the horizon, and the ocean was smooth as jelly. Late as we'd want to be, Keogh had warned. Surfers compete for waves, spearos for reefs. Early bird catches the fish, literally.

Rajah loaned us his car. At the bottom of Anzac Avenue I turned right onto the road up to Long Reef Headland and slowed past the golf club and boat ramp. I veered left into the bottom carpark and had barely rolled to a stop when Keogh was out the door. Ever since he'd kicked me awake that morning something had opened up in him. The glint in his eye was brighter than I'd ever seen it, like a kid at Christmas with his presents ready to be opened.

I got out of the car and Keogh pulled two spearguns from the boot. Both were double-rubbered with floppies for spearheads. The only difference to my untrained eye was that one looked slightly bigger than the other. He passed over the smaller one and I looked it over unappreciatively.

'This the crappier one, I guess.'

'There's nothing wrong with that one. This'—he held his speargun up proudly—'was made for me.'

'What is it?'

'Finest damn piece ever made. Got me more fish than the others put together. I'm going to be buried with it.'

'Just like those warriors out of the old times, hey?'

Keogh smiled in a significant way, like I'd made a connection.

Suiting up in the carpark I barely managed to keep up with him, once he was finished there was no hope. He took off like it was the start of a race and I trailed him to the rock platform at a speed just under a trot, dropping pieces of gear in my hurry. If this is what I was in for, I knew I was in trouble.

I looked north, toward Collaroy and Narrabeen. The swell humped and broke in perfect curls about a hundred metres or so offshore where dozens of surfers freckled the ocean, waiting their moment. This early in the morning and I could see there was already a queue for waves.

'Look at them,' Keogh said, following my gaze. 'Spend their whole lives on top of it. Gotta wonder how often they stick their faces below, see what's down there.' I turned my head in the direction we were going and saw empty ocean. At least we had that over them.

The platform at Long Reef extends seawards a couple of hundred metres, flat as the deep blue yonder we were headed into. Water slapped about my ankles and nice bare rock gave way to rubbery Neptune's necklace, and barnacles and periwinkles I had to aim my feet between.

'What's the tide doing?' I asked.

'Going out,' Keogh answered.

'Does that make a difference?'

'Not where we're going.'

'And where's that?'

Keogh flipped a hand at the ocean. 'Out there a way.'

'How far?'

'Dunno. Never measured it.'

'Okay. How long will it take?'

'Depends how fast you swim. Fifteen minutes or so, give or take.'

'Are you kidding?' I asked horrified. 'That must be at least a mile out.'

'Get real.'

Close to the edge of the platform we stopped. Keogh spat in his mask and wiped his saliva around while I contemplated the ocean. It looked far less inviting now I had to swim . . . however far out. I'm a landlubber, got no problem with it. To me the ocean is a world full of razor-sharp teeth and armour-plated hides, of stinging tentacles and peanut-sized brains that stopped evolving once they'd learnt all that was needed to mangle their prey. Ted Hughes was spot on.

'Can't we just hang around here in the nice and shallows?' I asked.

'If it weren't this late in the season it might be worth a go,' Keogh said. 'A few good jew holes in close, but this late in the year they've had a flogging. Best chance is out on the ledge where we might pick up a snapper or kingie.'

'Don't you worry about sharks?'

'All the time,' Keogh replied. 'Bastards steal my fish.' He bent down and picked up the diver's float and rope. 'Don't worry,' he smiled, 'I'll tow the float.'

We reached the perimeter where the ocean deceived us with small, harmless waves that crawled over the rocks and foamed about our ankles. Keogh heaved the float high out over the ledge and the rope arced out neatly behind it. It plopped into the sea just as the slack ran out, about thirty metres or so. The diver's flag bobbed up and down and settled. Balancing on one leg, he slipped his feet into his fins and then began walking backwards, heel first toward the ocean. At thigh-depth he did an about-face and threw himself in. His head popped up through the whitewash and he levelled off and aimed himself toward New Zealand like a U-boat.

I sat myself down on the rocks and fit my fins the conservative way, small waves breaking about my waist. Once fitted I stood and began walking backwards like he'd done, fins flopping about like duck's feet, until water was breaking about my knees. A small wave knocked me off balance and I guided my fall in the direction of the ocean. The wave retreated and I push-upped over the cunji-coated rocks like a salamander, chest-bumping and finning madly until the platform dropped and I was floating freely.

Clear of trouble, I treaded water and used one hand to drain the water from my mask and adjust it so it didn't bite into my face. Ahead, Keogh was waiting. Soon as he saw me, he flattened out and took off. I pulled the gun-rubbers back, nocked the spear, and kicked off after him.

Visibility improved the deeper and further out we went; I could see about fifteen or twenty metres. The bottom faded, colours lost their hue and clear-edged rock fuzzed and faded until it disappeared altogether. I was floating in a green-blue space. A sense of helplessness overcame me, a fear of being way outside one's element. I stopped and raised myself vertical, treading water as I rotated my head this way and that, but with the swell rising around me I couldn't see far in any direction.

Just then the orange float bobbed past, bouncing away in stops and starts. I timed myself to the rise of a swell and kicked up to gain height. There was Keogh about thirty metres away, horizon-bound. I kicked for the float, grabbed it and decided he could tow me until he noticed. The line went slack and I lifted my head.

Keogh turned his mask up. 'What's up?'

'You wanna slow down?'

'Sorry.'

After that his speed was more respectful. It felt a tad better with him swimming alongside, knowing my chances of being chewed were reduced by half. I could never do this on my own. And this nutcase did this regularly, on his own too I'd been told.

Streaks of light pierced the blue depths, fading into nothing. It was impossible to allay this fear; fear of the known, fear of the unknown. To me it made perfect sense. As far as I was concerned it was wired into the mind of rational human beings for good reason. It kept one out of trouble. If I'd never known what a shark was, or if someone told me the nearest one was fifty kilometres away, I'd still be as jittery as a rabbit. Since year zot there was always something swimming around in the ocean with big teeth and a nasty temper – plesiosaurus, megalodon, the Loch Ness monster – and I didn't feel like bumping into any of their descendants on account of my guide being a gene short of common sense.

Just keeping up was a challenge, let alone darting my head impulsively to each phantom shade of blue that crept into my vision. I thought I heard a shout and looked up. Ahead, Keogh pointed urgently to his left. I slid the mask up my face to see him better. 'What's up?'

'Over there,' he said, pointing again.

About fifty metres away the surface was awash with a myriad of small eruptions. Hundreds of seabirds hovered above, and as I squinted away the salt water dripping into my eyes I saw them take turns dive-bombing into the disturbance. I'm used to seeing this sort of thing from the safety of land or on TV, not in there with them.

'What is it?' I asked, my voice slightly panicky.

'Baitfish.'

'Yeah, so?'

'Something might be under them.'

'Like what – a bloody Great White?'

Keogh laughed. 'Man up!' he lamented loudly. Then he was down again, heading straight for them. It was a choice of treading water in the big blue or following. What the hell.

As I got closer to the commotion I saw the flash of a striped body – thankfully less than a foot long – shoot past. Another one followed and began doing crazy circles into a shimmering, swirling mass I realised was an immense school of fingernail-sized baitfish. The water was so thick with the tiny things I could sense the ocean's rhythm stilled; an electric presence that gave the water a virtual warmer feel. I pulled my head out of the water and saw Keogh treading water right in the thick of it.

'Hey!' I shouted. 'What's that in there with them?'

'Just bonito,' he said. 'Don't worry about it.'

Don't worry about what? I thought annoyingly. *That it's not a pack of sharks in there with them?* I was near shaking. I just wanted the damn thing over with. Keogh resumed his former direction, and with no alternative I followed.

There was, despite this feeling of helplessness, something surprisingly invigorating about this. I could feel my senses hum, the finely-honed nerves inside me working for my protection. And the freedom, a sensation not unlike what I often felt in my dreams, flying like a bird.

Without a watch I had no idea how long we'd been going. Once I heard the low drone of a powerboat and looked up surprised to see it more than half a kilometre away. The damn thing sounded like it was almost on top of me.

At last the seafloor materialised out of the murky depths. And now

I could see things moving below, silent shapes on secret business, teasing me with their lack of clarity. Then my eye caught something big. Seriously big. It glided along the bottom in no hurry at all, a ray-shaped shadow moving as effortlessly as a dark cloud. The last time I'd seen something as big was behind the safety glass at Manly Aquarium. It was a showpiece of the depths, big and strong and sure of itself, its wicked barb-headed tail trailing out behind; six feet of sophisticated, antipredator weaponry designed to check the most sinister denizens of the deep, and here I was with the equivalent of a popgun.

I stopped to see where Keogh was and saw his face-masked head about thirty metres away.

'Okay, we're at the Wall,' he said. 'You see that school of kingies before?'

'No.'

'We'll run parallel to the ledge, see how we go.'

I followed him to the dropoff, keeping the ledge in sight once the bottom disappeared again. He must have had somewhere in mind, which was confirmed when I saw him arch his back like a humpback whale, invert, and then kick gracefully down into the murk with his fingers pinching his nose to equalise. The tow-line attached to his gun followed him down, arcing like a bow with the current.

He blended into the gloom, and was gone. I was all alone again. The seconds passed and I did a vague mental calculation of time. Long after I'd have run out of breath, he was still down there. I lifted my head to see if I'd missed him surface somewhere, and saw nothing.

So I waited. And waited. A string of tiny bubbles rising from the depths let me know he was still down there. After what I reckon was a minute, I heard a sharp metallic snicker below, then nothing.

A few seconds later he ascended from the deep, real slow. He was moving funny, kicking both legs as one, like a dolphin. One hand clutched the spear-shaft, the other was pressed up against his chest trying to hold a fish still. The gun trailed down, suspended by the mono. The fish fought madly, a silver blur of scales flashing like polished diamonds in the shafts of sunlight. Not once did Keogh break his rhythm, porpoising calmly upwards until his head broke the surface.

'He's gut shot,' he told me. 'Grab the float, I don't want to lose him.'

I hauled on the rope and the float bobbed closer. 'Undo the clip,' he said when I got it, and I grabbed the loop of wire and fumbled with the clip. Every time I tried to squeeze it open, it slipped out of my fingers.

'Sometime today would be good,' Keogh goaded me. At last the clip sprung open and I passed him the eye of the wire. 'Take the shaft,' he said.

It was a messy exercise, the fish kicking for all its life, slapping my facemask with its tail. I held the shaft as Keogh pushed the wire through its gills and out its mouth and clipped the eye secure. He manoeuvred the shaft out of the hole in the fish's guts, which had torn open as wide as the mouth of a middy glass. The floppy on the spearhead barely stopped it slipping free.

'Okay,' he said. 'Done.'

We let go and the fish shot away, shaking its head furiously, trying to dislodge the wire. It gave up quickly and bobbed listlessly just below the float.

'What is it?' I asked.

'Blue morwong.'

'You got what you came out here for then?'

'You had enough already?'

'How much longer do you want to hang around?'

'You don't want to have swum all this way for nothing.'

'Shit, I'm happy to call it quits.' I'd seen a doco taken somewhere in India. When villagers went into tiger territory they'd haul a sacrificial goat along with them at the end of a mighty long rope. Given the choice, the theory went, the tiger always went for the goat. Though I searched my mind hard, I couldn't recall a similar test applied to a two-tonne shark. I redid the maths and told myself my odds of being chewed had been reduced to a third, give or take, but then I needed to balance this with the fact that there was now a bleeding two to three kilo fish sending *come get me* death quivers out through the ocean like a sonar pulse.

Keogh said, 'We'll give it another half-hour or so, eh?' He didn't wait for an answer; just flattened out and was on his way again.

The closest I got to anything worth shooting was a giant kingfish that sped by quicker than a bird. The few times I actually could see the bottom I tried to follow Keogh down, but as soon as I got there my lungs were bursting and I had to abort the effort and kick back to the surface. I'd look below and see him gliding along effortlessly, and console myself with the thought that I'd kick his butt at chess.

Long after the promised time he was still at it, dropping down every few minutes to inspect the domain of Captain Nemo. 'Hey,' I said after about his twentieth dive. 'You finished?'

'You want to go in?'

'If it's not too much out of your way.'

'All right. There's nothing here anyway.'

I sighted the mainland, which looked about a mile away, and pointed myself eagerly toward it. This time I set the pace all the way back.

It was a long swim, although it didn't feel as long as the trip out there. The bottom showed again and I felt a comforting relief as it gained clarity. Keogh came alongside and I knew what he was going to say before he opened his mouth.

'We'll just do the shallows around here, hey? Scoot around the edge of the whitewash.'

I thought of a smartarse reply, then reminded myself if it weren't for me the guy would still be enjoying himself way out in the watery wilderness. Before I could reply, he shot off south.

I took stock of the situation. I hadn't shot at a single thing and he was right, I ought to try and bag something. The bottom was only about five metres down max, and it felt good having my back to a wall of rock. Anything coming at me had to do so from the ocean side, and worse-case scenario I'd launch myself over the ledge and onto terra firma like a flying fish.

For no reason at all, I decided to go the opposite direction to his. I finned closer to the edge of the platform, keeping to the calmer deep where the ocean sucked me back and forth, back and forth, playing with me; one moment trying to fling my sorry arse over the rocks, the next hauling me back to safety. Occasionally I swam over large circular holes, so unnaturally round they looked man-made. I was hovering over one, not paying attention to the swell, when a surge caught me and flung me over a submerged ledge. The next thing I knew I was sucked helplessly down into the trough on the other side. A blinding vortex of bubbles and froth nearly ripped the mask off my face and the fins off my feet, and I kicked madly but my fins wouldn't grip. But I knew it would pass, so I held my breath and waited for the pull on me to weaken, which didn't take long. The suction died, the froth parted and I was surrounded by swirls of rising bubbles that looked like mini whirly-gigs. I'd just begun to kick for the surface when I looked down to see how deep I was.

There were two of them, eyeballing from below like they had all the time in the world. Perfectly aligned, facing the same direction. Motionless as goannas soaking up the sun, big and fat as bullmastiffs, streamlined as torpedoes. Diamond studded along the lateral line, like tiny lights. Never had I seen this close up as big and magnificent an eating fish as these.

I was all out of air and had to keep going, had to break surface. I filled my lungs quickly and arched into a dive position but I was too jerky, full of the excitement of the amateur. My free arm flayed like a bird with a broken wing and then I saw their fan-shaped tails come to life and beat thickly, slowly at first and gathering speed remarkably – *thwoop thwoop thwoop thwoop* – the vibrations pulsing through the water. They were too fast for fairness and my only advantage was that the tip of my gun had a lead on them as they ascended to clear the trough. They disappeared into the breaking wash and I pulled the trigger purely out of frustration.

The shaft followed them in with a blur. Then suddenly there was an almighty jerk in my hand and my fingers clawed reflexively over the grip. I was hauled forward as if a horse was on the other end.

I didn't know what I was supposed to do, bloody Keogh hadn't briefed me. Without a float-line to play the fish I suspected there was way too much tension on the mono. And now I was being dragged down. My head went under on the inhale and I was tugging madly, trying to bust the mono. My lungs were bursting for air. I didn't want to lose the shaft, let alone the fish, but it was either that or let go of the entire speargun if I didn't want to drown. I didn't relish the thought of either. Forking out a couple of hundred bucks to Keogh to replace it was one thing, having it broadcast all over college was another.

The whitewash cleared and the massive fish was revealed, swishing its tail slowly and pulling me like a Great Dane on a lead. It had it all over me in this tug-of-war well below the surface, but then it did something positively stupid, even for a fish. Against all logic it rocketed up suddenly, dragging me with it, and as soon as my head broke surface I blew the sea out of my snorkel and got a couple of good breaths in. I had just flattened out again when a chance swell caught the fish and lifted it over the exposed ledge. The wave sucked back, the mono went slack and I was temporarily blinded by froth again. I raised my head, water slid down my mask and there was this monster of a fish stranded on the rock, flexing madly.

Another swell gathered beneath me. Timing myself perfectly, I rose with its lift and rode it onto the ledge, glory bound. The swell receded back into the ocean with a gush like a river rapid and I felt my full weight pinch into pointed nasties. I lunged after the fish and sharp edges scratched and bit at my hands and knees, but it's amazing what you can ignore when you're grabbing for a prize like this. I hauled on the mono and the spear shaft clunked closer with the fish skewered at the tail, thrashing desperately. I grabbed the shaft with one hand and went with the other for the only hold on the fish I thought I could make, sliding a finger between a massive gill plate and parting it enough to get my whole hand inside. My fingers curled over the sharp serrations of the bony gill-rakers and despite it feeling like I was clutching a handful of broken glass I held on solidly. I knew I had him then. My fingers sent me clear messages of damage but I'd lose the lot of them before I'd let go.

I was just in time. A wave barrelled into me and I went with it. My chest and torso bounced over the barnacle-crusted rocks and my neoprene suit caught once or twice, and it was all I could do to hold onto my prize. The speargun bashed into my ribs and I gave passing thought as to where the spear was; I couldn't have done a thing to stop it impaling me.

Then I rolled into the merciful emptiness of water. I was safe and the fish was going nowhere. My hand was jammed tight through its gill-plate and my fingers were so glued to its rakers that I didn't think I could get them out anyway. The fish started bucking furiously and I jerked with it each time, my arm feeling like it might rip from its shoulder socket.

The water cleared, the fish stopped fighting and I saw a single rubbery eye staring at me. I hugged it to my chest and looked down to where its long silver body tapered into a fan-shaped tail that swayed weakly next to my fins, and it was way down there that the spear-shaft protruded. The speargun trailed safely on the mono behind it.

The sea was too rough to exit here, so I kept swimming north. Now and again the fish bucked desperately in my grip and my fingers protested in pain, but it was easy to ignore. I swam to a relatively calm spot protected from the swell, and after a graceless struggle on all fours managed to haul my scratched and bleeding body onto the platform while dragging fish and trailing speargun. I crawled forward like a baby until I was in ankle-deep water, then carefully manoeuvred my hand out of the gills, sacrificing a bit of skin as I did. Panting heavily I sat on my butt, slid my facemask up and snorted the saltwater out of my nose.

I looked for Keogh. Fifty or more metres away a pair of fins pointed skyward like a whale's fluke, then slipped beneath the surface.

There was a grunt beside me. The fish flopped miserably on the barnacles, gnashing itself and probably oblivious to the pain, like me. It grunted again; a strange, almost human sound that might have been outrage, might have been sadness, gills venting in futility. The early morning sun gave its scales a sparkle like tiny jewels and a beautiful golden tint.

I kicked off my fins and leaned over it. I tried to lift it by the head but it weighed a tonne and bucked easily out of my grip. I grabbed a gill plate and managed to drag it a good distance away from the wash foaming over the rocks, then let go. The fight was over. There was nothing more to do.

Then I did something I've never done before. I clenched both my fists, tilted my head back and threw my arms skywards.

'*YES!*' I screamed it out. Several times.

It was hard to describe the emotion. I'd killed a fish. A monster of a fish, but still just a fish. I'd hit the winning runs at cricket matches a few times. I recalled when I'd heard my name read out for NSW Combined High Schools Cricket. I recalled my first century at representative level and how great it felt; that buoyancy of emotion that had left me with possibly my proudest moment. Such achievements seemed paltry now. This was different. My hands were tremoring. I balled a hand into a fist, opened it up again. It was still tremoring. It occurred to me then how sloppily the term *adrenalin rush* gets thrown around. This was the real deal, the sort that made pain go unfelt, your limbs turn so light that your extremities vibrate, your breathing turn short and your heart beat so hard you feel it thumping against your ribcage. Relevant and irrelevant flash in your mind for instantaneous sorting; your attention jumps randomly from one thing to the next while taking everything in with remarkable detail: the beautifully timed cadence of a crab's legs as it scurries into a rock pool, the subtle contraction of a cunjevoi as it squirts seawater skywards, the barely perceptible quiver of a fish's tail as it lay dying on the rock. My veins were singing with it.

I inspected the hand I'd stuck through the fish's gills and saw my palm scratched to buggery, crisscrossed everywhere and rough like sandpaper. I barely felt my countless cuts and abrasions. Everywhere I looked my skin was coated with an impressive veneer of blood. I couldn't have cared less.

By the time Keogh crawled out of the ocean the fish had stopped gulping. He straightened up, removed his facemask and fins, and came over with his face all twisted in confusion. He stared down as if he'd never seen a dead fish before. Then he turned his head every which way, frowning.

'Where'd he go?'

I followed his gaze. 'Who?'

'The bloke that shot the jew. Where'd he go?'

'Mate, I done told yuh . . .' I beamed with assumed superiority. 'You wanna catch the big ones, you gotta follow me.'

'Hang on a sec . . .' Keogh slapped his cheek repeatedly '. . . hang on . . . just wait . . . trying to wake myself up here. I thought I got up this morning.'

I smiled gleefully. 'You want to show me what to do with this thing now?'

Keogh looked at me like I was from another planet. He shook his head disbelievingly, then began to chuckle. 'Mate, I've seen some arsy luck in my time, but this breaks my heart.'

'Arse is class.'

Keogh knelt and slapped the fish on the side. Its brilliant golden sheen was fading to patches of mottled grey before my eyes.

'Where'd you get him?'

I explained where and pointed. Keogh took it in with a nod that made me think he knew the exact hole I was talking about. 'Let's go,' he said.

The fish was all I could carry, so he carried the rest. He hardly said a thing to me on our way back. Plenty of guys I knew would have misunderstood his silence, would have been miffed if he'd reacted like that to them. It was all about ego. They'd say his had been checked, and he was too vain to acknowledge it. But I was getting to know how this guy's mind worked. Like so much of his behaviour, this was just another filter he used to determine his friends. His patience for attitudes as superficial and shallow extended only as far as it applied to him, which meant bugger all. Take it or leave it seemed to be his silent dictum. I knew he was happy for me. Happy enough not to spoil the occasion with needless flattery. With that thought, I was glad to have shared this moment of mine with him. Just him.

We diverted to the cleaning table near the clubhouse. It occurred to me then that I didn't want to butcher it up until everyone had seen it. I was disappointed not to have brought a camera.

Keogh read my mind perfectly. 'It's a good fish,' he said, 'but you haven't broken any records. You can take him back in one piece for showing off but we should at least gut and scale him here, otherwise it'll stink the place out. Add another kilo for guts if you want to weigh it. I'd say we're looking at about twenty-five kilos or so.'

After gutting both fish and throwing the offal to some patient pelicans, we arrived back at Rajah's where my big jewfish got all the attention from the guys, aghast looks from the girls. I dumped it onto the grass and they backed away as if thinking that butchering it up was an automatic delegation to women. Keogh assumed the role generously enough. Rajah collected a saw from the shed and a large knife from the kitchen, and Keogh set to work. None of us knew how to butcher the thing anyway, so we stood back watching with beers in hand while the ladies prepared salad and crackers.

We were in high spirits the whole time. I'd never seen Keogh grin so much. He couldn't get over it, just kept going on and on about it.

'Mate,' I interrupted after an eternity, 'enough already. Get over it. It's just a fish.'

'Nuh,' he said. 'You don't get over something like this. Took me years to bag my first jew, and *you* . . .' he said with a raised voice, pointing a finger at me and laughing. 'You! This softcock who can barely pull the rubbers back comes along and bags a monster on his first date. I'll never be the same again. I've found religion. There is a god.'

We fired up the BBQ and cooked up a heap of thick steaks, flipping them over the BBQ until the meat turned a toothy white with a crispy brown layer on top. Rajah bagged up what we didn't throw on the BBQ.

'Plenty left here,' he said. 'What do you want to do with it?'

'I don't know,' I answered, and turned to Keogh. 'Can we sell it? Plenty of fish shops around here.'

Keogh shook his head. 'Illegal.'

'Freeze it,' Mick suggested. 'We can take it back to college, spread it around.'

'Not in my car you won't,' Gabe warned. 'You're not stinking it up with that.'

Rajah threw some large chunks of fish into a bag and tied it closed. 'I don't think I can fit much more into the freezer. If this is enough then

I'll chuck the rest.'

'Like hell you will,' Keogh answered, and muttered something that included the words 'bloody sacrilege.' Rajah shut him up by agreeing to put what he could in the freezer and the rest in the fridge, which Keogh assured would keep for a couple of days. We'd take it all back to college and hand it over to the kitchen staff. They'd cook it up at a mutually agreeable time if we gave them some.

It felt good, this curious synthesis of bonding and feasting on freshly slaughtered meat. Added to this was a deeply rewarding feeling that I'd caught another bug. The sport held far more appeal to me than it did that morning. One fish, one kill, had done it. But one fish wasn't enough now. I couldn't wait to get back out there. Mightn't be ready to stomach the fear out wide just yet, but surely there were more big jewfish in close. Bigger even. We had more than enough fish to eat, to take home, to give to charity, and here I was gripped by an irrational greed that compelled me to go and catch more.

The sun had almost sunk when we finished tidying up. We went inside and spread ourselves out across the lounge room. Time to chill. It felt wrong to clutter one of the healthiest meals I'd ever eaten with a nip or two of Scotch, but I couldn't help myself.

I always look back on that evening. Keogh stretched out on the sofa, Rajah sitting at one end, both transfixed by the TV. Mick slothing on a lounge chair with Gabe laid back against his knees. Joey sunk into a beanbag, strumming his guitar to the soft chords of Mark Knopfler in the background. No one smoked that night, didn't even suggest it. I felt healthier and better than ever and JW warmed my veins. It was the archetypal image of college for me, relaxing with some of the best friends I would ever make, and I see it as lucid as if it was yesterday, a snapshot of a memory so strong as to etch into my DNA. One day my kids will sit around in a similar situation and be jolted by the weirdest of sensations.

They'll call it *deja vu*.

It blew up during the night, turned the ocean ugly. Keogh wanted to check it out anyway. We parked the car at the top of the headland and walked up the track beside the golf course that led to the lookout. Near the top we diverted to the edge of the drop. Sky dark and brooding with thin rain blasting my face, cleaning my eyeballs and tickling my neck. The ocean that floated us so peacefully the day before was now end-to-end rolling whitecaps and horizontal spray.

'Look at it,' Keogh said. 'Like a bitch in a foul mood. Gotta love her though.' He stared ahead, lost in another world. 'After a while, she owns you.'

The wind was so strong it had me swaying. I leaned into it at an angle and spread my arms like the wings of a bird; a few feathers might have seen me airborne.

'I love this place,' he said affectionately. I'd never seen him so calm, the muscles on his face so relaxed. 'Been spearing here since I was a kid. Know every hole, every rock. Got my first big jew down there,' he pointed, 'just like you.'

Despite the soaking I enjoyed standing there letting nature run through me. I'd just closed my eyes to feel it better when Keogh distracted me.

'Don't know how they do it,' he said, barely above the wind.

I dropped my arms and opened my eyes. 'Do what?'

There was a strange look about him. He stared out over the ocean and mumbled so softly I only caught the end of it '. . . *keep on swimming*.'

'What'd you say?'

He turned toward me with eyes as far away as the horizon. I was sure he was about to answer, but a loud call killed the moment.

'Steve!'

I swung around and saw Natalie skipping up the path, holding her jacket up over her head against the side-blown rain.

'Oh great,' I grumbled. 'What's she doing here?'

'Hi Jase,' she said happily when she reached us. Keogh nodded politely, then resumed his watch over the ocean.

'What are you doing here?' I asked. 'I thought you had your aunty over.' It must have come out rougher than intended. Her forehead softened and there was a trace of hurt in her voice.

111

'I thought I'd surprise you.'

'That you did,' I agreed tonelessly. The water was trickling down my back now, and I felt the coldness of it on my spine. 'Can we go?' I suggested to Keogh.

He tore his eyes from the ocean and we headed back.

We spent the afternoon watching videos of *Goodfellas* and *The Abyss,* back-to-back. Keogh took off for a rain-run afterwards and Joey took off with Sal in her car for parts unknown. A deck of cards appeared in Rajah's hand and the rest of us sat around the dining room table playing Rickety Kate.

We'd been at it for a couple of hours when Rajah asked Nat if she wanted to stay the night. She glanced my way, like it was up to me. She must have known I'd been looking forward to time with the lads on my own. I studied the cards in my hand to mask my thoughts.

'No, it's ok,' she said after a bit. 'I didn't mean to stay.'

'Plenty of room,' Rajah offered. 'I can make up another bed.'

'That's there's one dream of a couch.' I flicked a finger in the direction without looking up. 'There's also the garage, eh Raj?'

'Why Steve,' Nat said with deep sarcasm, 'you're such a gentleman.'

I chuckled then. Rajah said, 'It's no problem, really.'

'Thanks, but no. I'll get going after this.'

Gabe lent her support. 'Go on Nat, stay the night.'

I'd had my fun, made my point. 'If you want to stay Nat,' I said amicably, 'just take my bed.'

'No, it's all right.' She smiled then, as if the offer was all she was waiting for. She plucked a card or two and rearranged her suit.

I watched her now; this was worth pursuing. Surely she knew that popping up unexpectedly – not to mention uninvited – put Rajah on the spot, me on the spot. I was curious to see how much we'd need to push her, particularly with the bed issue.

'If you want to stay Nat, and it's ok with Rajah, I'll sleep on the couch. I'm going home tomorrow anyway.'

'No, it's ok.'

She'd sounded more than genuine, and I warmed to her a little more then. Now came the awkwardness of an undeniable truth; if I wanted her to stay, I'd have made more of an effort. Or at least put the enquiry to Rajah, not let him do it.

I turned to Rajah. 'Can she stay for dinner, mate?'

'Of course,' he said with a sigh, like it was a tragedy I thought it necessary to ask.

I inclined my head toward Nat. 'You heard the man. You wanna stay for dinner, sweetie?'

'No . . . it's ok. I don't want to—'

'Please,' Rajah cut her off. 'We have plenty of food.'

She stayed quiet long enough for a yes.

'Fish especially,' I said.

She met my eyes. 'I like fish.'

Eight

A two-year hiatus from rugby had me wondering if I'd see out the trials with the necessary grunt, but each time I entered the change rooms to get kitted up the smell of Dencorub hit me like smelling salts, and I knew I was back. The horsing around, the prep talk, the circular huddle as we fired up, and the run onto the field with the scent of crushed grass underfoot was all it took. I was a part of it again, that primordial clash of muscle and bone as natural to grown men as wrestling is to young boys. It didn't matter I played fifths, or those early games were trials, or no more than thirty people sat in the stands that time of morning. All that mattered was the far goal post and fifteen like-minded bullheads intent on getting in the way.

By the time lectures resumed after the Easter break, teams were sorted and the Shute Shield had kicked off. The Phil was commendably represented throughout the grades, and we had good numbers for our flagship intercollegiate team. We trained together, played together, ate together. The kitchen staff set our dinners aside wrapped in foil for us to eat after training in an empty dining room and we sat where we pleased and got treated like equals. Come game day it was great to go into combat with the boys, and a treat to have the same seniors who gave us so much grief off the paddock step in for us when things got heated. We were their boys and no one could kick our arse. Only they could do that.

It took priority over a lot of my activities; study included, Nat included. It pulled a heartstring or two when I noticed her sitting in the stands one afternoon watching us train. She stayed there the whole time. Though I was prepared to go over and say hello when we finished, she spared me the macho-awkwardness by wandering away during our warm-downs. I told her later on that that was sweet but unnecessary, which must have served as an invitation to come and watch me more often. There she'd be in the stands on her lonesome, black duffel coat and umbrella if raining, sometimes with a book, sometimes not. I got used to the sight and truth to tell, became so fond of it that I'd walk up to her after training and greet her with a peck.

It was almost out of guilt. I knew I wasn't being fair to her, not putting in the effort she did. We got on great and hit it off like best buddies. We'd lie in bed at night talking and joking so long that more than once a housemate of hers had to knock on the door and tell us to shutup. She said things that stuck, from little quotes and phrases to snippets of information totally unfamiliar to me. She educated me in a way my courses never could, exposed a side in me I didn't know I had: a witty side, a bright side, a fun side. I should have been happy. So why did I feel my eyes creep over every girl with a slim waist or short skirt? Why did they, not Nat, monopolise my dreams at night? I always thought the girl of my dreams would give me furballs in the stomach, set off fireworks – all those clichés that went with love at first sight. Given the opportunity, would I yield to temptation? Nat didn't deserve it. I didn't doubt her fidelity for a second. The only person she ever looked at was me, ever talked about was me. Now and then a girlfriend of hers would pass on a compliment she'd made that left me scratching my head. Nothing tickles your vanity more than hearing you have qualities you didn't know existed.

I thought I'd wait until we had a massive fight, take the opportunity then. But we never fought, at least not to a point that presented the option. I knew I shouldn't have dragged it on. I had a long road ahead of me and there were plenty of girls on that road. The problem was that I did like this girl. I liked her plenty. It added to the uncanniness of a lot of things she did that if ever I thought to tread that road, she did something to pull me off it. And the beauty of that was that she did it unintentionally, made it my choice.

Gabe lived in a house in Surrey Hills a few blocks from campus with three other girls and a guy called Skimp who, in his own words, owed his place to taking the garbage out, moving furniture around, and changing blown fuses. In that tinderbox of high-spirited ladies I'd have thrown in peacemaker; he was a tactful, laid-back young gentleman.

One Saturday night midterm Nat and I were invited over for a quiet night in front of *Hey Hey*. We drove over in Nat's Mazda. I had it over most guys in that my girlfriend owned a set of wheels, and a relatively fancy one at that, with its electric wind-down windows, power-steering and central-locking. That day I'd played a bruising game against Wests and most of the team had headed for the Grange, but I thought I'd earned a night off from our sponsors. My left quad had pillowed a Samoan knee in the first half and I played the game out with a raging cork that seized up so tight afterwards I could hardly bend my leg when I stepped into Nat's car. I groaned loudly as I plonked onto the passenger seat but the only sympathy I got from my tender-loving came in the form of a raised brow.

'Just like men,' she said. 'Play the game out with a broken leg, moan like a whale just getting into the car. Why didn't you come off, then?'

I didn't know where to start, so I didn't.

Stragglers pushed numbers up to a dozen and we all chipped in for Dominos, beers, and a couple of casks of fruity white. Red Symons was giving the final act on Red Faces the blasting it deserved when Gabe turned to Nat and asked, 'Shall we play Truths?'

'Wouldn't be his thing,' she answered quickly.

I scraped a melted cheese dreg from a pizza box and glanced at her askew. 'What thing?'

'Just a game we play,' Nat said, shrugging it off.

'What game?'

'An honesty game,' Gabe took over. 'A trust game.'

I looked around suspiciously. The girls chewed away like this was their thing, and I didn't qualify. 'You mean like truth or dare?'

'A slight variation.'

'Yeah?'

Nat shot me a glance. 'You wouldn't like it.'

Mick and Skimp sat there quietly. Too quietly. 'These guys part of it?' I asked, and they smiled secretively. 'You better tell me what it is, otherwise I'm gonna think you're up to something kinky.'

'It's an honesty game,' Gabe explained. 'You say anything you like about someone in the room, and they can't take offence. Something you might find annoying, something they can work on. Anything at all. No arguing, all constructive.'

'What, you pick on anyone?'

'You don't *pick* on anyone. We draw names out of a hat, so it's not taken personal.'

'Criticising someone to their face isn't personal?'

'The whole point is not to take it personal, Steve.'

'This a Psych 101 assignment?'

'No.'

'Then it has the makings of chaos.'

Nat said, 'That's why you shouldn't play.'

There was an empty silence. All I heard was the munching of pizza. 'Let me get this right. You say something bad about someone—'

'Not necessarily,' Gabe corrected. 'Something they could work on.'

'Like I said – something bad about someone – and they aren't allowed to take offence, even if they do.'

'It's called openness. People need to know their faults.'

'Sure. They just don't want to hear them.'

'I told you he'd be no good,' Nat reminded.

'Well, that's something he can work on, right?' Gabe said. A couple of the girls giggled, but Nat grimaced painfully.

'Go on, give it a go,' Gabe encouraged, as much to Nat as me.

'Can I say good stuff?'

'Saying good stuff is easy,' she said, her voice purring. 'Saying bad stuff to someone is harder. You'll do it when you're angry, when you're not thinking straight. When you want to hurt them. The beauty of this is that you're actually trying to help. We're all friends here. What better way than to hear it from one of us?'

I didn't like the sound of it. I really, really didn't like the sound of it. We boys were on our third beers, the girls keeping pace with cheap white. This needed clear heads, at a minimum.

'This'd be like . . . I don't know . . . reading people's minds. And there's a reason we weren't made to do that. We'd end up extinct.'

'Just forget it,' Nat said.

'It's all right, Nat,' Gabe offered. 'He'll be okay.'

Nat stayed quiet. Gabe lifted the cask and poured herself a wine. I'd said this had the makings of chaos and I couldn't see how I was wrong. I didn't want to appear like I couldn't handle a bit of negative comment, but this was different. You can forgive someone for firing off a nasty truth in the heat of an argument. But firing off a nasty truth when they're not? Had a hell of a lot more potency about it.

I kept my eyes on Nat. She took a sip of wine and her deep hazel eyes flashed me a warning. Then it hit me: what if I drew her? There ends the night. No lift home and definitely no sex, for who knows how long. Then again, I suppose I could tell her she needed to lighten up occasionally, like the other night when she snapped at me for suggesting Lisa was a serial flirt. After all, she wasn't supposed to get angry, right? And what did I have to lose if she did? Wasn't this the opportunity I'd been waiting for? What the hell, I could tell her she needed to work out a bit; she was getting flabby around the thighs. She also wore too much makeup lately for a simple trip to a pub. I could tell her to stop showing up unexpectedly to places where I preferred to be on my own. I could tell her I hated that little kissy sound she made when she sucked salt off her fingers, or that pesky giggle of hers, or the. . ?

'Okay, I'm in.'

Gabe put everyone's names into a bowl and we drew them out one by one. I didn't know whether to feel relieved or disappointed when I drew Skimp. I'd been psyching myself up for a stab at Nat.

One of Gabe's housemates was an unassuming, shy little piece called Karen who volunteered to go first. 'Okay,' she started hesitantly, glancing at one of her housemates Donna, a loud busty thing with oily hair and droopy cheeks.

'I drew Donna,' she said. 'Donna,' she faltered, 'we . . . sorry . . . I mean I . . . find it a bit uncomfortable how you and Jock make out so openly in front of us all the time.'

I had to stifle a laugh. Donna and her boyfriend's brazen sex practices were a frequent topic of discussion behind their backs. What most people did behind closed doors they thought was okay in a lounge room with people present as long as you covered yourself with a blanket. I didn't know or care what either did at Uni, or what they did for kicks, but I sure knew more about their sex life than I wanted to.

I thought this was going to be a dumb exercise, but my interest piqued when I saw the way Donna reacted. A startled frown appeared on her face, like this was the last thing she expected to hear. Her mouth opened and words gathered on her lips. I could sense her hunch, the effort she put into restraint. But nothing came, and her expression slowly corrected. Karen offered her a friendly smile that wasn't reflected in the look Donna gave her back.

'Okay,' Gabe said. 'We'll go around clockwise. Jen, you're next.'

Their other housemate Jen was a brutally honest, fiery woman and I listened with interest. 'I drew Mick,' she said, looking straight at him. 'Mick, you tend to kill a conversation a lot when you say "I think this," or "I think that." Like your opinion's the only one that matters. To you, anyway.'

There was a pause as we soaked it in. Mick looked like he'd been given the gravest of news. Gabe gave him a sly smile, one that seemed to say *there . . . see?*

'Give me an example,' he asked.

'Like when we were watching *Full Metal Jacket* the other night,' Jen explained. 'We're talking about the good points, the bad points, conversation is flowing and you come in with "when I was in cadets, we did it this way" or "if that was me, I would have done this." Things like that.'

'Just making conversation,' Mick responded.

'The trick is to do it without making yourself the subject all the time.'

'I still don't get it,' he said, frowning now. 'I'm not—'

'No,' Gabe cut in. 'We don't want arguments.'

Mick rolled his eyes while he mulled it over. Okay, I thought, this wasn't so bad.

'Donna, your turn,' Gabe said.

Donna bored us with a gripe about Gabe not cooking enough, and

119

Gabe filed it away with a mature nod. Then it was Nat's turn.

'I drew Joey,' she said. She glanced my way with a sour face. Nope, she certainly wasn't happy this game was being played. Or more correctly, with me in it.

'Joey, I've noticed you tend to interrupt a conversation a lot. We'll be in a group talking and you just come up and say: "Hey Steve" and off you go. The polite thing to do'—she spoke with soft emphasis—'is to *wait* until there's a break in the conversation.'

Joey dipped his head agreeably. 'Fair enough.'

'It's not that you do it intentionally.'

'Sure,' he agreed. 'Point taken.'

Everyone liked Joey Prentiss. He meant what he said. Just like Nat.

Gabe went next. 'I drew Jason,' she said, squirming a little in her seat. 'I . . . um . . . I find you a bit stand-offish. You don't seem to make much of an effort to get to know people, like you're not interested in anyone.'

Keogh accepted this with a faint crinkle of bemusement. She had a point, but to me it wasn't all vice. If he was so particular about his interest in people, sure made me feel all the more special.

'Would you like to respond?' Gabe asked politely.

Keogh shrugged. 'Fair enough.'

'Ok, let's move on. Skimp, your turn.'

Skimp had drawn Donna's boyfriend, Jock. 'Jock,' he spoke with ease, 'when I first say something to you, I always have to repeat myself. You always go "Uh?" and I have to say it again.'

Jock rubbed his chin, thought for a bit. 'Maybe you mumble.'

'No,' Skimp said. 'It's just easier to have someone say it again than for you to tune in the first time. It's like we have to make a phone call . . . *ring ring* . . . before you pick up,' He offered a good-natured smile, and his intentions may have been harmless, but you can't say something like that without leaving a pinch of hurt. The look on Jock's face seemed to confirm it.

'Ok,' Gabe said. 'Steve, your turn.'

Nat pored over me like I was about to disclose the meaning of life.

'I got Skimp.' I barely knew the guy and there was only one thing I could think of. 'Hey Skimp, stand up for yourself man. Next time one of the girls asks you to change a lightbulb, tell her to iron your shirt.'

It drew a guffaw from the boys, grim silence from the women, and a belated vent of despair from Natalie. Gabe waited for the laugher to recede.

'That's not what we're trying to achieve here, Steve,' she humoured me with a diplomatic smile. 'This is supposed to be constructive feedback on people's personalities. You can't *tell* him what to do.'

'Okay,' I said. 'Maybe I said it wrong. Skimp, you're a girl's blouse. There you go. Nothing I wouldn't tell him anyway.'

'Gee, thanks,' Skimp replied morosely.

We exchanged a few more witty taunts before Gabe got the game back on track. 'Hey, stop it! Can we get serious please?'

'Sure!' I agreed, and with effort assumed the proper demeanour. 'Continue . . . please.'

Lisa was next. She turned my way and I felt the sting of her glare. 'I got Steve.' *Oh for. . .* 'Steve,' she started, and I braced myself. 'You have to be the most sexist man I know.'

Relief washed over me and I relaxed, astounded. Not because I'd just been called sexist. I got that from Nat all the time. I was astounded I'd gotten off so lightly.

'You left the 'e' out when you said sexist.' It was the same line I always used on Nat.

No one laughed. Lisa pursed her glossy lips like a spoiled child, and the eyes beneath those perfectly angled brows of hers lost their shine of arrogance when she saw I wasn't offended.

'Steve,' Gabe adjudicated, 'would you like to respond?'

'No. Move on.'

Keogh was next. We all waited expectantly. This was a guy that hardly ever said a thing about anyone.

'I drew Flip. And I can't think of much to say.'

'Aw, come on,' I encouraged him. 'I can think of a million things.'

Keogh's face contorted awkwardly. 'All right – player's player then. I wouldn't go voting for yourself, mate,' he mumbled, almost apologetically. 'It's indulgent.'

Flip was way too upbeat to ruffle easily. He even took it in with a nod that implied concurrence. Like he'd never thought of it that way, but now that you mention it . . .

'What's this players' player?' Gabe asked. We waited for Keogh to answer, but he probably thought he'd said too much already.

'In the change room after a rugby match,' I spoke for him, as I often did, 'the players all vote for who played best. Person with most votes gets the players' award for that round.'

'Can't you vote for yourself?'

'Sure.'

'What's the problem then?' Gabe asked. 'People vote for themselves all the time. Look at politicians . . . school captains . . . board members . . .'

'That's different.'

'How?'

'Do women vote for themselves in a beauty contest?'

Nat shifted uncomfortably. 'Steve . . .'

'What?' I searched the girls' faces, got no help there. I suspected I'd made another faux par, though I didn't know how. 'Must be a guy thing,' I proposed innocently.

I heard a hiss from the side that had Lisa's ring to it. 'What's that supposed to mean?' she asked, lining me up for cross-examination. 'That only guys vote for themselves? Or that we girls are too dumb to understand?'

My pulse sped up a little. This was the warning bell; this is how we bounced off each other. It always annoyed me how mine seemed to be the only opinion that could make hers depart so radically from a group consensus, and her interpretation of things offensive narrowed remarkably with it. And though I'd never been an overly aggressive drunk, the mouth more than compensated. I'd learnt the hard way to never say or do anything sozzled that I wouldn't sober – good or bad – but around the likes of her rules like that tended to fly out the window.

'He might as well say he played better than everyone else,' I explained politely.

'That's not the same as voting for yourself,' Lisa said, in that condescending tone of hers.

'A matter of perspective. What if someone said: "I baked this delicious cake." Don't you think that's up to those who eat it?'

'That's a dumb example.'

'Ok,' I took an agitated breath, 'how about this one then: "I wore this gorgeous dress."'

That shut her up. Her eyelids flickered and her mouth parted, then closed. Seconds ticked by while she sat there speechless.

'What's wrong with that?' Gabe sprung to her defence; she knew exactly what I was talking about. She'd been there when Lisa had made the comment.

'You don't reckon it might sound like "I looked gorgeous in this dress?"'

'That's not what she said.'

'Doesn't matter.' I held Lisa's eyes as I spoke, for everyone's benefit. 'It's what some people hear.'

'She just giving her opinion,' Gabe pointed out.

'Fairly presumptuous one.'

'Just how'—Lisa weighed in, shaking her head irritably—'do you go from a vote after a football game to a shot at me?'

Keogh's gaze flicked between me and Lisa. 'What's this all about?'

'Nothing,' I replied.

'Then why bring it up?' Lisa asked hotly.

'Hey, we're all friends here.'

'All I was trying to say at the time was—'

'It's okay,' I cut her off. 'No need to get defensive.'

'Then don't bring up shit like that.'

'Lisa . . .' Gabe held up her hand. 'Steve, you had your turn.'

'I'm just trying to be constructive.'

'Bullshit,' snapped Lisa. She was blinking angrily now.

'Please,' Gabe interjected, 'we don't want arguments.'

'Hon,' Keogh added his voice, 'he probably didn't mean anything by it.'

'Like you'd know.'

Keogh sighed, retreated back. His features softened, seemed to fade a little. Lisa was the only person I knew who could do that to him. The silence that followed reminded me of the night we'd met at the Manning. I chuckled at the thought.

'What's so funny?' Gabe asked, frowning.

'This,' I said. 'Shall we move on?'

But it seemed everything had been said. Lisa sat quiet as a mushroom. Gabe leaned forward to collect the cask. She poured her glass full and the trickle of it hung in the air. One or two girls took a sip of their drinks while the boys sat there unfazed as ever, or at least pretending to.

I stood up, had a stretch. 'Are we finished?' Lisa and Nat hadn't received their critiques yet, and I was keen to hear them, but no one made a peep. I reached for the remote on the table. 'Can I change the channel?'

As I flicked through the stations, Nat broke the quiet. 'Said he'd be no good.'

I gave her a cheeky smile. 'And I said we'd end up extinct.'

Lisa and Keogh took off soon after. Jock and Donna obliged previous comment and retreated to the bedroom for business. Gabe and Mick stayed up a little longer, then followed suit. The rest of us settled for *Ghostbusters* and watched it till the end.

As Nat went to unlock the car door when we left, she paused and gave me that hooded-eye look of hers.

'You wanted to get me, didn't you?' she asked, more like a statement.

Damn. It wasn't the first time she'd seen through me. I pulled the door handle but the car was locked. 'What are you talking about?' Lame I knew, but I needed to stall while I thought about it.

'You know what I'm talking about. The game of truth we played tonight. You wanted to get me.'

'Why do you say that?'

'Why else would you change your mind to play so easily?'

I gave the door handle another useless tug; flight reflex I suppose.

It slipped out of my fingers and snapped back down.

'Go on,' she urged. 'What would you have told me?'

'You're the mind reader, you tell me.'

'*Steve . . .*'

'*Nat . . .*'

'Really,' she said, a little too easily now. 'It's okay.'

'Unlock the door.'

'Not until you tell me what you would have said.'

'Okay. I think you're smart, that you can—'

'No, you can say that anytime. Tell me something you think I don't want to hear.'

'Nat, it doesn't do any good. All you'll do is get upset. You saw what happened in there.'

'Try me.'

'What?

'Try me.'

'Oh . . . *please.*'

'If there's one thing you wanted to say, just one, what would it be? Now's your chance. You'll never get another and get away with it.'

I looked her over, thought it over. I'd lost count of how many beers I had and I didn't want to hobble all the way home on one good leg. But the face she gave me told me she was ready. That she wanted it. That for all the crap I gave her about how gender-emotional, hormone-emotional, and everything-else emotional she was, this was the litmus test.

'We're not going anywhere unless you tell me,' she warned.

'I'm worried I won't be going anywhere if I do.'

'Oh, come on!' she said, smiling. The sort of smile a hangman wears just before he pulls the lever.

Okay then. I'd prepared myself for it earlier anyway, right? What could I say that would be construed as constructive? Something we'd both benefit from, and not too degrading. Something that wouldn't cut her to the core so bad she wouldn't speak to me for an aeon, let alone have sex.

'Okay Nat. I think you could shed a little weight in certain places.

Happy?'

As soon as I said it, I knew I'd stuffed it. The fight-light flashed on in her eye and her jaw clamped tight. Yep, I certainly stuffed it this time.

'See?' I said irritably. 'What did I tell you? Now I'm in the—'

'Of all the things you could have said,' she interrupted, 'you chose that.'

I opened my mouth to defend myself, but she beat me to it.

'It's okay,' she said regretfully, like she knew she only had herself to blame. She unlocked her door and her flash central-locking popped my doorknob up. She got in the car. I was still standing there in sin when she turned the ignition on.

'Are you coming?' she asked, quick with impatience.

We didn't speak on the way home. She put on a brave face and drove at regulation speed. She also smacked at the indicator, squealed the tyres around corners, braked too hard and changed gears too early, shoving the gearstick mercilessly and clashing the teeth.

She said she was tired when she dropped me off out front of college. I stood there in the dark and watched the car drive away out of sight. I suppose I should have been grateful. At least she'd given me a lift home.

Later that week a bio prac ended early so I hit the gym for a bit of lower bodywork, thought I'd focus on this blasted thigh of mine giving me grief. To get to the weights room you pass through a corridor that has on one side a room used for aerobics with a glass wall. Lined up along one side of the room are a series of steppers and treadmills. Like most boys I'd spare a glance whenever I walked past, me being interested in the latest leotard fashions and all.

There on one of the steppers was Nat. Her face was red and sweaty and her legs were hard at it, pumping up and down. She was side on and didn't see me. I stopped and watched her for some time. Watched how focused she was, how those tight little calf muscles of hers bunched and how her rosy cheeks puffed in and out, doing all they could to strain air into her overworked lungs. I went to tap the glass but stopped myself. For some reason it was important that she didn't see me.

Throughout my gym session I couldn't shake the image. I sat through dinner and it was the same. There was nothing remotely erotic about it. It was something else, a warm blend of affection and respect that left me with an ache in my heart.

After dinner I hunted about campus for a nice flower. A late bloom of petunias lining the flowerbeds along Western Avenue provided me with a drooping, sad-looking specimen I felt ashamed to pick, but it suited my mood. From there I walked to Nat's place. Parking was usually a nuisance for tenants but tonight I found her car close to her place. I tucked the flower under the windscreen wiper and went back to college.

Later that night as I sat at my desk there was a soft knock on my door. Nat came in, walked up to me doe-eyed and gave me a hug. We weren't due for a catchup and this was an unscheduled visit. She never said a thing, just kissed me on the lips for so long I thought she'd never pull away.

'It was just a flower, Nat,' I said when she finally did.

'And that was just a kiss, *Steve*.'

'How did you know it was me?'

I have never forgotten the look on her face that came with what she said next, so humble it puts a lump in my throat just thinking about it. Nor the tone of her voice, made all the more poignant by its weight of truth.

'Who else would do that for me?'

She stayed over that night.

Nine

In fact, she stayed over lots of nights. By then I had a good feel for which dumb-arsed rules in this place were meant to be stretched. Like the rule about drugs. Hard stuff wasn't an issue because it didn't exist, but you'd have to be in denial not to smell the gigglyweed occasionally.

One day I caught the whiff as I passed Metcalf's room, prompting me to knock on his door and ask if there was an inhouse supplier, maybe even him. With squinty red eyes and a crooked grin he suggested I might have a source more reliable than his? I told him I'd look into it. That night I rang Saunders from the payphone at reception.

'What?' he asked in a mocking tone of voice. 'Can't get any green in that toffy-nosed joint you're in?'

I pointed out that it was a bit early for me to go around making enquiries about suppliers of illicit drugs when rooms were regularly got into by seniors looking for excuses to dole out punishment.

'They toss your cells, like in the movies?' he asked.

'Yep.'

'They probably do full body searches.' He laughed at the possibility. 'Rubber gloves and vasso, yeah baby!' He punctuated the suggestion with an obscene howl. 'You'd like that wouldn't you, butt boy?' It was this brand of humour that made me think our days as friends were numbered.

A week or so later I went home with the oldies for dinner after they'd come to watch a rugby match, and that same night I caught up with Saunders who slipped me a bag. By midweek I was lounging in Metcalf's room sampling the goods with a couple of older boys. You couldn't dismiss such intimate proceedings as idle fraternisation. As I reclined on his couch, proud of my special exemption, it occurred to me I'd scored some handy friends.

That's the way it worked. The only consistency with the rules here was that there was no consistency. College was a microcosm of the greater world it insulated us from. Life ain't fair, folks. Get used to it, get over it. Adapt and prosper, fight it and suffer. Some guys had a blind eye turned their way for major infractions, some copped both barrels for the tiniest slipup. Take Babs.

David Schiffer. There had to be one in every college.

We were sitting in a chemistry tutorial when someone complained he had no hope of passing an upcoming test. Our tutor offered his little gem about the greatest barrier to success being mental, citing the four-minute mile example. Experts had said it was physically impossible but as soon as Bannister broke it in 1954, a flood of runners followed in quick succession. 'How soon?' someone asked, and Babs responded in a bored voice. 'Six weeks later, Finland. John Landy. Another six weeks later was the Miracle Mile in Vancouver where they both ran under.'

While flicking through a magazine in the college library, someone asked why watch adverts always show the hands at around ten past ten. The answer given was along the lines that the watch is a face, and people react best to a smile. It also keeps the company logo below the twelve visible . . . *duh*.

Babs took it a step further. 'After the war global advertising took off. Back then it was often a frown, supposedly a show of respect for victims of Hiroshima. Little Boy detonated around eight sixteen am.'

In the games room, Babs and I were playing Pronk and a senior med for the pool table. Pronk balled a sitter and blamed it on alcohol poisoning. 'Think I need a new liver,' he declared painfully, rubbing the left side of his chest. His partner corrected him. 'Liver's on your right side, dopey.' Pronk said, 'Mine must be on the left.' His partner said, 'Then you're one in a hundred thousand,' and went on to explain the rare condition, fumbling over the name. 'Sivus . . . vissus or whatever . . . my mind's gone blank.' Babs said, '*Situs inversus*. Site inverted. And it's one in ten thousand, actually.'

Whether the trivia was men get struck by lightning six times more than women, or the Pythagorean theorem was in use by the Babylonians a thousand years before he was born, or 3000BC texts prove people weren't that dumb to believe the earth was flat, or that oodles of scientific literature supports epidemiologic evidence that stretching before or after exercise does bugger all to reduce the risk of muscle injury, or that finger length ratios correlate with penis size, or to settle the debate once and for all the chicken came before the egg Ref: Genesis 1:20-22, Babs would work it seamlessly into any conversation. His brilliance spanned so many disciplines I suspect he had a good lend of us now and then. The only trivia that ever caught him out was Women's Weekly type rot staple for housewives and drama students, and even then the fact that he wasn't up to speed with Tom Cruise's dating habits spoke more for him than against. He scored 495 for his HSC, or something hideous. Never crowed about it, the school did that for him. When a school gets a pupil in the top one percent of the state it's pretty well splashed into every parent notice. We only found out through a former schoolmate of his when the subject of university medal candidates came up.

From what we could figure, Babs couldn't care less. The only comment I ever heard him make on the subject was when coaching was mentioned. Back then most of us got into selective schools the old-fashioned way; natural ability. Coaching was killing all that. Babs gave us his opinion: 'Cheats. Give any dumb monkey a key and you can teach it how to unlock a door. Smart one figures it out itself.'

It was clear that the seniors had singled him out. For all his brains, he was hopeless. They hung out the bait and Babs would not only bite, he'd give them the fight they were looking for. Every time. It didn't help that some older boys harboured a grudge for the earbashing they'd been given after Babs' parents lodged a complaint about that Brisbane business early in the year.

We tried to explain it to him one night He'd just got his dinner and was heading for our table with his baggy tracksuit pants flopping against his legs. His hands balanced a tray replete with steak, bangers and vegies, cordial, fruit, bread roll, and side dish of salad. The sight was too much provocation for Pronk. As Babs walked past him he stood from his seat, snuck in behind and dropped Bab's pants in a flash, undies included. The dining room was full, the roar went up and Babs' religion was narrowed down for everyone to see. He calmly placed his tray on the closest table, pulled his pants up real dignified and gave us a wave like her Majesty acknowledging the crowd. Applause thundered around him and he took a bow.

He reached our table and sat down. 'Prick,' he muttered.

We kept on chuckling. 'Babs, you ought to know by now not to wear loose-fitting tracky-dacks to dinner,' said Mick.

'They decide what we should wear as well?'

'That's one way to look at it.'

'You know what your problem is, don't you?' said Joey. 'When the joke gets played on you, just take it. Laugh it off with everyone else. The more you react, the more they'll dish it out. Trust me Babs, just go with the flow.'

'Why?'

'How many times do you want to get your room turfed?'

'It's a matter of principle.'

'So is getting your room turfed.'

The flipside to his brilliance, as there always is one, was that he was hopeless with women. The closest I came to seeing him hitting onto a girl barely qualified, and even that was true to the guy's form. Babs was in a class of his own.

Our calculus lecturer was one of those blinkered geeks who must have thought the way to impress people was to baffle them senseless by scrawling ridiculous equations across the board at running pace. There was a cute little girl in class who Babs planted himself beside whenever he could, or close enough to. That he was keen on her was patently obvious, equally so was that he had no idea what to do about it.

We were all scribbling away frantically one morning, bobbing our heads up and down to the point of nausea, when this girl spoke up for everyone.

'Excuse me, could you just go a little slower?' Her voice was as gentle as her looks. 'It's too hard to follow.'

Without turning around our proud professor said, 'Then I suggest . . .' his scrawl never wavered '. . . you go to our . . . Tuesday afternoon .

. . tutoring sessions in E204.'

Over one hundred students snickered behind his back but he kept on writing, arrogant enough probably to think it was directed at the girl.

Babs' voice rose above it all. 'You made a mistake, third line.'

At once the prof's marker stopped and hovered over the board. 'What?'

'Third line down, second parenthesis from the end, where you got your partial derivative fx as a function of your ordered pair x zero y zero. You forgot to cancel the square value of your variable.'

Professor Hathaway MSc. PhD. Ass Dean Fac Maths, Member ARC, FAustMS and ANZIAM medallist went curiously still. His marker homed in on the offending parenthesis and dangled over a digit. It danced back and forth in the air a bit as he redid his math, and then stopped. Without a show of expression he put a line through it, then went along the rest of the equation correcting his mighty calculus where needed, pretending not to hear the entire class whispering and giggling behind him.

As we exited the theatre I snuck up to the girl from behind and gave her a nudge. She looked at me and I gestured toward Babs walking away on his lonesome.

'For what it's worth, that was his way of hitting onto you,' I said.

Even that didn't do him any good.

Ten

Then there was Keogh.

Like Babs, he had a way about him that didn't go down well with a lot of folks. In fairness to said folks though, that might have come about in response to him having some issue with them. Perhaps it was that stubbornness that went with seeing things they missed. Or being blind to things they saw. Probably both. Not that he was daft; far from it. On paper he was cruising. The side to him that had it over the rest of us was so antiquated though it made him look eccentric. Titters aplenty sounded behind his back. Even Lisa, to my contempt, contributed to the sport on occasion.

But that's as far as anything went. Seniors tended to spare him. It couldn't have all been owed to his commanding presence or killer visage. There were plenty of kids equal to that. He was no Ferris Bueller in the popularity stakes. His parents weren't members of the Senate, College Board Appointees or sponsors of scholarships and bursars. It was a visceral thing; one you couldn't put your finger on.

He talked me into a gym routine. Put me on a program tailored for loose forwards, one that worked select muscle groups without bulking me up to a point that compromised speed or aerobic fitness. Worked me hard that first session and the next day my muscles felt like a steamroller had run over them. It might have ended there had he not talked me into following it up two days later. My tender muscles groaned in protest to start, but a bench-set or two later the pain went mute. By the end of the following week it had become a weak sensation, more of a background presence, something to push. The weights came up easier, the reps went quicker, and the breaks between each were shorter. As the weeks passed I'd steal a glance in the mirror and try not to feel too vain about the transformation I was seeing; the swell of pecs, widening of shoulders, division of muscle beneath skin turning paper-thin. It amazed me how much of a difference those early sessions made. Liken it to the law of diminishing marginal returns, Keogh told me. The greatest gains are made at the start. And when you start to plateau off, rest assured the hardest part is behind you. By then it's a habit, and habits are easier to keep than to break, right? It's all about attitude.

I don't know about the attitude, but I did have *him*. If not for his keeping at me I reckon I'd have gone the same way as anyone else with good intentions and better excuses. He knew what to say and how to say it. Just like Nat. With that pearl of wisdom in one ear and him in the other, I didn't need to think for myself.

Wasn't long before two to three gym sessions a week became the norm, which included a bit of cardio on the treadmills and high-intensity interval training on the bikes. Add to this my two sessions of rugby training and the games Saturday, I left more and more boys blowing behind me at training and felt less sting in the hits I took on the paddock. I played meaner, hit harder, covered more ground and wouldn't you know it, jumped a grade into thirds. One to go to catch up to Keogh.

For my part, I got him into a habit of chess. I kept a board in my room and pulled it out on spec one night. Keogh was good, but not great. It takes a certain quality – 'equanimity' a champion once put it – to be down that end of the bell-shaped curve. I beat him easy, which seemed to make it his mission to square up.

It was during these sessions, with considerable persuasion, that he opened up a little about his past. He was always focussed when he played – I liked that about him – and getting him to talk about himself was harder than getting someone like Flip to shutup about himself. He'd lived in Sydney's north until year ten when his father had absconded to some nameless hole in Tasmania so far off the grid it drew alleged sightings of the Thylacine. His mother moved to Newcastle for work, and it was there that Keogh and his older brother had finished high school. On blowing his HSC, his older brother had gone feral like his dad and joined him down south, and Keogh hadn't heard from either of them in over two years. The old man sounded as weird as his two sons and I suspected it was from him that Keogh had been introduced to his arts: boxing, hunting, diving. I asked him once if he missed his dad. 'Not the beatings,' he'd replied. There had to be more to the story but his reticence wore me down. I did have one burning mystery solved though. When he told me the name of the high school in Sydney he'd gone to, I made the connection with two cricket guys I knew from there who'd been at that party early in the year. He must have kept in touch.

One night, well into another whipping, he lost his queen to a fancy move I'd pulled. 'Didn't see that coming,' he said.

'Variation of the Caro-Kann,' I explained. 'You think you're all over me, then I castle kingside and these guys,' I pointed, 'turn defence into attack. Favourite trick of a Chinese bloke Dong Wung, or Wong Dung, someone or other. Created carnage with it at the world championships a few years ago.'

He stared down at the chessboard for a minute or so. I thought he was just trying to work out his next move until he said, 'I cannot figure you out, Chambers.'

It took me back a little. I stayed quiet, trying to work out if I'd just been paid a compliment. Two moves later I cornered his king, he tried to counterattack with his rook and I immediately relieved him of it.

He looked at me meaningfully. 'What else you hiding?'

I moved my queen in for the kill. 'Ever play cricket?' I asked. It was worth exploring. Keogh was one of those mutants who'd pick up a bat for the first time and whack the ball into the stands as smug as a gum-chewing Viv Richards.

'Years ago.'

'Didn't keep going?'

'Thought better of rugby.'

Bit by bit I drew out his rugby background. Early on in his career they had him at Manly Juniors, by age fourteen he was representing Northern Districts Schoolboys and flirting with higher fixtures. Moving to Newcastle killed that line of progress, but within a year or two he'd returned to rep level up there. Speaking from experience, I'd say he was a certainty for some serious rep stuff in the near future. Doesn't matter what game it is, the principles are the same. Playing rep relies as much upon getting noticed as being good enough, and getting noticed by the right people. You build on your reputation through consistency, get so many people talking about you behind the scenes that when you run onto the field you're already being watched. They were doing it with Keogh here already; plenty of heavyweights were talking him up. He'd do his spell in seconds but it was only a matter of time before he was locked into firsts. It wasn't just his rugby skills that would get him there either. The guy had a quality about him common to elite players; that blend of maturity, determination, and professionalism that both gave and commanded respect.

'But why rugby?' I asked after he'd briefed me. 'No money in it.'

'Substitute.'

'Substitute for what?'

He said nothing for a while, and then: 'Why do you play?'

'Go figure,' I said. 'I'll tell you one thing I like about it, though. Watching people. Football brings out personalities. You can't hide it out there on the paddock. Take Jeffro. Lazy and slow and that's all he'll ever be. Cappo . . . plays dirty, always going for the cheap shot. Milks a penalty for all its worth, dignity doesn't come into his set of rules. Guys like Mick . . . never gets flustered, easy-going to the point of despair. And Flip? Overrates himself, tries things beyond his ability. The real world's gonna cut him down to size.'

His eyes stayed on me then, and I knew what he was thinking. 'And before you ask – no,' I said. 'Me criticising your rugby would be like you criticising how I play chess.'

'You just did a good job on a few of the boys.'

'They ain't here to bitch back.'

He didn't take it further. I was tempted, though. I would have told him that *he* was too hard to figure. That his style of play was full of contradictions. Aggressive yet fair, thoughtful yet reckless. With the speed, agility and ball skills of a glory-seeking back, yet choosing to tough it out amongst the pigs. He'd do speculator straight busts, leading with his shoulders and never dodging the defence, but going too far; going those few extra yards and getting isolated when he should have gone to ground. Trying to do it all himself, not putting enough trust in his teammates.

I'd planned to drag this game on a bit more, but changed my mind. I moved a bishop and cornered his king. 'Checkmate.'

Keogh pulled a face. 'Yeah, saw that coming.' He stood to leave.

'Wanna go again?'

'Nuh. No point getting my arse kicked.'

'Never stopped you before.'

It came out in reflex. It was always there in the back of our minds, and that's where it should have stayed. And yet it stood between us. If it never came up again it would have been too soon, and there it was, out in the open like a goddamn bad smell.

He stopped at the door and smirked at me knowingly. 'Yeah, well,' he said, 'I'm working on it.'

Eleven

Around 4.30pm one Tuesday I was at my desk going over past exam papers, putting circles around questions that seemed to pop up year to year, when Nat knocked on my door. It was my only free afternoon of the week and I'd make good use of the desk time before training; a habit she knew well.

'Glad you're in,' she said once she'd swung the door open. 'Can you come with me?'

'Where to?'

'Women's College.'

'What's up?'

'I heard something today that I'm following up on. I think you'd be interested.'

'I got training in an hour.'

'Please, it's important.' When Nat said something was important, it usually was. I followed her out for that reason alone.

Clear of college I asked again what was up, but all she said was that a girl in her hockey team appeared to know the identity of our knicker-snipping friend. Before I could ask her anything else, she took my hand and changed the subject to some banal work issue she was having at The Oaks where she'd recently scored work as a bartender a couple of nights a week.

We reached the entrance of Women's College and Nat pulled the door open. By habit I kept an eye out for stray glances as I walked through the place and caught a smile or two from some pretty faces that I filed away for future reference. A couple of stairways and corridors later, Nat knocked on a door. A girl I recognised from Nat's hockey team appeared.

'Hi Marion,' Nat greeted her. 'Steve, do you remember Marion?'

'Sure.'

'Can we come in? We won't be long.'

Marion let us in and closed the door. I leaned against the door and Nat sat down on the bed.

'Sit, Marion.' Nat reached out with a hand and urged her down beside. 'I spoke to Belinda today. She told me about the conversation you had with her about Charles,' she said, fixing her eyes deeply on the girl.

Marion's cheery face flattened out and she shifted uneasily. 'Oh, it's nothing.'

'Marion, it's not nothing and you shouldn't keep this bottled up. Is it all right if we talk to you about it?'

I pulled the chair out from her desk and sat down. Marion squirmed a little more and the smile she summonsed was far from convincing.

'What's all this about? I asked, flitting my gaze between the two of them.

'Marion used to go out with a guy from your college,' Nat explained, and waited for Marion to take over. When she didn't, Nat went on. 'Since they broke up he's been saying some pretty nasty things to her. From what I heard though, it's more what he did to her while they were going out that's of concern.' Again she checked with Marion, and again the girl stayed quiet.

At once I felt an instinctive need to help this girl, whatever her problem. She had a small, petite frame, and with her oval face and matching eyes she presented a picture of innocence.

At Nat's gentle bidding, Marion let out how she'd gone out with a guy at Phillips named Charles Beeman for about six months; a guy I could only put a face to after her lengthy description. In his second year he was the type that didn't draw attention to himself; a fringe dweller amongst fringe dwellers. He had dark greasy hair that always went uncombed, an acne-cratered face and shifty eyes I'd never had the pleasure of looking closely into. About a month or so into their relationship he began asking her to do weird things, depraved things. It was a sensitive topic and Nat had to coax the finer details out of her. Despite my stomach turning queasy from what I listened to, I felt the mild thrill of witnessing a side to Nat I'd never seen. She'd chosen the wrong career path. A professional counsellor would have done a lesser job. Her face was grave, yet strong and understanding; her questions direct, yet voiced with compassion and empathy. It was a character defining display of integrity I could never hope to emulate, and I took far more interest listening to her than her subject. She was an angel into the girl's soul. I felt guilty for being so surprised. That was the thing about Nat's surprises; each one stumped me more than the last. It wasn't that I thought she didn't have it in her, I just didn't imagine her true potential often enough.

The impression Marion gave me was of a gentle and shy thing, naive and dependent and eager to please, easy prey for the seediest of Kings Cross rejects. And here she was revealing the most explicit details about their sex life not only to Nat, but to a complete stranger.

Sounded like the two lovebirds had started off harmless enough – blindfolds and bondage and a bit of porn – but then he'd gotten more experimental, moving onto devices and sadomasochism. Here Marion was quick to say that she didn't let him go too far with it, but then Nat frowned in a way that suggested she'd heard something to the contrary previously. From there the conversation went from weird to disturbing and I wondered what else was going on here. The coaxing became redundant; it was as if Marion wanted her story told. And though I felt for her I didn't want into this screwed up mess that is the fallout of the behaviour she signed up to; its listening or its remedy. I suspected this little sitting in itself might have served the same need for attention that inspired her to take part in Beeman's perverted fantasies in the first place.

It was none of my business, and for all our sakes I thought it best she didn't air any more details, but to show some semblance of concern I asked in the mildest possible terms if he made her do these things. She shrugged and gave me an embarrassed, if not nervous smile, which I took to mean she played along with it, which made it consensual. I raised my eyebrows at Nat, assuming she'd read my mind: What am I doing here?

Without taking her eyes off me, Nat said to Marion, 'Is it true what he did to your underwear?'

My ears pricked up a bit. Marion's look of embarrassment deepened.

'Marion?'

I decided to step in, use my own charm. 'Nat, if she doesn't want to—'

'When he used to tie her up,' Nat interrupted determinedly, 'he'd cut the crutch out of her underwear with scissors.'

She waited for me to react accordingly. I didn't. All I was thinking was: *Yeah, and . . .?*

'That's not the worst of it.' Nat looked at Marion in a significant manner. 'Do you want to talk about the time—'

'No,' Marion said forcefully, shaking her head.

'Okay, that's fine,' Nat reassured her. She put an arm over the girl's shoulder. 'That's good Marion, we'll leave it there.'

I sat there, said nothing. The last thing I wanted to do was ask unnecessary questions and have the girl in tears. If she was after counselling, Nat could do it. There was one thing I needed to ask though, something many of us had speculated on from the day we first heard of this joker.

'Why did he . . ?' I mimed the action of scissor-snipping. Nat sent me a frown that hit the dumb spot, and I waved the question away. 'Never mind.'

I leaned back and took a heavy breath. 'Well then, assuming he's the man – so what? Doesn't make him psychotic.' I didn't mean to sound dismissive, but the face Nat gave me suggested it came out that way.

'I've asked around,' she said. 'There's another girl he went out with last year – Andrea Walters, second year. She said he tried similar things on her, but she told him to fuck right off. Not long after she split up with him there was a function here in college that he came to. He joined her at a table and they got talking. He acted fine, even bought her a drink. A short time later, all of a sudden, she felt she was going to pass out. The arsehole tried to take her back to her room but a couple of her friends brushed him off. They helped her back to her room and she passed out as soon as she hit the bed. The next day she couldn't remember a thing.'

'Close call, huh?' I asked. It mustn't have come out with the serious ring I'd intended. Nat gave me the evil eye. 'Did she report it?' I went on smoothly.

'No,' Nat answered.

'Okay,' I said, nodding. I stood and motioned for the door. 'Nat, can we . . ?'

Marion asked quickly, 'What are you going to do?'

I twisted my cheek. 'Dunno, sweetie.' It seemed like a natural term to use. I know some women hated it, but it went with this girl like *your highness* went with the Queen. 'It's a lot to take in. Nat and I will have a think.'

'I don't want people to know about . . . certain things . . . we did.'

'Sure.'

Nat put a hand on Marion's shoulder. 'Thanks sweetie.' I liked that Nat used it as well. 'It's good you told us.' She stood up and I opened the door. 'Goodbye Marion, we'll talk again soon,' she said on our way out.

I waited until we were safely out of the building and into open space before speaking. '*Jesus H*, Nat,' I moaned. 'What do you want me to do here?'

'Give it some thought, at least!' she retorted, a little more loudly than I'd expected. 'You saw the poor girl! She feels like shit!'

'Okay, okay,' I said ruefully, rubbing my chin. Normally, I wouldn't' let an unsubstantiated, one-sided version of events sway me. Throw in the emotional ex-girlfriend factor, and I'd be even more objective. But something in her story rang of the truth. I even suspected I was hearing the milder version of events, which added to the story's credibility. Then there was the Nat influence. I got the impression she believed every word Marion had said, and when Nat believed something, that swayed me. The thing I gave her most points for was her ability to read people. Hell, I was her best example.

'Okay,' I said, 'I've given it some thought. We still got nothing.'

'I think he should be reported.'

'Report what? To whom? What do you have? A guy and a girl played a few kinky games, she busted up with him and now she's all upset. Big deal.'

'What about that business with Andrea? Spiking a girl's drink is no big deal?'

'Don't give me that.'

'You know what he did to Marion that she didn't want to talk about?' She looked at me hard. 'One time he asked her to do a pretend-rape. She said no but he went ahead anyway. When he was finished she balled her eyes out and he called her a baby.'

My take on the guy had been sliding downhill from the start, and it dropped further then, but I still wasn't sure where this was going.

'Look, it makes me crook, but we need to look at this rationally, not emotionally. Any first-year law student would tell you you got nothing. Forget that rape business; they obviously kissed and made up. Aside of the drink spiking, which happened last year and you'll never prove now, I don't think he's broken any laws. Even that girl didn't report it.'

'Maybe she will.'

'She didn't then for the same reason Marion won't now. *Shit*—' I cut myself off, knowing I was losing to frustration. 'What does she expect?' I asked, then mimicked in a high-pitched falsetto, 'Please do all the dirty work, just leave me out of it?'

'She never said that. I'm the one who's pushing.'

'Pushing to do what, Nat?'

'Report him!'

I stared at her disapprovingly, her face mirrored mine. 'And you think by doing that, they'll handcuff this guy and drag him away? It's not going to happen.'

'So you're going to do nothing?'

I took a deep breath, let it out in a big sigh. She glowered at me ruthlessly, shaming my sense of duty. 'I didn't say that,' I said defensively.

'I just thought that since he's in your college you'd have the up on me. But if it's all too much, forget it. I'll look into it myself.'

She kept watching me with those intense eyes, a boding look that

143

reminded me of my vulnerability. It was a familiar look. That purposeful, read-my-mind look that had bent men's wills since Eve first used it on Adam.

'All right then,' I said, running a hand through my hair. 'Leave it to me for the time being. I'll make some enquiries.'

'What sort of enquiries?'

'Geez Nat, I dunno. I have to think about it. I'm first-year science, not a bloody private investigator.'

She mellowed a bit then. 'Thank you.'

I could see she meant it.

The guy who'd done the rounds in April had left his calling card with Admin, so I gave him a ring and told him they'd been some developments. He told me to ring Newtown Police station and be sure to be put through to the Detectives. I did all that and got onto a Detective Senior Constable Allworth who told me he'd been briefed on the business earlier that year, though I suspected he rated it as seriously as a barking dog. Without mentioning names I passed on everything that Marion and Nat had told me, confessing at the end that I knew it didn't prove much.

'Do any of the girls want to make a complaint?' he asked tonelessly.

'Doubt it.' There was silence then, and I sensed that spelled the end of it. 'It's not likely anyone's going to move mountains on this one, are they?'

'Well, it makes it easier for us if we had a complaint.'

'If I got these girls to come in, would you do something then?'

'That depends on the nature of the complaint.'

'Could you go through his room?'

I thought I heard a snigger. 'To search for what?' He used the same sceptical tone that I'd used on Nat. I felt like hanging up then, and might have done so if not for the promise I'd made.

'I don't know,' I said. 'You tell me. A stack of stolen underwear?'

'Sure. If we traced their origin, we might be able to charge him with property theft.' He sounded bored.

'But you could go through his room, theoretically?' I was throwing up scenarios for the sake of it, leaning on my ignorance. No one was going to go down that path and I knew it. I just wanted to be able to tell Nat I tried everything.

'If or when the situation calls for it. This one doesn't.'

'What about the drink spiking?'

'Any witnesses?'

'No one actually saw him do it, no.'

'How long ago was that, did you say?'

The tone in his voice made my chest tighten. 'What can you do, then?'

'If what you're asking us to do is to roll up there and turn his room inside out – not a chance. Nor would we want to. Even if we did, we'd need a warrant and there's no way we'd get signoff on this one. There's nothing—'

'What if one of us let you in?' I cut in eagerly.

I took the silence that followed as encouraging, thinking he was considering the possibility. But then he said, 'It doesn't work like that. That'd be no different to the manager of a holiday park for instance saying we could go into a rented cabin, and that still needs a warrant. In any case we're talking about malicious damage to a girl's underwear, not sexual assault or rape. Think about it. We can't have a team of uniformed police turning his room over on the basis of hearsay for something like this. The repercussions would be hard, particularly if he hasn't done anything to deserve it.'

It wasn't the logic of this I found irritating, but that someone had given us a big lecture about keeping our eyes and ears open, and I go to the police with a suspect and get told there's nothing they can do.

I pestered him a bit longer, and he summed it up with the comment: 'Bottom line is we'd need a complaint from the victim, a serious complaint, something with a little more substance before we went fishing. If we questioned the guy on the basis of what you've said we'd just be going through the motions. We need evidence of some sort of crime,' he explained patiently, 'so if *you* were to find anything incriminating, by all means let us know.'

I read him loud and clear. I thanked him for his time and hung up the phone.

Metcalf leaned against his desk, rubbing his chin. He'd listened to everything I'd said without a peep. Watching him now, I wondered if he was plagued by the same reservations that occurred to me now that I'd given this business more than a passing thought.

There was no fun to be had in this one. This was serious business. This wasn't turfing someone's room for some menial college infraction. This was snooping into someone's private belongings to see if he was twisted. If we found a diary, we'd read through it to see if it contained perverted fantasies. If we saw a pile of photos, we'd flick through to see if there was anything kinky. The guy might be a closet gay, or he might have taken some harmless porn with an obliging female. For the first time in my life, I understood what invasion of people's privacy really meant. Here we were, proposing violations on someone who might well be completely harmless, and on the strength of a claim made by an ex-girlfriend, in her teens at that.

'Stuff him,' Metcalf said at last. 'I know he's got tutes tomorrow afternoon at two, which will keep him out of college for a couple of hours. We can have a squiz then. You around? You don't have to be.'

He was giving me the easy way out, and I respected him for that. 'I'm around.'

'Okay. We'll do it.'

As I opened the door to leave he added, 'Don't go telling anyone.'

I hoped he knew how dumb that statement was.

The corridor was empty when Metcalf opened the door with his master key. I followed him inside and closed it softly. Though I hadn't expected to see ribald porn plastered over the wall, or medieval torture devices dangling from the ceiling, I was disappointed by how ordinary it looked. I doubted then we'd find anything.

'Don't make a mess,' Metcalf warned unnecessarily.

While Metcalf went through his drawers, I directed my efforts to the wall cupboards, brushing aside shirts in their racks and carefully lifting folded pairs of jeans. I slid his chair over, stepped up and checked the compartment above. More clothes, a tennis racquet and balls, books and papers and folders and loose junk.

Ten minutes was enough for a thorough search. The only thing we found of possible interest was a locked steel casket about three feet long beneath his bed. We hadn't found any keys and there was no way of opening it.

'That's where I'd hide my handcuffs and whips,' I suggested.

Metcalf knelt to inspect the keyhole. 'Ok,' he gave in. 'Must keep the key on him. I'll have to think about this. Let's go.'

As I walked out the door, I turned for one last look. I didn't have a clue if we left it the same as before, nor did I care. We'd come up with nothing and I hoped that would be the end of it.

But Metcalf pushed it.

A couple of nights later after dinner he told me to follow him. We arrived at the room of a senior named Brad Draper I'd gotten to know through rugby. Upbeat and balanced with the arched brows of a thinker, he was never too tough on us freshers and well positioned in the pecking order here. With him were two able-bodied seniors named Keith Tory and Pat Fisk, neither of whom I'd spoken to much before. They were spread out over the room on what passed as seating.

Draper gave me a distorted grin. 'Been doing a bit of detective work, Chambers?'

I froze. I could only assume I was in for a dressing down.

'Relax and take a seat,' he invited, sliding a chair my way. 'We're discussing options.'

'I'll leave you boys with it then,' Metcalf said, and turned to go. He gave me a wink as he closed the door. Very strange.

I sat down and they got straight into it. Sounded like they'd been well briefed, courtesy of Metcalf talking it up like the salesman he was. I learnt quickly that Beeman wasn't the most liked guy in college, which made him fair game. Andrea and Marion weren't the only girls to spread rumours about the guy. When you hear enough consistencies between unconnected sources, you got a case for the prosecution.

I'd thought some of the things these guys did were over the top, a flow-on from their boarding school culture. Or one could take a more philosophical point of view, regard college and its pranks as a sort of last stand, a subversive challenge to a system designed to slot us into templates of conformity as soon as we're out of here. Listening to them now, I was impressed at the different aspect they'd taken on. The room had the feel of a war room briefing. For all their pranks and grief doled out, when the business called for serious ruminating, they gave it its due. College was a close-knit affair, regardless of its cliques. No one wanted to share the same table, breathe the same air, or sit on the same toilet seat as some deviant. If Beeman was one, they wanted to know.

No one assumed leadership on this, they spoke as equals. The decision sounded like it had been made before I'd entered the room, and I took heart thinking that my presence was more a gesture of recognition for bringing it to their attention than anything I could contribute. Unless of course I was a set of hands or eyes for what they had in mind. Which, as it turned out, was the case.

The easiest option for everyone would be to front the guy and demand him to follow us to his room and open the box, but then of course if he did have anything to hide, he'd likely say he lost the key. Or he could simply refuse. Pulling his fingernails out to get him to cooperate was voted down, and even if he did open the box, it was possible we'd find zip, and gone would be our element of surprise. Not the preferred option.

So we'd open his box without his consent, which meant without his knowing, which meant somehow getting the key off him, assuming he pocketed it during the day. Two windows of opportunity were discussed, shower and mealtime. No one knew his daily schedule well enough to know when he showered, nor was anyone willing to spy on him to find out, so hitting his room during mealtime became the preferred option. Most boys went straight for the dining room if their courses intruded into lunch or dinner and just dropped their bags along the walls of the JCR. It was one of those things about our college at least that thieving was virtually unheard of. Most kids didn't lock their doors. Bags strewn about the JCR or the foot of the stairs didn't rate a stray glance, unless you tripped over them.

They examined Beeman's movements, pooling knowledge of his timetable and deciding that lunchtime midweek provided the best opportunity. They'd try for that week. My only input was that we use more bods, people we could trust. I would have liked Keogh in on this but they dismissed the suggestion on the grounds that the less people involved, the better. But I suspected there was more to it than that. Keogh was too much of an unknown quantity. It wasn't that they didn't trust him, rather they had nothing to gain by doing so.

I left the briefing far more motivated than when I'd entered it. What started as nothing more than a spurious claim by a frightened girl had developed into a well-planned, covert operation run by respected college seniors. And my girl had gotten the ball rolling.

It made me proud. So proud I called Nat straight away to let her know we were onto it. That's all I told her, and I was grateful she didn't prise. I didn't doubt her discretion, I just wanted to have something to surprise her with if or when we found it.

Our first attempt failed. Beeman came into the JCR, dropped his bag and took off up the stairs to the tables. Soon as he was seated Draper grabbed his bag and rummaged through it in full view of passers-by, none of whom gave him a second glance. He zipped it back up and gave us a nod in the negative.

A week had passed and exams were looming when everyone was next available for another try. Everything went the same, except this time Draper's hand withdrew from the bag clenched and he gave us the thumbs up with the other. Seconds later, Tory and I were following him out of the JCR. Fisk stayed back to keep Beeman under surveillance. We'd need only ten minutes or so. If Beeman broke from lunch before we finished our search Fisk would delay him on some pretext or other.

We got to his room and checked the corridor was clear. Draper fumbled with the keys and opened the door with his first attempt. We followed him in and I closed the door softly. Draper dropped to his knee, reached under the bed and slid the chest out. Tory told me to go stand by the window where I'd be able to see Fisk signal us from the courtyard if Beeman was coming.

After trying one or two keys, Draper found success. The lock clicked and he lifted the lid open. I caught a glimpse of a stack of magazines, then Tory got in the way.

Draper lifted a magazine from the top of the pile and flicked a page or two, but I couldn't see. Tory began to chuckle. 'Ooh you naughty, *naughty* little boy,' he said. I moved closer.

The last time I'd seen something similar was in year seven. Saunders had pinched a magazine from a friend of his older brother and shown it to us for the shock value I'd assumed, like a kid bringing a dead rat to school for show and tell. Without proof of it there in graphic technicolour spread, I wouldn't have thought people were capable of engaging in things like this. Back then I'd given a groan or two and shrugged it off like I might some freak-thing I'd seen in books, like the wolfman with hair all over his face, or the women with three breasts.

I wished I could have shrugged it off now. I wish I could have treated it with a chuckle like Tory was doing. I wish I didn't occur to me how sophisticated the collaboration of twisted minds had to be in order to turn aberrations like this into an industry, from the girl contorted on the barnyard floor to the squinty-eyed deviant Beeman providing the market. I wish I didn't think that one day we'd let him loose in the world, armed with a degree and all the character credits it implied. That there'd be no warning on his resume, that someone would make him boss, that he'd have authority over better souls, date decent women, mind people's kids . . .

Tory kept chuckling away, but Draper and I just stood there. I could see the disgust work its way up from Draper's stomach and onto his face. He flicked another page and I had to remind myself we weren't looking at trick photography.

'Well, it's not really a smoking gun,' observed Draper, 'but we're getting close.'

'If I didn't know any better,' Tory mused, 'I'd accuse you blokes of setting this guy up.'

Draper dropped the magazine onto the bed. 'I suppose you can forgive the dumb horse,' he muttered, then leaned down and lifted the stack of magazines away. 'What else you got in here, dickhead?'

I went back to the window, looked down into the courtyard. This business had a different feel to it now. The levity was gone. Every so often I checked progress. My colleagues fingered their way through the contents of the casket gingerly, as if a decaying corpse lay inside. In all they found about five hundred bucks in cash, about an ounce of weed in a plastic bag, a bong, and bingo – three pairs of girl's undies. That and a pile of magazines that made me ashamed to be part of the human race.

Draper straightened on his knees. 'That's all there is,' he said, and then very carefully placed the items back into the casket in the same order he took them out. Then he locked it and slid it back under the bed. A minute or two later we were striding across the courtyard, bound for the hall.

We met Fisk in the JCR as he stood by the stairwell to the dining room. 'How'd you go?' he asked, and while Draper briefed him I climbed the steps to check on Beeman. He was still eating, chatting between mouthfuls to someone. A thought suddenly occurred to me and I returned to the boys.

'Hey Brad,' I asked. 'Does Beeman have a car?'

'Yeah.'

'Well?'

Draper traded glances with the other two. 'All right. Keith and Pat stay here,' he instructed. 'If he makes a break, one of you stop him and the other come give us a warning.'

We walked briskly through the main building and came out into the carpark. Draper pointed. 'There it is,' and I followed him to an old, beat-up white Datsun. It was locked. Draper fumbled with Beeman's keys and opened the door. He slid himself inside and opened the glovebox.

'Pop his boot,' I said. Draper found the lever and gave it a tug. The boot popped open and I went over.

The first thing that drew my attention was a box stacked with magazines, still in their plastic wrapping. The front page alone would have kept them from any respectable distributor. Again, I felt my stomach curdle. My queasiness gave way to serious concern when I observed that they were all the same copies. I shut the implication from my head and focussed on the task we were there for. I lifted the box and put it on the ground, then pushed aside items of clothing and a smelly pair of joggers. A half-full bottle of Southern Comfort clunked out of a towel. I pushed it to the back of the boot and lifted the cover of the spare-tyre housing.

Draper joined me as I checked the housing. There was nothing incriminating in there. I lowered the housing cover and put the box of magazines back over it. Draper picked up the one at the top and grimaced in disgust. 'He has more of this shit?'

I spread the items of his boot around to make it appear normal. 'See how they're all the same copies?' I pointed out, and Draper picked up another magazine to confirm. 'Makes you think there's a secret society of rock-spiders here, and he's their main supplier. For all we know he's Grand Master, holding rituals in black robes and jerking off over severed goat heads.'

Draper pointed to the bottle of Southern Comfort. 'What's that?'

I picked it up and showed him.

'Strange place to keep a bottle of Southern,' he commented.

I unscrewed the lid and took a sniff. The big C wasn't my preferred beverage and I was no judge of quality. I wrapped it back up in the towel and didn't give it another thought.

Between Draper and my proud set of marbles, you'd think the penny would have dropped. Perhaps I was too focussed on finding girl knickers. Perhaps I was trying too hard to shunt images of horse appendages out of my mind. I was wholeheartedly fed up with the whole business, didn't want to give it another thought. Exams were closing in and I didn't have time for this creep's sicko fetishes.

I waited for someone to make the next move. A day turned into two, then three, then it was stuvac. Fearing inertia, I finished my dinner and headed to where Metcalf and Draper were seated on the big boy's side of the room. I knew I was being presumptuous crossing the line like that – literally – but hey. Hopefully they'd see it for the initiative they lacked.

They saw me coming and looked at me like I'd committed a heinous crime. I sat myself down and their frowns deepened.

'You boys decided what to do about Beeman?'

Their gazes went to various parts of the room and they resumed their meals with utmost concentration. Draper grunted what sounded like a no through a mouth full of veal.

'What'd you say?' I asked.

'What do you suggest, Steve?' Metcalf asked.

I was relying on their lead. Truth being I had no idea either.

Draper downed his mouthful and said, 'We're keeping it up our sleeve,' and then stuffed another forkful into his mouth.

'What's that supposed to mean?'

'Steve,' Metcalf said through a full mouth, in a tone that signalled to let it drop. Maybe it shouldn't be discussed at the dining room table. Later on though, after I'd knocked on his door and pressed him on the issue, he told me in all honesty that no one had any plans. If we fronted him now about his farmyard porn he'd know someone had busted into his casket. They wanted to watch and wait.

I took it in with major disappointment. Watch and wait. The slogan of many a man you won't find in the history books. What made it harder to bear was my certitude that it was just a matter of time before Beeman found out we'd been into his treasure chest. You can't keep a secret like that bottled up in a place like this for long. People talk. Right now only a handful of boys knew about his penchant for bestiality, soon it would be all of college. His alter ego, if that's the way to put it, would dive underground.

I decided it was time to bring Keogh in on this. Straight after leaving Metcalf's room, I paid him a visit. He sat at his desk and listened to everything I said without interrupting. I finished up and watched him think it over.

'Doesn't it make you crook?' I asked.

'Sure.'

'So?'

'So what?'

I flayed my hands about. 'Don't you want to do something about it?'

'Like what?'

'You're as bad as them.'

'Don't know why you're so uptight about this cockroach,' he said. 'You shake hands with guys just as bad all the time, you just don't know it. You'll do your head in trying to squash every one of them, mate. There's just too many.'

'Well, if the boys come up with a plan, would you be in?'

'Yeah, right,' he snorted. 'You reckon they're up to it?'

With that, I felt the same drop of enthusiasm that had become an affliction for everyone involved in this. We weren't dealing with a serial killer. I figured we all had better things to do.

I passed this all onto Nat at her place later that night, and her mood turned quiet. But I knew she'd be bubbling like a cauldron inside. Considering her fierce interest in this, she'd been commendably patient. I tried to mollify her by explaining it from their point of view, drawing from almost the same words they'd used until I felt ashamed of myself.

I didn't need her to tell me to shut up.

Twelve

By the end of exams college was more than half empty, which gave it a ghostly, depressing feel. Straight after lunch I packed what I needed and headed for Redfern Station without delay.

It was all over for a month. No studies, no assignments. We even had a bye that first weekend of holidays. The fun police tried to schedule a training run for that Saturday but one after the other the excuses rolled in. Before I needed to give mine, they called it off.

By mid-afternoon I was sharing a coffee with mum, who shared my cautious optimism that I'd passed through exams okay. I rang Kep and learnt that the boys would be up at the local that night. I also rang Nat; part formality, part to confirm she was working and that I had the night to myself. I was ready for a huge one.

A bus got me there around 7pm. The place did good business on Thursday nights and this one was no exception. I found my crew over at a table near the window, on their own. Manners and Saunders were absent, which at first didn't strike me as odd. After a round of handshakes we settled back and Kep asked me what I'd been doing, I replied not a lot, and no one said anything after that.

Something was out of order. I'd expected a round of good-natured taunting and at least one or two serious questions, after all I'd barely seen these guys for months. The last time I'd sat at a table as gloomy was at the wake of a high school friend killed in a car accident the year before.

'Saunders and Manners coming?' I asked.

'They're keeping very low for the time being,' Fin mumbled. Then he gestured out the window. 'Pete's out there.' I stood from the stool and looked out the window.

Grigg was over the far side of the road, standing on the footpath with his head down. Two rough-looking blokes were in front of him, facing our way. I put them at mid-thirties. Shoulder-length hair and unshaven faces gave them a grizzly appearance, and save a difference in height, they looked cut from the same cloth. One of them had to be the biggest man I'd ever seen. The top of Grigg's head stopped just short of his neck. The other guy was smallish, had his hand in his pockets and seemed to be doing all the talking. A protective kick of loyalty raised me in my chair.

'Pete in trouble?'

Kep filled me in.

On the ladder of street-thuggery, these friends of mine were bottom rung. They weren't the type to stick their noses into the domain of serious crime, nor were they savvy enough to do it for profit. They didn't deal drugs or commit petty larceny, though they did bust into a car now and then, and if anything of value was found in in the glove-box they'd call it finders-keepers. Manners had even hotwired a car or two and gone for a joyride, but the owners always got their cars back intact. In every instance I knew of, or more to the point was told about, it was no random hit. Some poor sod would give Manners or Saunders grief, and having their prize possession broken into was considered justifiable payback. I steered clear of these things, didn't want to know about it. The closest I ever got to being an accessory was when Saunders gave me a cassette player he'd nicked from some 'prize dickhead.' I found out where this guy lived, drove over one night, and with a skill equal to that which had pilfered it, stuck it back inside his car real quiet. I couldn't help leaving a note: *Mate, you need to lock your door more often.*

They were, for the most, just hoods. Gangs weren't common around our neighbourhood and there was no driving force to morph them into something more sinister. They'd caused some serious havoc over the years and gotten away with it for so long they were getting sloppy. About two weekends ago, it appeared to have caught up with them.

They'd gone to do their business on a guy we called Cranky,

another no-hoper made for a career in a place like Dominos, which by no coincidence was where he worked delivery a couple of nights a week. Saunders had taken interest in a blissfully naïve woman Cranky knew, or was possibly keen on himself, and when Cranky got word of it he'd dutifully gone to the woman and given her a scathing review of Saunders, sprucing it up with terms like 'self-centred arsehole' and 'psychopath.' Word got back to Saunders, which followed swiftly with a roundup of whoever was available and a trip to Dominos one Friday evening. They waited until Cranky stepped outside to make a delivery and gone to work on him in the carpark in front of half a dozen witnesses, including a mother and her three kids sitting petrified in a car. To his credit Cranky brushed himself down, politely excused himself from work for the rest of the night, and bled his way back to his car and off home.

The manager though, pissed that fifty bucks worth of pizza lay scattered around the carpark, reported it to the police. According to the rumour mill he'd let them at his security footage, but if it had captured anyone's mug you'd assume some of the boys would have been rounded up by now. Equally evident was that Cranky hadn't snitched by providing names to the police. But in the mysterious way these things get around, they must have picked up a scent. A few days later they paid a visit to Spiff, who'd enthusiastically lent his muscle to the boys that night.

Spiff was more a friend of Manners and Saunders, and as far as I knew the only one of us known to police. He had this changeability to his nature that always made me wary as to which way it would jump, and I'd seen it jump from harmless to berserk in the blink of an eye. The year before he'd beaten someone senseless and been charged with 'assault occasioning actual bodily harm.' Spiff's parents, low-income earners who knew as much about the law as they did about their own son, fluked a good lawyer. Spiff claimed the most traumatic thing about the whole affair was sitting in court trying not to piss himself laughing as he listened to his lawyer describe how the side-effects of ADD medication (which he'd stopped taking years before) had turned him into a manically depressed, mood-swinging, sleepwalking victim of pharmaceutical greed and professional malpractice. They'd given him youth justice counselling that consisted of a face-to-face session with the victim's family, the parents of both parties, and a police youth liaison officer with a stern voice and huge tits. According to him, the only discipline to be had was trying not to gawk at them. Not even a two-year good behaviour bond could stop him reverting to old habits less than a year later.

One thing the whole affair did achieve was to wise him up on how the system worked. When the cops paid him a visit, he'd called their bluff on everything they threw at him, and they'd left mighty pissed, he boasted.

The boys thought that had been the end of it. Then these two uglies across the road had shown up here a couple of weekends ago, asking questions. When Spiff found out they were looking for him he started asking around himself. Wasn't long before someone whispered the word *bikies* and he stopped asking questions. I could only guess that Saunders and Manners were tipped off. The other boys' penchant for a beer at the local though had always been stronger than theirs.

All I could get from anyone was that these two had been waiting for them when they got here. Spiff was invited across the road first. He hadn't argued. Neither had Fin. Now it was Grigg's turn.

A lot of questions went through my mind as we waited at the table, the most obvious I asked out loud. Who were these guys to take an interest in a bit of biff in a carpark? How did they get the finger pointed here? What else was going on? To assume Cranky was connected with outlaw motorcycle gangs required too great a mental contortion. But I was the only one who wanted to talk about it. I'd never seen them so hushed up about anything. They sat around staring into their drinks and glancing out the window every other sip like they were counting the minutes.

About half an hour later Grigg trudged through the door and stopped at our table looking like he'd been parleying with the Grim Reaper. Spiff pulled a seat out and Grigg slid onto it mechanically.

'Hey Pete, you wanna beer?' I asked him.

Grigg spoke in a subdued voice. 'Kep, they want to talk to you too.'

All eyes turned toward Kep and his face fell into a slump. 'I wouldn't keep them waiting.'

Kep emptied his glass and set it down. He stood from his stool and without a word walked to the door and pushed it open. Through the window I saw him stop at the curb, look left and right, then skip over the road to face the music. The two guys watched him come with hawklike focus.

There were no handshakes, no smiles. The smaller guy's lips moved, Kep dropped his head and it stayed there. He put his hands in his pockets and didn't move. The smaller guy kept on talking.

'Hey Steve,' Grigg gave me a soft pat on the back. 'Good to see you.'

'What'd they say?'

Grigg stared ahead and gave a barely perceptible nod in the negative. It was his cue to leave it.

For the next half-hour I kept a diligent watch on Kep over the road. I cared a lot more for his welfare than I did for the other guys. Despite the trouble he'd land himself into, he was a good kid. The paradox to his nature was that he'd do almost anything for most people. That was his weakness; he was your classic follower, always going with the flow, even if it meant stepping into a fray one of his buddies had started. When I was around, I'd keep him out of trouble. I felt I'd let him down. If these guys did anything I'd be out the door in a second. I doubt I'd have moved as fast for any of the others though.

Now and again he lifted his head our way, for reassurance I figured, but for the most it stayed down. He put on a show of courage, but by the crossing and uncrossing of his arms and the shuffling of his feet I knew he was scared plenty.

At last they let him go. I watched the mystery men walk off down the road and felt mighty relieved. The way everyone relaxed in their seats suggested the same.

A minute later Kep was at our table and quiet as the others. I went to the bar and returned with drinks but it wasn't enough to clear the air. Spiff, Finlay and Grigg bailed out as soon as their glasses were empty looking like dogs given a whipping. I'm sure the only reason Kep hung around was because of me. We joined a table of local lads, and with the others gone and me there to cheer him up he returned to his happy self.

The night had taken a turn for the better when I felt a tap on my shoulder. I turned around and there was Nat.

'Hi!'

Oh, for . . . 'Oh, yeah – hi. What are you doing here?'

'I finished early. It was a slow night.'

I checked my watch: 11.27pm. 'How'd you know I'd be here?'

'You told me, remember.'

I almost said: *that didn't mean it was an invitation,* but my friends were listening. 'Kep, this is Nat. Nat, this is Kep . . .' and I went along the table. She offered her hand with each introduction and the boys shook it and nodded approvingly. Everything went peachy, bad jokes were bounced around and before I knew it she'd assumed her place at the table as if we'd been waiting for her. It reminded me of a line I'd heard in an old Australian movie. 'Ducks on the pond!' someone had cried when the boss's daughter had the gumption to walk uninvited into a shearer's shed full of sweaty men.

After a long stretch of obligatory, who-gives-a-rats' conversation, she touched my arm lightly. 'Are you ok?'

I put my drink down. 'Dandy.'

She leaned a little closer and spoke into my ear. 'Do you want me to go?'

It was tempting, but the humility in the offer took the bite out of me. It was also almost closing time and she was a handy lift home. 'No,' I sighed. 'It's all right.'

'You don't have to sit here just to keep me company, you know. If there are other people you want to talk to, just go.'

'Gee, nice to have your permission.'

If I hadn't been with company, I reckon she'd have pulled me into line. The temptation in her eyes was there, but in them was hurt as well. I softened up a bit then. One of the things that always endeared me to the girl was her inability to fabricate emotion.

'Look . . . sorry Nat,' but I wasn't as sorry as I made myself sound, 'it's just that I haven't seen these guys for months. No offence, but I was looking forward to the night on my own.'

She gazed at something distant. She pressed the straw of her drink between her fingers and played it around her lips. 'Sure.'

'And yeah, I wouldn't mind having a chat with some other guys I haven't seen in a while, before the place closes.'

'Go then,' she urged, a little too forcefully. 'Go.'

An unconvincing smile formed on her lips, then died. Her compliance shamed me.

'Listen . . . Nat. Something I've been meaning to ask for some time.'
'What?'

'That day when you first spoke to me in the library,' I said. 'I know what I was doing up on that floor. What were *you* doing there?'

She wrinkled her nose and spoke dryly. 'Maybe I was looking for you.'

I kept my eyes on her but she wouldn't meet them. It was a sweet thing to suggest and I tried to imagine the truth of it. She might have seen me come into the library, walk past perhaps, and the time it would have taken to find me on the eighth floor fit neatly with how long I'd been sitting there before she did. I wanted to take it further, but she had that sulkiness about her that warned me she'd take it back if I did, true or not. Just to spite me.

I wandered over to another table of boys I knew and got talking. I checked Nat's way every few minutes and she appeared to be doing fine. Kep had been in her ear since I'd left her and they were hitting it off like pals.

When it was closing time, she shook his hand. By then he was the only one at the table, so it didn't look exclusive. But it did tell me a lot about what she thought of the guy. In the car on the way home I asked her what they'd been talking about.

'Lots of things,' she said.

I didn't push it.

Dad worked for an insurance firm. He'd pulled a few strings over the years and got me some handy work in one of their city offices –

thankfully nowhere near his – earning me some prize bucks for a student. Between the work I did there and catching up with some former high school buddies, I didn't see as much of the home crew during the break as I'd planned. Nat joined us a couple of times. She and Kep spent so much time coddling each other that if I didn't know them better, I might have made a scene.

Then there was football. The powers-that-be didn't arrange the Shute Shield draw just so Uni students had time off over a break. It was tough on Keogh, having to travel down from Newcastle all the time. Lisa put him up for a few consecutive nights the first week but that arrangement proved short-lived, so he'd stay at my place after that.

Like our chess meets, he was good company when it was just the two of us. He opened up to me in a way I knew he didn't with others. We'd stay up late watching videos, something would pop up on the screen that warranted comment and we'd yak away until the movie was background noise. With him though, that yak was often a drift toward the ideological, the existential. The bigger picture. Deep inside that composed shell of his there seemed to brood a dark and restless energy, a silent scream. He had this brutally clinical take on life, while at the same time a profound yearning for the betterment of things, a poet's love for the world's beauty. Philosophically at ease one minute, doom and gloom the next.

Sometimes though it got too much. I'd remind him there was a movie to watch, and he'd shake himself out of it and apologise with a laugh.

He was an odd fellow.

Thirteen

The danger with hazing is that there are always those who take it too far. *Stasi* minions like Pronk and sundry who made it their duty to go beyond the call of duty. The sort of guys that put a face to truncheon-toting guards in Gulags and concentration camps, the sort of guys that turn friendly rivalry between colleges into a punchup. The sort you don't want on your case. And don't they love that very reputation. Fortunately, there's only so much damage these guys can do in a civilised society. Still, they try.

Poor Babs. They pulled just about every prank in the college arsenal on him and still his spirit prevailed. There were times though it had to be just a brave face. I'd sat through a couple of one-on-ones with the guy and dug into his moods often enough to suspect it was taking its toll. You can roll with the punches in here as long as you had a senior or two of influence to rein in the bad guys before things got out of hand. I got the impression Babs had no one. Not even Metcalf, who always went batting for freshers.

Helpful as our tutors were, they weren't paid to do assignments for us. I'd run out of time with a nonparametric assignment and knocked on my RF's door to see what he could do. Now and then lecturers got lazy and doled out an assignment that differed little, if at all, from a previous year, and Metcalf had obliged me before with past papers of his. After flicking through a few pages, he said he'd look into it. A couple of days later there was a knock on my door.

'Keep it to yourself,' he said after he poked his head in. He passed me some papers and left without another word.

It was a photocopy of the completed assignment. *Babs'* assignment. As I flicked through the handwriting I knew so well I could see he was in for another high distinction.

At first, I didn't know how to feel. I assumed Metcalf's advice meant he'd lifted the assignment from Babs' room and photocopied it without his consent. We'd cut down on pestering the poor guy months ago after one of our lecturers, all out of patience, warned us that those caught copying answers from fellow students risked the dreaded FF. Whenever Babs had helped us out in the past it was with his full cooperation. Now I faced a moral dilemma.

Babs was not a bad guy. He was witty, well-liked, and respected by a lot of us here for being his own person. But some alpha males had him marked, which was all it took for the rest of the pack to follow suit. By being party to Metcalf's transgression, I felt contributory to his victimisation.

But then I thought, stuff it. You want to be careful how close you get to guys like Babs, lest you catch his curse. I also needed these answers, bad enough to have made the decision already to cheat. The source was irrelevant. So I took it. That was the unfortunate thing about Babs. Without meaning to, he had a way of bringing out the dark side in all of us.

We were celebrating some random intercollegiate sport victory in the courtyard when Camilleri and another lad were caught leaving prematurely. Prematurely meaning the kegs weren't finished. They were summonsed back and kangaroo court was fittingly convened. Of course, the occasion wouldn't be worthy of its name unless they boosted numbers.

Sproule jumped up onto a table and shut everyone up with a piercing whistle. When Pronk hopped up beside him I knew something dreadful was in order, especially now that the seniors we usually relied on for rescue had abandoned the field.

'Right!' Sproule announced after everyone quietened down. 'The following students are accused of breaches of the St Phillips Code of Conduct. When you hear your name called, step forward.'

Our self-proclaimed judge and his right-hand man then conferred amongst themselves. Pronk did most of the talking, Sproule the nodding. 'Peter Hurst!' Sproule cried suddenly. 'Take a seat and face your peers, please.' He pointed down at the bench directly below.

Hurst stepped heavy-shouldered through the crowd and sat down on the bench facing our way.

'Blindfold!' cried Sproule, and a senior stepped forward and blindfolded him eagerly. After so many months in college I suspected some guys carried the things around in their pockets. Along with God knows what else.

'Peter Hurst! The charge is having an insufficient quantity of nominated beverage when visited by Brother Garrett on the 20th July, that being approximately two fluid ounces of Johnny Walker against the prescribed minimum level of five fluid ounces. How do you plead, guilty or not guilty?'

The plea offer was moot. This was kangaroo court. You get charged, then by Jesus, Joseph and Mary, you were guilty. After a short deliberation of weighing the options, Hurst conceded.

'Guilty.'

'The Shute Shield is named in honour of Robert Shute who died after a tackle during a trial game in 1922. What was the lesser-known tragic coincidence of the day?'

'The tackle was made by a player of the same surname, Jack Shute.'

'Very good, Master Hurst. You may take off your blindfold and leave your seat.'

A couple more boys were called forth for misdemeanours real or imagined and had it easy. The first to get stuck on an answer was Camilleri. The tittering grew loud very quickly.

'We can't hear you, Master Camilleri! And I see Mr Pronk unzipping his fly! What *is* he doing?'

My pity for the guy turned to surprised amusement when Pronk leaned forward with a kettle someone handed up to him. After taking careful aim, he tilted it forward and a stream of water splattered Camilleri's head. A cry of disgust sounded from the crowd to feed the illusion. Camilleri leapt to his feet and wiped his hands over his head in horror.

'We have our first casualty. Camilleri, you may return to your place. Next – Andy Kelpin!'

Camilleri took off his blindfold and sniffed at his arms and hands with his nose screwed. Beaming delightfully, his RF sauntered over to him and spoke the words he desperately needed to hear. A second later Camilleri was shaking his head in relief and grinning along with the rest of us.

Two freshers either gave no answers or got them wrong. One had a bucket of iced water mixed with food leftovers emptied over his head, the other a tub of some kind of syrup followed by a generous sprinkling of pillow fluff – the college equivalent of the good ol' tar and feathers. After the celebration of that died down, Pronk spoke into Sproule's ear and our secretary nodded and jumped down. I'd already guessed who Pronk was going to call.

'David Schiffer!' he called loudly. 'Take a seat!'

Babs came forward, bent over and suitably miserable. He sat down on the bench and was promptly blindfolded.

'Our Latin *and* bible aficionado,' Pronk resumed. 'The charge my good friend is *hominem absentia,* to wit: failing to participate in the scavenger hunt during O-week and letting your team down. Yes, Master Schiffer, our memories are better than an elephant's. Guilty or not guilty?'

'I was at a med school induction.'

'In the Great Hall on either side of the western window are two angels holding scrolls. Had you gone on the scavenger hunt, you would know that on one is written the words "Scientia inflat, Caritas oedificat." Translation please.'

Babs was quiet for so long I thought they had him. Then when he did speak his voice lacked assertion, as if he knew whatever he said would never be enough.

'Knowledge puffeth, but charity edifies.'

'Yes, Master Schiffer!' thundered Pronk. 'Knowledge may get you high and mighty, but it is charity that saves you!' He raised his head to the heavens and stretched his arms out as high as he could.

'AM – EN!'

The table served well as a pulpit. He looked like a mad preacher, doubtless his intention. He'd taken to the role so convincingly it didn't rate as acting. He lowered his arms and looked down.

'But you don't get off that easy. Bible passage, please.'

The seconds passed and Babs said nothing. Pronk shuffled forward until he was directly above him, then unzipped his fly and aimed down. 'Corinthians, 8:1,' he said, and let loose. '*Actually.*'

I'd like to think most of us were hoping he'd miss. I'd like to think that had Babs not caught on so quickly, had he not pulled out the instant that first trickle arced onto his scalp and shoulders, someone would have knocked Pronk flying off his perch. Someone like Keogh. He was standing beside me and started forward as if to do just that, stopping only when he saw that Babs was out of harm's way.

Where there'd been hooting and hollering before, the cry was less enthusiastic this time. Some older boys guffawed and a few freshers clapped dutifully, but most of us stood around in a sympathetic silence.

Babs ripped off his blindfold and threw it away. Pronk strained to extend his reach but Babs was well out of range, sniffing at his hands. He had a vile look about him, an expression of fierce loathing I'd never seen in him before, and yet there was a shakiness to it, that crumbling of spirit that is so often the precursor to tears. He walked away and no one called out after him.

'You arsehole, Pronk,' Keogh muttered, and we all watched him take off after Babs.

Pronk finished and zipped himself back up. 'You're next, Keogh,' he promised through his signature wicked sneer.

Keogh ignored him. He caught up to Babs put and put an arm over his shoulder.

After that little event, on top of everything else, I was ready to believe they had him. That it was just a matter of time before he broke. There was a droop to his posture that had to have come from more than just lack of sleep. Yep, the Phil and Babs were never meant to be.

I should have known better. Babs was way too proud a cookie to let any of that get the better of him. For all he might not have been, he was a survivor. And if I'd known him anywhere near as well as I thought, I'd have known he was always going to triumph.

But not in a million years would I have guessed how. Not a soul in Phillips would have, either.

Like all colleges, ours had a history of proud traditions. Some never found their way onto our Academic Calendar, for good reason, even though they were as much a part of the culture as formal dinners and VD awards. Take the Drink Olympics.

Second semester, third weekend. For reasons to be made apparent it was held outdoors, down the cosy end of the courtyard where there were seats and tables and tiles that could be washed down easily. I was surprised to see a lively spread of women in attendance, mainly regulars of our student club activities or those with boyfriends. I'd invited Nat myself but she'd pulled out after hearing accounts of what she might see.

After dinner we assembled ourselves in the courtyard and Sproule took to the role of MC. Wouldn't you know it, there were rules.

'There shall be no finger-pointing during the Games,' he explained.

'There shall be no arguing with the judges.'

'There shall be no raised voices, foul language or calling of names.'

'There shall be no induced vomiting, or fingers down throats.'

'Entry to the bathroom will be preceded by a mandatory nip of JW.'

'Any breach of the aforementioned rules is punishable by a mandatory scull.'

'Dry retching is punishable by two sculls.'

'Major infractions will incur Dr Jekyll, aka the *Cup of Death*.' The older boys cheered knowingly at this one.

'Dr Jekyll!' Sproule picked up a schooner glass and poured it half full of beer. He finger-scooped some dip and flicked it into the cup, sprinkled in a crushed cracker and added a glob of Tabasco sauce. Not-so-crisp crisps and a sorry clump of chicken skin came next, met with howls of encouragement. He found a spoon and gave it a stir. He held it up to the light and I swear it actually fizzed and frothed.

On a positive note, Sproule announced awards for this and that – not the sort of thing you'd brag about beyond the college walls. Two judges replete with flowing back robes and wigs positioned themselves at a table. The robes were the real deal – academic gowns – but the wigs must have come from that secret wardrobe of theirs that delivered for any occasion.

'Group Captain bottom floor, A-Wing,' Sproule cried, finger-pointing with impunity as he read from prepared notes. 'At one hundred kilos, gold and silver medallist, blood type Bourbon and a major sponsor of the Grange. Majestic on the outside but in his guts lies the means to change history, at four to one for first barf of the night we have Brother Franks, aka the TROJAN HORSE!'

Franks clasped his hands together over his head and gave himself a bravo. The whistling died down and Sproule reviewed other favourites and wannabees and gave them odds for this and that. Keogh stood to one side with his arms folded. At one point he caught my eye and shook his head like he was watching a bunch of clowns trying to run a circus.

After the last favourite had taken a bow, Sproule cried: 'Lay your bets boys! All categories, don't be shy!' and there was a flow of kids to the bookies.

With everything sorted, Sproule set a wok of whisky alight. It flared and puffed weakly with a thin blue flame and I found it fitting that it died the moment he declared the Games open. No one, least of all him, seemed to notice.

What followed was a variety affair unlikely to ever make a sports page, and yet familiar in some form or other to any residential student on the planet: *the Bucket*, *the Wheel of Ill Fortune*, *Master's Apprentice*, *Blind Man's Bluff*, *Russian Roulette* . . . take your pick. Most chose something called the *Funnel Relay* on account of the requirement to lick tequila and salt from a brave girl's belly. By the time they called first heat for the boat races my stomach felt tight as a football. I'd assumed proceedings up till then were designed to weed out the weaker stomachs but the Phil, proudly, had no weak stomachs. I wondered if Charles Darwin had witnessed something similar during his stay at Christ's College.

There were so many infractions throughout it all that the judges could hardly keep up. By the number of penalty sculls doled out, you'd think they served more as a badge of honour to the recipients than to speed things up. The drinks got stronger, faces turned sicklier, and Dr

Jekyll grew uglier. Every time Sproule lost order, he added some unidentifiable dreg to the mixture and threatened anyone who wouldn't shutup with drinking it. That always worked.

About two hours into it, all heads turned to the sound of splatter we'd been waiting for.

(Excerpt): *The Drawl.* Edition 6, August.

The 23rd Drink Olympiad: St Phillips College:

Master of Ceremonies: The Honourable Carl Sproule
Judges: Terence Redcliffe, Simon Merrick
Chundermaster: Ricki Vlahos
Sponsors: J Daniels, J Walker, J Beam.

Official placings:

Gold Medal: Sprint
Stephen Reynolds: Bach. Music Year 2
Time: 114minutes, 25seconds +/- 5
B-Wing, ground floor
Coach: Dwayne Springer

'Step back now gentlemen! Step back! Give the man his breathing space,' our chundermaster ordered, parting the crowd with a wave of his hand. A clipboard was tucked under his armpit. Second-year Reynolds was sitting on a chair, doubled over and gagging. Someone gave him a congratulatory pat on the shoulder.

Vlahos reached him and stared down at the arrangement on the floor. Our two judges Redcliffe and Merrick pushed through and joined him. Redcliffe rubbed his chin thoughtfully, then gave the thumbs up. Merrick did the same.

'Folks, we have a winner!' Vlahos declared. Reynolds lifted his head weakly, then his eyes widened and his chest heaved . . . once . . . twice . . . there was a cry or two of encouragement from the crowd, and then *wullah!* – the follow through. Vlahos barely managed to step back in time.

A sick stench floated in the air. With the seriousness of their bona-fide Olympic counterparts, Redcliffe and Merrick stretched a measuring tape over the greatest diameter of puke and Vlahos scribbled on his scoresheet. He kneeled down, picked here and there at the chunky bits with his pen, and made some more notes. As a finale he produced a spoon from inside his gown and waved it majestically in the air like a wand, then scooped up a sample of the horrid stew and lifted it to his nose and took a sniff.

In the manner of a gourmet tasting some hot, exotic dish, he nibbled off a small portion. 'I detect a hint of smokiness and salty character within a dark, smooth base of various rustic colours and firm elements of . . .' he tasted it again '. . . malted barley, I believe.' After adding some notes on his clipboard, he read out marks for categories ranging from colour and consistency to aroma and taste, and declared an overall score of 36 out of 50.

That was the cue for the sounder-minded of us to bow out. More boat races and penalty sculls followed until even they became obsolete. Stomachs emptied faster than the judges could keep up with. The noise got louder, the stink stronger, the sick sicker.

By 11pm Dr Jekyll was a curdled, dark lumpy mess that looked like the stuff you pull out of a blocked drain. It would have sent a cockroach packing. Commanded an impressive amount of respect though. Die-hards who dismissed penalty sculls with a finger-birdie turned meek as mice when threatened with that smoothie from hell.

There came a point though to go on with the affair might not be in our best interests. Pouring every conceivable beverage down someone's throat in order to send it back out again was one thing, getting stomachs pumped out in a hospital might cast the college in a dim light. As faces went from green to purple our Event Officials wisely wound proceedings down by gathering up all near-empty liquor bottles and screwing the lids on. All that remained on the table was Dr Jekyll.

Sproule picked it up and inspected it with a contortion of face that suggested he was at pains to even look at it. 'Righto boys!' he announced. 'Last formality of the night. Calling for nominees for the *Cup of Death!*'

Heads turned every which way. Pronk called out: 'Jason Keogh!' and the nomination received a loud, drunken chorus of support.

At that stage he was sitting beside me. His chair was about-faced and he was leaning over the backrest. I was surprised he'd hung around this long, didn't think it was his thing. He'd had a few beers, and though he hadn't participated in boat races or sculls or elbow pointing or throwing drinks over people I suspected he'd sat through the affair for the same reason we of compos mentis did. Call it morbid curiosity.

Sproule was cheered loudly as he approached. Keogh watched him coming with his own variation of a grin.

'Dr Jekyll!' Sproule beamed delightfully, closing in on him and holding the glass out at arm's length.

'Come near me with that thing,' Keogh warned with a menacing smile, 'you'll be wearing it.'

You could see he meant it. Sproule withdrew the precious offering and held it protectively against his chest. 'Come on mate, you know the way it works.'

'Wanna bet?' Keogh sniggered.

Sproule turned away and held the glass up for all to see. *'Ke-ogh! Ke-ogh!'*

The chant caught on, got louder. Sproule turned back to Keogh, more courageous now that he had the support of just about everyone in the place.

Keogh just shook his head in the negative, stayed still. Sproule held the glass out gingerly, torn between having the precious drink slapped out of his hands or thrown over him, and following through with his own directive. The chant continued, but like the horse led to water – *you can't make it drink it.*

I was surprised that someone supposedly savvy enough for a spot in our student leadership would assume Keogh would cooperate. It was a mistake, made it look worse than Keogh's refusal, and too late Sproule knew it. You could see the disappointment grow on his face, the realisation it was never going to happen. That he had as much chance of getting Keogh to drink that dreg-riddled concoction as he did in getting him to wear a dress. The chant died down as reality set in.

There were scattered boos and murmurs of disapproval, mainly from the older boys. Sproule turned around in a circle searching for a suitable substitute and crinkles of delight replaced the disappointment on his face when he lined up with Babs standing behind everyone on his lonesome. Despite our suspicions, Schiffer's bean proved made of mortal stuff whenever he soaked it in alcohol, and I found it comforting he hadn't shied away from this glorious occasion.

'David Schiffer!' he cried, and the cheer was as loud as what greeted Keogh's nomination. Sproule raised a clenched fist as if he'd scored a direct hit.

'Schi-ffers! Schi-ffers!' Sproule moved in for the kill, leading the chant.

Babs' eyes went wide as an owl's. Though I felt sorry for him he should have seen it coming. Of all the guys present he was always going to be a prime candidate. I didn't know who was dumber; Sproule for assuming Keogh would submit, or Babs for hanging around when he didn't.

'Schi-ffers! Schi-ffers!'

Sproule was dancing on his toes when he got to him. He held Dr Jekyll out for him to take, careful not to spill a drop. Babs looked at it mortified.

'Take it!'

Babs stared at it for a moment, his face oddly serene. Slowly his hand lifted and took the glass. Sproule clapped his hands together in rhythm to the chant. *'Schi-ffers! Schi-ffers!'*

For some time, Babs didn't move. Then, in a curiously authoritative manner, he held a hand up to quieten everyone. The chant receded into silence. Even the older boys stopped gabbing. Most of them didn't listen to Babs at the best of times, but they all listened now.

Sproule was standing a lot closer to Babs than what I'd have thought safe. He would have made an awfully tempting target.

'For what it's worth,' Babs announced in a clear voice, 'I think this is wrong. You guys go too far sometimes. I'm with Keogh, no one should have to drink this shit.' Heads swung over to Keogh, who looked as taken aback as the rest of us.

Babs looked at the glass regretfully. 'I fight it, I know. I shouldn't, but I do. Cheers.' With that he lifted the thing to his lips, tilted it, and we witnessed a miracle.

I watched in disbelief. His Adam's apple bobbed up and down and I expected spew to erupt from his mouth any moment like a burst of lava. But he emptied the glass without the slightest hiccup.

The courtyard had gone into silent shutdown. Someone had hit the pause button. Babs lowered the glass mouth-down and not a drop fell out. A milkshake-like film of goo lined the inside, and one or two globs of something scary stuck to the rim, but that was it.

Then the place exploded. There was an ear-splitting cheering and clapping and hollering. Glasses were thrust skywards and their contents shot out in long silver streaks. Fists banged on tables and whistling pierced the air. Babs' entire body started to convulse and shudder and his face took a form of excruciating pain.

Sproule stepped forward and patted Babs on the back as he doubled over and gagged. A voice cried 'Stand back!' just as Babs gave the tiles beneath him the full force of a projectile vomit. It hit with a dreadful splat and spread out like a shock wave.

The ruckus continued for a good minute or so. All the while Babs stood doubled over with his hands on his hips, breathing deeply and giving his head a shake. At last he straightened and wiped his lips. He looked us all over pink-faced, then pointed his finger down.

'Try some of that.'

Official placings (continued):

Gold Medal: Taste
Gold Medal: Aroma
Gold Medal: Colour

Overall winner: Most Outstanding

David Schiffer: Bachelor of Medicine
C-Wing, Floor (2)
Coach: Roland Hardy

Had they broken him? In a way he'd lost some of his self-esteem. But that little display of conformism won him something from those hard-arse bastards long overdue: respect. Respect for him stepping down from his assumed airs. Respect for him accepting that he was part of an order. Respect for him acknowledging that he had no more rights than anyone else to buck rules and traditions. Not exactly the R's they were looking for, but close enough.

They never bothered him after that. I even caught Pronk joking with him on occasion. And Babs, for his part, didn't push it. Obeyed the rules from that day on, just like the rest of us. He was still our Babs, but he was also something else now. He was one of the team.

It was a truce.

Fourteen

'Chambers, your missus called,' Flip mumbled as he walked past. 'Asked if you can ring her back asap. She's over at Women's on this number.' He gave me a piece of paper. 'Tell whoever picks up that she's in that room number there.'

I read the room number he'd scribbled, and it clicked.

The dining hall was full. It was Monday evening, dinner was corned beef with that grotesque white sauce, and talk at our table was dominated by Babs and Keogh arguing over the range of an English longbow. Babs seemed to have met his match on that one.

I called after Flip through a full mouth. 'When did she ring?'

'About twenty minutes ago,' he said over his shoulder.

'Gee . . . thanks.'

I left my half-eaten meal at the table and rang the number from the internal phone in the JCR. Nat came on within a minute of someone going to get her.

'Steve, thank God. I'm in Marion's room. Can you come over? I'll meet you at the door.'

'What's wrong?'

'I'll tell you when you get here. Just come over now. *Please*.'

'Let me guess,' I groaned. 'It's that loser Beeman again.'

There was a pause. 'You need to hear this yourself.'

'Ok,' I sighed. 'Give me ten minutes.'

I scoffed down the rest of my dinner and headed off. Nat met me at the entrance of Women's College and I followed her speedy step all the way to Marion's room.

Nat tapped on her door, then opened it. Marion was sitting on the bed with a girl called Louise I'd met before. Attractive to the point of distraction, she wasn't the type I forgot easily.

Marion's eyes were red-rimmed and puffy, and our entry instigated a fresh burst of tears. I raised my hands defensively and turned to Louise for help. She put a hand on Marion's knee and rubbed it.

'What's he done now?' I asked in that *not again* tone of voice.

'She doesn't remember,' Nat said. 'But we can guess.'

In dribs and drabs from Nat I learnt that after our last chat, despite everyone's warnings, the girl had capitulated and gotten back with him. Hang on – Louise was quick to correct – not necessarily back with him, but . . . you know . . . just on occasion. Isn't that more accurate, Marion? And Marion nodded.

I preferred Nat to talk; I put far more faith in her objectivity. She also knew how to cut to the chase. I prompted her with the appropriate look and she obliged.

The on-off arrangement Marion found herself in reached its climax about a week ago when he came doorknocking one night and she wouldn't let him in. A friend of Marion, wise to the slug, chased him away, but then on Saturday night he'd rung using the bleeding-heart approach, and Marion had foolishly agreed to a 'talk' after dinner. Soon as he was safe inside her room he'd tried a move or two on her which she brushed off, and after that he seemed to let it go. They had what she thought was a friendly chat. He was all mature and accepting of the situation, after which he'd opened up a bottle he'd brought. This wasn't unusual; in their happier days they'd often share a nightcap.

That was the last thing she could remember. The next thing she knew she was standing by the sink in the bathroom naked from the waist down early Sunday morning feeling seriously nauseous. A girl had walked in and found her, and assuming she was just hungover, led her back to her room. Marion had holed up all day, gone to dinner late, and retreated to her room again. At breakfast this morning someone made a joke about her walking around butt-naked the day before, and she burst out crying. They'd shut up at that, but when a giggled account reached the wiser ears of Nat during a coffee between lectures the joking stopped and the serious questioning began. Nat had tracked her down at first opportunity and it didn't take long after that. So here I was.

A series of emotions were vying for hold inside me: sympathy, loathing, anger, shame. I didn't know which was greater, or which I should act on. I settled for shame. Shame that this guy was part of our college. Shame for our gender. Shame that I'd let it go like everyone else.

'What was the drink he gave you?' I asked, though I knew the answer.

'Southern Comfort,' Marion said.

'How many did you have?'

'Just the one, I think.'

'Did you see him drink any of his?'

There was a delay while she thought about it. 'No,' she answered wistfully.

'Did he . . ?

Marion didn't answer. Nat said, 'She thinks he did.'

'Thinks?'

I turned to Marion and her desultory eyes darted away. I raised my hands in silent enquiry, but only Nat spoke.

'Marion, you have to report him this time.'

Marion sniffed and wiped a tear away with a finger. 'No. It doesn't matter. I'm not that sure anything happened, anyway.'

'Yes you do Marion,' Nat said firmly. 'You just don't want to believe it. He wouldn't have drugged you for nothing.'

'Did he hurt you or anything?' I asked, and Marion shook her head.

'Jesus Steve,' Nat answered. 'This is fucking rape. Why should that make a difference?'

I said to Marion, 'Is that what you think happened?'

She sniffed and stayed quiet.

'Marion?' Nat prompted.

'I don't know,' she said wistfully. 'I'm ok, really.'

'Marion, you have to report it this time, for everyone's sake,' Nat said. 'We don't know how many other girls he might have done this to, let alone tried it on. You're not the first. Remember Andrea? Please report it.'

'I don't want to.'

No one spoke. I looked at Marion. 'You showered since?' I asked, and she nodded shyly. 'Does anyone know how long this stays in the system?' Louise and Nat shook their heads no. 'What has it been?' I was thinking aloud, it helped get the message across. 'Sunday night. . . Monday,' I did the finger count, 'almost forty-eight hours.'

'Are you worried that you won't be believed Marion,' Nat asked. 'Is that it?'

'Nat . . .' I inclined my head toward the door. 'We'll be back in a sec, Marion.'

Nat followed me out and I closed the door. 'What?' she asked impatiently. I walked her down the corridor until I was sure we couldn't be heard. A door opened and a girl came out, and I waited until she disappeared into the bathroom.

'Listen, first things first. Ease up. You're putting pressure on the poor girl.'

The heat left her face a bit as I saw it sink in.

'Second,' I said with a sigh, 'I don't want to sound like a drip, but I'm worried it's the same all over again. We got nothing.'

'I knew you'd say that!' Nat flared instantly. 'Not this time, Steve.'

She was fuming, shaking with rage. She might have been a mother whose daughter had been violated. I felt for her, I truly did. I felt for Marion, and I despised that piece of filth more than ever, but that didn't help the hard facts of the matter, or more correctly, the absence of.

'Nat, don't get me wrong. I'm on your side, but again it has to come down to proof. Do we have it?'

'I've done some checking,' she said, a scale softer. 'There's plenty of examples of rapists getting locked away on the testimony of the victim. That's right – just one woman, one person's word against another. Nothing else. No fancy forensics, no other witnesses.'

'Rape? Come on Nat, she's not even sure he did that.'

'What, you don't think he did?'

'Oh, I'm sure he would have done something; he's twisted enough to do things normal people don't think of. But rape?' I said with a deep sigh. 'She's out cold, can't help us there, and there'd be no traces now. And even if they can prove he knocked her out, what then?'

'Isn't that enough?'

'You'd think so,' I speculated. 'There's some law, something about administering a drug to someone without their knowledge. But seriously, look at the girl. She'd need to cooperate, and right now it's as if she's trying to protect the guy. Do you think she'd make a reliable witness?'

'With the right talking to, the right persuasion, I think she might, yeah!' She stared at me with fiery eyes, and I could feel the red-hot will behind them. I felt weak in the face of such determination. I was surprised at her stance on this. Marion was a friend of hers, but not that great a friend. This went deeper than that, and I admired Nat for it. If she was prepared to go this far for her, how far would she go for someone she really cared about? Like me? It was a selfish thought, one I couldn't help gloating over. I had me a wild one.

'Okay . . . okay,' I relented. 'But this is serious shit, Nat. We need to tread delicately here, ok?'

We went back to her room. As soon as we stepped inside Marion said firmly, 'I don't want you to do anything.'

Nat and I stared at her, speechless. For a girl who had teetered on the point of breaking minutes earlier, her recovery sure was bold. 'I just want everyone to forget about it. He can't have done anything I haven't let him do before, so what difference does it make?'

'Marion . . .' Nat said, almost pleading, and I could see the defeat in her eyes few people can achieve. 'If we can show—'

'Stop it!' Marion said with grit in her voice. 'I don't want to do it. I'd like you all to leave now, please.' Her face was set hard as granite. 'You've been here long enough. I just want to be left alone.'

No one said a word as we headed back through the corridors. At the top of the flight down to reception we stopped.

'What now?' Louise asked.

'I'm going to report him,' Nat said staunchly.

'Nat,' I said, 'she doesn't want you to. You'll be making a mess.'

She grunted something I didn't catch and took off down the stairs.

'Natalie!' I called after her. I swapped glances with Louise, who had nothing to offer. I set off at pace and leapt down the stairs two or three at a time. Even at that speed I only got to Nat after she'd pushed the front door open. I caught it on its backswing and followed her out.

'Nat! Slow down, will you!'

She kept going and I hurried after her. 'Just stop for a sec. If you want to help, listen to me.'

She stopped then, and I went on hurriedly. 'You want to haul Marion through something she doesn't want to go through? You'll make a lot of noise for nothing and she'll end up hating you.'

'Oh, for fuck's sake!' With both hands she clutched her head and shook it, as if in horrible pain. 'What do *you* propose, Steve?'

She buried her eyes into me, the seconds passed slowly. She gave me a low curse and took off again.

'Nat!'

She kept going, didn't look back. I took a long breath, let it out in a beaten voice. 'Just give me a day or two, will you?'

She stopped and turned around, and I saw the tears rimming her eyes. 'All right.' She lifted up a single finger. 'One day.' Then she walked away.

Each step I took closer to college, I could have kicked myself. *The bloody bottle.* I'd seen it, picked it up. I'd been handed the gamebreaker on a silver platter and been too dumb to see it. Sure, it might have been pure, unadulterated, 38 proof Southern C. Kept in the car for the odd occasion he felt like a cap, a leftover from a harmless night out. Perhaps a lot of things.

Yeah, right. The prick kept it there like a crook kept a loaded gun. Ready for when some poor, naïve girl let him into her room and said no. If I had taken one tiny sample – poured it into a stray cup or bottle or whatever – he'd be history.

I got back to college and strode into the carpark. Beeman's piece-of-shit Datsun was parked on the far side. I reached it and gave the door handle a yank. Locked. I pressed my face against window and cupped my hands over my eyes to block the reflection. God knows what I expected to see. Slam-dunk evidence like a bottle of laced alcohol on the seat?

This wasn't going to happen. That bird had flown.

I pushed myself off the chassis and gave the door a decent kick. I stared at the car and let the rage fizzle out. This was going to nag me to death, I knew. The utter uselessness of it all left me sagging as I headed back to my room.

The nature of the critical point (0, 0) and the type of its stability is also given along with a typical phase portrait for each case, that is, if (0, 0) is the only critical point of the linear system dx/dt = ax + by, and dy/dt = cx + dy, then it is asymptotically stable if and only if the real parts of the two roots . . .

Asymptotically stable? What the hell is that? Stable? Horses? Horses as in—?

I thrust my half-finished assignment into the book and snapped it closed. I shoved it to one side of the desk and reached for my to-be-done-later pile. Next.

Top of the stack was an organic chemistry assignment. For several minutes I stared down at meaningless ink, sliding my hands through my hair. I checked my watch. Monday nights were video nights in the epicentre of college and round about now they usually started.

I got to the JCR and stood at the back wall to see what was on. Bruce Willis showed up in a white singlet and I made the connection with *Die Hard*. I scanned the room and settled for a seat to the side.

To me at least, the next most annoying thing to whispered natter while watching a movie is the crackle of a bag of chips. You can tell how long you'll be hearing it by the intensity of the crackle they so gallantly try to suppress. The effort I heard now suggested whoever was responsible was going to make that bag last the duration of the movie. I suffered about ten minutes before screwing my neck to locate the source.

Though the room was rather dark, Beeman's insipid face stood out like a beacon of disease. He was only a few seats away, slouched low in his seat. The bag on his lap crackled softly and his hand lifted robotically up to his face. I watched the slow-motion masticating of his jaw with distaste until his tongue gave the corners of his lips a lick and I couldn't look away quick enough.

The sight incensed me. There was just no escaping this guy. I tried to watch the movie but I couldn't focus now. The timing of this was like a sign from above. This was rubbing it in. For all our valiant efforts this is what mine amounted to: watching movies with the guy and his frigging bag of chips crackling in my ear.

Around me I could see Draper, Lanky Shanks, and Hardy. These guys were serious winners, future leaders. I knew I should fill them in on this latest development but some vague instinct stopped me. Perhaps I thought that shifting ownership of the issue might be regarded as violating some principle this place was trying to teach. Or that these lofty impressions of mine might be sullied if they gave the guy nothing more than a dressing down and nasty slap on the wrist. This was out of their league. They could refer it to the law, and even I didn't put much faith in that quarter.

I thought of Marion and that fawn-like innocence of hers, that willingness to please without question. I thought of Spiff and Grigg and Fin and their ash-grey faces after the heavies from God-knows-where had put the fear of death into them. I thought of Beeman and those rat-shiny eyes of his, his filthy tongue. I thought of that bloody bottle of Southern Comfort and the moron who missed a golden opportunity to nail him without anyone else having to lift a finger.

Now I felt a burning need to make up for it. I'd go talk to Draper and we'd have another crack at Beeman's safe and car. It would have to be tomorrow, or the day after, latest. Or we could just front the guy. Put the allegation to him, go to his car and open his boot, or go through his room and his safe again on the off chance we'd find something. Of course, there was the real possibility he'd disposed of the evidence. Surely he wasn't that dumb to rely on Marion keeping her mouth shut. If things heated up he couldn't risk having her story corroborated. No. I'd have to assume that bird had indeed flown.

And even if we did find it, what then? We'd take it to the cops, they'd do whatever fancy stuff they did and he could just say sure, that's mine. I'm on Rohypnol, here's the prescription. I like a little Southern C to wash it down, works better. Never gave it to Marion. Yeah, she knows I'm on it, I suspect the bitch is setting me up for that time I kicked her car door in.

Or he just could say someone planted the bottle there. Someone doesn't like me, is trying to set me up. Didn't you say you took my keys, broke into my room and my personal effects? And my car?

But at least then the issue would be out in the open. Who knows, maybe we could rattle him enough for a confession. Even if he didn't, the scumbag would be on notice. If he sneezed out of line, we'd be onto him. He'd be shaking at the knees. He'd curse his evil ways, find religion. He'd be a model citizen, donate to charity. Yep. Give the guy a break.

I was grinding my teeth without realising.

The next thing I knew I was sidestepping past chairs out of the place. I hit the door to the JCR open and nearly broke into a trot across the courtyard. I bounded up the C-wing stairs and hurried through the corridor to Keogh's door.

'Yuh,' was the reply from inside after I'd knocked.

I swung the door open. 'I'm going to deal with Beeman. You in?'

Keogh turned his chair around and cocked an eyebrow. 'Something happen?'

I filled him in and he never said a word. Just sat there taking it all in with that look on his face that made me wonder again what lurked in his depths.

'It's up to you,' I said, and gave him a while. No answer came and it felt like a kick in the guts. I was closing the door to leave when it got the better of me.

'What is it with you?' I asked testily. 'Pronk pisses on Babs and you're ready to rip his head off. A girl gets drug-raped for all we know and you don't even twitch.'

'I'm thinking this through,' he said evenly. 'Sounds like you haven't.'

'Oh, give me a break!' I raised my voice. 'That's all we've been doing! Sitting on our arses, thinking it through! How about actually *doing* something?'

He stared at me and didn't answer. Looking into his eyes was like looking into a dark well. I huffed loudly and made to leave.

'Okay,' he said, rising from the chair. 'Let's go.'

My mind was working fast as we walked. I wanted one more person in on this and that needed to be a senior. My initial preference was Draper but my gut went with Metcalf. He had the Res Fellow tag. I'd be using up a lot of credits I had with the guy but it was worth the gamble.

We got to his room and I knocked on the door. Metcalf opened it and I spoke quickly.

'I'm going to have a yack with Beeman and I need you to make sure we don't get interrupted. Can you give me a hand?'

He glanced at Keogh, then back at me. 'What kind of yack?'

'Just a talk.'

Lines of suspicion wrinkled his forehead and his eyes narrowed a little. Here was a Resident Fellow elected by College Council, dutybound to its resident students. To lead by example with integrity, honour, and decorum. To instil unconditional respect for college laws and codes of practice as if he'd written them up himself.

'There's been an incident,' I decided to give him more. 'We think he drugged his ex-girlfriend and who knows what he did with her after that. It can't go on. You guys don't want to deal with him, fine. But someone has to, before the cops do.'

Putting him on the spot like that was a shitty trick, but after everything I'd gone through as a first-year I felt a sense of poetic justice. As the seconds ticked by I was tempted to add that I'd do this with or without him, but thought better. It suddenly became very important to me that he make the decision without it. Out of all the seniors here, I looked up to this guy the most.

'Steve,' he sighed, 'you don't want to—'

'You know what sucks?' I said impatiently. 'You all pick on guys like Babs all the time. Call it tradition, character development . . . whatever. They're good kids. Yet here's this fucking weed you just don't want to pull.'

He studied me for a few seconds more, then gave me his back. I thought he was retreating into his room, but he shut the door and said, 'All right, let's see what we got.'

I couldn't help feeling proud of myself as I led the way. One more roll of the dice was left. The adrenalin was already kicking in; there was a spring in my step and an edge to my senses. I didn't try to fight it. There was a good chance I'd calm myself down if I did, and that would just lead to an about-face. The wisdom of this wasn't lost on me, but neither was the notion that it was now or never.

'He's watching a movie in the JCR,' I explained. 'I want to take him to the games room and if anyone's in there that won't leave then I need you'— I dipped my head Metcalf's way — 'to kick them out. Then just go stand by the door, make sure no one comes in for about five minutes.' I delighted in giving instructions to an RF. Keogh said nothing, just walked obediently behind.

'Listen,' Metcalf said, 'I think I should deal with this.'

I glanced over my shoulder, said it all with the look I gave him. Metcalf didn't argue and my respect for the guy went up another notch. We made a right-angled turn into D-Wing cloister and I increased my pace. We reached the JCR without further discussion. Once inside, I told Keogh and Metcalf to wait and negotiated my way between the chairs.

I came up to Beeman from behind and tapped his shoulder. That bag of bloody chips was still there on his lap. 'Hey Beeman,' I said affably, kneeling down so as to not obstruct people's view. 'Can we have a word? I need to talk to you.'

I turned my face Keogh and Metcalf's way. The gesture was deliberate and I wanted him to notice. Sure enough, Beeman craned his head and his beady eyes squinted with suspicion when he saw them. The thought occurred to me then that I could have planned this better. I'd never spoken to the guy and here I was with two henchmen standing by.

'What about?'

'Something important. It's pretty serious and we need to hear your side of the story.'

I saw it kick in. His eyes widened a little and he sat up more in his seat. 'What'd you hear?'

A couple of heads turned our way now.

'Not here,' I said, just above a whisper. 'Is the games room okay?' I had to will my show of insouciance. This was it. Without his consent, it was all over. 'Trust me. It's important.'

More seconds passed. 'Okay,' he said, and I smiled falsely. He was playing it cool, probably thought that whatever we had on him would never be enough. He stood and left his unfinished bag on chips on his seat. I led the way out and Metcalf and Keogh fell in behind us. We strolled through the corridors like regular folks and arrived at the games room.

I opened the door and saw two chaps inside. They were good guys I'd come to like, on the level. Perhaps it was our expressions, perhaps it was their intuition, but at once they sensed something was up. They stopped what they were doing and gave us their full attention.

'Gents,' I said, 'can you give us a moment in here alone?'

They looked us over, glanced at each other. Without a word they put down their pool cues. I held the door open and they stepped through. I ushered Beeman and Keogh inside and closed the door. Surprise showed on Beeman's face when he realised our RF hadn't followed us inside. He watched Keogh go over to the pool table and lean against it, then he turned back to me.

'That's right.' The charade over, there was venom in my voice now. I stepped right up to him and stood face to face. 'This is between me and you.'

His face lost a little colour and he shuffled back a step.

'You've been upsetting your ex-girlfriend.' I only said it so he'd know where I was coming from.

'That's none of your business.'

My hand came up quick, a fake to hit him in the face, and at the last instant stopped short. Beeman raised his hands reflexively to block his face, and when nothing came his arms stayed that way long enough for me to grab his right wrist and pull his whole body forward and off balance. I transferred all my weight on my left leg and drove my right knee deep into his guts that were soft as a pillow. Air whooshed out his lungs as he doubled over and I knew the groan that followed was no exaggeration.

Without pause I drove my elbow down hard onto his spine. From personal experience, when done properly this feels like a knife in your back. With two strikes I'd taken the fight out of him. I mightn't have been a match for Ali or Frazier, but hit a gorilla like this properly and it'll turn as defenceless as a lump of jelly. I wasn't interested in complying with the Geneva Convention of fight rules.

I belted him in the face a few times and made his nose and lips bleed before he went down. As he lay curled up and wheezing on the ground I got a few groans out of him with a kick or two, not hard enough to rupture a spleen or burst a kidney, though by the sound he made you'd think so. He didn't offer the slightest resistance.

It would have lasted no more than half a minute. Beeman lay whimpering on the ground like a wounded puppy. I stood over him.

'Here's the story. You bother the girls again, I've told them to come to me. You take advantage over any of them, they wake up somewhere not knowing how they got there, they'll be coming to me. Only next time it won't be just me sticking the boot in.'

'Thanks for hearing my side of the story,' he moaned weakly.

'If it makes you feel any better,' I booted him in the guts again, 'it wouldn't have made a difference.'

I knelt down, grabbed a fistful of his greasy hair and hauled his face closer. 'No one likes you here, mate. I have it on good authority that it would be in your interests to fuck off out of this college. You want to take your chances, you want to make noises, then we let everyone know how you have a thing for horses' dicks. We might even bring the cops into it, tell them a thing or two we know about. Do you hear where I'm coming from, you sick maggot?'

I stood up, wondering if there was anything I'd missed. Not much.

'Fuck off out of here,' I repeated, and kicked him once more for good measure.

He stayed on the ground and didn't move. I glanced over at Keogh, leaning against the wall. Pumped as I was had me ignorant to as minor an issue as what he might be thinking, but I did notice that his face was strangely without expression. Not that this fooled me. Something was going on in there, it was just impossible to fathom what.

That was it. I walked to the door and stopped to wait for Keogh. He went over to Beeman lying on the ground and stood over him with a look that seemed a blend of pity and loathing. Then he joined me at the door and I pushed it open.

Outside, Metcalf and the two boys were waiting. Their gaze went to the crumpled mess lying on the floor and they didn't say a thing.

'Beeman and I didn't see eye to eye on something,' I obliged their wordless enquiry. 'For the record, it was just me and him. The guy's a pussy and can't fight for shit.' It was important to get that side of it straight.

Metcalf looked at me like a lost kid.

Fifteen

When you start to get glances from people you barely know, when someone's gaze from a distance lingers on you a little longer than normal, you know people have been talking about you. When someone like Pronk taps you on the shoulder while you're eating lunch and asks out of the blue, 'What's this job I hear you did on Beeman, Chambers?' the talk dries up and you have the table.

It's not as if they were ignorant. A remark here, a rumour there, and you know snippets of the backstory had been well and truly circulated. Dots had been joined and a picture formed. The feedback I got reassured me that that picture was pretty close to accurate. Beeman didn't have a lot of friends, or at least none that mattered. The consensus indicated that he deserved it, one way or another. I wasn't so sure about Keogh, though. He'd barely talked to me since.

The powers-that-be ignored so much that went on in this place I'd assumed my fling with Beeman barely raised an eyebrow, but then Sproule cornered me as I headed across the courtyard after dinner Wednesday night. He took me to an empty corner and in a straight-faced, business-like fashion, chewed my ear off. I stood there quietly taking it in, feeling less respect for the guy with each word that left his mouth. That's all the guy was to me – one big mouth. Of mice, not men. All title, no mettle. Just another art student with two much time on his hands. I'd had my suspicions ever since that little speech of his at our inaugural JCR meeting, and this confirmed it. I shut his sanctimonious rot out after a while and settled for an image of him scarpering from a fray with his tail between his legs, coming back only when it was safe to bravely vow retribution upon those not around to hear it. I'd seen it plenty.

When at last he gave his tongue a rest, I offered my case. Told him how everything pointed to this prick, that he needed sorting, and so I sorted. Asked if he'd heard what he'd done to Marion, got no response and so I elaborated. Told him about the bottle Draper and I found in his car, and to my surprise he said he'd heard about that. Just stood there like it didn't mean a thing. That stumped me. I gave up after that.

'You don't go beating up on guys just because you got a hunch,' he said in an authoritative manner, like he had it in him.

'This was more than a hunch.'

'You don't know that for sure.'

'Yeah I do. You do too, just don't want to admit it. And for all the tough talk that goes on in here, you'd let this slime crawl around campus doing whatever sick shit he feels like.'

He shook his head as if I was beyond help. It was tempting to tell him one of his lieutenants had given me the all clear, but it appeared our secretary wasn't all up to speed, and out of respect for Metcalf I didn't want to bring him into it. I put it to him another way.

'I wasn't the only one that thought he had it coming. Plenty of your boys wanted it, just didn't say so.'

'No, you got it wrong,' he said firmly. 'I don't know what hole you were brought up in, but you don't bring that ghetto-shit into this college, mate.'

It was my turn to shake my head. 'You can stand by and watch Pronk piss on Babs, and say something like that.' I'd said it with as much disgust as I could muster. 'You gotta be kidding me.'

A shade passed over his face, left him stuck for a second or so. But he recovered quickly. 'What are your movements tomorrow?'

I shrugged. 'The usual, why?'

'Will you be here at one?'

'I could be.'

'Do it then,' he said, like it was an order. 'I gotta go see Keogh.' Then he made to go.

'What for?'

'Chris and Trent want to talk to both of you,' he said over his shoulder. There was a triumphant note in his voice. 'It's out of my hands now.'

I barked a short laugh. 'Don't flatter yourself.'

'Just be here after lunch.'

I retired to my room and tried to focus on modes of development in triploblastic animals, but that bloody Sproule had put a monkey on my back. After an hour or so of study, five minutes of which might have been productive, I tossed my pen aside and took off to Keogh's room.

I gave his door a couple of knocks and pushed it open. Keogh never locked his door.

'Come right in,' he grumbled. He was sitting at his desk and as I walked in he pushed a drawing away and put some papers on top of it.

'What's that?'

'Nothing.'

I moved closer. 'Show me that.'

He flicked it up reluctantly. I caught a flash of black crayon, then he tried to hide it again. 'Here, gimme a squiz.'

With a snort, he handed it over. Drawn in sharp black strokes was a man in tattered clothes carrying a lifeless woman in his arms, surrounded by rubble. Skyscrapers stood crumbling in a smoking, apocalyptic background. Despite the gloominess of the image, even I could recognise the talent in the hand that drew it. The list with this guy just didn't stop.

'Not bad Jase,' I said. 'Bit morbid though.' I handed it back and he placed it aside. I mind-filed it away for the time being and sat down on his bed.

'Sproule come see you?'

'Yeah.'

'What'd he say?'

Much the same as what he'd said to me, by the sound of it. Keogh had made himself available for the Principal's office after lunch the next day. The Principal's office. What were we in for? A high school caning?

'You going?' I asked.

'Do we have a choice?'

I watched him closely. 'You got a problem with what we did, don't you?'

There was a pause before he answered. 'Been thinking about it.'

'And?'

He regarded me deeply. 'Okay.' He flicked his crayon away and leaned back. 'Don't you think it's dangerous?'

'What?'

'Think about it. We beat into this loser and it pays off. Makes it easier for next time. You think you got it under control so you stretch it, and stretch it, and before you know it, you're beating into guys like Babs for eating dinner before a senior sits down. You know what I'm talking about.' He said it in a tone that made me shrink. I turned my head away. It wasn't fair to use that against me.

'It's all been tried plenty,' he went on. 'You think you'd be different, and there lies the danger. Every bastard tyrant in your history books would've started off with the same noble intentions.' He shook his head sadly. 'We're just not good enough, mate.'

I stared at him long and hard, feeling my surprise flip into anger. He said it all with such a righteous tone of voice it felt like I was getting a sermon from dad. I could ignore Sproule's lecture. I was ready for our principal. I'd give as good as whatever Nat threw at me. I didn't give a rat's what anyone said. But Keogh's opinion mattered to me. I realised then that his was the only one that did. That he was the only person that could give me cause for doubt. And I didn't like it, not one little bit. I'd stuck my neck out for the betterment of the human race, been silently backed by just about everyone that mattered, and here he was taking the moral high ground.

'What . . ?' I stuttered, gobsmacked. 'How can you . . .' The words wouldn't come. I felt like a kid stumbling over impossible dictation. 'And you can't work me out?' I blurted. 'You of all people, always standing up for the moral principle?'

'Sure, I got caught up in it at first,' Keogh admitted. 'And truth to tell – this dropkick – probably good for him. For that reason I went along with it, and for that reason I can live with it. Just this once. But don't ask me to do it again. Shake hands with the devil mate, one day he'll come knocking.'

'Oh shutup.'

'It's like this hazing bullshit,' he said tiredly. 'It gets out of hand. You wait. Someone's gonna get killed one day.'

'Oh, come on. Don't go all bigger picture on me now. This one's a no-brainer, your worship. This guy bloody deserved it.'

'And he'll get what's coming to him, in the long run. The way he's wired up, the factory spat out a dud. One way or another it'll catch up with him.'

'That's the bloody point!' I raised my voice. 'He did get what was coming to him! In the only language he understands! All this crap we get told about how no one's above the law – what do you do when it don't work? Let the deadbeats of the world get away with it?'

'And you think you can make a difference, working your way through them one by one?'

I stood up. 'Screw you,' I said on my way out the door.

I got back to my room and flopped onto my bed. I stared at that ceiling for a long time. It occurred to me that I might have screwed up on this one. Though I hadn't expected backslapping from the boys or thankful women lining up at my door, I hadn't expected an investigation from high command either. Hopefully I was in for nothing more than a repeat of the diatribe I got from Sproule.

Tonight was my mid-week appointment with Nat, and the hour was approaching. She'd want an update on this Beeman business and I wasn't sure I wanted to give it. She must have been one of the few oblivious to what I'd done because she'd have tracked me down by now otherwise. And not for the reasons I'd have hoped. Despite her eagerness for me to fly into this, I doubt she'd have endorsed me giving the guy a hiding. Nat detested violence. Stories I'd told her about the havoc my local crew had wrought over the years made her bristle with contempt, a lot of which was directed back onto me. I'd get all the adages like *what goes around comes around*, and *violence begets violence*, etcetera, and I tended to agree with her. Some guys just had that way about them. Was I one?

Best I not mention it. Not tonight. If she knew I was booked into the Principal's office the next day, it would only fire her up more.

Keogh's take on this had depressed me enough and I didn't feel like the double whammy.

I lay on my bed, soaking up the time. The later I got to her place, the less chance for discussion. I knew I should hit the books before heading over, but the effort eluded me.

When I got there her roommates had all gone to bed and she was the only one up. I apologised for my lateness and gave her some fib about an assignment due tomorrow. She said that was okay and asked if I wanted to watch a bit of TV, and I was grateful I didn't have to lie a second time when I told her I was tired. There was nothing altered in her demeanour other than her unlikely silence once the greetings were done. And that I'd prepared for.

'Nat, there's been a development and I'll fill you in when I know more. I'm not in the mood for an interrogation tonight.'

I'd used a tone that left no room for misunderstanding. Her mouth half-opened and I saw a question coming, but she let it go. I brushed past her and marched up the stairs.

'It's late,' I said over my shoulder. 'I just want to go to bed.'

I'd never been into the office of our college principal. Shiny wooden desk and not a paper clip out of place, out-tray full and in-tray almost empty. A nice little picture of smiling family angled toward us. Tightly wedged books on every shelf. White walls decorated with cheap art and a framed Bachelor of Psychology Degree (Honours) awarded to Christopher Hatchett.

Finch closed the door behind us and Chris stood from his desk and leaned forward to shake my hand, then Keogh's. The glass panels on the wall cupboards behind him were so polished I could see the grin on my face.

'Boys, thanks for coming,' he said. 'Have a seat.'

Keogh and I sat down opposite. Finch dragged a chair forward and positioned himself to one side like an umpire at a tennis match; a symbolic gesture of neutrality I wondered. Though I barely knew him, I was glad for his presence. I'd come to like our college president. What won me were his speeches. Thoughtful and well-spoken, he had the rare ability to engage rather than bore, to be frank without being blunt, and his humour always came with tact and intelligence. Brave was the man who dared to heckle because our Pres had a lightning wit that gave far better than what he got. In him I sensed a genuine pride and commitment to what college stood for, to what we stood for, and I suspect he didn't turn as blind an eye to what went on in this place as it might have appeared. The most serious blights to our good college name always seemed to occur when he wasn't around – like the things they did to Babs – and I would have loved to be a fly on the wall at their Senior Common Room meetings because the conduct of many a habitual offender tended to moderate in the aftermath. For a little while, at least.

There was a bit of small talk about how our studies were going, and how rugby was going, before Chris got down to business.

'Okay gentlemen, I understand you've assaulted Charles Beeman. I've heard his version, now I'd like yours.'

I'd only spoken to him once, doing the rounds the year before when I was exploring which colleges to apply for. In his mid-fifties, he had an easy smile and a persona as crisp and neat as his office. Being on a first-name basis with the students implied a certain amount of respect, and it occurred to me then that I hadn't heard a single derogatory remark made about him. He had a presence about him, a wise old shine in his eyes that called for the truth. So I gave it to him. With omissions, of course. After all, truth told with omissions is still the truth, isn't it?

I told him I'd seen magazines in his room to make any respectable gentleman of St Phillips puke, but not that we'd busted into his room. I was up front telling him I'd gotten into his boot and found suspect liquid in a bottle, but not that Draper had been with me. I told him I knew of two girls he might have used it on, the last one only recently. At that his face took on a serious fold.

'Did she go to the police?'

'Didn't think she'd be believed.'

He squinted then, like he'd picked up a flaw. It did occur to me to say, 'Well, the last one was his ex, and they played dangerously kinky games on occasion, but I've already thought of that, and I'm still of the opinion that she told the truth,' but I held off on that one.

When I arrived at the affair he was really interested in, I watered it down by saying I'd taken Beeman to the games room with the intention of talking to him, things got heated and he started swinging. Not my fault he can't fight his way out of an air bubble. By the time I'd finished I knew I'd told a barefaced lie, but something in Chris's piercing gaze made me think he preferred to hear it that way. Like it would have made things more difficult for him if I'd admitted going in there with the sole intention of belting crap out of the guy.

'Charles claims Jason was involved,' Chris said at the end.

I glanced over at Keogh, sitting there quietly. 'He went in with me, but he didn't touch him.'

'That's not what Charles said.'

'Then it's a matter of who's word is more reliable.'

'Okay,' Chris said. 'We'll deal with what we know happened.'

The speech that followed surprised me. Similar in content at least to Sproule's courtyard effort, there was a subtle, yet very important difference. The more he went on the more I listened for it, listened to every intonation in his voice, every word. They were carefully chosen, like he was reading from a script. It reminded me of a politician's speech; a speech that had to be said. He was chastising me but his tone lacked punch, and his steely gaze never stayed on me long enough to hammer home the point he was making. Someone must have been in his ear, someone with integrity enough for Chris to take seriously. That ruled out Sproule. It must have been the Pres, or Metcalf.

Having said what he had to, he let out an exaggerated sigh and finished with what mattered. 'The point is we can't tolerate an unprovoked attack on a fellow college student. You even drew your Resident Fellow into it, persuaded him to accompany you on the pretext that you were only going to talk with Beeman, correct?'

He raised an eyebrow. I felt more relieved now than ever for having chosen Metcalf over Draper for the games room finale. Whatever I was in for, Metcalf was spared. After all you can't have someone punished too severely in this place when his dad is a respected alumnus who sits on the Standing Committee of Convocation. I obliged him with a short nod, and he went on as if the enquiry had never been put to me.

'Despite what Beeman may or may not have done, you've taken the matter into your own hands and assaulted him, rather badly I'm led to believe. The colleges are under a lot of pressure to stamp out bullying and intimidation and this goes well beyond that. Had you reported him there are any number of ways the matter could have been handled. Yours isn't the first report of sexual assault in the colleges.'

'With respect Chris,' I said, 'that approach doesn't seem to work very well.'

'That's not true.'

I shrugged indifferently. 'I saved you the trouble, then.'

He looked me straight in the eye. 'We're suspending you both from college for eight weeks. Any fees you've paid will be credited back to you.'

Now *that* caught me off guard. I think I was more surprised than angry. Who on Earth ever got suspended from college? I looked over at Keogh staring into space, and then the gravity of what I'd done really did hit home.

'Are you for real?' I groaned. 'With all the crap that goes on here, you take issue over this?'

'Eight weeks almost takes you to the exams, so you may wish to consider not returning this year at all,' Chris suggested. 'You can reapply for residency next year if you're still interested, and your situation will be reviewed. Consider yourselves lucky that Beeman hasn't taken it up with the police.'

A dry laugh escaped my mouth. 'I dare the bastard.'

No one said anything. I glanced over at Keogh. The guy hadn't reacted to a thing during the whole discussion. A show of support would have me firing on all cylinders, but my one and only ally stayed quiet in his fathomless world.

I dropped my head and scoured my brain for what I knew about the College Act, which was zip. No, I had to assume Chris was acting in full accordance with its wonderful prescriptions and by-laws and umpteen commandments. It was a bitter disappointment, but not the end of the world. The rugby season was just about over, as were most of the intercollegiate sporting events I was interested in. A couple of weeks more of silly season, two of holidays, and then a month and a bit until exams and the end of the year. It wasn't that bad. A glimmer of hope seemed to brighten the gloom.

'Okay,' I said, nodding my head resignedly. 'Okay, fine. If the decision's been made, I'll wear it. But this has nothing to do with him.' I jerked a thumb at Keogh. 'This was my idea. He never touched him.' There. I'd fallen on my sword and our principal was a reasonable man.

'That may be,' Chris said, 'but he was there, and that makes him complicit.'

'You're kidding.'

'I'm afraid not.'

I felt my temper flare. My respect for Chris went south and I didn't hold back. I gave it everything save swearing and shouting, using every argument I could think of from a matter of principle to burning the innocent. But the Principal and President sat there like rocks. Just like Keogh.

We went around in circles for five minutes before Chris put an end to it. 'Steve, this isn't up for negotiation. The admissions officer has already been notified and there's nothing more to discuss. You and Jason have until the end of the term – two weeks away – to find alternative accommodation. Your Resident Fellow will sort out anything that needs taking care of. Let Sandra know when you're departing and she'll credit any fees back to you. You'll need to leave her your keys.'

A spell of heavy silence passed. I heard someone call out to someone a long way off. The thump of a door closing somewhere. The world moving on.

I stood stiffly and looked Chris in the eye. He looked back. What the heck, another principal might have taken in much further. I nodded defeatedly and held out my hand for him to shake. He took it and I tightened my grip as I spoke.

'Just one more time, for the record,' I said. 'Please leave Jason out of this.'

Chris gave me the thinnest of smiles and said nothing. I let go and stepped back. Keogh moved into my space and held out his hand for Chris. They shook hands and Finch opened the door for us.

'It's just eight weeks, Steve,' our Pres said consolingly, and I felt my morale flutter a little. As I stepped through the door Chris spoke.

'You scared Beeman off, by the way.'

I stopped and turned around. 'Say again?'

'He's given notice. He's leaving St Phillips.'

I turned away so he wouldn't see me smile.

We walked into the courtyard with our heads down. It was a typical weekday lunch hour with boys idly standing or sitting around, talking. A game of volleyball had good numbers. Sights I would soon no longer be a part of.

'Shit,' I muttered. 'Didn't see that coming,' I turned to Keogh. 'Sorry man.'

'Yeah,' he said. 'Now I'm late for my chem prac.'

He walked away and I thought I saw a little less spring in his step than normal. Was certainly a lot less in mine.

Back in my room I hit the bed and curled into a ball. Damned if a film of water didn't blur my eyes. It wasn't the inconvenience of being turfed out of residence that got to me now, or the things I would miss. It was that soul-crunching feeling of being not wanted. Being dumped, big time. I'd been shunned, spat out by a respectable academic institution with all its officialdom and Acts of Parliament and lord knows what else behind it. The hard yards were behind me. I'd kept my head low, ducked the worst of the crap thrown my way and slotted in. And I'd blown it. Whatever it was that college required, I'd failed. I was no better off than Beeman.

Naturally my thoughts turn to my one-and-only, and even then I didn't presume for a second she'd offer the comfort I needed. I thought to give myself a day or so, get my hard-luck story pitch perfect. But I knew she'd get word soon enough – from Lisa no doubt – and so I decided to get it over with. I could just imagine the rot she'd throw into a version of events.

If ever I'd earned the right to miss a tute or two, today was it. I think I drifted off for a while but couldn't tell. A presence hovered over me like bad company.

Around five I changed for rugby training and had just stepped from the door when a passer-by asked if it was true that we'd been kicked out of college. Wow. We were news already.

Heads swung my way when I entered the JCR, and my face flushed warm as a globe as I plodded toward my teammates. They treated me to a generous cocktail of humour and commiseration before we left, and kept right at it until our warm-up laps on the oval put space between us.

Training was good for me. I focussed on what I was there for and burned up a bit of angst. Only when I'd sat down for dinner afterwards did I start stewing over it again. Keogh came into the dining hall a bit later with the boys of the higher grades and we talked openly about options for appeal, which sounded bleak. Those in the know let me know that the colleges were obligated to keep these things low-key. In-house. The College Act gave the Principal the power to suspend students for up to eight weeks. Period. Throw phrases like *due process* back at them and I'd only incur the wrath of bigger guns. A few minutes on the subject were enough to convince me that we were on our own.

I retired to my room and took a shower. The warmth of it was as soothing as a Nat massage and breathing in the steam gave my mind a fresh lift. This was a tough assignment, but not impossible. The oldies weren't a problem. I'd tell them a place to live off-campus had come up and I felt like a change. The truth again, with omissions. As long as college refunded the balance, they'd be happy.

Nat was a different story. By the time I was ready to leave I was having second thoughts about going over at all. I'd worked myself up a bit. I suspected I'd be in for the same roasting Hatchett and Sproule had given me, and when I thought about it, who was she to give it? This woman who for months I'd been procrastinating about? Maybe this was the opportunity I'd been waiting for. Soon as she started in on me, that'd be my cue. See yuh round, kiddo.

In this ambivalent frame of mind, I headed off. It was a route I knew to the step. Ever since I started taking it, I'd wonder if it was the last. Six months later and I was still wondering.

The wind moaning through the crowns of the trees was apt for the occasion I thought, had me ruminating deeply on these up and down feelings I had for the girl. I'd criticise her often enough for being indecisive but situations like this made me think I was worse. There was a good chance we were in for a fight and here I was walking into it. I kept telling myself she could take it or leave it but somehow it wasn't as easy as that. *I am the captain of my soul,* wrote Henley. I wondered if he was a bachelor when he penned it.

One of Nat's flatmates let me in. I kept my greeting brief and climbed the squeaky stairs. At Nat's door I stopped and took a breath. A knock or two later and the door opened.

'Oh, hello,' she said, and her face brightened up. She always liked my unannounced visits. She closed the door and I sat on her bed.

'Listen . . . Nat . . . thanks for being patient throughout all of this.' My head felt heavy and my voice came out soft. 'Did you hear what happened?'

The look she gave me said no. So I told her. As it happened, the whole truth. Her gaze went far-off and she didn't say a thing, just sat there beside me like she'd gone into torpor. I finished up by trying to make a joke of it.

'So, if you know anyone who needs housemates, let us know. We haven't been swamped with offers.'

Her prolonged silence made me edgy. Soon as it sunk in, I knew I'd be getting a blast.

'I'd better go Nat. Sorry for the drama.'

I rose from the bed and she followed me up and took my arm. 'I'm so sorry.'

'What?'

She pulled me close and gave me a strong hug. It felt good. Really good. 'God, I'm such a . . .' she mumbled something I didn't catch, but I did hear the last bit. 'I'm so sorry.'

'Sorry for what?' I genuinely had no idea what she was talking about.

'I got you into this. I shouldn't have . . . made you . . .'

'Hey . . .' I pushed a space open for her to see me. 'You didn't make me do a thing. This was my choice, all of it. You're not responsible.'

She looked at me misty-eyed, then dipped her head onto my chest. 'Do you want to get a coffee?'

My head felt so buoyant I thought it'd float off my shoulders. 'Sure.'

She gathered her purse. 'My shout,' she said, and opened the door.

She took my hand and gave it a squeeze. I waited until she turned her head away before shaking mine clear, but it didn't work. I was still in a daze as she led me down the stairs.

You knew where you stood with most people in college. Priority was those casually scribbled but damningly significant marks atop those papers you've invested with your finest. Interpersonal skills was a phrase to learn for job applications, years later. You got away with being yourself.

For someone I'd rate as one of the most honest and direct people I'd ever met, Keogh was hardest to figure. It would have been a burden off my mind to know what went on in his. There was no dip in his mood, no remark one way or another. Not even in jest. Didn't bring it up at all. Went about his business in a way to suggest he'd shrugged it off. His quiet dignity though was so much a part of his habitual demeanour you couldn't read into his silence like you could with most people.

Our last home game was that weekend against Randwick. We were up on the hill enjoying a couple of quiet ones, gloating over our lower grade wins and barracking firsts on loudly. Keogh was a rare inclusion in our gathering. After playing seconds he usually benched for firsts, but he'd carried a nagging shoulder injury for a while and by questionable coincidence today he'd sat out.

For the first time in weeks, our firsts showed form. Twenty minutes into the game they'd taken the lead, and when our fly-half intercepted a pass thrown by the opposition fullback to score a length of the field try the cheer turned deafening. Their fullback was an ex-international and a legend even now, but in his twilight years he'd lost the edge to keep him out of first division on weekends. We could see him beneath the far posts with his head down and hands on his hips while his teammates stood to one side in a huddle. Pronk, standing not far from us, had singled him out for heckling long before then. This latest gaffe put him in heaven.

'Not so flash now eh, you big hero? You should have retired years ago!' he shouted delightfully, the beer in his hand perched on his gut. A bit of a balancing act would have seen it stand there unassisted.

We scored two more unanswered tries before half-time, the home crowd lapped it up. It was one of those rare games when just about every one of their star players chose that day to have a shocker. It got worse second half. The teams swapped ends and now every time we scored the opposition had to assemble along the goal line down our end of the oval, well within hearing of the mildest taunt. Leading the merciless chorus was Pronk.

'Take a look at yourself, Wonderboy!' he shouted for the umpteenth time. 'You're on the slippery pole, heading down! See you in fifths next year, you has-been!'

'Hey Nev!' someone shouted. I turned around and saw Keogh glowering at him. I switched back to Pronk and saw him glance around, dopey enough probably to assume the call had been to someone else.

'You there – Nev!' Keogh called again, louder this time. Pronk turned his head the right way.

'Yeah, that's right,' Keogh continued. 'You! Neville fucking never-was. When was the last time you played for Australia?' I don't think I'd ever heard Keogh use the f-word before.

Pronk glared back at him, the boys around me fell into a hush. The entire hill fell into a hush. Pronk didn't flinch, Keogh didn't flinch. Not a set of eyes was pointed anywhere else.

'No?' Keogh taunted. 'Then how about you shut up, *wanker.*'

'Pull your head in, idiot,' Pronk snarled back at him. The ref blew his whistle, our conversion was successful. The Randwick players jogged off to restart play.

Pronk didn't have much to say after that.

Sixteen

As a kid, I tried to imagine what it was like to have a brother. There were a lot of lonely rides home on the pushbike, a lot of balls bounced against walls, a lot of board games that gathered dust. No one to practice judo throws with, how to block a punch. I'd hang around kids with brothers and wonder how they could trade blows over something as trifling as whose turn it was on a tricycle, then take turns pushing each other on it as soon as their mother pulled them apart. I wondered how a guy who always bagged his kid brother could have a glow in his eyes as proud as any parent when he watched the little shit kick the winning goal in a soccer game. Or how he could belt crap out of him one day and be prepared to take a hiding himself the next if some bully tried to do the same.

I envied them. For me, loyalty was a choice. With siblings, it was a birthright. Natured and nurtured. They'd been born into a pact free from the scruples of taste, the pitfalls of judgment. The links in the chain that bound them were forged by the hand of the Almighty. . . mother nature . . . call it what you will. Like it or not, they were unbreakable. This was my idea of brotherhood.

As the years rolled by I'd try to plug the hole with kids from various backgrounds, but I never found the proxy I was looking for. It wasn't necessarily the fault of either one of us. The flaw in the deal was often parents. They went where the work was, took the kid with them. Or sent him to a different school. Just one more thing that siblings had over us. They never had to start over with each other.

I'd grown so fond of the notion that I couldn't abandon it. When someone offered loyalty, I offered mine cheap. Friends are supposed to keep you out of trouble. A lot of mine didn't. They were valiant, considerate, and loyal in their own daft way, but true friends don't go the distance by admiring each other at their best. They go the distance by accepting each other at their worst. The local boys didn't protect me from what really mattered – the wrong path. That was up to me. The bonds I shared with a lot of them were straining at their weakest links. That I was giving it less thought with each passing day bore testimony to the stock I put in the friends I'd made since.

To say I felt like a hypocrite for getting Keogh into this mess was to let myself off way too lightly. *Shake hands with the devil mate, one day he'll come knocking*. And come a-knocking he had. Keogh had every right to ditch me. I desperately wanted to make it up to him. The least I could do was assure him he didn't have to do a thing, that I'd find us both lodgings if he didn't mind moving in with the goose responsible for his exile. 'Get me a room furthest away from yours,' was his toneless consent. I couldn't tell if he was joking or not.

A room came up at Palmer Street. They'd had a gutful of Donna; I got the whole story from Mick. In a show of solidarity her housemates sat her down one night and suggested it would be in everyone's interests if she found alternative accommodation. She'd asked why, they'd replied she knew why. She'd raised her voice, they'd raised voices back. They were sick of having to listen to her and Jock's virtual shagging on the couch while they were trying to watch TV, tired of them using up all the hot water in the shower doing the real thing. When Donna retaliated by saying Jen and Karen were just pissed because they couldn't get laid, it got personal. Long before the little sitting was over any goodwill shared between the two sides was as brittle as mouldy bread. She'd stormed off to her room and they'd hardly seen her since. They couldn't wait to get rid of her.

Straight after Mick's briefing I'd gone for a phone and spoke to Gabe, even offered to speed things up by taking Donna's stuff and dumping it on the lawn, after all I was on a roll. But my services were politely declined, and as it turned out, unnecessary. Two days later Mick tapped me on the shoulder during lunch and told me Donna had vanished, personal effects and all. We could move in right away. I must have heaved a sigh of relief louder than her housemates did. I finished lunch and headed eagerly up to Keogh's room.

'Hey,' I said as I entered. 'Hear the news?'

Keogh was sitting at his desk. He glanced over his shoulder, then gave me the back of his head. 'What've you done this time?' he asked in his mortician's voice.

'Donna's moved out,' I said, and closed the door. 'You still interested?'

He moved a paper or two. 'How soon do they want an answer?'

'Soon, I guess.' I waited for him to turn around, but he kept writing. 'You got a better offer?'

'Nope.'

I'd have been disappointed if he'd changed his mind, and I couldn't hide the note of it in my voice. 'You in or not?'

Keogh put down his pen and let out a big sigh. The last time I'd heard that sigh was during the mentoring he'd given me on Beeman. I thought I was in for more but he said nothing.

'Can you have a think and let me know tomorrow?' I asked.

'Sure.'

'If you're in, we can move in this weekend. Nat'll loan us her car.'

He nodded absently. I decided not to push him; I owed him that. I thought what I'd say next might extract a little more enthusiasm.

'By the way, I've been meaning to ask. You know I work for my old man's insurance firm in the holidays. Want to earn some bucks? There's some days there for you if you're interested.'

I'd put it to him by-the-by, but there was far more to it than that. I had to plead with the old man. I'd even offered to work fewer days so the two of us could share the workload.

'What sort of work?' There wasn't the slightest flutter of interest in his voice.

I explained all that and he showed about as much enthusiasm as he did in moving out with me. At the end he even gave me a snort that suggested it was beneath him.

'You want an answer to that right now as well, I suppose?' he asked, drearily almost.

'Well, soon as possible. I have to let the old man know,' I said, almost apologetically. 'We can start next week.'

He picked up his pen, stared off into space. I dipped my head into his line of gaze and peeked into never-never land.

'What is it with you lately?'

He shook himself back, tried to shrug it off. 'Nothing.'

I kept watching him to see if he meant it, and couldn't decide. 'Lisa giving you grief?' It would have taken a load off my mind if that was the reason.

'No.'

'All right, spit it out then.' I'd added a little attitude to my tone. I waited politely but the seconds passed and he didn't say a thing.

I gave him my back and went for the door. 'Shit,' I mumbled faintly, more to myself, 'throw me a bone here.'

I'd almost closed it behind me when he said, 'Hey Steve.' I turned around and he offered me a moody smile. 'Sure. I'll take it. Thanks.'

'Which one?'

'Both,' he said, and shrugged his shoulders. 'What the hell.'

It was like a ray of light on my soul. Our eyes met and held. It was only for a second or two, but that sealed it for me. I don't remember thinking much about brothers after that.

Our last supper was that Friday night, just before the holidays. I walked into the JCR with an image in my head of a guard of honour clapping me through, high-fives and all. There was none of that. No one noticed me.

Keogh was by the noticeboard looking troubled. I went over and saw that the team list for the combined college squad to play Newcastle Uni was pinned up. Though Keogh was always a safe bet, it was good to see his name written there.

'Hey, congrats man.'

He grimaced. 'See the date.'

I did. 'What about it?'

'It clashes with Lisa's hockey presentation.'

Only then did I remember the function he was referring to. I was supposed to be going as well, having made the same commitment to Nat. 'So? That's no big deal.'

'She thinks it is.'

I waved it away. 'How's the shoulder?'

He gave it a rub and screwed his face. 'All right I suppose,' he said, almost regretfully.

I took it with greater encouragement than he did. The fixture was a still month away and I wondered if the timing or the team announcement had something to do with his imminent departure. Perhaps they needed to secure his inclusion in the team while he was still, technically, a member of one of the colleges. I also found it promising that they assumed he'd be fit to play at all. With an army of flankers to choose from they could have easily overlooked him on account of his shoulder, but they'd afforded him that decency cherished by all players – the opportunity to decide for yourself if you're fit to play. The combined college team had their hides kicked for two years now and they wanted their best. Keogh might have been a bit of a stiff, but he was a damn fine rugby player.

During dinner I caught snippets of conversation from the table where Keogh had been invited over by the seniors. They were talking up the rep fixture and he was carrying on like there'd been a death in the family. When I could stand it no longer, I got up and invited myself over.

'Let me get this right,' I said, settling into a vacated spot opposite him. 'You've been picked to play in a rep side against Newcastle, your old stomping ground. Besides catching up with your old buddies, selectors will be there, including those who've watched you these past years and will sure as bugs to a light be watching you this time. And you're worried because Lisa's pissed that you won't be her dinner date for this Mickey Mouse function of hers.'

Keogh put another forkful of mash and steak into his mouth. 'She's in the running for the big one,' he said between chews.

'And that makes a difference because . . .'

'I committed myself weeks ago. She'll be coming to our rugby presentation; I should go to her hockey one.'

'That was before this came up.'

'Yeah well, it's not like things haven't changed since.' The tone he used stung me.

'Aw Jase,' Fuller crooned, 'don't be like that.'

I turned to the big unit. 'Slap me in the face, will you?'

'Slap him in the face.'

Hardy came to my aid. 'You're not thinking of bailing out, are you?' he said to Keogh.

'The game, no,' Keogh assured him. 'But if I headed back here straight afterwards I'd make it back by what – eight or nine?'

'You nicking off before the post-match dinner won't look good when they ask,' Hardy explained cordially, but there was a stern message beneath. 'Playing rep is as much about rubbing shoulders off the field as on, trust me.'

'Help us out here Jeffro,' I pleaded.

Fuller growled obligingly, 'Keogh – you're going, you big pussy.'

Keogh sat there in a shadow of gloom.

'Feel bad about it if it makes you feel better,' Hardy went on, 'but we go up on the bus as a team, and we come back on the bus as a team. The next day. Hungover as hell hopefully, but as a team. That's the deal. Tell that to your missus.'

Keogh nodded like a broken man. It was the first time I saw him rely on an excuse to get his way.

'I'll remind her on the night anyway, since I'll be there.' I'd add a bit of spite when I did, too. I couldn't believe she expected Keogh to piss it all away on account of him filling a chair.

'Nat play hockey, does she?' Hardy asked.

'Nah,' I said. 'I'm wearing a skirt and inviting myself.'

'So what's new?'

The boys chewed their dinners without speaking. 'I can't believe you need talking into this,' I said to Keogh. 'Wish I was going.'

I meant it, too. I could only dream of something like this. I imagined how happy Nat would have been for me. She'd have thrown her arms around me and told me how proud she was, and not a word would she utter about some dinner. Not for the first time I wondered how she and Lisa could be such good friends.

We moved into our new lodgings the next day. I offered Donna's room to Keogh, said I'd take the study. He nodded and said nothing, which was fine with me. I knew that was his way of saying thanks.

That night our partners joined us for a big dinner. Talk revolved around the merits of living off-campus but the more they tried to console us, the more it added to my melancholy. Nat stayed over and added a woman's touch to my study-cum-bedroom the next day, turning into a nest more hers than mine. She cemented her claim by planting a few discreet female bits and pieces in my drawers, along with a toothbrush in the bathroom. She couldn't hide her enthusiasm as she went about it, either.

Seventeen

When the old man first got me the job, like Keogh I'd asked what sort of work it was. 'Mind-numbing tripe good for comparing when you're old as me and feel like moaning about your career choice,' was his fairly accurate call. My resume would shine with skills like filing, binding books, opening the boom-gate when it got stuck, emptying recycling bins, changing water bottles and lifting things people were too lazy to lift themselves. The greatest challenge came in the form of sending notices off to members when their cheques bounced. They gave us a desk in a corner where we could listen to a radio quietly and not be bothered. Enough people our age floated about for conversation, along with a couple of decent girls who didn't mind a flirt.

Doing the introductory rounds that first morning, Keogh was at his consistent best. Desk to desk and office to office, he wasn't one to waste his words or force a laugh. The jokes got dumber, the questions more mundane, and everyone got the measure they were due.

There was a woman in ledgers called Emily Skinner I'd learnt early on to avoid. She had a tired, dour face, and enough grey in her hair to suggest an age far older than she was. As one of the managers she had her own office and gotten there more from longevity than performance I figured, but by the amount of framed credentials on her walls you'd think it was from them. No photos of family though, and certainly none of partners. Though I didn't report to her directly she assumed it her right to delegate jobs my way as she pleased.

I showed him in and made the introductions. She stood from her desk, put on her best smile and held out her hand all precise and formal, and he shook it. Please to meet you and all that followed, she asked what he was doing at Uni, and after his hallmark short answers Keogh turned his attention to the wall. He glossed over each nicely framed qualification one by one, like he was appraising paintings in an art gallery. Emily watched him with a big smile; probably thought he was awe-struck.

I tried to make a joke of it. 'See anything you like?'

Without turning his head, he floored me. 'What's she trying to hide?'

It reminded me of a time my five-year-old niece asked a woman straight to her face how she got the huge mole on her chin. The smile vanished from Emily's face as if it had been slapped away. Deep creases folded her forehead and her eyes turned dark. Only years in the job, years of training in interpersonal skills and dealing with difficult clients, backed up by the real thing, stopped her from reacting like she'd been thrown paint all over her.

I tried to cover it with a candid laugh. 'Jesus, mate.' It was a fruitless laugh, embarrassment lurking beneath.

'Thank you, Steve. You might want to teach your friend some manners.' She turned her attention to her papers and dipped her head. It was a dismissal.

Heading down the hallway with Keogh following, I turned around and rolled my eyes. 'Mate,' I groaned, 'do me a favour and don't say stuff like that in here.'

'It always intrigues me,' Keogh commented, 'why someone supposedly so good at their job needs to back it up with displays of vanity all over the wall.'

'She got where she is, didn't she?'

'Yeah, and I bet that's all she's got. I know the type. Nothing framed except overrated reminders of her own achievements. What does that tell you? I'm not falling to my knees just because she's trying to compensate.'

'Jesus,' I lamented. 'Aren't you two off to a flying start.'

Later that afternoon the phone rang. I watched Keogh pick up the receiver and give his monosyllabic greeting. A few seconds later he put the phone down and scowled heavily.

'She wants me to bring her the radio.'

'Emily?' I asked, and he nodded.

It wasn't a first. Emily had no qualms expecting service like this from runts like us. I tapped another letter or two on the typewriter. 'So take it to her.'

'Don't think I will.'

I stopped typing and stared at him. 'What's up buddy?'

'She got two legs, she can do it herself. What sort of ask is that?'

'Listen,' I sighed deeply, 'something you should know about this place. It doesn't need us as much as we need it. This is the sort of shit they pay us for. For a fiver an hour, just take it.'

But he didn't move, and I knew there was nothing I could say to make him. I reached for the radio and Keogh pointed a finger at me.

'Don't you do it,' he warned. But I stood up, unplugged the cord and took off with it down the hall. Mail left the office in about half an hour and I usually did the rounds now anyway.

The surprise that showed on Emily's face when I entered her office was quickly replaced by an expression that made me think I'd thrown her a challenge. Words formed on her lips, then she dropped her head back down without a whisper of a thank you. I put the radio on her desk, reached for her out-tray and scooped up a wad of letters. Another habit of hers was to paperclip the letter to the envelope for me to insert and seal. Today her tray was relatively empty, about ten letters or so, and still her royal tongue hadn't wet a single envelope.

I got back to our desk and dropped her wad of letters in front of Keogh. 'Present from Emily. Start licking.' I was only rubbing it in, wanted to see his reaction.

He stared down at them like it was a pile of dog turd. 'What is it with that woman?' He flung the letters to one side.

'Best that I answer the phone from now on, hey Jase?'

He didn't answer.

There's an old saying that if you want to find out the true nature of a person, make them boss. Here everyone was my boss, so I got to know them quite well. On paper I reported to the Manager of Customer Support, a lovely woman who oddly enough gave me the least amount of work. Unofficially, going by the number of menial tasks she made us do, the ballbreaker award went uncontested to Ms Skinner. After a couple of days of her style of management, Keogh went quiet. The office just wasn't big enough for both of them. Any enthusiasm he had for the job, if there ever was any, rewarded his employers with the bare minimum.

On Friday there was a birthday lunch for a staff member. About twenty of us went, including Emily, who congenially sat at the far end of the table. About two minutes after we got back to the office, our phone rang. Keogh was closer to it than me and got it before I could.

As he held the phone to his ear a grin broke from his lips, which made me curious. It took a lot for him to give humour in here its due.

'She wants me to collect some photos,' he said, hanging up the phone. 'If I heard her right, it's between here and where we ate.'

He spoke with such contempt I thought it was directed at me. I knew the shop because I'd picked up photos for her before, and he was right.

'Yeah, so?'

He stared at me and said nothing.

'Just pretend you're back in college, taking shit from the seniors,' I recommended. 'That's what I do.'

Keogh gave me a moment more of fierceness. Then he scooped up a pile of letters, stood from his chair and headed off. It was a determined pace, like he was about to break into a trot. I hurried after him.

He stopped at the door of Emily's office and knocked a couple of times. On receiving an invitation to enter, he opened the door and stepped inside without closing it behind him. I stopped at the doorway.

'Hey there,' he said, and Emily looked up from her work. 'I gotta ask – couldn't get your photos on your way back from lunch?'

The surprise that showed on her face didn't last long. Her manner remained professional, but the effort it required tightened her lips and made her voice snappy. 'I forgot, Jason.'

'Let me show you something,' he said, waving the wad of letters. 'See these letters? None of them are yours. You know how I can tell?

They're all stuck down. Yours are almost always the only ones that never are. But you're definitely on your own when it comes to getting us to bring you a radio, or showing one of your friends all the way up here, or getting milk for your coffee, or picking up photographs . . . just to name a few. Does that bother you?'

'These things take up time, Jason, and I have more important things to do.'

'Crap. You must get a kick out of, surely. Which one of these papers on the wall says your tongue's more delicate or your feet more precious?'

'Excuse me,' she said, frowning heavily now. 'I think you're being very rude. What we pay you for—'

'Woah,' he waved a finger at her, 'you don't pay me, and I'm not your personal assistant.'

They glared at each other, still as desks. Emily was the first to break the spell, glancing at me as if noticing me for the first time. She dropped her gaze to her lap. 'Well, if you think you can come here and choose which jobs you want to do, then you have—'

'Save it,' Keogh interrupted. 'You know that's not what I mean.'

He pressed the point home with his trademark, ice-cool glare, then turned on his heels. I don't think he even saw me on his way out. I about-faced and followed a step or two behind him.

Keogh returned to his seat and gave the typewriter cylinder a twist. 'Don't you say a word,' he warned without looking up. I settled down opposite and watched him hunched over the desk, smacking the bars onto the cylinder roll hard enough to break them. He looked as much at place in front of that typewriter as a gladiator.

I obliged him with peace those last few minutes. Then one of the senior managers walked in; a tall, grey-suited man in his fifties called Brian Reay. He gave Keogh the undertaker's look.

'Jason,' he said, 'I'd like a word with you.'

Heads turned our way almost imperceptibly, followed by a quietness that seemed to turn the volume up our end of the room. Oh yes, people were tuning in now, even if they pretended not to. Reay was too high up to visit our humble section without a good reason.

Keogh kept on typing. 'I'm listening.'

'Could you come with me, please?'

'Something wrong with here?'

Creases of irritation appeared on Reay's face, and he glanced at me in a way to suggest I take heed of the show to follow. 'Will you come with me?' he said. 'There's been a complaint and I'd like your version.'

Keogh stopped typing and gave him his attention. 'I'm sure it's the same as hers. We didn't talk long enough to get confused.'

Reay watched him intensely. 'Do you like working here?'

'Do you?'

Reay broke into a chuckle. 'Okay,' he said, rubbing his hand over his forehead. 'I think I can see what the problem is. I take your answer then as a no.'

'As a matter of fact, I don't mind.'

'It seems you do.'

'Some things, I guess,' Keogh agreed. He leaned back and folded his arms in a way that made it look casual.

'Do you think what you said to Emily might have been out of order?'

'No more than the demeaning crap she asks us to do.'

'Okay . . . okay. Maybe this place isn't suited for you, then.'

'Not if it means being someone's lackey.' He stood from the chair and pushed it into place beneath the desk. He opened a drawer, pulled out his wallet and keys, then yanked the paper out of the typewriter and placed it in his in-tray.

'Well then,' Reay said, adding a note of sarcasm, 'I'm sorry we haven't lived up to your expectations.'

'No you're not,' Keogh sneered. He put his keys into his pocket and held out his right hand. 'Thanks for the time.' There wasn't a trace of spite in his tone; he'd meant it. Confusion slipped over Reay's face as he offered up his own hand hesitantly, like it weighed a bit. Keogh gave it a firm shake.

'You'll need to fill in your timesheet,' Reay told him, dreamily almost.

'Just put in whatever time you reckon. If Steve can collect the pay

I'm owed, I'd appreciate it.'

And with that, he walked out.

Jen and Karen were seated on the lounge in the living room when I got home. 'Jason in?' I asked.

'I think he's in his room,' Jen answered, raising an eyebrow. 'I thought he was working with you today.'

'That he was,' I muttered, and walked off. Once inside my room I flopped onto the bed, hands behind my head. A couple of minutes later there was a knock.

'Steve?' It was Keogh.

'Yeah.'

He came in and closed the door. 'Hey,' he greeted me in an embarrassed sort of way. That was a first. 'Sorry about that business this afternoon.'

'Which part?' My ignorance was politely feigned.

'You made the effort to get me a job . . . your old man has connections there . . . and I carried on like a bit of a dick. Sorry man.'

Until then I hadn't thought of it that way. And now that I did, he had a point. 'Yeah, thanks for that,' I agreed. 'Don't ask for a reference.'

'Did anyone say anything to you?'

I sat up on the bed, exhaled deeply. 'Not especially. A few people asked what happened, but that was it.'

'How much did I make?'

'Let's see. Three and a half days . . . close to the hundred mark maybe, less tax. Was it worth it?'

'Nope.'

'Payday is fortnightly, which means I won't get yours until next week.'

'Sure.'

I thought about my next question, not sure if it was proper. 'Say Jase . . .' I fumbled. 'Is this the first job you've had?'

'Course not.'

'And by that I don't mean working at McDonalds or tossing bricks around. I mean a job where it's all about how you deal with people.

You know – saying nice things you don't really mean, smiling at people you'd rather spit in the face, winning good folks over so you can squeeze them for all the money they're worth. Which often means sucking it up and doing whatever you're told.'

I waited for him to answer, but nothing came.

'Oh well, doesn't matter I suppose. You'll learn.' But part of me wondered if he would. His first proper job by the sound of it and he'd lasted less than a week.

'You and me both,' he said.

'What's that supposed to mean?'

He grinned and gave me the eye. 'You learn how not to get kicked out of college, I'll learn how not to get kicked out of a job.'

'Deal!' I chuckled. 'Probably take us more than one lifetime, though.'

A laugh rolled out of him, and it was like a burst of warm energy. That was the thing about Keogh. The tiniest smile was enough to crack his façade, make you feel you'd won something.

We changed the subject, tossed around some ideas about what we might get up to over the rest of the holidays. I'd be working the next week and only had a couple of free days, there were the homeboys to connect with, Nat was badgering me for some 'you and me' time, but maybe we could hook up with the Phil boys one weekend. As we talked I found it strange he never referred to any former school or football buddies; he wasn't that socially inept not to have made a few. I asked him once if he kept in touch with them and he said he did, but if my own experience with him was any guide I reckon the effort would have been one-sided. The guy was hard work. If not for people ringing him, I reckon he'd turn into a recluse.

We resolved to make an effort, but something always got in the way and it never eventuated. Before I knew it, the holidays were over and we were back at Uni for the home stretch.

Eighteen

Plenty of students don't take to college life. A couple of weeks away from it was enough to realise I wasn't one of them. Despite its inconsistencies, college to me was the beating heart of campus, feeding us like corpuscles into every extremity to see it energised and nourished and given to a soul. It was a world away from the real and less important one, filtered the irrelevant happenings beyond its walls and kept me focussed on what I was there for in a way no friend or parent or scholar ever could. It kept you at just the right distance from people, liked and disliked. Making friends was as easy as knocking on someone's door. And that's not even starting on the academic support it offered.

Fortunately I'd involved myself heavily throughout the year in the sporting and social calendar, so if there was a game to be played or a race to be run, a function to attend or an excuse to be made, I'd be back in the place as if I'd never left it. I became so common a sight you'd think I was still in residence. 'Hey Steve, get kicked out of your new joint as well?' was the standard ribbing. Every now and then, just to heckle them, I'd loaf about the JCR with some fruit or bread I'd pinched from the kitchen.

In my eagerness to find lodgings I hadn't given much thought to how Keogh and I might fare living together. Or with the others. After the episode at the workplace I feared a domineering, value-guided temperament would run the same course in a small house as a large office, but as usual I was wrong. His iron-hard will never surfaced during negotiations about chores, or whose turn it was to buy milk, or what TV show we should watch. He did his share of cooking, cleaning up, gardening. He didn't leave crumbs on the table or the toilet seat up. For a guy prone to vent his strongly-held beliefs whenever they were challenged, he kept oddly quiet during our dinner debates, never argued those radical and outrageous opinions students feel compelled to air. Without saying it in as many words, the girls adored him. I began to wonder though if this strangely agreeable side to him belied some other issue. He'd lost interest in the goings-on in college. Though he'd never been a crowd person, he'd never shied away from them like he was doing now. He'd pass up most offers for a quiet drink or catch up with the boys, preferring instead to hole up in his room where I figured all he did was study, read, or draw those weird pictures of his. The only break in his routine was gym, a swim in the pool, and one or two nights a week over at Lisa's. I asked if he wanted to join Uni's archery club, told him I'd sign up myself if he did, but he scoffed at the offer. 'Fancy darts' was the term he used. He did promise however that he'd be happy to target shoot with just me, if I was interested. His impressive compound bow sat idle in his cupboard and I resolved to make the effort more for his sake than mine.

Oddly enough he hit it off with Skimp, who even managed to get a laugh out of him occasionally. A Bachelor of Business undergrad, our new friend was tidy and fastidious to the point of anal. Tailor-made for accounting. He took care of our bills, rent, and petty cash like a happy pastime. Add to this a complete lack of interest in playing, watching, or commenting on sport, I'd assumed zero compatibility in any department until I discovered his unlikely passion for guns and hunting. We swapped stories and places we'd been, and he mentioned a property he knew out Oberon way. The owner leased it out to a neighbour who ran some cattle. Skimp shot out there with his father on occasion and made it sound like they had an open invitation. There were goats in the hills and even the odd pig or two. I'd been shooting with the old man enough times over the years to catch the bug, and I knew Keogh was into bow-hunting, so I badgered our blood-sport housemate to get us out there as soon as we all had a free weekend. This wasn't easy. The seasons were a-changing, there was a shift in the air and it felt like campus was drawing a deep breath before plunging into the business end of the year. Every weekend there was some ball or presentation or dinner thing on.

We pencilled in a date in November that gave us a bit of breathing space before exams. The track to the property was four-wheel drive, so a friend of Skimp called Barndo who was also into hunting qualified for an invitation, along with his Toyota Land Cruiser. We asked some others to come but everyone seemed to have better things on. Suited me fine just the four of us.

They held the hockey presentation in the Main Hall. Nat wore a sleeveless, high-waist black flowy dress that had me groping as soon as she walked out of the bathroom all dolled up, but even at her best she paled alongside Lisa when we met up for snapshots in the foyer. The girl was a living cliché. In her dazzling yellow dinner dress, lacquered hair, and glowing makeup she would have stood out in a crowd of models. Seated at our table were two girls that didn't have a date either, but even that didn't mollify her. When one of them asked where Keogh was, she lifted her nose and purred with sarcasm, 'Oh, at some football thing.'

She might have meant it lightly, and everyone else at the table might have treated it so, but little barbs like this had set us off on the wrong foot from day one, and kept us there ever since. What annoyed me most was that I tended to hear them when Keogh wasn't around. It took some effort to will my eyes away.

Entrée was a prawn cocktail I devoured in two mouthfuls or so, the main was a slice or two of marinated beef edged with fluffy greens and lovingly sprinkled with . . . something. It would have fit neatly beneath the fifty-dollar note I paid to be there. A saucy red glob of chef's hard work went wasted to one side. My appreciation for how much time and effort must have gone into the meal lasted as long as it took me to devour it – about a minute – after which I settled back with a beer resolved to sneak off to McDonalds at first opportunity.

They'd reeled in some suitably handsome dude from the national hockey side as guest speaker, famous apparently, who sounded like he was prepping for a career in motivational speaking. The girls gave him a standing ovation when it ended while I slapped my hands together like a performing seal, distracted by an image in my head of the rugby boys up north whooping it up.

'You okay?' Nat put a hand on my shoulder.

'Think I'd rather sit through a physics lecture,' and she grimaced and turned away.

From there it was awards and more speeches. A ceremony free of testosterone was a pleasant change, nevertheless I started to yawn as they limped toward Sportswoman-Of-The-Year. When the name Lisa Howard sounded out of the loudspeaker everyone at the table leapt to their feet to applaud her. I followed them up slowly, leaned into a geriatric bow and gave one or two lazy claps before plonking back into my seat. Nat, still clapping, protested my indiscretion with a nudge from her hip. I pinched her backside playfully and she glared down at me. The speech Lisa gave us was nothing to knock I guess, and when she sat down and everyone showered her with praise I even managed a respectful nod her way. She gave me a tight smile, then looked down at her trophy and sighed.

'Pity he isn't here to see this,' I commented. I'd meant nothing but what I said; it was my offer of condolence.

'Yeah well,' she said with sting in her voice, 'I guess he had better things to do.'

That set off a cracker inside me. I couldn't stop what came out next, or the glare I shamed her with. 'He was selected in a rep side the rest of us would have given our nuts to play in. A good game won't just cement his spot in firsts next year, it'll line him up for the next rep fixture. This is what he's busted his arse to do ever since he started playing rugby. And I reckon he'll get there, too.'

I sensed a squirm or two around me. Nat kicked my shin and Lisa toyed with her glass. A sadness stole across her magazine-cover face that reminded me even she was mortal, and I did feel sorry for her. This was her moment, with no one special to share it with, and here I was spoiling it.

'Hey, sorry, but if the two of you want to be elite athletes, this is what you're in for.' I felt another kick on the shin, but this time I kicked back.

'Guess I should wake up and smell the roses, right?' Lisa said wistfully.

I had an answer, but kept it to myself.

The formalities over, the DJ took over and the floor filled quickly. For the most I sat at the table with the other boys enjoying the spectacle of our girls getting tanked. I watched Nat in circular huddles of girls laughing and swaying and singing at the top of their lungs, and if I truly enjoyed myself that night it was because she did. Of all the guys present it was clear our guest speaker had it best, what with all the attention he got from the starry-eyed females keeping him company, including Lisa, who must have assumed it went with her award.

Occasionally a song came on that Nat liked and she'd haul me onto the floor for a dance. By midnight she was unsteady on her legs and using me for balance, but it was only when I felt her grab me in certain parts that I realised how drunk she really was. For the first time ever, it was my turn to push *her* hands away.

'Nat, you're embarrassing me,' I said, and she flashed a smile and tried to do it again. It was my cue to lead her back to the table.

I sat her down and poured her a glass of water. She buried her face into my shirt and wrapped her hands around my neck, more to stop herself sliding off the chair I figured.

'*Steey . . . yeeve?*' she moaned.

'Yes Nat.'

'I love you.'

'Love you too, honey,' I said out of habit, and patted her on the head.

'*Steey . . . yeeve?*'

'Yes Nat.'

'I'm sick.'

Just then Lisa came over. 'How's she doing?'

I put a hand on Nat's forehead and pulled it up to check. Her eyes were gone. 'Nat, you okay?' I asked.

'What . . . time is it?' she slurred softly.

Time for bed, Lisa and I agreed. We helped her up.

'Are you coming back?' Lisa asked. I thought it unusual that she cared either way, but it was nice that she asked.

'Nah, might call it a night.'

I took a big share of Nat's weight as I led her unprotestingly across the floor. At the door I turned around and saw Lisa rejoin the guest speaker and his harem. I grimaced in distaste and retreated with Nat away from the place.

Getting home I had to prop her up with my shoulder under her armpit, giving me an ache in my spine as bad as a late hit from a front-rower. I reckon I burned up more calories on that trip back to her place than a gym session. She had little energy for anything save dropping her head on the pillow once I'd got her undressed and into her bed. Her eyes were shut when I pulled the sheets over her. It sure was refreshing to see our roles reversed.

I sat down on the bed and put a hand on her forehead. Her warmness seemed to pass into me, filled me with a moving sentimentality. I sat there a long time watching this girl of mine, wondering what it was that held me back with her. Wondering what resolved me to think our days were numbered, apparently the only one who did. I tried to think of words to describe it, what stirred this curious affection I felt for her now. Maybe it was because she was oblivious, or helpless, to my scrutiny. She was like a child to me then. I knew her every inch, from her banana-shaped big toe to each silver filling in her mouth. An image of Lisa flashed in my mind, and when I recalled how I'd compared their appearances earlier, I found it all weary. More importantly, unfair. I lived in a place surrounded by privilege – a slice of wealth here, a dose of good breeding there – privilege nonetheless that tends to make people forget they get where they're going from a running start. And that included me. Whatever privilege Nat had been born into came with virtues a lot of us here seemed at pains to refine. Selflessness. Modesty. Compassion. Humility. *Low maintenance* flashed in my mind, and I think I learnt something about myself right then.

Maybe it was just the alcohol. Time for a walk.

I brushed a strand of hair from her nose. She stirred and I thought she was awake. 'Nat, you gonna be sick?' I asked, to no reply. I put the waste bucket at the foot of her bed within easy reach, took her keys and headed off to put solids into my stomach.

The fifteen-minute walk served well to deflate my bloated belly. I got to McDonalds and saw it still doing good business despite the time of night. Nat and I sat here on occasion, making a game of people-watching. Every type found its way in here, from homeless drunks to expensively dressed kids poised to make their mark on the world. I always found the pointless exercise comforting. You don't worry about what you might have been when your whole life's ahead of you.

A late winter westerly shivered the crowns of the eucalypts lining Missenden Road as I headed back. Bows squeaked and groaned and papers skidded across the street. My light dinner jacket soaked up the chill and the icy clamminess of it stuck to my chest like something wet as I walked with both arms folded. My teeth were chattering when I turned into Nat's street and I looked forward to sliding into a bed made warm by her lovely body heat.

It was the dress that gave her away, the eyecatcher it was designed to be, bright enough in the night shadows thrown by the trees to create the impression of trailing an afterglow. I didn't need to see her escort's face to know it was our immaculately dressed guest speaker. Their pace was rather quick for a post-midnight stroll.

I was behind them a good fifty metres or so. I veered off the path and followed from the road, keeping them in sight through the windows of the parked cars I used for cover.

They crossed over where I thought they would, and though her gaze went every which way an owl wouldn't have spotted me behind the car where I'd crouched. At that point my disdain for the girl had sunk to a new level. It wasn't just what I saw that did it; she'd reduced me to the low of a frigging stalker.

After that I let them get ahead a little. I knew where Lisa lived and wouldn't lose them. I was a good distance away when she passed through her gate and reached for the door with her keys but I hunkered down behind a station wagon anyway. If my guess was correct, she'd take a furtive look over her shoulder before stepping inside.

My precaution was unnecessary. Her glance was too flighty, had too much ground to cover. They went inside and I walked a bit closer. The window of her room lit up, and not long after that I saw a hand pull the blind down. I toyed with the idea of giving her a shout, or knocking on the door, but quickly dismissed both.

I settled for a spot down the road where I could keep the house covered. The terraces here backed onto other properties and I knew the front door was the only way out of the place. To keep warm I paced back and forth, blowing into my cupped hands. Tempted as I was to skip off to Nat's for a warm jacket, I stayed put the whole time.

About half an hour later the thin sliver of light edging her blind went black. I pressed the button of my watch and it flashed 1.48am. I watched over that front door for another twenty minutes, then left.

Nat was snoring like a grizzly bear when I left her place the next morning. Compared with the night before, walking down the footpath in broad daylight made me feel like I was heading to Lisa's on invitation. As far as I was concerned an interrogation was moot, but it would make me rest easier, vindicate the course of action I'd decided to take.

I was glad that she opened the door and not one of her housemates. With her hair precisely brushed and her jeans and shirt neat and crisp, I could see she'd been up a while. I saw behind her that the lounge room was empty. The look she gave me went from mild surprise to a wariness I thought fitting. She even checked over my shoulder to see if anyone was there.

'Oh . . . hello Steve. What are you doing here?'

'Yeah,' I agreed. 'What would I be doing here?'

A flash of surprise showed on her face that might have been genuine. 'Is something wrong?'

'Have a guess.'

'Excuse me?'

'Do I have to spell it out for you?'

'Steve, I don't have time for—'

'To kick this off, just how much do you like Jason? Because if you're not into him, fair enough. Happens to all of us. But don't play him along. He likes you a lot and you know as well as me that he'd never try to hurt you. He's not in this for show, so if you don't want him, get it over with. He isn't one of your fashion accessories.'

She kept her rigid composure. She was either too dumb to pick up where I was heading, or a very good actress. I thought the latter. 'What are you on about?'

'Get lost on your way home Lisa? Need someone to show you the way?'

For a second her eyes ballooned and her jaw dropped a fraction. She recovered expertly though, dropping a mask of innocence over her face. 'Oh, I get it,' she said in a tone of voice made to patronise me. Like how on *earth* was she supposed to know that *that's* what I'd been alluding to. 'If you mean Andrew . . .'

'Yeah, the guest speaker you were chatting up all night.'

'You spied on me?'

'Gee, I couldn't have picked a more innocent mark.'

'Listen,' she gave me a snide laugh, 'he just wanted the addresses of some ski resorts I stayed at when I was in France last year. He's going skiing there later this year, you know.'

'Is that how you got him here?'

A flash of annoyance took the prettiness out of her face. 'Excuse me, but what has this to do with you?'

'Take another wild guess.'

Her eyes darted away, but not the irritation on her face. 'Nothing happened, Steve.'

'How long did he stay?'

'About twenty minutes, I guess,' she answered drolly. She found it hard to look at me.

'And he left after that, did he?'

'Yes!'

'What did you do then?'

'I went to bed.'

I almost said *with him in it*, but caught myself. 'Twenty minutes, eh Lisa?'

'I said I don't know. It might have been longer.'

I pored over her intently, watching that smooth face of hers play its part, a matching expression for what left her mouth. Oh yes, stage was denied a fine actress while she was Uni. 'But it was longer than that, wasn't it?'

'This is none of your business.'

'Wrong. Jason's a mate of mine, and you got some convincing to do.'

'Fuck you.'

'No!' I retorted. 'Fuck you Lisa! Just answer the question. How long did he stay?'

'I don't know! I didn't time it!'

I almost said, 'but I did,' but I wanted to give her a little more rope. 'You just went to bed after that, eh?'

'You got no right to ask these sorts of—'

'Answer me!'

'Yes!' She virtually spat it out.

'After this guy left, right?'

'Yes!'

'Did he say where he was going?'

'I don't remember. I think he said he was going to get a taxi.'

'So you brushed your teeth, got in your jim-jams and turned out the light. That sort of thing.'

'Yes!'

'Which would have been only minutes after he left you? After he strolled out the front door, headed for that taxi. Right?'

She almost screamed at me now. 'Yes!'

I watched her closely, too closely. I think she saw through my poker face then, saw the hand I was about to play. 'I don't know,' she said now. 'I can't remember.'

I took a deep breath. 'Now I'm going to ask you something and I want you to think very, very carefully about how you answer.' Her glare was brutal and I could feel the hot contempt at its source, months and months of it pent up and ready to explode. 'I'm asking you to be honest. You can 'fess up now, or you can bullshit and take your chances.'

Backed into a corner, she still regarded me through the guise of composure and dignity. Nothing came out of her mouth.

'I know this is hard, but I'm trying to make it easy for you,' I said in a kinder voice; something I'd last used on her long before we learnt to despise each other. 'Just be honest. If you can't say it, fine, just nod your head or say you're sorry. Or stand there and cry if you have to. After that, it's between you and Jase – you're right, that's none of my business. Go over the finer details with him but give me something better than *I just gave him the addresses of some ski resorts.* You hearing me?'

I thought I'd connected. I could see the hint of a soul in those wicked eyes. But it didn't last long.

'I already told you Steve, nothing happened,' she said, with an earnestness that even sounded genuine. 'I didn't let him.'

I inhaled deeply, let it out in a big sigh. 'Fine. Then I'll tell him what I saw, and that ain't the way you said it, baby.'

There was dead silence behind me as I headed for the gate. I closed it behind and took off down the footpath.

'Don't you dare tell him shit!' she shouted after me.

'No,' I said over my shoulder. 'I'll leave that to you.'

I caught a bus home and holed up in my room. Keogh returned from his foray up north after midday. I heard the clatter of kitchen stuff as he made lunch and Jen's voice when she came out for a yak.

I couldn't face him. I was screwed either way. I couldn't look into those lie-proof eyes of his and pretend I didn't have the worst news he'd want to hear locked up inside me. And if I did reveal all, I'd be denying Lisa the opportunity to atone herself first through confession, if only minimally. I stayed in my room buried in my books, glad he never came in.

We crossed paths in the kitchen as I banged about making French toast for dinner, but I kept my head down and answered in low mumbles the question or two he sent my way. I'd started back to my room balancing my plate and glass of juice when I asked in passing, 'You gonna see Lisa later?'

He squashed a meat patty onto the frypan with a spatula. It sizzled and spat, cooked on too high a flame. 'After I've had a bite.'

He paused then, eyed me over his shoulder. I hadn't asked him a thing about a weekend we'd been discussing for a month. Not even if they'd won. Something had caught his antennae and I left quickly.

On Monday night I stayed at the library until closing and didn't get home until after 10pm. By dinner Tuesday I'd had enough. Soon as he retired to his room after we'd eaten, I followed. I gave his door a courtesy knock and invited myself in.

'Hey Jase.'

He turned his tape player down; the Doors by the sound of it. 'Steve,' he said. His greetings were more of an acknowledgment.

I watched him and waited. He shuffled a paper or two and then looked at me like it was just another day at his desk with me intruding. Nope, I decided. Lisa hadn't told him a bloody thing.

'Good weekend?' I asked.

'Super,' he said, and we swapped stories. Though he didn't mention any names it sounded like a few of the boys had got lucky in the nightclubs of Newcastle. It opened up the conversation I wanted to have.

'Did you? I asked.

'Did I what?'

'Get lucky.'

'I'm spoken for, mate.' There was pride in his voice, and a firm gaze let me know he meant it. It wasn't his thing, never would be. There are just enough guys like him around to give the rest of us a good name. The thought made it easier for me now.

'Would you ever fink on any of those guys, tell his girlfriend he'd dicked behind her back?'

'None of my business,' he said with a shrug.

'What if it was the other way around? You caught his girlfriend shagging behind his back. Would you tell him?'

'Depends how good a friend he was.'

'Up there with his best,' I said staunchly.

He thought for a bit. 'Would he want to know?'

'Yep.'

'Guess I would then.'

'What if she was a friend as well?'

'That's the choice of friends you gotta make.'

'So if you found out Nat was shagging behind my back, would you tell me?'

'Would you want to know?'

'Shit yeah.'

'Well, there's your answer.'

I waited to see if it would catch. There must be a block in all our minds when we hear what we don't want to hear. The clues just fly on past. But then I suppose Keogh was a naturally trusting guy. This should have made it easier for me. For some reason it made it harder.

I forced it out. 'What if it was you?'

He straightened a little and his eyes darkened. Again I could feel the energy behind them, a boding rage fit for a battlefield. By God I was glad this guy was a friend.

'What if it was?' There was a different note in his voice now.

'Has Lisa said anything to you about last Saturday night?'

'About what, specifically?'

'Did she tell you I spoke to her?'

'No. Go on.'

And I did. I explained exactly what I saw and left nothing out; he could draw his own conclusions. It hit him hard. The draining of his strength was plain in his face and his whole body went limp like something punctured. After I said all that was needed he sat there slumped, staring over my shoulder. I stood to leave.

'Sorry, bud,' was all I could think to say. I opened the door and he stopped me.

'Hey Steve.'

I turned back around.

'Thanks.' His voice was sincere. I nodded and left.

Boy, did I cop it. After dinner the next day the phone rang. I made the mistake of picking it up.

'Hello.'

There was a pause, then: 'Is Jason there?' It was Lisa.

'Yeah.'

'Is that you Steve?'

'Yeah.'

She let me have it in a voice so loud I had to lift the phone away from my ear. She must have gone a minute without taking a breath. 'You don't know what happened!' she screamed after an eternity, and I felt the receiver vibrate. 'How do you know he didn't go in and screw one of my flatmates? I live with two girls, remember! Did you ever think of that! Did you!'

'Sure Lisa,' I spoke into the mouthpiece from a foot away. 'Tried with you for about an hour before using his fall-backs.'

'That's right! How do you know it didn't happen like that!'

'Listen, now it's my turn to say *I don't need this*. If Jason's dumped you, you're just pissed because you didn't end it on your terms. Don't take it out on me because he beat you to it, first time a guy ever did probably.'

'You wanted this didn't you? Admit it. You just couldn't wait to catch me out.'

'Believe what you want, Lisa.'

'That's it, isn't it? Hope your happy with yourself, you fucking two-faced, sexist—'

For the first time ever, I hung up on a girl. I'd stayed calm and was proud of myself. Proud enough to wear a smile all the way to Keogh's room.

'You spoke to Lisa, I gather,' I said by his door.

'Yeah,' he said from behind his desk. He twisted around on his seat and gave me his attention.

'She just gave me an awful blasting.'

'Was that her on the phone?' he asked with sudden interest.

'Yeah. All of her.'

He chuckled then, and I took heart that he found the whole thing funny.

'She give you grief as well?' I asked.

'Not especially,' he said. 'I think she knew what was coming. She did call you one big bullshit artist though, amongst other things.'

I sniggered. I wasn't going to insult him by asking if he believed her. 'Just to know where I stand with this woman, is that it with you and her?'

'That's it.'

Inwardly, I smiled. I know I got some pretty ordinary vices, leave a lot to be desired. But at that moment I felt a shameless pride. She should have known not to contradict me like that, worse that she put his loyalty to the test. She should have known that my word would always trump hers.

Chew on that, bitch.

Nat came over later that night. We were lying in bed and I was feeling a little down. Going over events and looking for flaws. 'You reckon I should have told him?' I asked, which was followed by a lengthy pause. Not a good sign.

'You did what you thought was best.'

'Shit,' I grumbled. 'Sounds like a no to me.' I waited for her to elaborate, but all I got was silence. 'You don't think she deserved it?'

'What if she didn't do anything?'

'Oh, for . . .'

'We don't know for sure. She told me he must have slept on the lounge.'

'Took a while for her to think that one up.' I rolled my head to face her. 'Come on Nat, just because she's your friend isn't a reason to go into denial.'

There was another long pause. 'Ok, suppose you're right. What if she truly is sorry, though?'

'What difference should that make?'

'You don't think someone has the right to be forgiven?'

'Yeah, right. The only person she's ever felt sorry for is herself.'

'That's a bit harsh.'

'You should have heard that woman on the phone tonight. Didn't sound very remorseful to me. Beneath that pretty face is pure witch.

She's got a side to her I don't think Jason's ever seen.'

'You don't think you're being biased?'

'You're just taking her side because she's your friend.'

'And what are you doing?'

I tensed up a little. Seven months of practice had made us better at arguing, and we were heading down that horridly familiar path toward it now. 'So what are you saying Nat? Sorry makes it all okay, is that it? Praise Jesus . . . turn the other cheek . . . let he who has never sinned cast the first stone, or what the fuck ever.'

'She made a mistake Steve,' she murmured. 'That's all I'm saying.'

'Then she ought to have 'fessed up and apologised on her own accord. Too late now. I wouldn't want to hear it, wouldn't want her to even hint it.'

'Why not?'

'Because it'd be a farce. Isn't it funny how sorry some people can be when they're caught out. When remorse is their only option. I didn't see her choking up on guilt earlier, and unless I'm mistaken, neither did you.' I took a breather; my blood was up. 'And for that reason I wouldn't want Jason to hear it. He's too bloody naïve, too trusting. Like as not he'd give in to the honey-voiced bitch and take her back. She's good, I'll give her that.'

She was quiet for a while. I could hear her brain ticking over. 'He wouldn't.'

'Wouldn't what?

'Take her back.'

'What makes you so sure?'

She turned on her side to face me. 'You think you know him, don't you?'

'Better than most.'

'Then you should know he'd never take her back.'

'What are you on about?'

'Why do you think you two get on so well?'

'Never thought about it that much.' Or at least not as much as the situation between her and me, but I didn't add that.

Nat stayed quiet, which told me only one thing. I was going to hear something I'd rather not. She was sorting the right words out in her head, wanted to soften the punch. Yep, the maestro was at it again, and I was in for a free session.

'You're both idealists,' she said. 'Romantics in your own stupid way. And now he's had the illusion shattered. She's broken the rules; he won't take her back. It would go against his principles.'

My surprise at being spared a character demolition quickly turned to amusement. Romantics? Idealists? But I'd take that up later. 'I dunno Nat. He's mighty big on doing the honourable thing.'

'Forgive her, sure. But take her back? Not a chance.'

'I thought the two went hand in hand.'

'No.' She'd said it so abruptly it made me think she was speaking from personal experience.

I mulled it over. Okay, she had a point there; maybe he wouldn't take her back. But Keogh a romantic? Me, a romantic? It made me chuckle.

'What's so funny?'

'You,' I said. 'Me and Keogh romantics. You might as well say we're gay.'

'God, you're so bloody ignorant sometimes!' she said with a raised voice. 'All of you! You all think he's so tough. How many friends does he really have? True friends? You're more of a friend to him than you realise, and for the same reasons.'

'Yeah? Which are?'

'Look at you both,' she sniggered. 'Longing for the old ways, living in the past. You have your history books; he has his bows and spearguns. You're two of a kind.' She let her breath out and mumbled *'Bloody throwbacks'* in a voice so low it sounded like a curse.

She rolled away. I could hear how quick her breathing had become. I'd hit a raw nerve; something was bugging her. We lay for a long time without talking while I tried to figure out what. In the end I just gave up.

'Well, good to know where you stand on this, sweetie,' I said. 'You're a better person than me though if you reckon saying sorry is all someone has to do after they've—'

'Do that to me and I'll rip your fucking balls off,' she snapped.

The tone in her voice shocked me. I felt her body go taught and coldness creep under the sheets. I found it curious though that she said that. Rip my nuts off yes, but dump me – not a chance.

'I wouldn't be much good to you then, would I?'

She didn't laugh.

Nineteen

We drove out of Sydney in high spirits. I was far more comfortable with this one. Give me the Australian bush to the South Pacific any day. Yes sir, I was far more comfortable with this one. All I had to fear this time were a couple of trigger-happy amateurs.

A flaking sign showed us the turnoff to the property. We rattled over a set of cattle grids and onto a dusty track barred by a gate. Skimp got out of the car and bobbed down to lock the front wheels into four-wheel drive, then he swung the gate open and away from us. It took over half an hour to crawl about five kilometres. Every time the wheels fell into a rut or pothole we slammed against the doors or cracked heads against the chassis and Barndo got an earful for his driving skills.

At last we came upon an open patch that bore the hallmarks of a camp. Other than scattered clumps of Scotch thistle it was bare grass. We unloaded the car and kicked cow patties aside in order to pitch a large tent. It would have slept four with ease but Keogh opted for a swag he'd brought along. Preferred it that way, he replied to Skimp's offer of squeezing in with us. This was followed by the predictable taunt that he only wanted privacy so he could flog himself.

A sad creek gurgled alongside and my mind baulked at the thought of drinking water percolated down slopes sprayed with all manner of fertilisers and pesticides and things that caused cancer in rats.

'This drinkable?' I asked, pointing.

'If you're a cow,' Skimp replied.

We'd brought a wide range of firepower. Barndo had a .270 Browning, Skimp had a semi-auto .223 Remington, and I had my father's 30/30 Winchester. Keogh of course came armed with his trusty compound bow.

Barndo's face broke into a grin wider than a frog's when he saw

Keogh pull it from the back and gloat over it like some kind of treasure. It was a complicated looking thing, more bat-shaped than bow, with overlapping strings and a little pully system at the end of each wing. Screwed into the stock was a quiver with polished broadheads that glittered in the poor light.

'With all this firepower, you wanna use that?' Barndo asked. 'What is it with that thing?'

'It's a survivor,' Keogh replied lovingly.

Evening fell with a chill that bit through my clothes. We got a fire going and threw a hotplate over the top. Dinner was a bushman's staple of sausages, bacon and eggs, and a couple of fried half-tomatoes for our vegetable course. Science has yet to explain why smoke picks on certain people in the same manner mosquitos will, and I tend to act as a magnet for both. Though too cold for mozzies the smoke was pestilence enough, and my eyes dripped nonstop as I sat on my fold-up chair sucking it in with my overcooked sausage sandwich.

As we waited for the billy to boil we threw around tactics for the following day. Keogh was for splitting everyone up, me going with him and Skimp and Barndo taking off in another direction.

'I'm not trooping around the woods with you two shooting at me,' Barndo complained.

'I got a bow mate, not a cannon,' Keogh reminded him. 'And we'd take different directions, anyway.'

'Famous last words.'

Safety prevailed. We were all going off together. Keogh wasn't happy.

'If we find anything I'll need to get close with the bow, and I mean real close,' he said. 'Which means you guys are going to have to wait. That's why I'd rather go off with just one of you, better still alone.'

'Don't worry,' Barndo said. 'We'll let you go ahead, get you into a nice position for first shot. But once you've let loose – duck. Because then we're going to open fire.'

Keogh grunted. 'At the goats, please.'

We woke before sunup. After a quick breakfast of Weet-Bix dunked in ice-flecked milk we were on our way. The entire valley was clogged with mist thick enough to get us lost if we strayed too far from the gully we followed. My face and hands went numb in the frigid air and my breath came out in vapour plumes thicker than cigar smoke. My jeans went soggy from brushing past scrubs and grasses, and I could feel my feet losing their feeling despite my thick woolly socks.

We tried to tread stealthily but to the locals here I reckon we sounded like bulls stampeding through the scrub. Predictably Keogh set the pace, keeping point. As soon as we set off he hightailed it to the front like a dog on a scent and there was no point trying to stop him. Just like the day we went spearing, he had that glimmer in his eyes that let you know this was his element. If we hadn't constantly reined him in, we'd have lost him. The impatient frown he gave us each time he had to wait conveyed clearly what he thought of three novices slowing him down.

About an hour into the hunt the mist thinned and we could see the full scale of the hills looming above us either side, though the bush climbing the slopes was too thick to see anything browsing within it. We turned another bend and this time Keogh was waiting with a smile.

'Up ahead,' he said, pointing.

The early morning sun had yet to poke its head over the range and the slopes where he pointed were grey and featureless in the poor light. Bando unslung his rifle quickly. 'Where?' he asked, all hushed up.

'Up ahead, along that slope,' Keogh replied.

'I can't see shit.'

'Those far hills.'

'Which ones?'

'Open your eyes,' Keogh said tiredly, stabbing a finger in the direction. 'Up ahead – there!'

We all peered ahead, through the sparse tree cover of the gully. Far ahead on the slope of the furthest hill a bare stretch of what I guessed was grey shale separated the endless bush. It had to be more than a kilometre away. Now I could see small white dots, a few browns, and one or two blacks spaced out across the patch.

'What, those dots?' Barndo asked.

'Yep.'

'They're bloody miles away. By the time we'd get there they'd be gone.'

'They're goats, mate,' Skimp explained. 'Not a herd of migrating caribou. They're feeding, be there a while.'

Barndo snorted, and we resumed our march. After what felt like an hour trekking through the gully we came to another bend. Keogh was a fair way in front. We saw him climb up the hill a bit and then he stopped and signalled for us to wait. We watched him standing there still as a tree, gazing ahead while his mind did calculations I couldn't begin to conceive. Then he came down.

'Okay,' he said. 'There's about twenty of them. We'll need to climb, get above them.'

We discussed strategies. Barndo suggested we separate, leave half of us here while the other half headed up the hill.

'Sure,' Keogh replied. 'That way we can shoot at each other.'

Fortunately, Barndo was the only one needed talking out of that strategy. There was no option but for us all to go up the hill. As we got closer Keogh would peel away and approach the herd close enough to be in range for his bow. He would have first shot. After that the rest of us would fire at will.

We went about our business more seriously now. Keogh led, moving with the stealth of a seasoned hunter; a finger point here, a hand wave there. He made it look so natural. I reckon the effort Skimp and I made was comparable, but Barndo cursed whenever a branch flicked back at him and a stick cracked underfoot with every step. We managed to get ourselves within range of our rifles without giving ourselves away, and from there we dropped onto our hands and knees and crawled ahead to better our position. I settled behind a log and peeked over the top. I caught black and white movement behind a clump of bushes and ducked down again.

Keogh waited until Barndo and Skimp settled into their places, then he pointed to a couple of goats plucking at some bushes about thirty metres away.

'See those ones down there?' he whispered, pointing. 'I'll head over to those bushes on the right, that'll be close enough.'

I'd caught that look on his face again, same as when he'd pulled back on his bow that day of the archery contest. His face was flushed and his brows were contracted, while his eyes shone out from beneath with the glitter of polished metal. It was contagious. My senses were tuned to their limits.

Keogh dropped onto his haunches and duck-waddled away between the bushes. After a while of this he slunk onto his belly and elbowed his way forward like a crippled lizard, smothering the crackle of leaf litter with his weight, every move as unconscious as his breathing. From the other boys' impatient sighs and fidgeting, it was an agonisingly long wait. For me, it was an experience. Those who knew him as the moody college boy wouldn't have recognised him now. And yet this explained so much about him. Freed of moronic impediments like people he'd settled into himself, calm as a lioness in silent communion with its prey. Each flick of goat's ear, each flare of nostril or tremor of muscle was the trigger for some calculated response of his, some clue to go by. It was the concentrated form of the guy we knew, and yet so familiar – there on the periphery, heedless of his yawning company, absorbed in something lost on the rest of us. A stone's throw away, yet always so far.

Barndo crawled forward and took position beside me. 'Wish he'd fuckin hurry up,' he griped.

After twenty minutes or so, Keogh reached his clump of trees. Problem was that by then the goats had moved off a way. Knowing Keogh's proficiency with his bow, I thought he had a good chance of finding his mark regardless, but I also knew he'd want to be sure of himself and improve his position. These weren't balloons he was shooting at. These were living things that would die a painful and lingering death if his arrow hit more than an inch or two off the heart-lung area.

He gestured with his hands toward a patch of cover ahead of him. He wanted to get closer.

'Well, hurry up then!' Barndo hissed. Keogh frowned harshly and put a finger to his lips, then sunk down on his stomach and began edging forward again.

The sun broke above the hills and moisture sparkled from leaf tips and tussocks. Warmth flooded the gully and the goats moved into the sunrays, putting more space between us. The boys' frustration was palpable in the confined space of our cover. We'd underestimated the difficulty of stalking goats with a bow and arrow. If not for Keogh we'd have opened up long ago.

Barndo picked up a small stone and threw it Keogh's way. It hit a boulder and bounced downhill. Anywhere else it might've passed unnoticed, but in the pervasive silence of the bush it sounded suspiciously loud. Keogh lifted his head and gave us a murderous snarl before flattening out again.

'Come on, will you!' Barndo jeered, barely able to keep his voice down. He made a frantic motion with his hands but Keogh wasn't watching. 'Where's that chessboard of yours, Chambers?'

This time I couldn't help joining in with Skimp laughing. We tried to keep it down but a few chuckles broke through.

A wise old billy with a proud curl of horns lifted his head and began jerking it this way and that, shaggy beard swaying beneath. Something wasn't right, he just couldn't figure. He let off a warning bleat that raised the heads of every goat and had them scanning the surrounding bush in nervous, repetitive head-jerks. Keogh lay on his stomach, flat as a dead man.

The billy paced the ground nervously. It was that stage just prior to all-out panic, when the herd would catch on and take off in a powerful hurry. All that they were waiting for was confirmation, one way or another.

In a quirk of luck, the billy moved closer to Keogh and stopped well within range. Laying on his side, Keogh slowly brought his bow alongside and fitted an arrow. Yes, I thought. *At last.*

But then, inconceivably, the billy began to skip away. Either he'd caught a whiff, or that sixth sense unique to wild animals kicked in. Within seconds he'd moved out of range, and kept going.

'Keogh!' Barndo muttered loudly. 'What are you waiting for?'

The billy's head shot up and pointed back over his shoulder, aimed toward us. Barndo flayed his hands about and hissed *what the fuck*?

The billy blurted and broke into a trot, a signal for the others. As one they abandoned their feeding and followed. Loose rocks dislodged by their hooves clattered down the hill, spooking them further and speeding their retreat. Keogh raised himself up on a knee. The arrow was still fixed to his bow but he seemed undecided about using it.

An almighty crack of gunshot exploded behind my ear. My eardrum hummed like a gong and sound around me was muted. Beside me Brando quickly reworked the bolt-action of his rifle. Before I could curse at him, he fired again. Skimp's rifle cracked loudly as he joined in.

The hell with it. I swivelled my 30/30 in the direction of the billy goat as he clambered up the hill. I aimed the rifle-notch at his spine where the shoulder blades met and squeezed the trigger. The butt of the gun punched my shoulder and I saw a puff of fur where the bullet hit. He went headfirst into the ground and rolled over, his legs twitched a few times and then went still.

Around me was solid gunfire; the ear-splitting *boom* of Barndo's Browning, the *clack clack clack* of Skimp's Remington, and with every blast the hills echoed and a goat went down; they were all quite close. I worked the lever and slid another round into the chamber. A goat ran straight at me in blind panic. I waited until it turned broadside to step around me, then blasted it point-blank. It hit the dirt and didn't move.

Intelligence didn't elevate goats to their top rung position as feral pests. With their leader down they were like a bunch of kids that had lost the grownup. They ran back and forth in front of us desperate for an opening, bleating stupidly.

I swung my rifle around on my shoulder, searching for another target. Keogh appeared at the end of the barrel, standing there but not moving. I lowered the gun. Pumped as I was, with gunfire deafening my ears and targets distracting me in every direction, I found time to reflect on the look on his face. There was a strange sadness to it, like he was watching something that shouldn't be happening. Goats ran in panic-stricken circles around him, while at his feet lay utter carnage; goats twisting their bodies, flailing their feet and trying to stand, bleating in terror and pain while Barndo and Skimp yahooed and emptied their magazines into them. A goat trotted past Keogh slow and stupid, close enough for him to grab. But he didn't raise his bow, just stood there and watched it go past.

'Go on, scat,' he said, half-heartedly kicking a foot after it. It passed me by and I had to fight the impulse to lift my gun, despite Keogh being out of my firing line.

The break between gunshots lengthened until only the heavy-calibre was firing. I turned around and watched Barndo take aim at a nanny goat frantically limping away, dragging a shattered hind leg attached by a thin strip of flesh. The gun roared and bucked, muzzle-fire licked the air and a chunk of rock exploded at her hooves. Barndo cussed, quickly worked the bolt again and brought the gun back up to his shoulder. He fired and another piece of hill burst into a puff of fragments.

'That's it!' Skimp cried with laughter. 'Show us how it's done, Ace! We'll bring a machine gun for you next time.'

Barndo fired again and missed. 'Fuck!'

I brought the Winchester to my shoulder and lined the nanny up in my sights. At that distance and angling away she wasn't an easy target, but I fired anyway and was surprised to see her flip forward in a neat somersault. She rolled down the slope like a rag doll until she hit a boulder. Her legs kicked convulsively, then she shivered and went still.

We tied the ankles of the billy goat to a tree and skinned him, joking about and flicking bits of gore at each other. Keogh sat on a rock watching us, deep in some private research. He'd hardly said a thing since the shooting stopped.

'Hey Jason,' Barndo said over his shoulder as he tugged at a piece of fur. 'How's it going with that survivor of yours?' It brought out a chuckle from Skimp, but not me.

After another few minutes of slicing here, pulling there, I stopped to give my spine a stretch. I flicked some gunk off my fingers and looked at Keogh; his silence was bugging me.

'What's on your mind, buddy?' I asked. 'I thought you liked hunting.'

'You call that hunting?' he scoffed.

'Tell you what, Jason,' Barndo crooned. 'We'll finish up here shortly and you can take a shot at him then, if you like.'

Even I had to laugh at that one. Still not a twitch showed on Keogh's face.

'Why do you like hunting, Barndo?' he asked.

Barndo straightened and met his eyes, on the level. 'Why do you like sex, Keogh?' he asked with a snigger.

Keogh watched him impassively. 'You going back for lunch after this?'

'Yeah.'

'Ok.' Keogh slid his butt of the rock. 'See you back at camp.' He picked up his bow and started walking.

We all stared at him, as if guiltily. 'Where you going?' Barndo asked.

Keogh smiled in a conspiratorial fashion. '*Hunting.*'

'Hang on,' Barndo said. 'We might head off again after lunch. Don't want to be shooting at you.'

'You won't.' Keogh pointed down the gully. 'I'll go this way, follow the goats you just blasted. They'll stop eventually. You guys piss off somewhere else.'

'Hey, you can't—'

'Let him go,' I interrupted. 'If we go anywhere, it'll be in a different direction.'

'You know how far a slug from a .270 travels?'

'Shit Barndo,' Skimp spoke up. 'We're not shooting at birds in the sky, are we?'

'No, but—'

'Let him go,' I repeated. I needn't have said it. Keogh had disappeared already.

The day had lost its colours, we were sitting in a ring around the fire drinking our beers and complaining about how much of a pain in the arse it would be if we had to go looking for Keogh in the dark, when he strolled into camp with a kid over his shoulders.

'Timed that well,' Skimp commented. 'Snags are just about done.'

Keogh went to one side and dumped the carcass. It had already been gutted. He leaned his bow against a tree and took the knife out of the scabbard at his belt. Skimp and Barndo stood and walked over.

'What are you doing?' Barndo asked.

'Ever eaten goat?' Keogh answered.

'Nope.' Barndo regarded it in the same manner of horror the girls had shown with the jewfish.

'Hey Jase,' I called from where I was sitting, 'you don't have to eat everything you kill, you know.'

He looked over his shoulder with a grin. 'Well, I sure as shit won't be eating you then.'

'Seriously, mate,' Barndo said. 'We got snags, a bit of steak . . .'

'Yeah, and now we got goat.'

Keogh hacked at the carcass with his hunting knife until he'd torn off a leg which he skinned and skewered and cooked on a spit over the fire. It gave off a rich gamey smell that screwed our noses, and when a drop of blood landed sizzling onto our hotplate of sausages Barndo protested and told him to move it out of the way.

To Keogh's visible disappointment, the rest of us passed on goat that night. We sat around the fire eating our meals with one eye on Keogh as he ripped chunk after chunk off his goat leg with his teeth like something out of a horror movie.

'Happy now?' I asked him, and he smiled.

We got up the next morning to find him gone already. The previous night he told us he'd take off on his own this time, save us all the grief. We'd be leaving for Sydney around lunch and he promised to be back by then.

To give him a wide berth, the rest of us took off by vehicle up the track in the opposite direction. I sat in the passenger seat with a fully loaded Winchester half out the window while Skimp sat behind me cocked with his Remington. We bounced along that diff-cracking track for about an hour before giving in and footing it into the bush. There was nothing to see. Skimp and Barndo blasted a couple of roos out of boredom but I wasn't interested.

When we got back to camp Keogh was there packing up already. We asked him how he went and he shook his head, but I could tell it wasn't out of disappointment. He would have been happy as a dog off the leash out there on his own.

We'd almost finished loading the car when Keogh stepped forward carrying a large green garbage bag tied in a knot. He took it over to the food esky and lifted the lid to put it in.

'Woah,' Barndo stopped him. 'What's that?'

'Goat meat.'

'You kidding?'

Keogh straightened. 'Is that a problem?'

Barndo snickered. 'Just chuck the bloody thing,' he said, and walked off.

Keogh just stood there, looking down at his bag.

'Mate, no one eats goat,' I said. 'You can't give it away like fish. Leave it for the goannas.'

Keogh didn't move. I could sense this crisis of the heart going on inside him. Some moments had passed before he broke from his thoughts and went over to some tussocks. After another short hesitation he untied the bag, upended it and shook it free. Several large chunks of goat meat fell onto the ground, skinned and cut with the love of a butcher.

I'd hoped the trip might have drawn him out of his shell, but soon as we were home it was the same again. Anyone else would have put it down to a phase he was going through. After all he'd been banished from college, minced his first proper job, and busted up with his girlfriend.

But I wasn't anyone else. I was supposed to be his best friend, not his bloody curse. Directly or indirectly, he was where he was on account of me. Right from the start. I'd made him do things he'd never have done, and made him worse off for it. I'd even dragged him to the Manning Bar where he'd met Lisa. Having me for company always ensured things turned to shit.

I thought I had a Eureka moment the weekend after the shooting trip. I knocked on his door and pulled it open eagerly. He was lying on his bed reading *Jaws*.

'Wanna go shoot some arrows?'

He flopped the book onto his chest. 'What, now?'

'Or never.'

I saw the interest flash in his eyes, then it faded. 'Nowhere to go.'

'The park down the road, remember?'

'Got no targets.'

'Oh, for . . .' I lamented. 'I'll find one.'

I hunted around the house for something an arrow would stick into – a cardboard box, an old pillow cushion. Finding nothing, I tried my pathetic room. My eyes stopped on a big teddy bear I got from Nat for my birthday, and I smiled wickedly. I took it to Keogh's room.

'One target,' I announced.

'We can't shoot that.'

'Why not?'

'Nat'll have your nuts. Mine too.'

'You promised to show me how to shoot a bow.'

'Yeah, but . . .'

'Don't worry about her,' I said reassuringly, and saw it register. By then he'd read the writing on the wall. I'd given him enough clues and here was another. I'd even joked about wanting to be free for next year's intake of fresher women. Assuming college took us back, that is.

'Come on,' I urged. 'I'll buy another one if she takes offence.'

'No you won't,' he replied, but it didn't take long to talk him into it. Within the hour we were at the park and setting up.

It was a glorious spring day, full of blue sky and not a breath of wind. We sat Ted against a newly planted sapling on an incline adjacent to the playing fields. The ground conveniently rose behind it to kill any stray arrows, and about a hundred metres further away an unbroken line of fencing shielded residences from the impossible overshoot.

For my benefit, we positioned ourselves only twenty meters or so from the target. Showing how to do it, Keogh plugged Ted neatly with all six arrows before handing me the bow. I made a show of taking the affair seriously and listening to every word he said, which perked him up a bit. It wasn't long before I was hitting Ted virtually at will, albeit not exactly where I aimed.

I'd just retrieved a couple of wayward arrows from the grass and was walking back to the mark when I saw a paddy wagon pull up by the kerb. I stopped reflexively, like when you spot a speed camera and ease off the pedal. Two boys in blue got out of the car and headed over like a couple on a Sunday stroll.

I walked back to Keogh as he adjusted the poundage on the bow with an Allen Key. 'We got company,' he said.

'Yeah, I saw.'

I dropped the arrows and he handed me the bow. 'Try it on a 40-pound setting,' he suggested. 'It's harder on the draw but the arrows will fly straighter.'

I took the bow and lined myself up for the shot as the two policemen stepped into view at the corner of my eye. They stopped beside us and I let loose. The arrow thudded into Ted's cheek a little high of where I aimed. Nerves of steel, I thought proudly; the truest of battlefield tests.

I offered a smile as I lowered the bow. One of the policemen was older, about mid-forties, with patient eyes and a thin mouth. The other was young with the quiet manner of obedience; probationary constable I reckoned.

'Hello boys,' the older one said in a friendly fashion.

'G'day,' I replied.

'We've received a complaint,' he explained, pointing to the bow I held. 'You shouldn't do that here.'

'Why not?'

'It's a public place.'

'So?'

'That's a dangerous weapon.'

I held it up and regarded it with amusement. 'You're kidding me.'

'No.'

I raised a hand to take in the empty park. 'There's no one here.'

'It doesn't matter.'

'I don't see any signs saying no archery.'

'Boys, I'm not going to argue. There's plenty of archery clubs around. I'm sure you'll find places set aside for these things.'

'What's wrong with here?'

'I told you already.'

I couldn't believe it. I felt that rush of blood that heats the veins and steams the head and tends to make you forget who you're talking to and what the consequences might be. 'Who's complaining?'

'That irrelevant.'

'Are we breaking some law? This isn't a firearm, right? What if we just keep on going?'

'Then I'll have to seize it.'

'Why?'

'Threat to public safety.'

'Public safety?' I asked incredulously, raising my voice a little. 'Yep, I can just see an arrow ricocheting off the target there, powering through the air another hundred metres and going straight through the fence to stick some poor woman in the neck while she's doing the dishes. Happens all the time.'

'Mate, I said I'm not going to argue,' the older one said patiently. 'Just take it out of here.'

'The bloody magpies here are more dangerous than—'

'You know,' Keogh cut in, 'back in medieval Europe this type of thing was mandatory.' His voice had a strange hollowness to it. 'There was a time in England for instance when it was law for any man with a son older than seven to provide him with a bow and at least two arrows. When they turned seventeen, it had to be four.' He looked straight into the policeman's eyes. 'Every man was legally bound to own a bow and arrows, and be proficient at using them. When things turned tough all men up to the age of sixty had to put in at least ten hours of practice a week, punishable by fines or public floggings or imprisonment if they didn't. In some places all other forms of sport were prohibited, just so the focus was on archery. Places were set aside in villages for practice. If they couldn't find spaces long enough they'd just shoot along the streets or between houses. Soldiers would roam the countryside checking up on villages, arresting Mayors and Sheriffs who ignored the King's Statutes. Men like you.'

A flicker of amusement showed on the seasoned officer's face. 'We've moved on from then, mate.'

Keogh smiled; a sad, melancholic sort of smile. 'Tell me about it.'

'Better take your toys and clear off, boys.'

I opened my mouth to carry on with the argument, but Keogh cut me off.

'Let's go.'

Twenty

It was the Friday night a week or so before exams, just another night I thought I'd never remember. I'd only gone for Keogh's sake. His weirdness was getting to me and I thought a night with the lads would do him good.

'Come on, it's our last chance for a drink before exams,' I'd said. He told me that sounded more like an excuse than a reason, and sunk back into his mood.

Then I thought of something. 'We don't have to stay long. It's Cam's birthday.' This was days before and wasn't the real reason we were going, and I felt a bit dishonest for using it, but nothing else was going to drag him there. To my surprise, it worked.

Skimp drove. We got to the Grange around 7pm and I for one intended to be out of there by 10pm latest. I'd made myself available for a game of cricket with one of Uni's lower grades the next day, and needed to be up early.

The pub was at about a third capacity, mostly students. We joined the boys at their table and Babs and Mick took their beers and went to play pool. We were into our second round when we all heard the distinctive, machine-gun rumble of Harley-Davidsons outside. Voices around us were cut short and necks straightened. There were a few loud revs as they parked – just in case anyone didn't hear them – before they killed the engines. A minute or so later, they swaggered in.

They looked resplendent in traditional dress; heavy boots, faded jeans and mottled leathers as rough and worn as what they were glued to. Bearded or unshaven for the most with pierced ears and scraggly long hair, they had the air of a proud tribe. Faded tattoos crept up necks, down arms. Their expressions were all the same, set on doling out misery. There was the inevitable moment's hush when they walked in, doubtless people wondering if it was worth hanging around.

There was a dozen or more. About a third went to the bar, another third sat down at an empty table, and the rest headed for the pool section. Voices started up again and everyone went back to what they were doing.

Everyone but Keogh. He sat in his chair like he was ready to launch. His forehead was creased with sharp lines of disgust and his eyes were full of loathing. He reminded me of a dog at a gate when another one passed by. For no reason at all, the hackles went up.

'Wankers,' he muttered.

A little later I noticed three bikies get up from their table and join their buddies playing pool. Babs and Mick were still at it, having paired up against a couple of guys from college. One of the bikies sauntered over and pressed a coin down on the sleeve; nothing out of the ordinary there. Then he went back to his buddy.

Not long after that, I was talking to Skimp when my peripheral vision caught that abrupt, aggressive hand and arm motion one associates with trouble. I jerked my head reflexively and saw one of the bikies standing face to face with Babs, pointing a finger at his nose. You could see Babs was scared, but he had nevertheless that defiant pose about him whenever he was challenged. Mick stood discreetly out of arm's length. The other two students had retreated to the far side of the table.

The bikie's voice was raised but the ambient noise was too loud to hear his words. Clearly though Babs had done something to piss the guy off. Nothing extraordinary there.

'Hey – trouble,' I said, grabbing everyone's attention. Everyone but Keogh. He'd already cased them. I could feel the potency radiating from his frame, like a leopard hunched for the strike. His face was flushing red before my eyes. Anyone else showing those signs wouldn't have made me nervous. If you didn't know him better, you'd have thought he was working up the courage to intervene. But I knew it was the other way around. He was talking himself into staying put.

'Leave it,' I warned, but his eyes stayed so hot you'd think they'd have melted whatever they were glaring at. The rest of us waited nervously, no doubt thinking the same thing. *Walk away Babs . . . attaboy.*

Thankfully, it didn't last long. The bikie moved off scowling and went to the side of the table to put his coins in. There was the collapse of snooker balls and he and his mate began setting up the table. The tenseness left my muscles and I breathed normally again. Babs put the cue back into its rack, picked up his beer from one of the shelves and came on over. Mick, visibly relieved, followed behind.

'What was that about?' Keogh asked as they dragged their chairs forward. His tone was coarse yet concerned, like what a father would use on his son if he'd been picked on.

Babs shook his head feebly. 'Doesn't matter.'

'What did you do?'

'He thought I moved his frigging coin.' When there's a queue of coins lined up it's not uncommon for players, particularly after they've had a few belts, to sneak theirs ahead or push someone's back. Christ, I've seen more pub fights start over pool tables than over women.

'Have a beer,' I gestured.

Things like this take their toll. Within ten minutes the pub had emptied by more than half.

By nine o'clock the bikies had taken over the pool table section. I saw a large pile of coins on the tables; even they lived by some set of rules it seemed. All that was left was our lot, a mix of about twenty students and locals, and them.

We'd just ordered our last round when I heard raised voices. Over by the pool tables a couple of locals were surrounded by at least four bikies. A feral with hair knotty enough to pass as dreadlocks was giving angry lip to a kid leaning on a pool cue tucked under his chin, submissively silent. The situation was almost identical to the one Babs had found himself in.

Apparently satisfied with his stamping of authority, the bikie turned away. Then the guy with the pool cue did something incredibly foolish. He leaned over the table like nothing had happened and lined his stick up for another shot. His chin was about an inch from the nice green felt of the table when the bikie lurched forward without warning and grabbed a fistful of the guy's hair and slammed his face down hard onto the table. There was a thump like a football being kicked and we all heard the bikie's raised voice. 'I ain't finished!'

I saw Keogh tense up in his seat. 'Hey . . .' I pleaded. 'Don't.' My voice carried the pitch of panic. I was truly worried. These weren't a few young punks at a party. This lot had graduated from those classes long ago, with the odd murder between them for all I knew.

The guy who'd been picked on wiped his sleeve across his nose and stared at his hand. Blood was bubbling out of both his nostrils. The bikie grabbed the guy's lapels and shoved him hard against the wall with a loud thump. Sound in the pub went quiet as a church and everyone froze. Patrons sat where they were, bartenders stayed behind the bar, doormen were conspicuously absent. The only one to move was Keogh. He stood from the table.

'Leave it!' I hissed.

There was no doubt in my mind that when the call came to get tough, something kicked into Keogh's psyche some people would have called pathological. We could all see his eyes film over and glisten like a crazy man, his jaw clamp tight, the cords of his neck rise like little ridges. And still he held himself with the steadiness of a man in full command of his senses. As calmly as ever, he placed his beer on the table and walked toward them as if all he was doing was taking his turn with the pool cue.

Well before he got there, they saw him coming. It was impossible not to; he made too weird a sight. He stopped in front of them and his voice was clear as if it came out of a speaker.

'Let him go.'

The turn of expression on the bikie's miserable face would have been comical if not for the seriousness of the occasion. Somewhere inside that feeble brain of his, a chip had blown. He gaped at Keogh as if he'd seen nothing of the like in his entire miserable life. From the look mirrored on the faces of his company, nor had they.

'Just what is it with you blokes?' Keogh went on. 'The whole world your enemy?'

The bikie dropped his hands from the local's lapels as if he never existed. Now you could see the brutal nature of his default setting kick in; the red of his cheeks deepened a shade and he straightened to gain height. He was shorter than Keogh by a hand span at least.

'You onto me, tough boy?'

'Tell me – where do you think your beers come from?' Keogh asked. 'Your shit-hot bikes? Society makes it all possible. People like us, kids like him. We all do our bit, mate. Why do you have to piss on everything? You piss on the floor in your own house?'

'You gonna be pissing your own pants, my friend.'

'Listen to me,' Keogh said, waving a finger. There wasn't an ounce of fear in his voice. He spoke with all the authority of one of his half-time rugby briefings. 'We're just here for a good time. None of us want trouble. *I* don't want trouble.'

'Going about it the fuck of a wrong way.'

The bikie took a step forward. One of his gang, a medium-sized guy, reached out and lightly nudged his shoulder. It was a subtle gesture, one I took as encouraging. His comrade turned toward him briefly and there was some sort of coded communication only they would have understood. I took it as a signal to let it go. It had to be. This guy had a different look about him. His clothing was less stained and his hair was neater, and there was a calmness in his eyes that came with sentiment. Or respect. He didn't want Keogh beaten to a pulp any more than we did.

But his mate ignored him. He stepped right up to Keogh and they stood face to face. Tinges of grey stained his hair like mould on cheese and a wisp or two of it bobbed freely into his prematurely aged face. You could see he was getting angry; the frown deepened just enough to show the difference in expression. The contrast between him and Keogh was so stark you wouldn't have thought they belonged to the same species.

The bikie's elbow came up quickly, the sort of jab that came quicker than a punch ever could. It might not have been intended to do much damage, more to let him know who was boss, but Keogh was too quick. His head darted out of reach and the bikie's forearm brushed it only

257

lightly. As he recovered his balance Keogh's arm went back for the punch.

I could only watch in horror. Everything went slow, panic felt like ice in my veins. Keogh was going to do it. In front of a crowd of this guy's psychopathic brothers-in-arms, this greater nutcase friend of mine was actually going to hit him.

A prize boxer wouldn't have seen Keogh's fist coming. There was the crack of knuckle on bone and a puff of what might have been dust, might have been dandruff, from the guy's head. It wasn't a knockout punch but it would have hurt. The bikie staggered a little before recovering. Keogh's fists were back in boxing mode in the beat of a bee's wing.

The bikie glared at Keogh, but his eyes lacked their former confidence now. His cronies stood around in a manner I could only describe as shell-shocked. It lasted only seconds, but that look on their faces was one worth framing.

A big guy with a gut like a bowling ball raised his fists and came after Keogh. As soon as he was within striking distance he extended his arm in a huge overhand punch. Keogh blocked it easily but the guy's forward momentum kept him coming. Keogh backed away but didn't have a lot of room to work with. Perhaps that was why he hit this guy too. They had him cornered, literally.

Hit the big troglodyte with a quick jab that made his head fling backwards, but like the previous punch it didn't have the weight to knock him senseless. The big dude started swinging in earnest now, haymakers that went everywhere except what he aimed at. Keogh managed to duck and block those that might have found him, but then the pack stepped in. I stood up in reflex. I don't know what I was thinking, not least of which was self-preservation, and the last thing I was going to do was go in swinging, but I had to do something. Hopefully I could pull a couple of them back, pleading if necessary.

By the time I go to the fray there were about six of them beating into Keogh and still he fought back. It was a sickening sight, worsening by the second in its scale of viciousness. They queued for their turn at him, hissing and grunting like rabid animals with their jaws clenched tight and froth foaming about their lips. The sound alone was horror in my ears; cracking knuckles, thumping knees and heavy boots driven with maximum force, for maximum hurt. Had someone thrown a knife onto the floor these savages would have fought themselves to pick it up.

I muscled my way through the torsos and flying fists and reached for the nearest guy, grabbing him by the arm.

'Hey mate . . . come on.'

I had time to see him turn his face my way, an ugly, miserable thing that barely passed as human. His fist shot toward me, an explosive flash went off in my brain and that was the last I remember.

The first thing to come back to me was the ceiling light, painfully bright in my eyes. Everything around me was as vague as a dream. Instinctively I kicked my legs, I don't know why. For some reason it felt imperative that I stand.

'Woah,' someone said beside me. 'Stay still mate, it's over. Everything's okay.' But I knew everything wasn't okay. I don't know how but everything around me seemed very, very far from okay.

There was a fog-like atmosphere in the room. People knelt around me, talking softly. I knew these people. Hell, that was Babs beside me. I tried to sit up.

'Take it easy,' he said. Now I noticed Mick, Joey, and Skimp kneeling there. 'You okay?'

Slowly the fog cleared, and things started coming back to me. I rolled my head and saw that I was lying between pool tables. Another group was assembled nearby. There were far more people crouching and standing over there than around me. A space opened up and I caught a glimpse of a guy lying on his side. Despite my own condition, the faintness on my head, the fuzziness of shapes and forms around me, my mind reeled in horror. His head was swollen like something congenitally deformed, covered in blood. A gash on his brow oozed the stuff as thick as raspberry jam.

Everything kicked in then. I tried to sit up again and Babs put a hand on me. 'Just take it easy, we got an ambo coming.'

People hovered around me. I felt my face, which was numb and tingly. I could taste blood in my mouth. I ran my tongue over my lips and felt raw flesh, then rolled it around the inside of my mouth and concluded all my teeth were intact. There was a persistent, dull pain over my temple. I ran my hand over it and felt a tennis ball.

'Shit.' I pressed down, appalled by how much swelling there was. I pressed a bit more, wondering where the skull started, but it hurt too much.

'How you feeling?'

'Shit.'

Babs patted me on the shoulder and left his hand there. At any other time I would have brushed it off, but it felt too good. 'Jase all right?' I asked, rolling my head back his way. Now I knew whose face it was, I could see a partial resemblance. The pool of blood beneath his head crept toward me.

'Hope so. Bastards worked him over real good.' Babs patted me again. 'Cops are coming too.'

With help from the others, I raised myself into a sitting position. My head spun a little and it made sense to sit there until it stopped. A bartender came over with a glass of iced water and I took a sip but all I tasted was blood. He gave me a wet hand towel which I used to pat my busted lips, but it stung too much and I transferred it to the lump on my temple. I told them I was good to stand, several times in fact before they believed me. Joey and Cam guided me up carefully and kept their hands under my armpit while I tested my balance. I gave them the thumbs up and they led me to a chair.

I don't know how long I sat there. The world had gone surreal. When I tried to think of the seconds or minutes before it didn't feel like time had passed. I'd always thought you woke from being knocked out with a huge headache. There was no headache, just this numb, dreamy sensation of what was going on around me. I kept looking over at Keogh, willing him to come to, but his eyes stayed shut. By Jesus he looked bad.

At some point I became aware of someone fussing over me. I lifted my face and saw a guy in a flashy blue paramedic uniform. He knelt down and put a small case on the floor.

'Okay buddy,' he said, 'let's take a look at you.' He asked me my name, if I knew where I was, what day it was. When he started to bandage my head I tried to protest but he ignored me. I saw two other paramedics crouched over Keogh in the pool section.

'Better let us take you in,' the paramedic declared when he'd finished, 'just to be on the safe side.' Out of nowhere a gurney appeared. The idea of lying down appealed to me and the next thing I knew I was on it.

They floated me into the ambulance. I thought they'd load Keogh into the back as well but we pulled off without him.

The ride was smooth and the padding on my head was comforting. If anyone spoke that entire trip, I missed it. Upon reaching the hospital the first thing they did, and the last thing I wanted them to do, was ring my oldies. I tried hard to talk them out of it, to no avail. They were long since done with me when Dad arrived. They'd shone lights in my eye, taken my blood pressure, x-rayed my melon and fussed over me like I was royalty, and all I could think about was Keogh. They couldn't – or wouldn't – tell me anything. I was led to a comfortable chair and told not to move. I don't know if it was the knock on the head, but I sat in a stupor of the diametric extremes I'd switched between that night; thuggery and wanton disregard for human suffering one moment, gentle hands and total commitment toward the easing of pain the next.

A policeman came over and asked me what happened. I gave him a quick version of what I could remember and he took some details. Then Dad took him aside and they spoke for a long time.

Every time someone walked past in some kind of uniform I tried to ask questions but all I learnt was that Keogh had concussion and they wanted to run the full tests. Real helpful. After a while Dad came over.

'Are you ready to go?' He didn't give me an option, just stuck his hand under my armpit and tried to help me up.

'I can walk on my own, Dad,' I said sternly, shrugging him off.

He dropped his hand, embarrassed. 'Sure.'

It's sinfully more pleasurable walking out of a hospital than walking in. But this time I wanted to stay, at least until my friend came to. I tried to explain this to the old man but he told me there was no need, his mum was heading down from Newcastle and should be here soon. I must have been in fairyland because I kept repeating myself and the old man kept prodding me along, reminding me of when I was a kid in a toy store not wanting to leave.

I spent the night at my parents' place. Sleep made all the difference. The next morning my thought process had normalised and when I pressed the bruise on my temple the sensation of pain, unlike the night before, was sharp and specific. First thing I did was ring the hospital. They told me Keogh had come to and they were monitoring his condition. I asked if he'd be right for visitors and she told us he was on painkillers and we best leave it for a day or two. My response must have sounded desperate because after putting me on hold for a bit she came back onto the phone with perk in her voice and said it was up to me but I shouldn't stay long. It being a weekend mum wouldn't need her car, so a couple of calls later I'd organised to meet up with the lads at college that afternoon and we'd walk the short distance to the RPA hospital together.

We found his ward, shared with an old man surrounded by an aura of death and drips keeping him alive by all appearances. Keogh's bed was on the far side, next to the windows. A lady in her fifties I guessed sat on a chair beside him. One side of Keogh's face was bandaged and the other was puffed and stretched white as the bulb of a freshly sprouted mushroom. He was barely recognisable but fully conscious, and relief flooded through me. He watched us come with his one free eye, a tiny slit in the swelling of his face.

The woman stood as we walked in and I could see the ordeal of a sleepless night on her face. 'Hello boys.' She smiled and held out her hand. Her eyes were moist and bloodshot and puffy.

'Mrs Keogh?' I asked when I shook her hand.

'Well, sort of. Mrs Costa now.'

'Steve.'

We finished the introductions and she leaned over Keogh and patted his shoulder. 'I'll get going.' Without another word, she began walking away. The boys approached the bed.

'Hey man,' Joey said, 'how goes it?'

Keogh mumbled something incoherent as I trailed his mother out of the ward. 'Excuse me . . . Mrs Costa?' I said once we were outside.

'Yes?'

'I'm Steve,' I said again. I think I was nervous. 'I'm a good friend of Jason.'

'Yes, I can see that. Thank you for coming.'

'Is he okay? There's no way he'd tell me if he's not.'

'We think so. His cheekbone is fractured and they're worried about his eye, he can't see properly out of it. They think it might improve once the swelling goes down.' She encouraged herself with a smile.

'Anything I can do?'

'No, but thanks. I'm sure he appreciates you being here.'

'You heard what happened?'

'Yes.'

'I guess they'll look into it.'

'Of course.'

She was holding herself together well. *How do you do it?* I wanted to ask. I was damn near ready to punch walls down. 'All this just for sticking up for a couple of kids,' I said despicably.

'I know.'

I shuffled on my feet, gazed down at the floor. There was something she could help me with, something I'd been trying to figure out ever since I met the guy. 'Listen . . . I . . . um . . .'

'He's always done things like this,' she said sadly. 'It's just the way he is.' I saw the mist gather over her eyes, and she turned away. 'Go on in, he'll be glad to see you.'

Her heels clopped loudly in the corridor as she walked off. I was desperate to talk more, but I let her go.

When I got to Keogh's bed no one was talking. 'Hey buster,' I said cheerily. 'How you doin?'

'How does it look?' he answered dully.

'Didn't think working your way through the deadbeats of the world was your thing, mate,' I said, none too passionately. I was his best friend and thought I'd earned the right.

'Stop it,' he scoffed. 'I got it from the old lady already.'

With his face all bandaged I couldn't tell if he was being witty or cynical, but the brevity in his voice checked that line of discussion.

'Need anything?'

'No.'

'Eye all right?'

'Too early to tell.'

Babs asked, 'You gonna be right for exams?'

'They're the last thing on my mind.'

'Nurses in here looking after you?' Rajah asked chirpily.

Keogh let out a deep sigh. 'Guys listen,' he said. 'Nice of you come and all that, but don't expect me to go all rosy just to make you feel better for it.'

We all froze. Confusion turned into shock as we shuffled our feet. I didn't know whether to retort or apologise.

'That's the easy part,' he mumbled faintly.

Babs spoke for us all. 'Hey, come on mate. That's not fair.'

'Shit,' Keogh lamented. 'Seriously . . . just give me a while, will you?' He stared at the ceiling, motionless as a corpse. 'I just want to be left alone.'

The seconds ticked away, none of us knew what to say. We glanced sheepishly at each other. I leaned forward and put a hand on his shoulder. 'Okay buddy . . . okay,' I said. 'We'll leave you alone, come back in a day or so. You just get better, okay?'

We left the ward and no one spoke until we were alone in the elevator. Cam pressed the button for the ground floor. 'That wasn't him.'

'Well shit,' I said harshly. 'The guy's marbles are so rattled he ain't himself. Plus he's all drugged up, that's all. Give him a day or so, he'll be right.'

I couldn't have been more wrong.

Soon as I got home mum told me Nat had rung twice and wanted me to ring her back. I went straight to my room and had a good sleep.

Around six I woke and went into the kitchen. Mum asked me how I was, I mumbled fine, then she told me Nat had rung again and was coming to dinner. I almost started an argument with her right then. Nat had two mothers now, and I reckon mine saw a brighter halo over her head.

I was in my room when Nat came knocking around seven, and I stayed there until she came in. I suppose it was good to see her but I didn't feel like going over events again, which I let her know as soon as she started asking questions. She asked how Keogh was, I told her, and then she turned her full attention onto me. Her touch worked its usual magic and I did feel a whole lot better for her coming. The shine she put into the place prevailed throughout dinner, and after giving me a warm hug and a kiss, took off. I hadn't been the chattiest of boyfriends and she was right to assume I wanted the night to myself.

Dad dropped me back at Palmer Street the next day, and I got a lot of attention over those that followed. I rang the hospital each morning to see if he was right for visitors and got told each time he didn't want any and he'd be out soon enough anyway. Plenty of people wanted to see him and needed a fairly persuasive argument to be talked out of it. Lisa was the worst. She just didn't get it. She'd rung me full of dutiful concern, differences forgotten. She might have been genuine but I lacked the patience to be diplomatic with her. She took offence when I told her he didn't want visitors. She must have thought it her right, or that I was lying – probably both – but I told her bluntly that's what he said and if she wanted to test it, then off and go see him. That shut her up.

I rang the hospital Wednesday evening and a nurse told me happily that they'd discharged him that morning. I took this as a good sign and asked if that meant he was ok. Aside from the eye, it sounded like he was. I rang his home and his mother put me onto him. His voice sounded better but it lacked life; muffled-like and monotonic.

He wasn't coming back to Uni this year. There had been negotiations behind the scenes and the powers-that-be had offered him replacement examinations that would take place a few weeks after normal exams finished. The cops had visited him in hospital and taken a statement. They'd be in touch with me soon. We didn't say a thing about the night, about the culprits, or about the investigation. He wasn't in a talkative mood and I considered myself lucky I'd got that much out of him.

I told him to look after himself and hung up the phone.

Twenty-one

The next day I got a call from Detective Allworth of the Newtown Police, the same guy I'd spoken to over the Beeman business. He asked me if I could come to the station asap. Given that memories are best served fresh I could see his point, but I wondered why it took him five days to get around to me. The rest of the boys had given their versions the day after it happened.

I delivered myself up to the counter of the police station at the time arranged. Allworth and I shook hands and he led me through to an office with a desk and a typewriter. For two hours or more he tapped away in a manner that told me it was just another day on the job for him. The questions never stopped. Describe the first guy. The second guy. Who hit who first? How far away were you? Was your view obstructed? How did Keogh hit him? Open fist, closed fist? Every time I answered he hardly broke rhythm, like he knew what I was going to say before I opened my mouth.

Besides the feral and the guy with the gut, I couldn't single out anyone. My lights went out early in the fracas and the focus was on how much I saw before they did. I couldn't accurately describe everyone I'd seen laying into Keogh, and the detective lingered on this for a long time. I made sure to mention Keogh was cornered, and I didn't need to exaggerate the thrashing they gave him, but by the end of it I knew my statement wouldn't be putting anyone away.

'Do we know who they were?' I asked.

'We got an idea on the main players.'

'Are you going to charge them?'

The detective winced. 'It's difficult. We need someone to say he saw this guy hit him, that guy kick him . . . things like that. You said a guy started beating into him, and you've described him reasonably well: shoulder-length brown hair, unshaven face, etcetera. You might even pick him in a line-up. But come court day you'll have a tribe of brown-haired, bearded bikies sitting in the room and a lawyer saying you got them mixed up. That the guy we've put in the dock was just trying to break it up. Then there's the problem of your mate taking them on. After all, who walks up to a group of bikies and starts mouthing off?'

He gave me a lot of negatives, not a lot of positives. But there was more to it than that. There was this weariness about him, a numbness he couldn't hide in his professional voice and demeanour. He wore the unflinching expression of a man who'd seen in all, typed it all, disconcerting to me in the way it tended to normalise the matter. He'd come to terms with a world the rest of us spend a lifetime trying to avoid, and I wondered if he envied or despised us for it. I suspected Keogh would have to be dead before they put too much effort into it. I reminded him that the guy had suffered major damage and his vision could be permanently impaired, and he didn't waver. He opened a manila folder in front of him and picked up some papers.

'We got a good statement from this guy . . . David Schiffer,' he said, holding it up. 'The problem is that appears he had a bit of a scuffle with one of these guys earlier.'

'So?'

'Well, it might look like he's trying to finger the guy who bullied him, just to get his own back.'

'You're kidding.'

'That's how they'd argue it. You have to understand that these guys are getting sophisticated. They have lawyers in their ranks.'

I asked what else they had. Though he wouldn't let me read anyone's statements, I got the impression most were consistent with mine. The detective didn't sound enthusiastic about any of them. No one singled out anyone, the bar staff didn't see jack. One of them even said Keogh 'threw the first punch.'

I stood up and we shook hands. I asked what happens next and he answered in the same tone he'd used the whole time.

'We'll continue with our investigations, and let you know.'

It was the worst time of the year for this to happen. We settled back into study, what else could we do? I rang Keogh's home once or twice over the following days and his phone rang out. The last time his mother answered. She told me he'd gone out and didn't know where. I asked about his eye and learnt about hyphemas and orbital blowout fractures. For all our wonderful medical miracles, not a single doctor could say if his vision would improve. I tried to cheer her up with optimism, reminding her that Keogh was your classic freak of health, but don't think I succeeded. I asked her to pass on the message for him to call me but I never heard from him. I figured there was a lot he was going through and he'd be in touch when he was ready.

Exams started mid-November. I sweated those nights till all hours trying to cram in as much as I could, getting about four hours of sleep on average. Images of that night kept distracting me. I'd seen plenty of guys get a thumping over the years but the sight of Keogh lying on the ground like some roadkill scorched an image into my mind I couldn't erase. Part of the reason was that I hadn't seen what happened. I had to imagine it, which only made it worse. I gave it no limits. This led to visions of me barging into their clubhouse on one of their monthly meetings or drug nights or whatever the fuck they did and letting loose with a semi-automatic, U.S. style. I'd take Skimp's 7.62mm army assault rifle and build on the fantasy, imagining how I'd go about getting away with it. At some stage in the delusion I'd realise my breathing had quickened and my heartbeat was banging away. I'd have to consciously wind myself down. I'd look in the mirror and see the snarl of someone losing the plot. I'd look down on my Lotka-Volterra equations and Laplace Transforms and get depressed by how trivial they were.

Nat's exams ended before mine. She packed her things, took off home and graciously let me be. The glorious end to my exams came on the Thursday afternoon of the second week. Needing a drink to clean out the brain, I rounded up some like-minded boys of the faculty and headed for the Manning where we'd be trouble-free. I drank hard, gloated over the poor sods still with exams to do, and let thoughts of

Keogh losing vision in one eye and me being on a bikie hit-list dissolve into an alcoholic haze. At one stage I caught sight of Louise, Marion's friend. I swaggered over with a big smile.

'Hello Louise.' I leaned forward to give her a peck, which I doubt I would have done sober, and definitely not if Nat was there.

'Hi Steve,' she replied, offering her cheek.

I took a step back, had a good eye-feast. She had that rare poise of a woman at ease enough in her own skin not to plaster herself with unnecessary makeup or cringe under the gall of my scrutiny, which I hoped she'd read as no different to me admiring a precious sculpture. In my sober moments her dark liquid eyes, effortless smile and rubbery lips would have me thinking long-term, deep discussions and playful bed wrestles; right now she had a butt worthy of poetry and I just wanted to jump her bones.

'You're looking good,' I said.

'Thanks,' she replied, smiling politely. 'How do you think you went in the exams?'

I kept that part of it brief, then cut to the chase. 'You here with anyone?'

'A few girls.' She gave me their names and I felt confident that there were at least a couple of degrees of separation between them and where Nat lived, Nat's hockey team, Nat's faculty . . . A table went vacant and she accepted my invitation to sit down. I offered to buy her a drink and my confidence lifted further when she said yes.

She sent me some encouraging signals after that. She leaned so close when we talked that her lips grazed my ear and I could smell her breath, as clean and fresh as peppermints in bloom. Did she really need to touch my shoulder every time she laughed? Were my jokes that funny? Did she offer to buy me a drink only because I bought her one?

I contemplated my half-empty glass. 'I'll get them,' I said. 'You right for another?'

'My turn.' She stood up. 'What are you having?'

I conceded only because it meant she'd come back. She walked away and my eyes followed her all the way to the bar. I leaned back, had a good stretch and let my gaze wander around the room.

There was Nat.

The place was crowded and my table was tucked into a corner, not the first place you'd check. The way she kept turning her obliviously happy face everywhere but my direction was a safe bet she hadn't seen me. I cussed lightly, drained my glass and stood.

Careful not to stray into her line of sight, I negotiated my way through the crowd to the bar and nudged through the layers until I was an arm's length from where Louise stood ready to be served.

'Louise!' I reached out and tapped her shoulder. She turned around. 'I'm going to have to take a rain cheque. Sorry.' I back up the apology with a wink. 'Maybe another time.' She looked at me uncomprehendingly and I turned away before she could see my rather ugly turn of expression.

I stepped away from the queue. A nasty feeling was growing inside me, slithering around in my belly like a snake about to strike. Nat was standing next to Skimp and both were scouring the pub with their eyes. Skimp saw me first. He tapped Nat on the shoulder and pointed.

Whenever Nat gave me one of her *there-you-are smiles,* her lips stretched wide and her cheeks became tight little balls with a dimple on either side I always thought cute. I saw nothing cute in them now. I walked over.

'Hi Steve,' she said, as ignorant to the scowl I wore as to what might have caused it.

'Nat . . .' I took her arm and led her away a bit. 'Why are you here?'

'I had some stuff to collect from my place.'

'What, you had to do it tonight?'

Her face lost a little of its lift. 'Is that a problem?'

'I didn't think you'd be here.'

'You thought wrong.' She pressed her body up against mine and guided my head down with her hand to speak privately into my ear. 'Your exams are over. Don't you want the icing on the cake?'

Right then I caught sight of Louise. She'd positioned herself in a way to clearly see me but was pretending not to. I glanced at the table we'd been sitting at and saw a batch of people pull the chairs back and settle in.

'Maybe I wanted the night off,' I said.

'You have the night off.'

'I meant all of it.'

'Well, you should know I'd always find you,' she said cheekily, the dimples reappearing on her cheeks. 'Like I said, you can run, but you can't—'

'Shit Nat!' I raised my voice. 'This isn't funny!' A couple of girls close by twisted their necks and gawked at me. 'You always do this, pop up unexpected!'

The grin fell from her face and she scrunched her brows. She dropped her hand and took a step back. 'What sort of welcome is that?'

I rubbed a hand through my hair. 'You don't get it, do you? If I don't ask you to be somewhere, it's a pretty good hint I want to be alone.'

'What? Are you telling me where I can and can't go now?'

I shook my head in frustration. 'Why are you here, Nat?'

Her lips wavered and her cheeks went tight. She was seeing a side to me she'd never seen and hadn't the faintest idea how to deal with it.

'Why are you doing this?' she asked morosely. 'Am I stopping you from something?'

I shook my head, more out of despair than denial, and looked away.

'Is that it?' she asked, adding a bit of fire to her voice. 'Is that what this is all about? You want to pick up, is that it?'

'Oh shutup,' I said tartly. 'Sometimes a guy just wants to be alone. For his own reasons.'

The noise was loud, people were having a good time, and we stood there like a funeral was going on. Her gaze went somewhere over my shoulder and she blinked once or twice. Her mouth opened to speak, then closed again. Her eyes watered over and sparkled in the dim light.

Abruptly, she swung away. I thought she might head for somewhere else in the place but she made a beeline for the door.

Okay, I'd overstepped. The alcohol in my system probably gave me a more aggressive touch than normal, but that was no excuse. I stood there in limbo. If she had looked behind I might have waved her back and apologised, but she never did. Grabbed the door, tugged it open and was gone.

I went to the bar and bought a beer. I joined the boys and got talking. Now and then I scanned the pub for Louise, but I didn't see her again.

I stumbled back to Palmer St after one in the morning and my head hit the pillow with the wonderful thought that it was all behind me. I had three months to enjoy. No study, no lectures, no assignments. This summer I'd have new friends to party with.

I went into those holidays on a high.

Twenty-two

To save on rent I pulled up stumps on Palmer St, thought I'd make a case for re-admission into Phillips next year. Failing that, I'd just find lodgings elsewhere. On Saturday I boxed my stuff and got Dad to pick me up, and by afternoon I'd resettled into my room at home. Keogh's gear was still at Palmer St but no one knew his intentions.

I felt well and truly free, for the first time that year. Just one more thing needed doing to make it all complete, something I'd let drag on way too long. After months and months of procrastination, months of putting it off, lo and behold I finally, yes finally, grew some balls and broke up with Nat.

She rang me obliviously the Saturday night for a catchup and I mumbled some lame excuse to get out of it. There was a steady silence on the other end of the phone before she spoke softly.

'You're dumping me, aren't you?'

The resigned, matter-of-fact way she said it was so moving that for a moment I felt myself buckle. But I brushed it aside quickly. I told her it had been fun, it had been great, but I didn't see us going the distance and I didn't want to lead her on. I told her it was the logical thing to do, that she wanted someone who put as much into a relationship as she did, and so on. What I didn't tell her was that I *did* think we were great together. It was the timing I was just starting out, needed to play the field; selfish I knew, and woefully primate, but hard to fight. The longer I left it, the more likely I'd stray. She was too good a person to have that happen to her.

And true to form, even as that final curtain fell, she had one more surprise left for me: her reaction. She'd always been full of fight, and I'd half-expected one. The other half was for her hanging up on me, which would have made it easier for both of us. She did neither. All she gave me were tears. Uncontrollable, broken-heart tears.

'Aw come on Nat,' I said impatiently, spitefully even; it was the easier path to take. 'Going from the number of times you've upped me about being rude, or sexist, or arrogant, or a plain shit, I thought I'd be doing you a favour.'

'That's not fair,' she blubbered.

Didn't matter what I said, I couldn't get her angry at me. She just kept on crying. Crying to the point I began to feel real pity for her, too much for my own good. I told her I was sorry, but I had to go. I could still hear her balling when I hung up the phone.

I met up with the homeboys early on in the piece, at the local. I'd barely walked through the door when Kep asked me if Nat was coming. I didn't have the heart to tell him we'd busted up; I thought it might break his own. Either that or give him ideas, and I didn't fancy either. I gave him a brusque no and changed the subject.

It was a totally unspectacular night. A free man, I thought I'd take to the place like a stallion put to pasture, but the urge never took hold. Nat had spoiled me, set too high a bar for her successors. I bored easily of girls rich in opinion and short of fact, laughing at their own dumb jokes, overstepping their meagre vocabularies. It got so bad sometimes I had to about-face while they were still at it.

Almost every weekend I got called in to make numbers for my old cricket team. I bought a three-month pass at my local gym and kept my shape tight. I caught up with school friends and beached on good days with anyone who was available. Between all that I welcomed the opportunity to just sloth on the lounge watching cricket or an old movie. It was bliss.

Keogh called in early December. It was a Saturday morning. A southerly had blown in and the trees were shedding more leaves and sticks by the hour. I was stuffing down bacon and eggs and answered the phone with my mouth full.

'Steve?'

My inner core lit up. 'Hey Jase! How you been man?' I swallowed quickly and spoke better. 'Good to hear you.' I meant every word and

275

wanted him to know. 'You okay?'

'Sure.'

'You doing replacements? Been studying?'

'On and off.'

'Great!' I was bursting with enthusiasm. 'You coming down to Sydney soon?'

'Don't know.'

'How's the eye?' I asked, making damn sure it didn't sound like an obligatory question.

'Not good,' he said. 'I can see things but they're all blurred. They're talking about an operation.'

I let it hang. There were questions I wanted to ask and I'd sleep better with the right answers. Keogh had always been a straight shooter and I knew he respected those who were.

'Is it permanent?' I asked.

'Could be.'

'Shit.'

And then it started to sink in – his football career, his spearfishing – the things he loved doing. Not to mention his future. Like everyone I'd taken the more palatable option of assuming he'd be fine, and if I was him, I'd have despised it. 'You don't know for sure though, right?' I offered hopefully. 'It's probably too early to tell.'

'Yeah, that's what the doctors say. Whatever.'

The tone in his voice had me worried. This wasn't like him. A different guy was on the other end of the phone, one I didn't know how to talk to. 'When you coming down?'

'Listen, Steve. I'm not going through with it. I'm going to tell the police to drop it.'

'What?' I'd be in denial to think I wasn't relieved. The fear of thugs stalking me for the next x years was something I'd rather live without.

'It's not worth it,' he said. 'No point dragging you all through a pile of shit for nothing. These guys aren't going to jail and one more assault rap on their sheets won't mean a thing.'

'You don't know that.'

'Yes I do. Thanks anyway. Thanks for going to the trouble. Tell the boys that for me, okay?'

'Yeah, but . . .'

'And listen . . . the main reason I rang . . .' I heard him take a breath then. 'Thanks for trying to help me that night. You stepped in when no one else did.'

It was so unexpected I was at a loss for words. 'Hey, forget it,' I said after a while. 'You'd do the same for me, only you'd have done a better job. So forget it.'

'No,' he said softly. 'That's the problem. People do forget, turn it into nothing. These things don't mean shit to anyone anymore. They're *breeding it out of us*, mate.' He gave a snort. 'Makes more sense to know how to straighten a tie and lick fucking envelopes. Squeeze people for all the money they're worth.'

Something wasn't right here. This went beyond his normal rants. I wondered if his brain had been rattled a little more than the doctors thought.

'Come down to Sydney,' I said. 'Shack up here. You in for a one-dayer? I was thinking of the Indies game next week.'

'Maybe. Might need a telescope.'

Even if I had the heart to take it up as a joke, I wouldn't have. 'I'm getting a ticket for you anyway,' I went on quickly. 'My shout.'

The line stayed quiet.

'Hey Jase,' I said hesitantly. 'There's something I've wanted to say for a long time.' I faltered then, and not because it was hard to say. Perhaps it was for effect. I wanted him to know how important it was that I say it. That it was long overdue. That I felt slack for not having said it way, way sooner.

'That night . . . at the party . . . at the start of the year.' I stuttered those first few words, but made damn sure the rest came out cleanly. 'I never did say I was sorry.'

There it was. Out. I've said a lot of important things in my life. Plenty of *sorrys* and *thank yous* and *I love yous* and *you're the best*, and no words ever felt better for leaving my mouth than the ones I just uttered.

I heard a snicker on the other end of the line, but there was warmth in it that came right out of the phone. 'That's okay,' he said faintly, and yet with a tiny kick of life in his voice. 'You made up for it since.'

I chuckled lightly, hoping it might draw the same from him, but his voice came back as hollow as it had been all along.

'You turned out all right, Chambers.'

And then he hung up.

The worst things in life hit you without warning. That's why they're the worst. They're born out of weakness, negligence. Ancient people gave them form, a presence. They danced and prayed and sacrificed, if for no other reason than to make themselves feel less helpless.

They're still here, they still happen. You can't fight them. They will have their way and when they're done, you will eat yourself with hindsight.

While they laugh and move on.

Twenty-three

After the phone call, I sparked. I finished breakfast and rang around. Keogh's call put me on a roll. We were on for the West Indies game and I wanted to round up as many of the lads as I could.

That night the wind picked up to fifty knots, blowing against the windows so hard I could hear the glass buckle. It was still roaring on Sunday night when I made the last of my calls. Besides Joey who was up at Byron Bay surfing, the Sydney regulars were all keen. They'd sounded even keener when I told them Keogh was coming to life and I reckoned I could tip the balance if I told him everyone was making the effort. That settled it; they stopped procrastinating. We'd hit town afterwards and make a night of it. I rang Keogh's number last, knowing he'd be more easily persuaded if he knew we were all in, but the phone was engaged and I went to bed after that.

On Monday I still hadn't heard from him. Not wanting to pester the guy, I let it be. I spent the day reading old MAD magazines and tuning in and out of the TV, enjoying the sensation of laziness while outside the city was being blown to pieces by a raging low. After dinner I rang Keogh's house again. Mrs Costa picked up.

'Hello?' It was a mechanical greeting, like a recording.

'Hi,' I said. 'Is Steve there?'

There was a pause, then she spoke in a husky voice. 'Who is this?'

I could feel her gather herself on the other end. Out of nowhere, an invisible claw gripped the nape of my neck. 'It's Steve Chambers,' I said warily.

This time there was a longer pause, a foreboding silence that tightened the grip around my neck.

'Steve . . . *oh Steve* . . .'

Ten minutes later I hung up the phone. I walked into my room without seeing a thing. I sat down and tried to think but my mind swirled like a washing machine. I tried to think positive. I'd kidded myself into thinking his eye would be fine. That his mind was fine. Wilful ignorance was the moderate term. Selfishly stupid was more accurate.

Keogh was missing. On Saturday morning he'd told his mother he was off to Sydney and taken her car. Right after he'd rung me.

Assuming he'd stayed there overnight, she only started ringing around on Sunday evening. It was out of character to leave her hanging, what made it creepy though was leaving her without a vehicle for work on Monday. First call was to Palmer St. Nope, he hadn't been there. She'd tried several known contacts after that, come up with nothing and gone a bit panicky. She'd called the police and got some relief hearing there were no road accidents, then spent a sleepless night through to Monday morning when the real panic set in.

She tried Palmer St again after that for contacts like me but the phone rang out. Then she'd rung St Phillips, hoping someone there would oblige her with a phone number or two. Sandra and Chris were on leave and the twit from the temp agency had rambled on about privacy and legal obligations and Mrs Costa lost her cool. The girl did promise to ring some friends of his that Mrs Costa nominated, including me, and pass the message on to ring her urgently. Mrs Costa had checked progress with the girl just before closing and was reliably informed the message had been passed on. When I told her I'd heard nothing, Mrs Costa burst into tears.

In between her sobs I learnt she'd rung the police again and spoken to an officer who dutifully filed his absence. No amount of a mother's tears or reasoning could persuade him to do much else. Too early for serious worry was his well-rehearsed, if not sympathetic encouragement. He gave her the stats: eighty to ninety percent of missing persons are accounted for within a week, and of those remaining, up to ninety-five percent are accounted for within three months. Keogh had only been gone two days. Could it be that her son just needed some time off? Does he have a girlfriend she might not know about? Has he been showing signs of anxiety or depression? Has anything unusual or disturbing happened to him lately? If the insinuation was supposed to put her at ease, it sure had the opposite effect.

My gut reaction was that Keogh had gone bush for a few days. A more worrying possibility was him prepping for some payback mission on the arseholes that did this to him, though that seemed unlikely. I put both theories to his mother, and though she didn't entirely dismiss either, the way she fell silent after my reasoning had me thinking her instinct pointed somewhere way, way more sinister. But I wouldn't go down that path. Refused to even encourage the thought by considering it. I told her I'd ring around and get back to her.

I rung around, got nothing. I even rang Lisa's number and spoke to the girl for as long as necessary to get the same answer. She sounded genuinely worried and told me to ring her back if I got nowhere. Every call I made I kept as brief as possible and only managed to finish up around 11pm. One call was left: the hardest.

I was sitting on the sofa, mum and dad were in bed, the house was silent and the cat was stretched out on the carpet with its paws pointed at the ceiling. I bowed my head into my hands. Mrs Costa was relying on me and I had nothing. I was at my wits end, just like she would have been. If Keogh didn't want to be found, he wouldn't be. Whatever he was doing was no cry for help.

She answered on the second ring. She spoke in a kind voice and was good to me. She was going to touch bases with the police in the morning; surely by now things were getting serious. But the hopelessness in her voice, born of a mother's instinct, was eerier to me than if she'd gone hysterical. It was like hearing the flatline that precedes death from cardiac failure. I told her I'd drive over to Palmer St first thing in the morning, then to several other places I had in mind.

She took a tired breath. 'Look for a white station wagon,' she said in a beaten voice, and added the plate number. 'Goodbye, Steve.'

Then she hung up the phone.

I couldn't sleep. A bug was crawling around in a dark corner of my mind

I couldn't squash. Hours had passed before I'd tired myself out enough to slip away.

Dreams came to me in a jumble. I was reliving previous events, former thoughts. I was hearing voices, mixed with my own. Past merged with present merged with neither. At one point I was down on the seabed with Keogh in front of me. I kept thinking I needed to go up, but then I found I could breathe like a fish. The ocean felt like a warm blanket. Keogh looked at me with an eerie smile. He was talking but I couldn't understand a word he said. I kicked closer and the ocean offered no resistance; it was like gliding through thin air. Then he turned away, swam off out of sight.

No one has given a valid hypothesis as to why we dream. Perhaps I'd been thinking too hard, clogging up the pipeline that gave flow to clarity. Sleep must have been the switch that shut it all down, let me reboot. Deep in the night it all fell into place, the hour of ghosts and voices that whisper to us from the otherworld.

I'm going to be buried with it . . .

. . . it's so peaceful down there . . .

. . . the factory spat out a dud . . .

. . . just keep on swimming . . .

There must be a block in everyone's mind when they hear things they don't want to hear.

The clues just fly on past.

It was dawn quiet, darkness was lifting. The wind had softened to a low moan. I sat up on my bed feeling like I hadn't slept at all. The digits on my clock glowed 5.21. I dressed dreamily in the faint light of my room, in slow motion.

My body felt heavy as I walked through the house. I took mum's keys from the hook in the hallway, opened the front door and closed it gently.

Mum would want her car for work, but this early in the morning there was no traffic. Barring holdups I'd be back before she needed it. It was a selfish and irrelevant thought; I thought it no more.

Very few cars were on the road. As I drove I'd glance at the faces of drivers stiff and intent on the road ahead. The day ahead, lives ahead. I was just one more in a robotic daze of people moving ever-forward, and I'd never felt further away from anything in my life.

I kept going over my reasoning. I hoped I was wrong. But that hope had grown as numb as the rest of me. I'd never felt this numb. All I felt was a vague appreciation that I was travelling freely on the road, like floating down a river.

About three-quarters of an hour later I pulled right into Anzac Avenue without having to wait for a break in traffic. I passed a man walking his Labrador and a girl jogging with headphones. The headland at Long Reef and the ocean came into view, surging under a mountainous swell that broke in foaming offshore waves as far as the eye could see.

I turned right at the golf club and idled ahead, keeping my gaze from straying too far up the road. I think I was plain scared, wanted to preserve the thought that I was wrong for as long as possible. I'd never felt like this before. If I was right about this, every day from hereafter would be *after*.

I passed the boat ramp and a white van with pipes and a ladder on the roof. A plumber possibly, out on an early morning swim or run. Far to the north, someone walked behind a dog scampering up the beach.

The turnoff to the lower carpark came into my field of view. I saw it and felt nothing. I think my mind had drained itself by then. It was like locking in that final piece of a jigsaw. You knew it was done long before then.

A single car sat in the carpark. One white station wagon, considerately parked within its own car space. I glanced at the rego plate, then let my head fall into my hands and my former life abandon me.

Twenty-four

A soft knocking woke me. I turned over on my stomach, groaned sleepily. What day was it? What time? I rolled my head to check the digital clock. 2.37pm, Friday. *Shit.*

'Steve?' Mum enquired in a polite voice. She'd been ultra-polite these last couple of days.

'What?'

'Natalie's on the phone.'

I lay on the bed, thought it over. Mum was supposed to take messages. She'd been doing fine till now. 'Okay,' I said weakly. 'Coming.'

I examined myself in the mirror, appalled at how crappy I looked. My eyes were red and squinty, sunken into my skull. A sickly presence in my gut had stolen my appetite and I didn't need a reflection to know I was in weight decline. I gave my hair a smooth over and it felt as greasy as butter. Sleeping had become so bad at night not even a catchup during the day made a difference.

I went into the lounge room and saw that Mum had made herself scarce. I sat down on the lounge and picked up the receiver. 'Hello?'

'Steve?'

'Yeah, hi.'

'Hi hon. You okay?' She sounded pretty wounded herself.

'Sure.' I rubbed a hand through my hair. 'You?'

'I've been away . . . I only found out about half an hour ago,' she said, and then waited for me to speak. I didn't. 'Are you all right?' she went on. 'Lisa told me no one's been able to get onto you.'

I'd only made two calls after I found the car. The first was to the police from the closest payphone I could find, the second to Rajah when I got home, and even that was just for someone else to spread word.

'I can't do it, Nat,' I said. 'I can't go over it with everyone who rings.'
Her voice came back softer. 'Is there anything I can do?'

Poor thing; I could hear her choking on her tears. 'No, but thanks for asking.'

'Do you want to talk about it?'

'No.'

'Okay . . . okay.' There was a long silence. 'Steve?'

'Yeah.'

'He was my friend too.' She'd said it stoically, but with a tremor in her voice. At that moment I felt deep sympathy for the girl. She was one of the few who could genuinely lay claim to the term.

'I know, but look . . .' I inhaled deeply. 'There's not a lot to say.'

'Have the police found out anything?'

'I don't think so. It doesn't matter.'

'He might have spoken to someone, or rung someone.'

I didn't have the energy to go over that last phone call of his, so I just said, 'Maybe.'

I heard a sniff or two. She was treading delicately and I respected her for that. 'You knew where he'd gone,' she said.

I took a few breaths. I didn't want to go down that path but I knew she wouldn't let up if I said nothing. 'Just something he said to me once,' I said dismissively. 'It was his place.'

'What did he say?'

I almost told her. Now and then some weird cosmic influence must play into our lives, when seemingly random events line up at just the right moment, and things meant to be fall into place. I thought back to that day on the headland at Easter when Keogh had mumbled the words that would haunt me forever, and how Nat had showed up with perfect timing, and wondered if the intrusion had been just a little *too* coincidental. Like she was supposed to be there. I'm not superstitious, yet I felt a boding sense of consequence not unlike what our hairy forebears must have experienced when gawking at a solar eclipse. A sign from above. It was eerie.

'Nat,' I said, a touch short of firmly, 'I'd rather not go into it.'

There was a delay before she resumed. 'Gabe told me Mick went in today to give a statement to the police. Have you?'

'Not yet. I was in a mess at the time, and they let me go. They told me to come in when I'm ready. I'll go in when I am.'

'Wouldn't sooner be better than later?'

'Shit Nat, there's not a lot of mystery here. We know what happened.'

'Sorry. I just meant . . . there's a lot of speculation.'

'Not if you knew him.'

Quiet for a few seconds, and then: 'Apparently they called off the search.'

'Yeah well, a five-meter swell doesn't make for a good search.'

'Is that it then?'

'I don't know. He's officially listed as missing, presumed drowned. It eases their workload.'

It felt good talking to her; I could vent my cynicism with impunity. She asked lots of questions and I couldn't blame her. I'd asked myself the same, along with a thousand more. She suggested someone should go up and talk to his mother, someone like me. It sounded like a good idea. I hadn't even worked up the courage to ring the poor woman.

'I could go with you, if you like,' she offered.

'Why?'

'It might . . . be good for her . . . if a woman was there.'

'Nat . . .' I let her think about it, then spelled it out anyway. 'I don't think that would be a good idea.'

There was a sniff or two on the other end of the phone and I imagined a fresh burst of tears rolling down her cheeks. It was bloody contagious.

'I better go,' I said, as my throat began to choke up. 'Thanks for calling.' I felt bad closing the door on her like that, but I had to.

'Do you want me to come over?'

There she goes again. By God this woman knew me. How easy would it have been for me to say *yes.* Sure, come over. She'd know exactly what to say, what buttons to push. She'd be so good to me I wouldn't let her stop. All the more reason to fight the temptation. I wouldn't do it. Refused to do it. I saw it as no better than guys who dumped their girlfriends and used them for sex afterwards, just because they could. I'd dumped her, I'd wear the consequences.

'Thanks, but no.' I'd barely managed to get it out. 'I'll see you around, Nat.'

A couple of days later I gave a statement to the Dee Why Police. It made me feel even more useless than the last time. I didn't mention that last phone call of Keogh's. If I thought it'd do any good I would have, but it was a private thing between me and him and no one else's business. They knew I was his closest friend and let me in on a few extras, like how a girl from the golf club on a smoko that day saw a guy wander off up the beach toward the rock platform carrying a speargun. Waves thumping into rocks were shooting up like depth charges had gone off beneath, and she'd thought it a bit strange. Unless some form of evidence was to show up to the contrary, and soon, they were prepared to file a report of suspected death to the coroner, presumed drowned. They didn't elaborate on the details and I didn't ask.

I kept at cricket, made it a weekly habit. Having no affiliations there with college was good for me. I bashed at that ball like there was nothing to lose, double my strike rate one week and get out for a duck the next. I'd have a drink afterwards and come home half-tanked.

I was invited to a party thrown by one of the Phillips boys, but only conceded to go when I learnt most of the lads were going. We gathered together in a corner and got stuck into the beers, laughing and carrying on, but a shadow hung over us thicker than storm clouds.

We'd been there a couple of hours when someone mustered the nerve to bring it up. I don't know how it started but before long the talk turned to possible events that day. We were all thinking the same thing but no one would say it. Ironically, it took a guy with mush for brains to bring it out. From the way he happened in on the discussion he must have been listening in. We knew there'd been a lot of speculation about what happened, the worst being how daft someone had to be to try spearfishing in such dangerous conditions, and the last thing I needed now was to hear someone as dumb as this guy support the notion.

'Oh for fuck's sake Sherlock,' I blurted out angrily. 'The guy was half-fish. Do you really think it was an accident?' I should have kept my mouth shut. When people don't know what to think, it can be worse enlightening them. After that we all got wasted. It was what we needed, to cut away the rotting flesh.

After much deliberation, I rang Mrs Costa. My trepidation was completely needless. A minute into the phone call and she asked if I could go up and see her, which I did the next day. She was an extremely stoic, kind-hearted person, and I could see where Keogh got it from. We sat down and she went through a lot of his life, things I never knew but didn't surprise me. As soon as we started talking we were on the same page. I'd gone up there not knowing what was worse for the woman – thinking her son died by accident, or thinking the opposite. She wasn't a daft woman, nor did she lend herself to denial, which made it easy to be completely honest with her. I told her about the phone call between him and me that Saturday morning, and the impact of seeing her face turn white made me open up about everything. I barely stopped. The parties, the fighting, the girlfriends. Some things made her smile, others brought a tear to her eyes, but I could see she needed to hear every word of it. Between us we filled in a lot of missing pieces and it was good therapy for us both. The sun had set when we finished talking and she asked if I wanted to stay for dinner, but I needed the long drive home to myself.

Presumed drowned means no body, no funeral. There was talk about a memorial once the coroner's report came back, but nothing set. It was as if we all preferred the delusion he was still out there somewhere. It wouldn't be the first time, our learned missing persons unit ventured. It was as close to closure as we got. We sent Mrs Costa a wreath of flowers and a stack of cards.

A strange bond developed between the closest of his friends over the weeks that followed, matched by a growing intolerance on my part at least for those who barely knew the guy positing theories about what happened, why he did it. Sympathy-seekers presumptuous enough to think they knew him so well it was like they were after absolution for not seeing it coming. I suppose they meant well but I couldn't help feel chafed by their piety. If people who barely knew him felt bad for not picking up the signs, then that spoke volumes about me. The best way for me to deal with the situation was to not let it show. That way it wouldn't reflect back onto me. I'd shed some tears, but tears were never my thing.

Saunders and Kep rang a couple of times to see what I was up to. I dodged their invitations to pubs and parties, gave them excuses that were pure lies. This time a year ago I never would have tried to deceive them. They were in another world now. After I'd turned down several invitations Kep rang one night and asked me straight up what my problem was, put it to me that I'd turned toffee-nosed and my old mates weren't good enough. Maybe he was right. It made me feel bad enough to commit myself to catch up with them soon. Truth is I didn't want to. Don't know why.

It wasn't me. My behaviour was all over the place. I found myself snapping at mum, at dad, at my friends, at some poor girl in McDonalds who took too long to bring me a thickshake I ended up throwing mostly full into a bin. I drove with road rage and blasted the horn more times in those couple of weeks than I had in my entire life. I put it down to the situation, but deep down I knew I was kidding myself. Something was building up inside me. I could feel it.

The Saturday before Christmas I took mum's car and met up with my local crew at Saunders' place. We started on beers and bourbons in front of the TV watching the 1-Dayer between Australia and India. I'd gone over hoping it would be just like old times, but an hour into it and I knew there was no going back. Their immature taunting and ribald humour no longer cut it for me. It grated on my ears. I watched the game trying to ignore Manners' views on which player took it up the arse, or the merits of the new muffler he'd put on Finlay's Ford. We ordered pizzas and I silently rejoiced when the delivery guy dropped them off. It shut everyone up.

I should have seen the start to that night as a bad omen.

By half-past eight Border was the only recognised batsman left, ten overs remained, and Australia needed more than a hundred runs to win. It was time to head off to a party.

Two others had joined us that night, Spiff and another guy I never had time for, which brought our total to eight, which meant we needed two cars. I'd lost the urge for serious drinking and I volunteered to drive. Kep got into the front, Saunders and Manners slid into the back, and two cases of beer went into the boot. Finlay took off first with the others because he was the only one who knew how to get to the place. I followed as close as I could but his driving didn't make it easy.

The back streets of home are dark and lonely long before then. Streetlights don't seem to make a difference. Three or four blocks from Saunders' house, Finlay's headlights lit up a pair of girls walking towards us on the same side of the road. Both were wearing flashy tight skirts; the sort that did wonders for a good figure and said a lot about the wearer when it didn't. And these two had good figures.

'Looky what we got here,' Manners said.

I was lucky I didn't. I caught the flash of red brake lights and slammed my foot down in reflex. I managed to keep my wheels from locking and only a faint squeal from the tyres as we stopped a foot short of Finlay's rear fender would have let him know how close his beloved Ford came to needing panel work. If I hadn't stayed off the drink, I'd have rear-ended him for sure.

'Fuck me Chambers, you trying to kill us?' Saunders jeered loudly behind my ear, and Manners laughed.

I was too angry to reply. On the passenger side of Finlay's car, Spiff wound his window down and said something to the girls but they kept walking. I shifted the gearstick into first, thinking that was the end of it.

There was a loud rev as Finlay swung his car into a tight U-turn. Tyres squealed and the girls glanced nervously over their shoulder as they passed us by. Finlay straightened into a harmless crawl and drifted over to the wrong side of the road behind us to follow them.

'Do a U-ee,' Manners said.

I was fast losing patience. I wanted nothing to do with this. But then, for the sake of the girls, I knew I ought to follow. I didn't trust Finlay or the guys with him.

I made a U-turn and caught up opposite, following on the correct side of the road. I thought to give the boys in the other car a blast of the horn but the stupid dicks would likely take it as encouragement. I wound my window all the way down and called out instead.

'Hey Fin! Can we get going?'

Manners unclipped his seatbelt and hauled himself up and out the window so his butt sat on the doorframe. 'Hey girls,' he called over the roof, 'where you going?' They ignored him. The taller one crossed her arms tightly over her chest.

'Chambers – get over to the other side of the road will yuh?'

'That's a no.'

Manners gave me a grunt, then said to the girls, 'Need a lift?'

'No thanks,' the tall girl answered.

Alongside them Finlay kept pace, eight cylinders grumbling through a modified muffler. The streets stayed empty, the dark stayed dark.

'Awful cold,' Manners said. It was that hot outside I had the air conditioning on.

'We're right, thanks.'

'Where yuz from?'

'Does it matter?'

'Just being friendly.' Their high-heels clip-clopped on the pavement. 'You live around here?'

'Just around the corner.'

Her voice sounded over-composed. At first I thought they were playing along, okay with it. Then I saw how tightly clutched the girls had their arms crossed. Their feet were moving faster than before and my idling speed barely kept up. I gave the pedal a nudge.

The taller girl put an arm over the shoulder of her friend and drew her closer. Only then did I see it from their perspective. Two cars tailing them in a dark empty street, one with a guy hanging out the door with tattooed arms and a beer in his hand. These poor women were petrified.

'Hey Manners,' I said. 'Shift your arse back inside. They're not interested.'

A car approached from up ahead and slowed down. The women lifted their heads and I saw the hope on their faces disintegrate as the car swerved wide of Finlay to avoid a head-on collision. It tooted as it accelerated away and Spiff stuck his hand out the window and gave it the birdie.

'Stop for a sec,' Manners said.

I slowed right down, thinking nothing of it. 'What for?'

Before I knew it, he was out the door. At the sound of it slamming shut the girls swung their heads and fear flashed in their eyes. Manners hurried across the road, caught up to them and walked abreast with a spring in his step.

'Hey Manners,' I called tiredly. 'Come back, you're scaring them.'

He ignored me. A pinch of anger tightened my breathing. Even someone as dumb as him would know he was going nowhere. It made me even angrier knowing I was a party to it, like some jerkoff loser. This was Beeman's M.O.

'Don't worry about him,' I said to the girls, changing my tone to sound reassuring. 'He won't do anything.'

'Hey Steve,' Saunders said. 'What's your problem? He's just having a bit of fun.'

'Like they know that.'

'You should listen to your friend,' the tall girl said, loud enough for us all to hear. 'Sounds like he's the only one with a brain in his head.'

Manners laughed. 'Yeah, but you should see what *I* got that *he* don't.'

Saunders hooted with laughter, the girls picked up a pace or two. The needle on my speedometer crept up a notch as I kept up.

'It's okay, we'll be out of here shortly,' I said to the girls.

'Thank Christ,' was the reply.

We came to a T-intersection. The girls skipped across diagonally, putting them on my side of the road, and resumed their former pace. Manners caught up and followed. I hesitated long enough for Finlay to beat me across the intersection. He slowed and sidled up beside them.

'What the hell's he doing?' I asked as I crossed over.

'You in a hurry?' Saunders asked.

'If he's not back soon,' I said, poking my head out the window and raising my voice, 'we're out of here!' I gave him a blast of my horn. 'And fuck the party,' I added for the benefit of the others.

'Steve,' Kep said, trying to cool me down I suppose. 'What's Nat up to tonight?'

I was too caught up watching proceedings to answer. Seated behind Spiff, Grigg now had his window down and his elbow out.

'Steve?' Kep said, a little more forcefully.

'Working at the Oaks I suppose, like she does every Saturday night.'

'She gonna join us later?'

'Nope.' My tone was pretty blunt.

He mulled it over. 'Things okay with you two?'

'We split.' My attention diverted to Manners, or more specifically his left hand. It dangled menacingly close to the backside of the tall girl he walked next to.

'You're kidding,' Kep said.

'Why would I be kidding?'

'When did that happen?'

'Weeks ago.'

There was a lot of feeling in Kep's voice when he spoke next. 'Sorry to hear that, man.'

'I'm not.'

An astonished pause, then: 'Tell me you didn't dump her.'

I didn't answer.

'Shit,' Kep lamented, in a tone of voice that suggested it was a personal tragedy. 'You're a goose.'

I turned on him sharply. 'What are you, my fucking counsellor?'

'The two of you got on so well. And she was good for you. She was really good for you.' He shook his head disappointedly. 'She was a good woman, mate.'

'Tell you what,' I said spitefully, 'she finishes around midnight. If you like her so much, go see her when she's done. Knock yourself out mate, she's all yours.' I was too angry to care if I meant it.

'You know,' he said sadly, 'you can be a real dick sometimes.'

Manners put an arm around the tall girl. I thought she may have brushed it off but she was probably too frightened. She just kept walking, huddled close to her friend for protection.

I was getting angrier by the second. 'For Chrissake Manners,' I called out the window. 'Can we get going?'

'Stop being a wet sponge,' Saunders retorted.

The only thing stopping me from getting out of the car and teaching Manners something about his nickname was that I knew the girls weren't in any real trouble. These friends of mine might have flirted with stuff bad enough to earn jail time, but they weren't rapists. This didn't mean that Manners wouldn't try for a poke or a grab, which ran the risk of receiving a slap or shove in return, and *that* might start a fire. It would have crossed the line for me. Friend or not, I'd be out the door. The thought of him taking a swing back at me didn't worry me the slightest.

But after another fifty feet or so, Manners disengaged. I braked to a stop and he trotted back grinning. 'See you later then,' he called to the girls.

'Goodbye,' was the thankful reply. They didn't look back.

Manner got into the car and slammed the door closed. *'Sluts,'* he said.

Saunders laughed.

We arrived at the party a little after 9pm. We settled for the backyard where a fair crowd had gathered. I sweated from the heat and a fireplace was aglow with a ring of kids seated around. Music droned out of two loudspeakers on the veranda where a battered dining table had been emptied of anything resembling food.

Later in the night I was seated with Kop and Grigg when I noticed Manners and the others standing amongst four or five guys at the back of the yard. Sure hadn't taken them long to stake out the weakest in the herd – skinny blokes with ironed shirts and peace in their eyes.

Manners was doing all the talking and his posture was all too familiar. Voices were muffled, too hard to hear with everything else going on. His body language gave it away. Jaw pointed forward, sinews standing out in his neck, frame as tight as a boxer in the ring. The boys he was confronting stood back out of reach, using their hands in a pleading, submissive way. I reckon they had a minute at most.

I rose from my chair and went over. A skinny guy with a mullet haircut said in an urgent voice, 'No, that's not what I said. All I said, all we were doing—'

'Nuh,' Manners disagreed. 'You told me to pull my head in.'

'No, I told you to stop arguing.'

'That's not what I heard. I asked a question and you give me shit.'

'Mate, I just said where I get my haircut is not your concern. We're not here to—'

'There you go again.'

'Where do I go again?'

'Mate, I'll ask the fucking questions. I asked you to—'

'You're not listening to me.'

'Don't cut me off, dickhead.' Manners jabbed a finger at his face. 'Don't cut me off again or I'll drop you, cunt!'

'Hey Manners,' I said, none too friendly. 'Do me a favour. We got friends here. So not now, okay?'

His head turned my way and a trace of annoyance arched his brows. His eyes had that killer shine and I could feel the hot temper behind them. I raised my eyebrows at him – a simple gesture to soften the impact of the tone I'd used – and slowly the anger on his face downgraded to disappointment. Saunders and Fin watched indifferently. As usual they weren't the instigators, just the backup.

'Come on boys,' I urged. 'Let's go sit down.'

'If it weren't for my friend here, dickhead,' Manners said grimly, 'I'd drop you.'

We walked away, Manners skipping ahead like a kid. By the time we sat down his demeanour had gone through a complete transformation. It was like nothing had just happened. His friendly grin came back and his face relaxed. I'd seen it before. It was the after-effect of pumping himself up. There was too much energy inside and nowhere to send it, all he could do was sit there in his high.

'What's with you tonight?' Saunders asked beside me.

The boys were watching me. I took a swig of my beer and

straightened in my chair. 'Say Manners'—I drilled him with my eyes— 'do you remember that party we went to earlier this year? You know, the one where you lost your chain after king-hitting that bloke.'

Manners' grin slipped away and he looked at me real suspicious. He'd heard the tone in my voice and knew I was serious. 'Yeah,' he said casually, but with a note of caution, as if I'd thrown him a challenge.

'You know that bloke that came at you at the end – big fella. The guy you all beat into.'

'Yeah, so?' The same steady, sure voice.

'His name was Jason Keogh. He went to the same college as me. We ended up best of friends.'

My gaze didn't budge. He said nothing.

'He drowned off Long Reef a couple of weeks ago, so they reckon. Just kept on swimming.'

Manners' eyes lost a little of their sheen. He could see what I'd said meant something to me. Though he didn't give a toss about most people, he was loyal to his friends. And that included me. He watched me closely as he digested the information, and I waited patiently. I was curious to see how interested he was. He might have asked, 'How'd he drown?' or 'What do you mean, just kept on swimming?' He might have asked more about him, his family. After all he had shared the life of my best friend at Uni, if only for a minute or so, beating into him like some godless sadist.

'Shit,' was all he said. 'That's not good.'

He turned his head away, guiltily I thought, and stayed quiet after that. It must have sunk in and I saw him in a better light. And as the silence lingered on, I saw them all in a better light. It was the quietness of respect. They were thinking it over, they were being human. They could see the mark it had left on me. It was an awkward break, made me very self-conscious.

Kep spoke up. 'What happened?'

I looked them over, but only Kep met my eye. 'Doesn't matter.' Suddenly I wanted out of this hole I'd dug. I stood up and wandered off to find alternative company.

Inside the house, I got talking to a couple of girls I had my eye on since we arrived. I perked up a little and half an hour or so later I asked them to come outside and meet my friends. They gave me the okay and out we went.

As I stepped off the veranda, I saw that most of our seats were empty. Kep and Grigg were the only ones there. The rest of the boys were at the back of the yard, same place as where I'd interrupted proceedings earlier. The guys they'd picked on were still there, outnumbered and with fear written all over their faces. Manners was back to his finger-pointing, beside him Saunders stood like a bodyguard. Finlay, Spiff, and the other two guys stood close enough to add their own brand of intimidation.

I left the girls I so gallantly tried to chat up minutes before, never to be seen or thought of again. A tingle of adrenalin lightened my step, turned my legs and arms weightless.

I heard Manners say in a harsh voice, 'When I say shutup, I mean it!' The hand he was using to point his forefinger at the guy's face balled into a fist. 'Now you tell me, right now to my face, what you been saying about me to everyone here.'

His gaze flicked my way as I approached and I saw him file away my presence as one more set of fists to back him up if needs be. The guy he was about to belt into was in mid-sentence – I caught a smidgeon of a denial – when I threw my punch.

I'd come in from behind and stayed in Manners' blind spot; he'd been a good mentor. I went for speed rather than accuracy, but it had a good arc and plenty of weight behind it. It caught him on the temple and barely lost force.

His head bounced away from my knuckles and his legs collapsed beneath him. There was a loud thump when he hit the dirt, followed by a flattening quiet. Everyone stood around in paralysed shock. I kept my eyes on Manners to see if he'd get up, and felt rather than saw everyone watching me. The fire in the bin crackled loudly.

Saunders reacted first, launching at me with both arms. I lifted my hands to protect my face but his arms went low, shoving me hard in the chest. I staggered backwards, keeping my fists up and cocked.

'*Are you outta your fucking mind?*' he screamed. His hands curled into fists and I saw in his eyes the last thing a lot of guys saw just before their lights went out.

I was that mad I hoped he'd lay into me. In fact, if no one intervened I might do it myself. I'd belt into him and anyone the fuck else that took a swing. On the ground Manners was gagging, out cold. But my so-called friends stood back in utter disbelief. The boys Saunders and Manners had picked on stood within arm's length of them, differences forgotten. They all stared at me like dumb sheep.

My temples throbbed with rage as I turned and strode away stiff as a tree, legs pumping. I exited alongside the house and strode across the front yard without looking back.

I fumbled with the keys when I got to the car. As I went to unlock the door, I noticed Kep coming after me across the yard. He broke into a trot when he saw me open the door.

'Steve?'

I slid inside and inserted the keys into the ignition. Kep rounded the front bonnet as I fired up the engine and gave it a rev. 'Steve, where you going?' he asked, worry spread all over his face.

I depressed the clutch, shoved the gearstick into reverse and gave the accelerator pedal another slice of my rage. The engine roared as Kep came up to my window and tapped on it. I wound it down a bit.

'Move!'

Kep stepped back and I reversed, somehow managing not to ram the car behind.

'Steve . . . you all right?'

I crunched the gear into first, roared away from the kerb and gave the car a lot of speed before changing into second. About fifty metres down the road I glanced into the rear-view mirror and saw Kep standing in the middle of the road. At the first T-intersection I shoved the wheel to the right and squealed around the corner.

On the open road I wound the window all the way down to cool my burning face. My foot eased off the pedal a little and the unhurried flow of Saturday night traffic kept pace alongside, soothing my temper.

It took about an hour to get to Long Reef. I turned into the road toward the headland smelling clean salt air and slowed to a jogging pace past the boat ramp. Seagulls and plovers scurried over the grass beneath the street lights and a steady northeaster ruffled the Norfolk pines lining the road. Wavelets flopped at the foot of the boat ramp and length of the beach, kicking up suds that swirled and danced up the sand.

A single lamp in the top carpark showed me I was here on my own. I parked the car and headed off up the hill, using the feel of gravel at my feet to guide me through the pitch black of the bushy stretch. I emerged on the other side with a starry sky overhead and saw the golf course on my right sprawl into the distance like the lunar surface, cold and lonely.

Near the top of the hill I diverted to the drop where Keogh and I had stood in the rain watching the ocean rage over Easter. Tonight she was quieter; a low boom rode the wind blowing moist and cool in my face. I sat down on the cliff edge and hugged my knees to my chest.

It made me terrified just looking out over it. It flexes its muscles and somewhere a tsunami hits, a seaboard crumbles. How many monsters had it spawned? How many lives had it claimed? And he had volunteered his, offered it up like some pagan sacrifice. I imagined him swimming on and on, driven by a heart made to beat for a hundred years; driven toward its own end. Did it fight for him? Did it drag his exhausted and freezing body back to the surface each time he went under, over and over as the ocean tried to choke the life out of him? Or had it given in sooner, like he had, so hurt and broken as to slowly stop beating?

I couldn't bear to think about it.

I could feel it coming, building up inside me like the surge of a goddamn ocean swell. It gathered force and pressed against my eyeballs with the weight of something physical. My chest began to shudder and my breathing caught in my throat, but there was no need to fight it anymore.

'*You bastard.*'

I buried my face in my knees, and let it flow.

A faint voice lifted my head. It rode the nor'easter, sounded like someone had called my name. My eyes were so puffed and my vision so blurred from all the balling I'd done I could barely distinguish the night sky from the seamless spread of ocean. My butt was sore and my spine was aching, but I was beyond pain. I had no idea how long I'd been sitting there, nor did I care.

'Steve?'

It was a guy's voice, familiar. I turned my head toward the path and saw a dark lump approaching.

'Steve, is that you?' His voice was all but muted by the wind and I could only see his dark outline. 'It's Kep.'

The surprise at him finding me lifted my posture.

'You okay buddy?' he asked.

Someone was with him. I knew who it was without looking, without thinking. Neither logic nor flutter of curly hair in silhouette told me. I felt her like one must feel a phantom limb, this part of me I'd severed.

'Steve?' her voice was light, with a ring of serious worry.

I felt my chest convulse. There were a few quiet seconds as they stood there, motionless in the wind that ruffled her hair and jacket.

Without another word, Kep headed off back down the track.

She came forward and knelt down beside me. I buried my face into my knees because I couldn't look at her. I heard her shuffle closer and felt her arms embrace me and it never felt so good. Then I caught her scent; achingly familiar and tender as my best memories. She nuzzled my face and I felt the slippery wetness of her cheeks. She sniffed thickly and it sounded like there were a lot of tears clogging up her nose.

I wanted to speak, but I didn't trust my voice. I wanted to ask her what she was doing, hanging around this loser. I wanted to say I was sorry for all the hurt and grief I had given her. I wanted to say I didn't deserve her or her pity. But I knew that as soon as I did my chest would start to heave all over again and I'd be blubbering until the sun came up. My eyes stung so much I wondered if I had a drop of moisture left to shed.

And then, in that angelic voice of hers, she said: 'Told you I'd always find you.'

We stayed there until dawn.

Twenty-five

Reunion.

A faint *toot* brings me back.

'Taxi's here!' my son calls from downstairs. I shake my head clear, switch off the bathroom light and skip down the stairs.

My wife is waiting at the bottom. She looks me over and nods an approval. We say goodbye to our two boys sprawled in front of the TV and they lift their hands without taking their eyes off the rugby and mumble words to the effect of having a good night.

She is as quiet as me in the taxi. I stare out the window. We stop at a set of traffic lights and I see a group of kids loitering around an adjacent park. I can't take my eyes off them. I see all my old friends standing around in the same fashion, waiting for something to happen. I see Manners as a teenager, compare him with the grossly obese man I saw sitting in a takeaway at Manly Corso many years ago. The woman he's with is his perfect match. Two kids of the beanbag-type stuff things into their mouths. He sees me and drops his head just enough to make it a nod, and I do the same back; a gesture of mutual understanding. I don't stop though, just keep on walking.

Weirdest thing about Saunders – I heard he turned born-again Christian. Re-baptised, bible study, church on weekends with the whole family, the works. I rarely saw any of those guys after that summer. The only one I made the effort with was Kep. I'd give him a ring on occasion, catch up if the others weren't there. He took longer to break away from the group than I did. About ten years ago I ran into him at a funeral. At the wake we got talking about the time he and the boys were paid a visit at the local by the dudes from hell. He said it was a turning point in his life.

Cops, Kep had told me. *Those guys were cops. I was too dumb to see it then, but I do now. The way they talked, the way they acted . . . cops . . . there to scare us stupid. Worked on me.*

The cab lurches forward. My wife takes my hand and squeezes. She smiles and I know she's been watching me, probing my thoughts as is her way. I return the squeeze and she rests her head on my shoulder.

We pull into the carpark at St Phillips. I hand the cabdriver a note and don't wait for the change I would have counted the last time I caught a cab ride here, a lifetime ago.

We're holding hands as we walk through the doorway. At the JCR doorway is a guy I recognise behind a table with long rows of alphabetically arranged nametags. He leans forward and shakes my hand. We barely spoke to each other at college, but it sure is good to see him now. His hand floats uncertainly above the nametags and I save him the awkwardness.

'Steve and Natalie Chambers.' I point to the tags and he hands them over.

We walk up the stairs and into the dining hall. I manage a few steps before the first slap on my back. It's Metcalf, and man, has he put on a bit. His cheeks are chubby and jolly and the crow's feet lining the edge of his eyes come to life as his face turns into one huge smile. He clasps my hand in both of his and shakes it vigorously. I look him up and down and tell him he looks like he's had a good life, and the laughter rolls out of him. Nat gives him a hug and he kisses her cheek. I pat his shoulder and promise to catch up with him later.

I find Mick and Joey and shake their hands like I hadn't seen them in decades either. We see each other all the time, but that didn't make the occasion any less now. Wives I know well get a hug; others get a peck on the cheek. I meet plenty of well-behaved yet watchful partners and task myself regardless of how tipsily honest I get to stop short of suggesting they should have stayed home.

There's a squeal from Nat; she's spied an old girlfriend in the crowd. A few of the boys left Uni with more than a degree. She excuses herself and rushes away.

'Love you sweetie,' I call after her, and she glances over her shoulder and blows me a kiss.

With every turn of my head, I see someone I want to greet. Over two hundred people were coming and at the rate I was going the night would be over before I'd shaken hands with a fraction. Barely a sentence is uttered about our careers. I wonder if they see me as I see them. I don't see them as lawyers or doctors or stockbrokers or directors. I don't see them clapped onto centre stage wearing expensive suits and head-mikes; I don't see them or in wigs and gowns blustering away at opposition counsel; I don't see them capped and masked bent over patients with scalpel poised and laser-sharp focus, the slip of a finger the difference between life and death. I see them crash-tackling each other on the dance floor, spraying beer over each other, passing out in chairs with drink in hand. I see them running nude out back of Women's College at two in the morning, lifting the Rawson Cup after our finals win, arms around me as we sing our team song, badly out of tune.

Major disappointment re: Babs. Rajah filled us in. Apparently brain surgery hadn't been challenging enough and he'd dawdled into the pharmaceutical industry. A firm in Munich had taken him under its wing and by the frequency his name popped up in a quick Google search, he seemed to be doing better than all right for himself. Knowing there was always more to Babs that meets the eye, we assumed this meant he'd been headhunted by a major conglomerate, learnt to speak fluent German in less than a month, kicked-arsed his way into the position of CEO, and now earned a salary that made a surgeon's look like pocket money. He might be a busy man but we all agreed that was no excuse for not jumping on a private jet and flying Downunder for the occasion. Rajah gave us his email address and we voted unanimously to jam his inbox with a rightful bagging.

In between the trays of nibblies come trays of beers, champagne, and wine. I keep glancing at my watch, reminding myself there was something I needed to do before I get too sozzled. I drain my glass, place it on a table and head out.

The grounds of St Phillips are bare and quiet. They look different to me now. Trees are twice as high, new hedgerows have sprouted.

Tables and benches colonise a once-empty lawn. I am headed for C-Wing; I am not interested in mine. The room I am headed for is one I never set foot in again after being let back into college. Oh yes, they did let me back – sympathy I figured – and I spent another two glorious years making the most of it before sharing a house with Nat and some others at the end.

The dining hall had been booked because it was the holidays and there was a good chance there'd be no one home, but you never knew. I enter the staircase and climb the stairs. I step into the first-floor corridor and the smell comes back to me. Light is leaking from under the door second from the end. I'm in luck.

I give it a knock. I hear the scrape of a chair and then the door opens. I'm perused by the sharp eyes of a young girl and remind myself that the college turned co-ed many years ago.

'Hi . . . hey . . . sorry to disturb you,' I stumble. 'I'm here with the reunion in the hall, just thought I'd do the rounds. I didn't know if there'd be anyone here.'

'That's okay.'

'A friend of mine had this room a long time ago. I just wanted to take a look.'

'You want to take a look?' she asks. A second or so passes as she thinks about it. 'Oh . . . okay.' She steps aside.

I peer inside. 'Yep, same room.'

A silence follows that would have made me uncomfortable if not for her smile, shy and sweet. 'Thanks,' I say. 'That's all I wanted to see.'

I turn to go and she stops me. 'Who was it?'

'Just a friend.'

'What happened to him?' The way she sees into me reminds me of Nat.

'He passed away.'

'Oh,' she says, in a heartfelt way. 'I'm sorry to hear that. What was his name?'

I tell her, and move on quickly by asking her name. We strike up a conversation and I learn she was pre-law, lived in the western suburbs, had a few issues at home and preferred staying here during holidays.

She speaks with an advanced tongue and sounds genuinely interested in the culture of St Phillips before it turned co-ed. At one point I notice a clock inside the room and I'm shocked to discover I'd been there twenty minutes.

'Oh Lord! Sorry, I didn't realise I've been raving for so long.'

'Not at all. It's been nice talking to you.' She holds out her hand and matches my grip when I take it. 'Go on and have a good night.' She closes the door.

So that was it. I hadn't heard his ghost. I hadn't killed any demons or undergone an epiphany. But I did feel better knowing the future had one more bright kid to send it in a rational direction. Perhaps that was all I was looking for.

And as the silence presses in around me, it occurs to me how far away from this place I really was. You could be in the same room as a student here, and you were a world apart. I had to envy them. So many of their finest days were still ahead, a large chunk of which they'd find here, when every cell in their strong young bodies was best placed to capture them. One day they'll walk out of here thinking they've left it all behind, when in fact within these walls, behind these doors, are born dreams that will visit them, deep in the night, for the rest of their lives.

As I head back through the corridors, I hear muffled voices. They play on my memories, but I know not to dwell. Viewed through the magnifying lens we give it, the past always looks bigger and better than it was, surely unrepeatable. Just like our heroes. We need them so much we contemporise all manner of media-spawned celebrities and icons we will never know, let alone meet, when all we need do is open our eyes to those extraordinary souls amongst us denied a place of honour in our history books by the cruelty of circumstance, the trump card of luck. Being born in the wrong crib, the wrong age.

I hear the soft thump of bass now, the light at the end of my tunnel. I have only to turn a couple more corners and open the door to an occasion I know I will look back on in the years ahead with a pang of nostalgia equal to that which creeps up on me now. A friend is a gift, and each day is a friend. They don't ask for much. I won't be the first to set foot on Mars, I don't think I'll find a cure for cancer. But if a man can keep his dreams realistic and his ambitions harmless; if he can make life a little more interesting now and then for the right reasons; if he can make people feel good about themselves, make them feel wanted, make their lives happier for having known him; if he can give what he owes and take only what he's owed; if he can recycle his plastics and keep his carbon footprint respectable; if he has children any man can hope for and a wife he can tell he loves at the drop of a pin three decades after he first said it – and mean it – then perhaps the world is that little bit better off for having him pass through it. Perhaps he doesn't have to look in a mirror and wonder if he's happy.

He *knows* he is.